THE *King's*

Daughter

A NOVEL

DANIEL HENDRIX

ISBN: 1482080214
ISBN 13: 9781482080216
Library of Congress Control Number: 2013902762
CreateSpace Independent Publishing Platform
North Charleston, South Carolina

TABLE OF CONTENTS

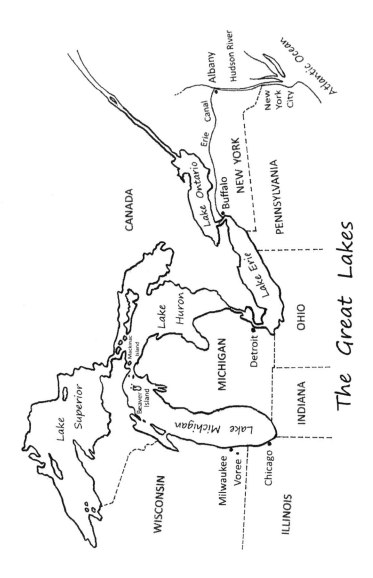

The Great Lakes

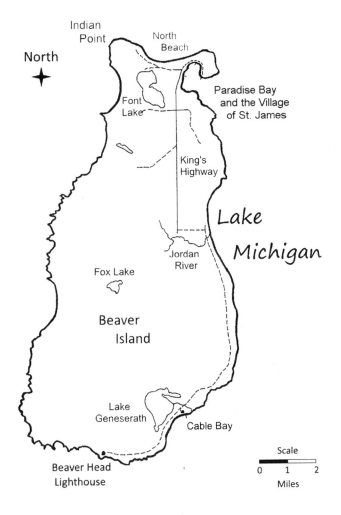

North

Indian Point

North Beach

Paradise Bay and the Village of St. James

Font Lake

King's Highway

Lake Michigan

Jordan River

Fox Lake

Beaver Island

Lake Geneserath

Cable Bay

Beaver Head Lighthouse

Scale

0   1   2

Miles

Beaver Island, 1856

North

North Beach

Andy's home
Nathan's home

Oren's home
School
Johnson's Store
Gurdon's home
Print Shop
Mormon Church
Sarah's home

Village
of
St. James

Cable's
Store

Whiskey Point

Paradise
Bay

Lake

Michigan

King's
Highway

Beaver

Island

Scale

0   0.5   1.0
Miles

Sarah Strang's Island Home

PROLOGUE:

On the Quay

F ar from the eastern shores of North America, three thousand miles across the Atlantic Ocean, lies the island nation of Ireland. Surrounded by a rugged and rocky shoreline, the countryside is covered with remnants of ancient forests and rolling green fields truncated by stone fences and clear flashing streams.

In the year 1849 Ireland was four years into a deadly famine. The annual potato crop had failed again. As rotten potatoes decayed in the ground, Irish tenant farmers were evicted from the land inhabited by their ancestors for thousands of years. Wealthy British landowners turned a deaf ear to their plight. Farmers lost their homes and many families starved or died of cholera. The lucky ones carried their pitiful possessions to the larger cities, seeking food and jobs. Many of them, completely destitute, ended up in British workhouses, which were little more than slave camps. In desperation, those with a little money bought passage on emigrant ships sailing to Canada and America.

Over a million people left their beloved homeland over a short period of six years, trading poverty and starvation for a sea voyage and a chance for a new life. The emigrant ships they sailed on were nothing more than converted hulks, unseaworthy and overcrowded. Passengers were packed below decks with no ventilation or sanitation. Many of them died on the voyage. If only one person with cholera managed to board a ship, the disease spread like wildfire, attacking the young and sick first. The bodies of the dead were unceremoniously dumped overboard. Those who managed to survive the disease faced exposure and starvation as the ships fought their way across the frigid Atlantic Ocean.

Still, it was worth the risk. The emigrants had no choice, for they faced certain starvation if they remained in their native land. Warnings of menial jobs and persecution in crowded American cities were overshadowed by stories of good farmland, schools for the children and, most of all, freedom from hunger and repression.

Most of the ships sailed from towns in western Ireland directly to Canada or America. Others sailed from Dublin across the Irish Sea to England and then on to America. A few ships sailed from small ports along the Irish coast. These were usually vessels owned by local families and converted to carry a cargo of human beings below decks. Toward the end of the potato famine these ships were not so crowded, food was more plentiful, and sanitation was greatly improved. The crossing of the ocean was still miserable, but at least the chances for survival had improved.

One of these ships was the *Dunbrody*, sailing out of New Ross, a village on the southern coast of Ireland. Built in Canada in 1845 as a cargo vessel, it was later converted to an emigrant ship as the famine spread across Ireland. Commanded by Captain John Williams, the *Dunbrody* was regarded as a "fortunate vessel" by the emigrants. It never had an outbreak of cholera and never lost a passenger to starvation.

On the night of March 12, 1849 the *Dunbrody* rested against the quay in New Ross, floating quietly in the dark waters of the Barrow River. All afternoon, sailors had been loading the ship with supplies for a voyage across the Atlantic Ocean. In the morning the *Dunbrody* would depart for New York with another cargo of emigrants, all destined for a new life in America.

CHAPTER 1:
Famine in Ireland

The village of New Ross was quiet except for festivities in a pub on the waterfront. A candle was lit in every window, an Irish band was playing, and the sounds of laughter and animated conversation drifted into the street. This was the sound of an American wake, a spontaneous celebration given in honor of the brave souls who were leaving Ireland for a new life across the ocean. Friends and relatives had gathered to see their loved ones off. It was a bittersweet celebration with both tears and laughter, for it was unlikely that these folks would ever see each other again.

Three men sat at a table in a dark corner of the pub. Two of the men, Ian McGuire and Patrick O'Donnell, had traveled from north Ireland and would board the *Dunbrody* in the morning. A third man was counting gold coins and pushing them across the table.

"Och, Ian, I'm sorry this is all I can pay ye for the *Emma Rose*," he said. "It's a good boat, but times are tough. I've got to feed me family, too."

"Don't worry about it, Barrie," Ian replied, his burly fists wrapped around a mug of ale. "I knew your grandparents and parents and I've known ye all my life."

"Sure, and now I'll be able to catch fish for my family, and if I'm lucky I'll be able to help out some of the other hungry families in New Ross."

"And we'll buy a new boat when we get to America," Ian said.

"It's a deal then," Barrie said, and the two men shook hands.

"Just promise me one thing, Barrie. Promise me that ye won't change the name of the boat. I loved my wife more than anything in the world, and it would break my heart to think of her name being scraped off the stern."

"Don't worry, Ian. Emma Rose was a fine woman and your son Andy is a fine lad. I give you my word, that boat will be named the *Emma Rose* as long as I own it."

"Thank you, my friend."

Ian and Patrick had been married to sisters from a family in County Mayo. Their wives both died in an outbreak of cholera that killed a quarter of the people in their village. Each man had been left with a young son, and the two boys were traveling with them to America to escape the poverty and disease raging across Ireland.

Ian raised his hand and waved across the room. A moment later a bar maid appeared with another pitcher of ale.

"Here's a toast," he said, "a toast to friends on both sides of the ocean."

"Hear, Hear!" The three men raised their glasses and they each took a hearty swig.

Barrie set down his glass and asked, "What's the news, Patrick? Were ye able to sell your wagon and team of horses?"

"I did sell the horses, and I got a good price for them. Unfortunately the wagon sits out on the street. I still have Hannah the cow, too. She's old, but she still makes good milk. No one's got any money to buy her."

"What are ye going to do?"

"I'll try to sell them early in the morning before the boat sails. If I can't sell the wagon, I'll leave it where it sits. If I can't sell Hannah, I'll just let her go. Someone'll take care of her."

"They'll butcher her for meat before ye even leave the dock."

"Not if she's still producing milk. Anyway, there's nothing else I can do. After we got evicted from our land we've had no place to live and I've got to take care of Nathan."

"Tis a sad thing when a man can't even live on the land of his ancestors anymore. There's just not enough food for everyone," Barrie said.

"Aye, the famine will kill us all," Patrick replied. "That is, if the English don't squeeze the life out of us first. And the landlords don't give a damn. They'll evict anyone who can't pay his rent. Why, last year alone, half of my neighbors were thrown out on the street."

"Sure, and there's nothing anyone can do about it," Barrie replied. "We each have to make a decision whether to stay or go. Myself, I'm going to stay at least another year. I've got a wife and four young kids. The famine can't last forever. At least with the *Emma Rose* I'll be able to fish."

"You'll do fine, Barrie. Just pray to God that you don't get sick."

"We already moved out of the city. It's safer away from the crowds. I don't want to risk an ocean voyage with my family."

"Yeah, we're worried about that, too," Patrick replied.

"It's a risky crossing, but I think ye and Ian are doing the right thing. Both of your wives are gone, God rest their souls, but you've still got your two boys and ye're all family. Ye'll have a much better future in America."

"Where are they, anyway?" Ian asked, looking around the room. "We've been sittin' here drinkin' all night. They probably left without us."

"I don't know," Patrick said, laughing. "They're still here, I hope."

Andy McGuire and Nathan O'Donnell were over by the band, listening to the fiddler and flute player and keeping time to the beat of the goatskin drum. They were only twelve years old, but they had already met some of the other young emigrants who were sailing in the morning. Andy had befriended a pretty red-haired girl and was dancing with her in front of the band. Nathan, standing near the back of the crowd, was talking quietly with some other boys who were also boarding the *Dunbrody* in the morning.

Barrie tapped his feet and beat out the rhythm with his hands on the edge of the table. "Ian, tell me about the letter ye got from your cousin in America."

"Jack? I heard from him in December, just after Emma Rose died."

"What did he say?"

"Well, he's living on the frontier, in the new state of Michigan. He wrote from a place called Mackinac Island on the Great Lakes. The fishing is excellent in those parts, or so he says. He fishes in a group of islands called the Beaver Islands. But he warned us if we decide to come we should be very careful about what ship we choose for the trip."

"That's what I've heard. How'd he go?"

"He took passage on a ship straight from County Mayo. He said the ship was overloaded and passengers were packed in like cattle. No sanitation and lousy food. The crew wouldn't even let them up on the deck for fresh air. About a third of the people died of the fever. Jack thinks the only thing that saved him was the captain recruited him to work as a sailor. He spent most of his time aloft in the rigging, away from all the disease below decks."

"That doesn't sound good. I'd say you were wise to come to New Ross to begin your voyage."

"Yep. The *Dunbrody's* small, but she's got a good reputation."

"Ye made a good choice," Barrie replied. "My wife and I will pray for ye and the two boys."

The band was winding down and people were beginning to leave the pub. There were tearful hugs, promises to write, and handshakes all around. The three men sat in their booth, sipping the last of their ale. Ian and Patrick watched the crowd in silence, thinking only of their lost wives and of the finality of their decision to leave Ireland forever.

In the morning, the street along the waterfront was a chaotic scene. A crowd of people, most of them dressed in rags and carrying only a suitcase or two, waited to board the *Dunbrody*. Men were shouting at each other, and women were calling frantically for their children as everyone crowded near the ship. A line of wagons blocked the gangplank and sailors loaded the last of the provisions for the journey.

"Can we get on now, Father?" Andy asked, tugging on Ian's arm.

"Not yet, son. We have to go through quarantine first. They don't want any sick people on board. Have you seen Nathan and his father? I can't find them anywhere."

"They were over in that alley, trying to sell the wagon. Here they come now."

Patrick and Nathan came toward them, weaving through the crowd. Nathan was struggling with the cow, which was tugging fiercely on its rope. She was terrified by all the commotion.

"We sold the wagon!" Patrick shouted. "Didn't get much, but we sold it."

"What about Hannah?"

"Don't worry. I'll keep her as long as I have to."

"Well, you better sell her quickly," Ian snapped. "Everyone is starting to get in line for medical inspection. We've got to hurry."

An officer supervising the loading of the ship looked up and came over to Patrick. "Are you a passenger on the *Dunbrody*?" he asked.

"Yes sir, I am."

"It's a little late to be trying to sell a cow, isn't it?"

"Well, yes it is, but don't worry, I'll get in line soon." Patrick's voice was starting to sound a little frantic.

"Does that cow make good milk?"

"She's getting a little old, but, yes, she still makes good milk."

"Listen," said the officer, "I'm the quartermaster of the *Dunbrody*. Would you be willing to take care of that cow and share the milk with everyone if I take it on board the ship?"

"Oh, yes sir," Patrick replied gratefully. "This was my wife's favorite cow. I'll take good care of her, I promise."

"All right, then. Bring her over here to the gangplank. We already have a pig and a few chickens, but we could use a good milking cow for the voyage."

"Thank you, sir," Patrick said, looking up at the quartermaster. "Thank you for saving my cow."

"Know this," said the officer sternly, "When we get to New York I'll pay you a little if she's still healthy and giving milk. Otherwise we'll have to butcher her for the return voyage."

"Anything you say, sir. Don't worry, I'll keep her healthy."

"You better get in line for your medical exam, then."

"Yes sir. C'mon, Nathan. Hurry up!"

Patrick and Nathan ran over to the quarantine area to get in line with the other passengers. They both turned and watched as several sailors struggled to get Hannah up the gangplank. The cow bellowed in anger as they pushed her over the railing. She landed on the deck with an enormous thud.

"That's the best sound I've ever heard." Patrick said happily to his son.

"Next!"

Nathan turned around in line and jumped in front of a weary medical inspector.

"Any sickness in the last month?"

"No, sir."

"Any fever?"

"No, sir."

"Open your mouth."

The man glanced briefly in Nathan's mouth.

"Next!" he shouted.

Nathan and his father were the last passengers to board the *Dunbrody*. They ran up the gangplank as fast as they could and jumped on the deck. Two sailors swore at them for being late and quickly raised the gangplank and pulled it aboard. Nathan ran over to Andy, who was standing with his arms around Hannah's massive neck. Patrick stood motionless on the deck for a moment, staring at the cow and gasping for breath. Then he went over to Ian, who was standing by the aft rail, casually smoking a pipe.

Ian looked at his friend with an amused expression. "Welcome aboard, Mr. O'Donnell. I'm glad that you left plenty of time to take care of your affairs this morning."

Patrick looked at him sheepishly. "I lost my hat in the river."

Ian put his arm around Patrick's shoulder. "I'll buy you a new hat when we get to America, my friend."

The officers of the ship shouted at the sailors, and the men ran to the bow and stern and let go of the dock lines. At first the *Dunbrody* remained still, snuggled up to the dock as if she was having second thoughts about her departure. Then, very slowly, the river current caught the bow and swung it around. The ship moved away from the quay and drifted slowly down the river. The passengers all ran to the stern and shouted and waved to people along the waterfront.

Ian saw Barrie in the crowd and shouted to him. "Take care of the *Emma Rose*, Barrie."

"God speed and best o' luck to ye!" Barrie shouted.

The ship drifted away from the village of New Ross and a quiet settled over the Irish emigrants as they took in their new surroundings. Most of them were poor and dressed in ragged and dirty clothes. They had lost loved ones to disease and starvation, and they all suffered from hunger and malnutrition. Now they were facing an ocean voyage to an unknown land. The weight of the permanence of their departure sank in as the ship floated past the green fields of Ireland.

"You know, even if you and I don't make it, our trip will still be a success," Patrick said to Ian as they watched the scenery.

"What makes ye say that, Patrick?"

"Look at us. We're just two old men. We sit at the stern of the boat and watch the shore go by. We look behind us and we see the hills of our childhood fading in the distance."

"So what?"

"Now look up there at the bow. There are our two boys, Andy and Nathan, climbing out on the bowsprit as far as they can go. They have no fear. They are looking in only one direction, straight ahead and out to sea, to their future."

"I never thought of you as much of a philosopher, Patrick."

"I wasn't, until the day I decided to leave my homeland forever."

As the passengers went below to find their quarters the ship passed Dunbrody Abbey, St. Dubhan's Monastery, and finally, the ancient Hook Head lighthouse, oldest lighthouse in Ireland. The captain gave the order to raise sails just as the ocean swells lifted the bow. The ship came to life in the offshore breeze and the helmsman set a course to the southwest, bound for America.

After six weeks at sea, the coastline of America emerged as a dark gray line on the horizon. The *Dunbrody* sailed along the coast of Long Island and entered New York harbor and the Hudson River. She arrived at New York City in early May with one hundred and seventy six passengers and no deaths at sea. She was indeed a "fortunate ship."

The New York wharves were swarming with people. Andy and Nathan leaned over the rails and looked in awe at the city. They had never seen so many people or buildings, and the line of ships along the wharves stretched as far as they could see.

The crew of the *Dunbrody* bustled with urgency as they worked to unload their cargo of emigrants and head back home to their own families. They pulled out the gangplank and hurried the passengers off the ship, throwing their luggage off after them. Ian and Patrick soon found themselves standing on the dock, holding their bags and surrounded by hordes of other passengers.

"What do we do now, father?" Andy asked, looking nervously at the crowds of people.

"Well," Ian replied, "we need to find a boat to take us up the Hudson River to the Erie Canal. Then we'll take a canal boat to the Great Lakes."

A man standing nearby turned around and greeted them.

"Welcome to America!" he said with a smile on his face. "I see you just got off that fine ship."

"Yes, we did," Patrick replied, "and we're mighty glad to be here."

"You've arrived in the land of opportunity. There's plenty of work and room for everyone, that's for sure. Say, I couldn't help but hear you were headed for the Great Lakes, is that correct?"

"Yep. We aim to go to Mackinac Island and buy a fishing boat."

"Well, you're in luck. I just happen to be an agent for the Erie Canal Transportation Company. I can sell you tickets right here that'll get you up to Albany and over to Lake Erie in no time. Here's my card: John Smith, Agent, at your service."

"How much are the tickets?" Patrick asked.

"Only five dollars apiece and a bargain at that."

"That seems pretty expensive. We just crossed the Atlantic Ocean for fifteen dollars each."

"When you see how high wages are in America you'll agree that this is a bargain, my good man."

"I don't know. It still seems expensive."

"I'll tell you what I'll do," said Smith. "These tickets were actually for someone else, but it's obvious that they aren't going to show up. I'll sell you these tickets for only four dollars."

Patrick looked over at Ian, who nodded his head in approval.

"That'll be all right, I guess." He reached into his satchel, carefully counted out a handful of coins, and handed the money to Smith, who examined the Irish money and shoved the coins in his pocket.

Ian turned around to pick up his baggage. "Now where did those two boys go? They were right here a second ago."

Andy and Nathan had returned to the side of the wharf by the *Dunbrody* to say goodbye to Hannah. They were talking to the quartermaster, who was standing on the deck.

"You're going to take good care of her, aren't you?" Nathan asked.

"Of course we are, young man."

"You're not going to butcher her, are you?"

"Certainly not. She still gives good milk. With Hannah on board the crew will have fresh milk for the return trip."

"But then what will you do with her?"

"The captain has a farm just outside of New Ross. I expect he'll take her there and put her out to pasture."

Ian and Patrick were looking everywhere in the throngs of people for the two boys. Finally Ian stood up on a barrel and spotted them.

"Andy! Nathan!" he shouted. "Come on. We're ready to go."

"But we're saying goodbye to Hannah."

"Well, make it quick. We already got tickets. Grab your bags and let's go."

Patrick turned back to John Smith. "We're ready to go now. Where would you like us to— hey, where did he go? Ian, did you see that guy? He's gone! I can't find him in this crowd."

Ian hurried over with a worried expression on his face. "He was right here a minute ago."

"I can't see him anywhere. We've got to find him. You go that way and I'll look over there."

"Patrick..."

"Hop up on that barrel again and maybe you can see him."

"Patrick, we just got robbed."

"But he's got to be here somewhere," Patrick said with panic in his voice.

"Patrick, listen to me. We got robbed. They warned us about this back in Ireland. Don't you remember?"

"What are we going to do? We need that money!"

Just then Andy and Nathan came running up.

"What happened?" they said in unison.

"That man selling tickets stole our money and disappeared."

"We can find him. We know what he looks like," Nathan said.

"Which way did he go?" Andy shouted, pulling on his father's arm.

"We don't know. You'll never find him in this crowd"

"Sure, we'll find him," Andy said. "C'mon, Nathan, let's go!"

The two boys took off running, weaving and dodging through the crowd. Ian and Patrick tried to stop them, but they were both gone in a second. They looked at each other ruefully, cursing themselves for being so gullible. Now the boys had disappeared again, lost in the crowd.

A man in a blue uniform stood nearby, leaning against a lamppost. Ian and Patrick noticed his uniform and hurried over to him.

"Excuse me, are you a policeman?" Patrick asked.

"Yes, I am. What do you want, Irish?"

"Excuse me, but we just got off the boat and someone stole our money."

"Well, who stole your money? Where is he?"

"We don't know. He ran away in the crowd."

"If you can't find him, then I sure won't be able to find him. What was his name?"

"John Smith."

The policeman let out a loud guffaw. "John Smith, eh? There's probably a hundred John Smiths down here today, and they're all pickpockets and con men. You Irish have to learn to watch your belongings."

The policeman walked away and Patrick and Ian looked at each other in dismay.

"I'm sorry," Patrick said. "I just looked away for a minute and he was gone."

Andy and Nathan came running back, appearing like magic out of the crowd. Their chests heaved and they bent over, gulping for air.

"We found him!" they both gasped between breaths.

"Where? Where is he?" Ian asked.

"He's over there on the next pier, where that other ship is tied up. He's talking to some people."

"Let's go," Ian said with a determined look on his face. "Grab your luggage, boys. Let's get our money back before he swindles anyone else."

The two men shouldered their way through the crowd, with Andy and Nathan following closely behind. They finally spotted Smith, talking to a young family who had obviously just disembarked from a ship tied to the dock. Ian and Patrick walked up behind him, one on either side. Ian didn't waste any time with niceties. He grabbed Smith by the arm and swung him around.

"Where's those tickets you just sold us?" he demanded.

Smith stared at him in shock and quickly regained his composure. "Do I know you?" he asked with a thin smile.

"You just sold us four tickets and we gave you sixteen dollars. I want those tickets right now."

"I'm sorry, but I've never seen you in my life. Now if you'll excuse me, I was just conducting some business with this fine young family."

Ian grabbed Smith by the throat and shoved him up against a barrel. "I said I want those tickets right now."

"Listen," Smith said, his voice rasping as his face flushed scarlet. "I don't actually have any tickets on me. I have to take the money up the road to the riverboat landing. If I buy a lot of tickets at once, I can get you a better price."

"Then we'll just take our money back," Ian growled. Still clutching Smith by the neck, he reached inside the man's vest and pulled out a satchel filled with coins.

"Where did you get all this money?" he demanded. "You cheated all of these poor people out of it, didn't you?"

"That's mine!" Smith managed to choke out. "Give it back to me or I'll call the police."

"I think I'll just give it back to all of the people you swindled today," Ian snarled.

Patrick reached over and grabbed his friend's arm. "Ian, we've only been in this country one hour. No one will believe you if you take his satchel. We didn't come all this way to spend time in an American jail."

"But he stole this money!"

"Then just take our sixteen dollars and let's get out of here."

"Yeah, just take your money and give me back the rest," Smith said, still struggling to get away from Ian's grasp. "I've only been in this country a short time myself. I'm an Englishman."

That was the wrong thing to say.

"Arragh! An Englishman! I should have recognized your accent. First you stole our land from us in Ireland, and now you follow us over here and rob us!"

"I never robbed you!" cried Smith.

"Oh, yes you did, but you won't do it again."

Ian lifted Smith off the ground with both arms, hustled him over to the side of the pier, and threw him off the edge with a mighty heave. Smith sailed through the air with his arms and legs flailing. He landed with a huge splash in three feet of water and mud. Ian calmly counted out sixteen American dollars, handed them to Patrick, and threw the satchel down on the dock. It burst open, and a cascade of coins spilled out, bouncing and rolling across the rough wooden planks.

"Good God, Ian!" Patrick exclaimed. "Now we're going to get arrested for sure."

"Why?" Ian asked with a smirk. "I didn't steal anything."

A crowd had gathered at the edge of the dock, staring down at Smith as he floundered in the mud. Several street urchins ran in circles, chasing the the wayward coins across the planks.

"Och, let's get out of here," Patrick muttered. "Come here, boys. Grab these bags."

The two boys were looking wide-eyed at Ian. Finally they picked up the bags and Patrick and Ian circled back to recover the rest of their abandoned luggage.

"Now," Patrick said, "we just need to find the boat up the river to the Erie Canal. Smith said the riverboat landing is beyond the last pier. Let's get out of here before someone comes after us."

Two days later, they arrived without incident at the town of Albany on the banks of the Hudson River. Albany was the starting point of the Erie Canal, a waterway that stretched from the Hudson River to Lake Erie, connecting New York to the Great Lakes and frontier lands beyond. They would travel by canal boat and then by steamer to Mackinac Island at the north end of Lake Huron. There they hoped to buy a fishing boat for the final leg of their journey to Beaver Island.

Andy and Nathan were sitting by a campfire near the banks of the canal, laughing again about the untimely fate of John Smith at the hands of Andy's father.

"I still can't believe your father threw that guy in the water," Nathan said with a snicker. "Did you see the look on his face when he went off the edge of the dock?"

"That was nothing compared to the look on his face when he landed in the mud," Andy replied with glee, "or when those little beggar kids ran after his money."

"I just wish they could have gotten more of it," Nathan said. "They looked just as poor as the kids back home in Ireland. I thought everyone was rich in America."

"Maybe not," Andy said. "But we're going to be rich, you just wait and see."

Ian and Patrick had gone into Albany to buy tickets on a canal boat. They returned in the afternoon, arriving at the campfire with four tickets and a sack full of food. They had purchased a large slab of beef, salted pork, potatoes, bread, apples, and a jug of apple cider.

"Hey, boys," Ian shouted, "throw another log on the fire. We've got dinner."

The two men walked up to the fire, kicked off their worn shoes, and plunked down the sack of food.

"We haven't had a decent meal since we left Ireland. Now that we're in America we thought it was time to have a feast," Patrick said.

Andy and Nathan jumped up and gathered more firewood. They suddenly realized how hungry they were. In just a few moments the fire blazed, potatoes were baking in the coals, and chunks of beef sizzled on a homemade grill of green branches. The boys both munched on crisp apples, staring at the meat ravenously.

"Do you see that boat tied up over there on the side of the canal?" Ian asked. "That's the *Canal Queen*. We board first thing in the morning and then we'll be on our way to Lake Erie."

"That's a boat? It looks more like a box," Andy said.

"That's because the canal is only four feet deep. You'll never see any waves on the Erie Canal."

"How does the boat move?" Nathan asked.

"See that path on the other side of the canal? They pull the boat along with a team of mules."

"No sails?"

"That's right," Ian said. "No sails."

Patrick flipped the steaming potatoes out of the fire and cut the grilled meat into four juicy chunks. Andy and Nathan both dug into the food and Ian sliced off some salted pork.

"No one's going to bed hungry tonight," Patrick said.

"That's for sure," Andy said. "We were starving."

"How long will we be on the canal?" Nathan asked between mouthfuls.

"About seven days. The good part is that we sit on top of the boat in the fresh air and sunshine, not stuck below decks like we were for a month on the *Dunbrody*. As long as it doesn't rain we'll be fine."

Andy and Nathan finished their beef and potatoes, ate a slice of salted pork and another apple, and settled down next to the fire. The sun glowed orange in the evening sky, and the boys began to feel drowsy. For the first time in many weeks they felt warm and dry and soon they nodded off to sleep. Patrick reached over and put a blanket over each of them.

"I think they're doing pretty well for a couple of twelve year old kids who just came across the ocean. What do you think, Ian?"

"They're going to be fine. They'll probably take to America faster than we will. We're already old and set in our ways. I suppose we'll miss Ireland for the rest of our lives."

"Do you think we made the right decision, coming here?"

"I do. I really do. We escaped the fever and we survived the ocean crossing. Now all we have to do is work hard and make something of ourselves."

"You know what I like best about this country so far?"

"What's that, Patrick?"

"These potatoes. No fungus inside like those rotten ones back in Ireland."

"You're easy to please."

"I know. I just worry about all those hungry people back home."

"So do I," Ian replied. "Sometimes I feel guilty about leaving, but there was nothing left for me after Emma Rose died."

"Aye. I don't know about you, but my house was empty without Orla."

The stars had come out and a crescent moon appeared from behind a dark patch of trees. Patrick grabbed a couple of blankets and tossed one over to Ian. They each pulled up a duffle bag to use as a pillow and curled up on the grass near the campfire.

"Good night, Ian."

"Good night, Patrick."

By noon the next day, the *Canal Queen* was already well on her way along the Erie Canal. A team of horses plodded along a path, pulling the boat through the water at a steady pace. The canal followed the graceful curves of the Mohawk River. Each turn revealed a new view of the river valley, a panorama of gently rolling hills and farm fields dotted with white barns.

Nathan sat on the roof, basking in the spring sunshine and taking in the scenery of a new world. He had already seen several deer in the fields and a family of otters playing along the bank of the canal. Earlier in the morning he spotted an eagle soaring above the river.

Patrick climbed up on the roof and sat down beside his son. "How're you doing, Nathan? This has been a long trip for you."

"I miss my friends in Ireland."

"I know, son. Don't worry, you'll make lots of new friends once we get to Beaver Island."

"I wish Mother was with us."

"So do I," Patrick replied. "She's probably watching us now from heaven. I know she would want us to have a good life in America."

"Do they have cholera here?" Nathan asked.

"Yes, they do, but only in the big cities. That's why we're headed for the frontier."

They sat silently for a moment, taking in the view as the *Canal Queen* rounded another bend in the canal.

"Look, Father," Nathan said. "Look at those hills over there. It reminds me of the hills back home."

"They are about the same, aren't they? Less rocky, though. I'll bet this would make great farmland."

"Father, why don't we stop along here somewhere? Why do we have to go all the way to the Great Lakes?"

"Well, Andy's father and I agreed to keep you and Andy together when we got to America. After all, he's your only cousin. It's best that we all stick together, don't you think?"

"Sure I do," Nathan replied. "I'd hate to be here all by myself."

"We heard the Great Lakes are going to become one of the best fisheries in the world," Patrick remarked.

"But do you really want to fish?" Nathan asked.

"Sure, for a while, but I have to admit it would be nice to settle down on a farm someday."

"How much farther do we have to go? I'm getting tired of traveling."

"About a week on the canal, and then maybe two weeks to sail across Lake Erie and Lake Huron. We'll stop at Mackinac Island and try to buy a boat. Do you think you can do all that, Nathan?"

"I think so, father."

Patrick was amazed at how well his son had handled the trip. Nathan had taken care of Hannah all the way across the ocean and slept in the damp hold of the *Dunbrody* for over a month. He had never complained during the entire voyage.

Three weeks later, Andy and Nathan stood on the bow of the steamer *Illinois* as it approached the harbor at Mackinac Island. By now they had forgotten completely about their difficult journey across the Atlantic Ocean in the *Dunbrody.*

Andy turned and called to his father. "Hurry," he shouted. "Come and look at all the boats!"

Ian came up along the starboard rail to the bow. When he looked out at the harbor, he was amazed at all of the boats tied to moorings and drifting in the calm water. Most of them were small sailing boats, rigged for fishing. The wharves were teeming with men, all rushing about and shouting. Some of them were loading supplies and others were hauling barrels toward the shore. At the end of the largest wharf, a group of men were gutting fish and throwing the entrails into the water. A flock of screaming seagulls fought angrily over the scraps.

"This place is really crowded," Ian said to the boys. "I've never seen so many boats."

Patrick came up behind them. "The fishing must be good around here. Maybe we should just stop here instead of going on to Beaver Island. What do you think?"

"I don't know," replied Ian. "There's hardly room in the harbor. Jack Bonner said Beaver Island's not as crowded."

"Yeah, but here the boats are bringing in plenty of fish. Look at that big stack of barrels over there. They must be full of salted fish, ready for shipping."

"Jack said in his letter that the best fishing is around Beaver Island. He only comes here to sell his catch and buy provisions."

"He's kind of a loner," Patrick remarked. "Don't you think the boys would be better off here? They probably have a good school and I see a church steeple in the village."

"I want a fresh start, away from the crowds and close to the fishing grounds."

"But fishing's not everything. They've got stores and boatyards and houses here. We might not want to fish forever."

"I don't care about all that. We're going to Beaver Island to fish and that's my last word on it. That's what we agreed on, isn't it?"

Patrick looked away, startled at Ian's sharp reply. They left Ireland as partners and made the journey together amicably, but now it was clear that Ian had set his course for Beaver Island with no thought of possible alternatives. Patrick, knowing his friend well, kept his silence. He didn't want to argue in front of the boys.

Ian, realizing the harshness of his words, dropped the issue of their final destination, at least for the moment. "First, we need to buy a boat," he said. "There's plenty of them here; we just need to find a good one that will suit our needs."

The *Illinois* had slowed to a near stop as it inched its way between the fishing boats, finally bumping gently against the wharf. The men on the dock yelled and swore at the massive intruder, but they kept on cleaning fish and tossing the guts into the lake.

Andy and Nathan were among the first passengers off the boat, running along the wharf and peering into the warehouses and shops clustered along the shore. They were glad to be on land again and they quickly disappeared into the village. Ian and Patrick trudged along behind, carrying the luggage and shouting to the boys for help, all to no avail.

"Oh, well, let them go," Patrick sighed. "They need to burn off some energy. It's a small island, so they can't go too far."

"They'll be back," Ian replied. "Let's see if we can find a boat. Maybe we should ask over at that warehouse."

A large wooden building stood at the edge of the village between two wharves. An ornate sign over the door stated: "Mackinac Fish Company: We buy fish; also fishing supplies, nets and barrels for sale".

Ian and Patrick entered the warehouse through a creaky door hanging by one hinge. Wooden barrels were stacked high along one wall and gill nets hung from the rafters. The floor was cluttered with coils of rope, anchors, sails, and boxes full of assorted fishing gear. A dapper man in a white shirt was sitting at a desk, writing busily in a ledger. When he heard the door close, he put down his pen and greeted Ian and Patrick with a friendly voice.

"Good afternoon, gentlemen. Martin Hedley, at your service. How may I help you today?"

"Good day, sir," Patrick replied. "We're looking for a boat."

"Ah, yes. You're both fishermen, I trust? I haven't seen you on the island before."

"Yep, we're fishermen. We just came over from Ireland."

"Ireland! Well, you're in good company on Mackinac Island, you can be sure of that. About half the people here are from Ireland. County Mayo, mostly."

"We sailed from New Ross, near the city of Watford on the Barrow River," Ian said.

"County Wexford, I believe," said the man after thinking for a moment. "You'll find a few neighbors here, I'll wager."

"That's good to hear," Ian replied. "Now, do you have any boats? We're in a bit of a hurry."

"Why, yes, I do, as a matter of fact. The terms are eighty percent of the catch for the Mackinac Fish Company, and twenty percent for you to keep. I require a one hundred dollar deposit in case you wreck the boat."

"Oh, no," Ian replied. "We want to buy a boat."

"You wish to buy a boat? No offense, my good men, but can you afford that, after just arriving from Ireland?"

"We think so, if we can find something we like."

"Begging your pardon, gentlemen! Please forgive me for being so impolite. I do have boats for sale. The company owns six of them. It's early in the season, so only one of them is leased so far. The other five are tied up on the other side of the wharf. If you want to look at them, I'd be happy to discuss a sale with you."

They all shook hands, and Ian and Patrick left the warehouse and walked across the wharf toward the boats.

As soon as the door closed behind them, Patrick turned to Ian. "Did you hear what Hedley said?" Patrick asked with excitement. "He said that half the people on Mackinac Island are from Ireland."

Ian responded with a dismissive grunt.

"He said that we'd probably meet some neighbors here. Maybe if we just stay here for a while we'll find some friends from home," Patrick continued.

"We'll buy a boat and be out of here in no time," Ian said, ignoring Patrick's suggestion.

"Wait a minute, Ian," Patrick said. "Let's not be too hasty. We need to be careful with our money. Remember John Smith back in New York? He cheated us and almost got away with it."

"You're right," Ian said, his enthusiasm chastened. "Let's just look at the boats first, and see they're even worth anything."

They walked across the wharf and looked down to see five weathered fishing boats tied to the piers. All of them had rigging, nets, and anchors and appeared to be ready to set sail to the fishing grounds.

"These aren't much different than the fishing boats back home," Patrick remarked.

The two men spent a long time examining each boat carefully. They finally selected a boat that was larger than the rest. It was worn and weathered, but it seemed to be well built. It had two sturdy masts, good sails, and a spacious cabin with four bunk beds in the bow. Most importantly, it had a complete set of fishing nets draped over the cabin to dry in the sun.

"This is a solid boat," Ian said. "It has a large cabin, which we'll need. We're probably going to have to live on board until we can build a house before winter."

"Let's make an offer," Patrick replied. "If he refuses, we'll stand firm."

They walked back across the wharf to the warehouse, where Martin Hedley was waiting for them.

"Did you find anything you like?" he asked.

"Well, we were looking at the one in the middle," Patrick said.

"Ah, the biggest one. You'll catch a lot of fish with that boat. I'll sell it to you for one hundred dollars."

"One hundred dollars!" Ian exclaimed. "That's too much!"

"As I said, that's my biggest boat," Hedley said. "Perhaps I can interest you in one of the smaller boats."

"But there are four of us. We won't even have room to sleep."

"Most of the men tie their boat up at night and stay in town."

"Not us," Ian said. "We're headed for Beaver Island, so we'll need to sleep on the boat."

"Why go over there?" Hedley asked. "The fishing's fine around here."

"We've heard it's better there, so that's where we're headed. Now, about that price…"

Patrick had realized by now he probably would not be able to convince Ian to stay on Mackinac Island. It also was clear to him that they would need the larger boat to safely make the trip to Beaver Island.

"Mr. Hedley," he said calmly, "we're on a tight budget and we have two young boys to take care of. We will gladly pay you sixty-five dollars in cash for the boat and we'll promise to buy our supplies here. How does that sound?"

Hedley laughed. "You might have to because there aren't many stores on Beaver Island yet. But you men seem to know what you're doing. I'll let it go for eighty-five dollars. I won't make much money on the boat but I'll wager you'll be back for provisions before winter."

Patrick and Ian looked at each other across Hedley's desk and nodded at each other.

"It's a deal," Ian said, "but only if you throw in some oakum to fill cracks. I saw a few leaks in the hull."

Hedley stood up and the three men shook hands. He went to a shelf and filled a bag with scraps of hemp and old rope. "This is the best oakum I have," he said. "It's been soaked in paraffin so it'll stop most leaks."

After they left the warehouse, Patrick looked over at Ian and remarked, "I didn't see any leaks in the boat."

Ian grinned. "Neither did I, but at least we got some free oakum."

Patrick laughed and changed the subject. "I wonder where those boys are. We haven't seen them in two hours."

"There they are," Ian replied. "They're over by our luggage."

Andy and Nathan were rolling around on top of the duffel bags, laughing and pushing each other.

"Hey, boys!" Patrick called. "Where have you been?"

"We went exploring, Nathan replied, pointing to a high ridge behind the village. "There's a fort up on that hill full of American soldiers."

"Yeah, we snuck inside and the soldiers chased us away," Andy added.

"You snuck inside a fort and got chased by soldiers? How in the world did that happen?" Ian demanded.

"They saw us hiding behind a cannon, and Andy stuck his tongue out at them," Nathan said.

"Andy, do you think that was very smart?" Ian asked, glaring at his son.

21

"We ran out the back of the fort and hid in the woods. We ran so fast they couldn't catch us."

Patrick sighed. "I can't believe we haven't been thrown in jail yet. Now we have soldiers chasing us."

"Didn't you get lost?" Ian asked.

"No," Andy said. "This is only a small island."

"Ian, remember what I told you on the *Dunbrody* just after we left New Ross," Patrick said. "These boys have no fear."

Ian looked at his friend for a moment and shrugged. "All right, boys, grab that luggage and bring it over here. We'll show you your new home."

The boys were ecstatic when they saw the boat. They gathered up the luggage and heaved it aboard. In a moment they were in the forward cabin, peering out the portholes and stretching out on the bunk beds. Ian and Patrick began to look over the sails and rigging. They inspected the hull and the rudder and then stowed the fishing nets and lines in the cabin. Ian got down on his hands and knees and checked the planks of the hull. It was a busy afternoon, but no one seemed to notice when the shadows lengthened and the sun began to set in the west.

Finally Ian stood up and pronounced the boat to be shipshape. "We'll leave for Beaver Island first thing in the morning."

"Yea!" hollered the boys. "We get to go sailing in our own boat!"

"Ian, did you think about my idea?" Patrick asked.

"What idea?"

"I think we should stay here on Mackinac Island for at least one season. We just arrived, and this looks like a good place to settle down. We can get to know the area and put the boys in school."

"What about Beaver Island?" Ian responded sharply. "I thought you wanted to go to Beaver Island?"

"I did, until I saw Mackinac Island. Look at all the fishing boats in the harbor. They must be here for a reason."

"I'm telling you, Patrick, there are too many people here. We need to be on the frontier where we can find new fishing grounds."

"But how do you know the fishing is better over there?" Patrick asked.

"Jack Bonner told me."

"Ian, that's only one person, and he's only been here a year."

"Patrick, if you want to stay here, then stay. I'm going to Beaver Island tomorrow morning, and that's the end of it."

After hearing Ian's ultimatum, Patrick gave up. He knew he could not win an argument with his headstrong friend.

"Ian, do you actually know the way to Beaver Island?" Patrick asked.

"Sure," Ian replied. "Jack Bonner told me in his letter."

"Did he send you a map?"

"No, but he told me the way. He said to head west from Mackinac Island through a wide strait and watch for a string of small islands to the south. Go past the last island, head south, and bear due west again. At dusk you'll sail right into a big harbor on the north end of Beaver Island."

"That's it?"

"Yes. Sounds easy, doesn't it?"

"Any mention of reefs, shoals, rocks, currents, or anything like that?"

"None. Just clear sailing all the way."

"I see," Patrick said, not at all convinced. "Well, just to be safe, let's look at the weather tomorrow morning before we start. If we don't make it to Beaver Island by sunset, I suggest we anchor for the night. It's not safe to sail in uncharted waters after dark."

"Sure," Ian replied. "That makes sense. We don't want to wreck our new boat."

Patrick grabbed a duffel bag and carried it below into the cabin. He threw it against the bulkhead in frustration. He had failed to convince Ian to stay on Mackinac Island. Even the welfare of the boys had not convinced Ian to stay.

As it turned out, the directions from Jack Bonner were reasonably accurate. After leaving Mackinac Island, they immediately encountered a steady wind that carried them westward through a wide strait with land on both the north and south horizons. Ian adjusted the set of the sail while Patrick held the rudder on a steady course. Both men were pleased with the performance of the boat, so Ian gave the order to raise the jib sail. Unfamiliar with the rigging, the two boys scrambled around and got tangled in the ropes on the bow.

"Grab those lines and pull!" Ian shouted from the stern.

Finally Andy sorted out the sail and Nathan grabbed a line which ran to a block at the top of the mast. As Nathan pulled, the sail rose up the mast and immediately began to flap violently in the wind.

"Grab that other line," Ian yelled at Andy. "Attach it to that cleat on the starboard side."

Andy jumped at his father's command and wrapped the line around the cleat, but the sail continued to flap.

"Now pull it in. Be quick about it."

Andy tightened the line and tied it off. The sail stopped flapping and the boat surged forward on the crest of a wave.

"That's more like it," Ian said with satisfaction. "Now see if you can raise that fore jib without tangling it up."

Patrick held the rudder and turned it slightly back and forth, searching for the best set of the sails in a following wind. "This is a fast boat," he remarked. "At this rate we'll be there in no time. We'll be able to run before the wind for most of the way."

Off the port bow they soon saw a string of small islands, just as Jack Bonner had described. After they passed the last island, Patrick pulled on the rudder and set a southerly course. As the boat turned, he instructed Andy and Nathan to let out the lines on both jib sails. Meanwhile, Ian let out the line on the main sail, the boom swung out, and the sails were set for the new course.

"She really holds her line to the wind," Patrick said.

"By the way, Jack warned that it gets pretty shallow through here by that island," Ian said.

"He did? You never mentioned that."

"Sorry. I forgot."

"How shallow?" Patrick asked.

"He didn't say."

"Oh, fine." Patrick immediately stood up and placed his foot on the gunwale to keep his balance. They were sailing through dark blue water, but in the distance he could see a band of bright turquoise water, indicating a shallow area or a rock reef.

"Andy! Nathan!" Patrick called, "Untie those lines to the jib sails. Just hold them, and let go if I say so. That will let the wind out of the sails. Ian, you do the same with the main sail. We may have to change course in a hurry."

Everyone took their positions, and Patrick watched with trepidation as they approached the shallow water. Soon he could see glimpses of the bottom, and occasionally the dark shadow of a boulder glided ominously underneath the keel of the boat. "We'll be in serious trouble if we run aground out here," he said. "Everyone keep a sharp lookout."

"Rock ahead!" Andy shouted.

Patrick immediately pulled the tiller, and the boat veered around a massive boulder barely six feet beneath them.

"More rocks!" Nathan called, pointing off the starboard bow.

"We're going to have to find a better way than this to get back to Mackinac Island," Patrick muttered to himself.

After dodging a few more boulders they sailed over a flat gravel bottom that gradually dropped away to deeper water. Soon the reef was behind them and Patrick changed course to the west. They all looked back, relieved to see the reef fading in the distance.

"No more rocks," Ian announced. "Now we're headed straight to Beaver Island. Andy, come and take the helm. Patrick and I are going to sort out this fishing gear."

Andy came back to the stern and took the helm from Patrick. Ian and Patrick began to rummage through the fishing gear, separating hooks and floats and untangling line.

"Just hold your course and head straight for the north end of Beaver Island," Ian said to his son. "Keep the sail full of wind."

"Father," Andy asked, "isn't it bad luck to be on a boat that doesn't have a name?"

"I suppose it is. I hadn't really thought about it."

"Could we name this boat after Mother? Could we name it the *Emma Rose*, just like our boat back home?"

"Well, I don't know, son. We're all partners. I'm not really sure that...."

Patrick, noticing Ian's hesitation, began to laugh heartily. "Orla hated the water. She got seasick every time I took her out. If I named a boat after her, she'd probably come down from heaven and throw me overboard."

"How about this," Ian suggested, "we'll call the boat the *Emma Rose* and we'll name that island over there Orla Island, after Nathan's mother. How does that sound to everyone?"

"Let's name both of those islands," chimed in Nathan. "We can call them East Orla Island and West Orla Island."

"That sounds good to me," Patrick said.

"In honor of naming the boat and discovering two islands, I think we should throw a few hooks in the water and see if we can catch some fish," Ian said. He pulled out some fishing line and attached several hooks at intervals along the line. Then he took a chunk of salted pork from their food supply, cut it into small pieces, and skewered a piece of meat on each of the hooks.

"This isn't the best bait in the world, but it's all we've got. Maybe we can catch some small bait fish first."

Patrick stood at the stern, tied a buoy to the end of the line, and threw it overboard. As the buoy drifted away, he fed the line into the water, carefully avoiding the hooks as they passed by his hands. Soon the entire line was out behind the boat and the buoy could be seen bobbing in the distance. The *Emma Rose* sailed steadily along, as Andy held the newly christened boat on a course toward Beaver Island. Ian and Patrick stared intently at the buoy, hoping to see it disappear underwater at the strike of a fish. They waited for about ten minutes, but nothing happened. Finally Ian, getting impatient, began to pull in the line.

"Let's see what we caught," he said. "Probably nothing."

But as they pulled the line in, small fish were squirming on most of the hooks. A couple of them thrashed about and managed to free themselves, falling back into the water with a tiny splash.

"Our first catch," Patrick said. "They look like herring."

"All we need is a million more of them to make a meal," Ian replied. "Let's use them for bait and try again."

He grabbed each hook on the line, removed the salted pork and impaled a fish on the hook, making sure it was still alive and squirming. Patrick threw the buoy back overboard and fed out the line again. The last baited hook had barely entered the water when the buoy at the end of the line bobbed violently and disappeared underneath the water. It immediately popped up, landed with a splash, and was pulled under again.

"We got a big one this time!" Patrick shouted.

"That's only one fish," Ian said. "Let it go for a while. We'll see what else we catch."

The buoy continued to bob up and down in the water. Sometimes it disappeared and sometimes it was pulled sharply to one side. Ian and Patrick watched the line as Andy steered the boat ahead. Nathan sat on the roof of the cabin, enjoying the midday sun and watching the buoy. From his higher vantage point, he occasionally could see the darting shadows of fish in the water behind the boat.

"Shall we pull it in?" Patrick asked.

"Sure, why not?" Ian replied.

Both men grabbed the line and pulled. A large fish was on the first hook, splashing and thrashing violently. Ian reached down and yanked it up on the deck. It was a plump lake trout, about eighteen inches long.

"Now that's a fish!" Ian cried. "Quick, get him in a bucket."

Nathan grabbed a bucket from the cabin and scrambled back to the stern. "There's another one. He's even bigger!" he hollered, looking over the transom.

Patrick pulled in the second fish, tossed it on the deck, and kept pulling on the line. Every hook had a large lake trout, each one bigger than the last. Nathan and Andy grabbed the fish from Patrick and dumped them in buckets. In the excitement Andy forgot to steer, and he had to grab the tiller and put the boat back on course.

After the line was all the way in, Ian baited the hooks again and Patrick tossed the buoy off the stern. Soon it was bobbing again, and after a short wait they pulled the line in with a second catch of fish. They repeated this routine again and again, each time pulling in a full catch of lake trout. Andy and Nathan began to alternate jobs, switching between steering the boat and pulling fish off the line. They soon filled all of the buckets, so they just piled the fish in the bottom of the boat.

Patrick and Ian were amazed at the success of their first attempt at fishing. They could not believe how many fish there were and how easy they were to catch.

"If we can catch this many with just a line, think how many we'll be able to get when we start setting nets," Ian said as he baited another hook.

"A lot of fish, I'll wager," Patrick replied. "Maybe you're right, Ian. Maybe Beaver Island is the best place for us."

Everyone was so excited about fishing that no one had paid much attention to the progress of the boat. When they finally looked up, they saw the boat was rapidly approaching the island. Directly in front of them was a wide passage leading into a deep circular bay with a few docks and log cabins lining the beach. The *Emma Rose* sailed ahead almost on her own, straight into the harbor. They had finally arrived at their new home.

"I guess we better stop fishing before we run ashore," Ian said.

He pulled in the last line and Patrick grabbed the helm and adjusted their course, steering near a point of land covered with pine trees. At the end of the point stood a ramshackle building with a weathered sign that said "Cable's Store." A set of stairs led from the porch to a short wooden dock. The water was dark blue almost up to the end of the dock.

"This is the finest harbor I've ever seen," Patrick said. "Look how deep the water is. We can sail right up to shore before we drop anchor."

"It's protected from the wind from every direction," Ian said. "There are plenty of places to moor, and look at all the timber on the shore. We can build a house right near the beach, and maybe even build a dock for the *Emma Rose*."

Patrick was enchanted by the beauty of the harbor. "This place reminds me of Ireland," he said. "We already named the boat and two islands today. I think we should name this harbor, too. I think we should name it Paradise Bay."

"Good idea! Paradise Bay it is," Ian agreed.

Ian and Patrick surveyed the pile of fish in the bow and they both began to laugh.

"We sailed across the Atlantic Ocean, up the Erie Canal, across the Great Lakes, and now we're pulling into Paradise Bay with our first catch of fish," Patrick observed. "What do you think of that, my friend?"

"This is the best catch I've ever seen," Ian replied, looking at the overloaded boat and the two boys squeezed in the bow. "There's only one problem, Patrick. What in the world are we going to do with all of these fish?"

CHAPTER 2:

Fish for the Mormons

In a log cabin on the other side of the harbor, Sarah Strang was tending to her younger brother and two sisters. Billy and Nettie were squabbling constantly and she had to keep separating them.

"Nettie! Quit teasing your brother! Billy, you can't hit her. I've told you that before. Now stop it, both of you."

In the baby crib Hattie began to cry again. She had a head cold and could not sleep. Sarah picked her up and rocked her in her arms, but Hattie only cried louder.

Sarah wished that her parents would come home. They had both been gone since early morning. Her father was James Strang, leader of a congregation of Mormon settlers working to establish a religious colony on Beaver Island. Strang was supervising the construction of a new temple, and his wife Mary had gone with him to prepare a noon meal for the workers. It was late in the afternoon, and Sarah had had enough of her younger siblings for one day.

"You two behave for a few minutes," she said to Nettie and Billy. "I'm going to take Hattie for a walk and see if I can get her to sleep."

Sarah wrapped the baby in a shawl and carried her outside, humming a lullaby and walking slowly toward the temple. In the distance she could hear the sound of axes and saws and voices of the workers. They had all come from farms in the center of the island to erect the log walls. Sarah's father had warned her that it would be a long day and that she would have to look after the children until evening.

Finally the sound of Sarah's voice lulled the baby to sleep. She followed a path along the shore of the harbor and stopped to rest in the shade of a grove of ancient oak trees. As the baby slept, Sarah closed her eyes and thought back to the day of her arrival on Beaver Island just over a month ago. She had been looking forward to her twelfth birthday when her family left their home in Wisconsin, and traveled to Beaver Island. Her mother had wanted to stay, but her father was anxious to start a Mormon settlement in northern Michigan. Now Sarah cared for the children while her parents built the temple.

Suppertime was approaching, so Sarah picked up Hattie and began to walk home. In the distance she saw her parents returning from the temple. She hurried along the path, anxious to get some relief from Nettie and Billy and the baby.

"Sarah!" called her mother, "There you are! How's Hattie?"

"She's sleeping. I think she's starting to feel better."

Sarah's father strode up to her and spoke in a loud voice. "Sarah, God love you. You are an angel to these blessed children. You have been patiently watching over them while your mother and I are conducting the work of the Lord."

Hattie squirmed in Sarah's arms and began to whimper. Sarah cuddled the baby and held her tightly against her body.

"Mary, take the baby. Sarah has earned a blessing today by caring for these dear children. They are all children of God. Now we must prepare a meal for the brethren who worked on the temple of the Lord today."

"James, there's hardly any food," Mary said. "All we have is a little flour and some rutabagas."

"Just ask the other sisters and gather what you can. The Lord will provide, I assure you. I'm going out to Whiskey Point to collect our mail. I hope to hear good news from our missions in the east."

"Father, can I go with you?" Sarah asked. "I've had the baby all day, and Nettie and Billie were fighting again."

"Of course you can, my dear child. Let's hurry, so we can get back in time for a feast with our brethren."

"James, are you sure you should take Sarah to Whiskey Point?" Mary asked. "Those men out there make me nervous. They..." She hesitated. "Sometimes they look at me."

"Woman, if your own heart is pure, you will not perceive the lust in others. Come along, Sarah."

James Strang took his daughter by the hand and strode down the path toward Whiskey Point without looking back. "How do you like Beaver Island, Sarah?" he asked.

"It's kind of lonely. I miss my friends back home."

"Don't worry, soon you'll have lots of friends. Now that spring has arrived, new converts to our church will be arriving every day. You'll see families with children soon, I promise you. Our missionaries have been busy in the east all winter."

"But why do we have to live so far away?"

"Beause God has commanded it. We must build a place where we can practice our own beliefs. It is best that we live apart from the gentile world."

"Do you think I can go to school again?"

"School? Of course you can go to school. In fact, you can be in the first class, beginning this fall. We're going to have a fine school on this island, I promise you that."

"But where will we meet?"

"At first you'll have to learn at home, but soon I'll build a school and hire a teacher. You deserve a good education."

"I can't wait! Will it be big, father?"

"It will be the biggest and finest school in Michigan. After we finish the temple, we'll build a school, and then we'll build homes for everyone and a road around the harbor. I also want to build a lighthouse out on Whiskey Point so boats can find their way safely to our docks. This will be a great city someday, and you'll be here to see it."

"Will I be able to climb to the top of the lighthouse?"

"Of course you will. I'll let you be the first one. I may even let you light the flame. How does that sound?"

"Mother won't let me play with fire."

"Oh, I think in this case she'll make an exception," Strang said with a smile.

Sarah laughed. "Father, can I run ahead?" she asked. "I know the way."

"Yes, but don't get out of sight."

Sarah let go of his hand and ran ahead along the path, dodging among the birch trees and juniper bushes. She forgot about her father's admonition and ran all the way to Whiskey Point, soon arriving at the back of Cable's store. She peeked around the corner of the building and saw a new boat tied up at the dock, one she had never seen before. It looked like any other fishing boat, but it was bigger and it had a cabin on the front with two round windows.

Sarah was curious, so she quietly stepped up on the porch and hid behind a post, peering at the boat. Several men were working on the dock, rolling wooden barrels and packing them with fish. She recognized one of them as Alva Cable, owner of the store.

"I've only got eight barrels," Alva said. "These are the last of them until next week. There are only four coopers on the island, and they can't make barrels fast enough to keep up."

"Will you buy these once we get them packed with fish?" another man asked.

"Oh, sure, I'll buy any good fish as long as they're preserved in salt and packed in barrels. A fish-dealer stops here once a week, buys every barrel I have, and ships them to Chicago. I'll give you a fair price for them and deduct the cost of the barrels. I can't help you with all of the rest of those fish, though. They'll rot before I could ever sell them."

Sarah looked at the boat and saw a large pile of fish in the bow. Her eyes caught a movement in one of the round windows and she realized that two faces were peering out at her. Suddenly fearful, Sarah remembered her mother's warning about the men at Whiskey Point. She turned quickly around to look for her father and came face to face with a man coming out from Cable's store.

"Whoa, there, young lady. What's the hurry? No need to run off."

"I'm sorry. I need to find my father. He was right behind me."

The man turned around and looked down the path. "Here he comes now, miss. Is that him? Must be, because there don't seem to be too many people on this island."

Still frightened, Sarah ran quickly to her father, her heart pounding.

Strang strode up the path to the front of the store. "Sarah, I thought I told you to stay in my sight."

"I'm sorry, father. I forgot."

"All right, come along, but stay with me. Good afternoon, sir. James Strang, at your service. Welcome to Beaver Island."

"I'm Patrick O'Donnell. We just arrived from Mackinac Island."

"Mackinac Island!" Strang said with a laugh. "With that accent I think you're from somewhere farther away than Mackinac Island."

"Well, actually we are. We're from Ireland. We've only been in America a few weeks."

"What brings you way out here? Most of the Irish stay on the east coast."

"We came here to fish. My brother-in-law's cousin lives around here somewhere. Say, maybe you know him. His name's Jack Bonner."

"Black Jack Bonner? Sure, I know him. I know everybody. He comes around once in a while to sell his fish."

"Hey, Ian," Patrick called, "this guy knows your cousin."

Ian was out on the dock, nailing the lid on the last barrel of fish. "You know Jack Bonner? I'm his cousin, Ian McGuire. How do you like our catch? We filled eight barrels, and the boat is still full of fish. At this rate we're going to be the best fishermen on Beaver Island."

Not to be outdone, Strang walked briskly out on the dock, leaving Sarah standing alone.

"I'm James Strang, leader and prophet of the Mormon church. All of my followers live in the village across the harbor. They're building a temple of worship. It's on that hill near those houses," Strang said, pointing across the harbor. "We're starting a new city on this island, dedicated to the Lord and free from gentile interference."

"Is that so?" Ian asked, looking at Strang quizzically.

Sarah took a tentative step forward. She was nervous about the faces she had seen in the window, and she wanted to rejoin her father, who apparently had forgotten her.

"I'm afraid we've been ignoring you, young lady," Patrick said in a kindly voice. "What's your name?"

"Sarah Strang."

"Sarah! That's a pretty name. How old might you be, if I may ask?"

"I'm eleven. I'll be twelve in July."

"Twelve! I never would have guessed it. Sarah, would you like to see the boat?"

Sarah nodded.

"Well, come along, then. We have two boys about your age on board. They're hiding down in the cabin. You know what I think? I think they're afraid of pretty girls."

Sarah looked up at Patrick and blushed. She still carried the gangly stature of youth, but she was blessed with her mother's eyes and grace and her father's wavy red hair and spirit. Patrick gallantly held her arm as she accompanied him out the dock and stepped on the stern of the boat.

Patrick knocked on the top of the cabin. "Nathan! Andy! Get out here right now. You have a visitor."

Andy came tumbling out of the cabin with Nathan following behind him.

"Boys, I want you to meet someone. This is Sarah Strang. Sarah, this is Andy McGuire and Nathan O'Donnell."

Sarah smiled shyly.

"Hi, Sarah," said Andy, stepping forward and shaking her hand. "I'm Andy, and this is my cousin Nathan."

Nathan stood in the doorway behind Andy, blushing and looking down at his feet.

"Sarah lives here," Patrick said. "I'll bet she can tell you everything about the island. She probably knows all the young people."

"There aren't too many...." Sarah said, hesitating.

Patrick helped her out. "How about school? Do you have a school here?"

"My father is thinking about starting a school this fall—"

Strang jumped aboard, rocking the boat and causing everyone to grab a rail. "Thinking about starting a school! My daughter, you do not do me justice. I *am* going to start a school, and it's going to be the best school in Michigan. You boys can attend, too. You want to go to school, don't you?"

Not waiting for an answer, he strode past Sarah and the boys to the bow of the boat. "This is a fine catch of fish you have here."

"We don't know what to do with them. I'm afraid we're going to have to throw them overboard," Ian said, following him to the bow.

"My people have been working all day on the temple. The sisters are preparing a meal, and this could be the main course."

"Patrick, what do you think?"

"You want to give them our fish?" Patrick asked, pausing to think for a moment. "I guess we might as well," he finally said. "No sense in letting them go to waste."

"Thank you, gentlemen," Strang said. "I would be honored if you would join us for a feast at the temple. You are generous men for providing this sustenance to our brethren. You will see that we are simple, hard-working folks, and we'll gladly welcome you into our community of the Lord."

"Let's just sail across the harbor with our catch," Ian said. "It's pretty calm, so we can put the bow right on the beach and walk to the temple."

"Can we sail the boat?" Andy piped up.

"Go ahead," Ian said. "Patrick and I could use a break."

"Grab the bow line, Nathan. I'll get the stern."

"Andy, why don't you let Sarah take the helm?" Patrick said.

"But I don't know how..." Sarah protested.

"Don't worry, I'll show you," Andy said. "Here, sit next to me."

Nathan cast off the bow line and pushed the boat away from the dock. He quickly ran to the mast and raised the mainsail. Andy grabbed the tiller just as the wind caught the sail and swung the boat around.

"Here," Andy said, "it's easy. Just hold the tiller steady and the boat will go straight. I'll help you."

"I don't know what to do. What if we crash?"

"We won't crash. Just hold it steady. If you move it either way, the boat will turn. We'll t sail across the harbor, straight toward the temple."

Andy put his hand next to Sarah's on the tiller. Sarah watched as he moved the tiller slightly to keep the boat on course. His eyes were fixed on the wind in the sail and the course of the boat across the harbor.

"Does this boat have a name?" Sarah asked.

"This is the *Emma Rose*. We had a boat in Ireland named the *Emma Rose*, but we sold it," Andy said. "This is our new boat."

"Who's Emma Rose?"

"She was my mother. She died before we left Ireland. Nathan's mother died, too."

"Oh," Sarah said. "I'm so sorry."

Andy moved the tiller slightly. Sarah thought about letting go, but she changed her mind and kept her hand on the tiller.

"Pull in on the mainsail, Nathan," Andy said.

"Aye, Aye, captain."

James Strang was busy showing the harbor to Ian and Patrick. He pointed out the site of the Mormon temple, the beginnings of a new village, and a new boat dock. He showed them where he planned to build a school and even a printing shop for a newspaper.

When the boat neared shore, Strang left them and climbed over the pile of fish to the bow of the boat. He stood up on the railing, holding on with one hand and waving with the other hand.

"What's your father doing?" Andy asked. "He's going to fall overboard."

"He's greeting his people," Sarah said. "He always does that."

The workers at the temple saw Strang standing on the bow of the *Emma Rose* and came down to the beach to greet him. Strang reached down, picked up a large whitefish by the gills, and held it up high for all to see.

"Brothers and sisters!" he said in a loud voice, "Our labors have been rewarded. I bring you fish for your dinner. God has smiled upon us. We shall prepare a feast in His name."

Several of the men from shore waded into the water as the bow of the *Emma Rose* touched the sand. They crowded around, admiring all the fish and looking up at Strang, who was still standing on the bow.

"While you were resting from your toil, I journeyed across the harbor. At Whiskey Point, in the lair of the gentiles, I met these Irish fishermen and persuaded them of the worthiness of our cause. They have seen our righteousness and have agreed to donate these fish, freely and in good will. We shall have a feast and we welcome them to join us in our celebration to the Lord. Our missionary efforts are destined for success, be it across the ocean or across our own little harbor."

Ian and Patrick had been watching Strang and listening to his speech. Ian looked over at Patrick and rolled his eyes.

36

"I don't know about you, but I'm getting hungry," Patrick said.

"Well, let's get these fish unloaded before they start to stink," Ian replied.

He grabbed the nearest fish and lowered it down to a man standing in the water. Startled, the man grabbed it and handed it to another man standing behind him. Patrick did the same on his side of the boat. Soon two lines of men were passing fish to shore as fast as Ian and Patrick could unload them.

In a field below the temple, Mary Strang and several other women were working at a wooden table near a fire lined with stones. They baked cornbread on the hot stones and boiled rutabagas and a few potatoes in a kettle hanging over the fire. One of the women had brought in several bundles of spindly carrots to add to the stew.

Strang jumped off the bow of the *Emma Rose* and waded ashore. He walked toward the women, his arms spread wide.

"I have come to supplement this meager meal with a fresh catch of lake trout and whitefish," he said. "These humble fishermen have truly been our deliverance today. We shall have a feast tonight worthy of our new temple. Now, shall we move this kettle so the men can cook these fish?"

"But the rutabagas aren't cooked yet," protested Mary.

"They will do just as they are," Strang said.

Two of the men moved the kettle off the fire and replaced it with an iron grill. They started to gut the fish as others came forward to clean and filet them. In just a few minutes the first fish landed on the grill and began to sizzle.

Sarah was still sitting next to Andy in the stern of the boat and Nathan had joined them. After sailing across the harbor, she knew she had made some new friends.

"Would you like to see the temple?" she asked.

"Sure," Andy said. "We've been on this boat all day. We're ready for some dry land."

Nathan jumped off the bow, dragged a rope to shore, and tied it to a stump. Andy climbed over the side and raised a hand to help Sarah. She reached for him and slid off the boat into the shallow water.

"Come on," Sarah said. "There's a big tree behind the temple. You can see the whole harbor. I'll show you!"

Sarah waded ashore, skipped across the beach, and took off running, excited to show her new friends around her island home. Andy and Nathan waded to the beach and ran up the hill after her. Behind the temple they came to the base of an ancient oak tree. Sarah climbed up a crooked branch that almost touched the ground. Andy and Nathan grabbed the branch and climbed up beside her.

"Look," she said. "This is the best view on the island."

"There's the point where we sold our fish," Andy said, looking across the bay.

"That's Whiskey Point. The gentiles sell whiskey there to the fishermen."

"This is a perfect harbor," Nathan said. "There's room for plenty of boats. It looks deep, too. Look how dark the water is."

"That's my house, over on the other side of the temple," Sarah said. "Beyond that is the village. It's small, but more people will be moving here this summer."

"We like your island, Sarah." Andy said. "Can you show us around the harbor some time?"

"Sure," she said, "but we'd better get back to the temple. My parents will be looking for me."

"We're hungry anyway. I can smell those fish cooking from here."

They started back down the hill toward the temple. Smoke was rising from the fire and they could hear voices of the crowd gathering for the feast.

"Hey," Nathan said, "look over there. There's someone hiding behind the temple wall."

"It's my mother!" Sarah exclaimed, running ahead of the two boys. "Mother, what's the matter? What are you doing back here?"

Mary was sitting on a log with her head slumped in her hands. She turned when she heard Sarah's voice.

"Sarah..." Her eyes were red.

"Mother, have you been crying?"

"I'm sorry, Sarah," Mary said. "I worked so hard to prepare a meal. I went to everyone's house I could think of. No one has any food to spare. All I could find was rutabagas and potatoes, and then your father brings a load of fish he got from those Irish fishermen."

"Mother..."

Andy and Nathan had come up behind them.

"Mother, these are my new friends. This is Andy and this is Nathan."

"Pleased to meet you, mum," Andy said.

Mary looked up, startled. She had not seen the boys standing behind Sarah. She rose to her feet and quickly regained her composure. "Hello, boys. I'm very pleased to meet you."

"Thank you, mum."

"Mother, would you like to sit with us for the feast?" Sarah asked.

"Yes, I would. I'd like that very much."

Sarah took her mother by the arm and led her down the hill, with Andy and Nathan following close behind.

James Strang was pacing back and forth in front of the temple, looking for the rest of his family. Most of the fish were grilled and the women were beginning to serve the food. Strang wanted his wife and daughter at his side.

Mary came walking around the corner of the temple with Sarah still holding her arm.

"Where have you been?" he demanded. "Everyone is seated. We're ready to eat."

"I'm sorry, father." Sarah said. "We were up by my tree showing Andy and Nathan the view of the harbor."

"You can do that later. The ceremony is about to begin. I'm going to speak, and so is Tobias Humphrey."

Sarah and Mary started to make their way to a vacant table.

"No," he said, "Mary, I want you up front with me. Sarah, you go sit with Gurdon Humphrey and Oren Whipple."

"But I want to sit with my new friends!"

"Gurdon is your friend, Sarah. You may sit with your new friends, but go back to Gurdon's table."

"Yes, father." Sarah glared at him and stalked through the crowd to the back of the temple. Andy and Nathan followed, wondering what the fuss was about.

Two boys were sitting at the last table in the back. They looked about the same age, but one was almost twice as big as the other.

"Andy, Nathan, this is Gurdon," Sarah said.

Gurdon was big, with a puffy face and a pale complexion. He eyed the newcomers with suspicion.

"And this is Oren," Sarah added, pointing to a scrawny kid with hollow cheeks. He looked like he needed a good meal. He didn't say much, or even raise his eyes.

"I hear you're Irish," Gurdon said.

"That's right," Andy said. "We just got here today."

"Those are some big fish you caught. You must have got lucky."

"I guess we did. We never caught fish that big in Ireland."

"Well, this ain't Ireland. This is Beaver Island. This is a Mormon island, you know."

"I'm sorry," Nathan said, "but we don't know what a Mormon is."

"You don't? Well, you should. Sarah's daddy is the head of the Mormons. He says that we're the chosen people, destined to inherit the earth. He's a prophet, ordained by God. Next to him is my pa. He's second in command."

Nathan turned and looked toward the front of the temple. He saw James Strang sitting at a table with a rotund man with long sideburns and a swollen, bulbous face. Nathan was surprised to see his father and Ian McGuire seated at the table on either side of them.

"Sarah, come and sit next to me," Gurdon said.

"I'd rather sit over here," Sarah said. "I can see better." Sarah sat down between Andy and Nathan.

"But——" Gurdon protested.

"Shhh. They're going to speak."

James Strang rose and stood on his chair to address the crowd. He was a short man with piercing eyes and a bushy red beard. Everyone in the temple looked at him expectantly.

"My brothers and sisters, I welcome you to this feast of the new Mormon temple. Today you have put up walls to bring strength to our temple, and I have provided food to the table to bring sustenance to your bodies. The Lord has worked through these men seated with me, inspiring them to donate these fish to our congregation. I introduce you to Ian McGuire and Patrick O'Donnell, recently of Ireland and now residing on Beaver Island. They join us in our feast, along with their two fine sons. When I met these men, less than an hour ago, they had just arrived. Even though their first landing was at Whiskey Point, lair of the gentiles, they were so taken with the beauty of our harbor that they called it Paradise Bay. For all of us who live here, who have been persecuted for so long, this truly is a bay of paradise. Therefore, I now name this harbor Paradise Bay, refuge of the true Mormon believers, today and for all time. Ian and Patrick, we welcome you to our Mormon community. You are free to live among us. We will help you as you have helped us, and we pray that someday you will join us in worship."

"Hey, Sarah," Gurdon said, "Your father sure talks a lot."

Sarah turned to face Gurdon. He had poked his fingers into a decapitated fish head and was moving its jaws to make it speak. Sarah jumped and grabbed Andy by the arm, clinging to him. "Stop it, Gurdon. That's disgusting."

At the front table, Strang took Ian and Patrick each by the arm and gestured for them to stand. Strang raised their hands up high. The crowd in the temple clapped and cheered. Ian and Patrick smiled sheepishly. They both looked like they wanted to be somewhere else.

After they sat down, Tobias Humphrey rose to speak. "My fellow Mormons, thanks go out to our prophet James. He has brought us to this island home and he has engaged our labor to build this temple of worship. Today he has named our harbor Paradise Bay, and a fitting name it is indeed. We truly have found a port of refuge. However, I would go one step further: I propose that we name our new village after our prophet and leader. I propose that we call our village Saint James."

Everyone in the crowd clapped and cheered.

Strang rose again. "Thank you, Tobias, and thank you, brothers and sisters. I humbly accept and endorse your proposal. We shall now call our home Saint James."

When the speeches were over, the feast began. After a hard day of work everyone was hungry, and they loaded their plates with fish as fast as the men at the grill could cook them. It wasn't long before the fish were gone, and the Mormon families gathered their tools and headed for home. Some of them lived in the village, but most had a longer journey to farms and homesteads south of the harbor. They climbed on horse-drawn wagons, and the children piled in back and snuggled down between bales of hay for the ride home.

The sun was beginning to set in the west behind the forest. The last rays streamed across the harbor and illuminated trees on Whiskey Point with brilliant shades of yellow and orange. Sarah and Andy and Nathan walked down the beach to the *Emma Rose,* followed by Gurdon and Oren. Ian and Patrick came behind them accompanied by Strang and Tobias Humphrey.

"You are welcome to spend the night here on the beach with your boat," Strang said.

"Thanks, but I think we'll go out in the harbor and anchor in deep water," Ian replied. "We're exposed to an east wind here."

"I would go over to the north side of the harbor," Tobias said. "You'll be protected from the wind over there. Just head for those big pine trees."

"That does look like a good spot to anchor," Ian said. "Thanks for the suggestion."

"That would be a good place to build a cabin," Strang said. "There's a flat building site behind those trees. The land is free and you'll be right on the trail to Alva Cable's store on Whiskey Point."

"Maybe we'll build a dock this summer," Patrick said.

"The water is deep over there," Tobias said. "You'll be able to tie up close to shore in the meantime."

Andy and Nathan were standing next to Sarah. They were both reluctant to leave.

"Will you still show us around the island?" Andy asked.

"I will, I promise," Sarah replied.

"How about this Saturday?"

"I can't on Saturday because it's our day of worship. Maybe on Sunday…"

"Sunday would be fine."

Sarah glanced over at her father. "Yes, I think I can."

"Great. We'll see you then."

The two boys waded out into the water and climbed aboard. The men shook hands and Ian retrieved the rope tied to the stump. "Thank you very much for welcoming us to Beaver Island," he said. "We did not expect such a warm reception."

"We are always glad to see new faces in our community," Strang replied. "This will be a big city someday, and this harbor will be full of boats. You, my friends, have arrived just in time to see it happen."

"Gurdon, why don't you and Oren push their boat off the sand bar," Tobias said.

"But we'll get our feet wet."

"It won't hurt you to get wet. Come on. I'll give you a hand."

Tobias and Gurdon and Oren waded out and pushed the *Emma Rose* into deeper water. Nathan raised the mainsail and the boat swung away from shore. Sarah watched and waved as her new friends set sail.

Andy looked back at her and waved. "See you soon, Sarah."

The harbor was calm and the boat moved slowly along the shore, catching a light breeze. Ian and Patrick stood near the stern, savoring the silence of the harbor after the noise and speeches in the Mormon temple.

"That was a bigger welcome than we bargained for," Ian said.

"I'll say," replied Patrick. "They seem like good people."

"Father, what exactly is a Mormon?" Nathan asked.

"I'm not sure, but I have the feeling we're going to find out soon enough."

CHAPTER 3:

The First Summer

It wasn't long before James Strang realized that he was asking too much of his congregation. It was his wife Mary who finally convinced him.

"James, you've got to stop summoning the men to work on your temple every day. They haven't even had time to plant their crops and some of them are still living in tents."

"I must have a temple for my kingdom," Strang said.

"Do you think everyone's going to live in your temple? They need houses of their own. They need to plant crops so they have something to eat. You're not going to have a kingdom if these people have no food and no shelter," Mary said.

"I have faith that if we all work together we will build a community."

"Faith? So far you've asked these men to build a home for us, and now you want them to build a temple and a building for your printing press. James, I know these people love you, but they must have time to take care of their own families."

"I have given them free land—"

"Yes, you did, but—"

"More people are moving here this summer. I am sure that we can finish the temple and still accomplish—"

"But the crops need to be planted right now. It's already late in the season. James, don't you remember last year when you explored this island? You told me you almost starved to death. You said that you had to cut firewood and beg for food from the gentiles out at Whiskey Point. Now here we are a year later and we still have to beg."

"Those Irish men donated their fish—"

"It's good that they did, because we didn't have enough food for a meal of our own."

"We had a feast. What's the problem with that?"

"The problem is that winter is coming in several months. Your people are going to starve, like you almost did, or they're going to leave the island."

"Leave? They can't leave. I brought them here."

"They most certainly can leave. Then where will your kingdom be?"

Strang thought for a moment and sighed. "I suppose you're right, Mary. I will postpone work on the temple until next spring so everyone can plant crops. But I do need a building for my printing press."

"That's fine," Mary said. "The island needs a newspaper. If you start with a just a small building you can always add to it later."

On Saturday Strang preached a powerful sermon. He told the congregation he had been visited by an angel. The angel spoke to him of the desire of the Lord to build a strong community that would last forever. To accomplish this, Strang said that all work on the temple must stop for the summer months so that the brethren could build homes and plant crops for their families. Strang himself would work on building a print shop, along with a few trusted volunteers. Furthermore, he announced that in the fall he would embark on a mission trip to cities in the east to spread the word of the Mormon community on Beaver Island. He would return with new converts, and they would all work together to complete the temple the following summer.

—⁓—

Sarah had been waiting anxiously for Sunday to arrive. She was hoping to see her new friends Andy and Nathan, but she was not sure her parents would allow her to visit them, for the *Emma Rose* was anchored near the trail to Whiskey Point.

After breakfast, her father announced that he was going to see Tobias Humphrey. "Sarah, would you like to come with me?" he asked. "Gurdon has been asking about you."

"I think I'll stay here and help mother this morning."

"I thought you wanted to get out of the house."

"But mother needs help with the dishes."

"All right, suit yourself, but Gurdon will miss you. Mary, I'll be gone most of the day. Tobias and I are making plans for the print shop."

"Don't be late for dinner," Mary replied.

Strang put on his overcoat and headed out the door, closing it behind him.

Sarah threw up her hands in frustration. "I can't believe it!"

"What, Sarah?" her mother asked, looking up from the table.

"I can't believe father thinks I like Gurdon Humphrey."

"Gurdon is a little plump, isn't he?"

"It's not that, Mother. He's odd. He's always showing me dead animals."

"Well, that won't do. Perhaps you are right to stay away from him. What about his friend Oren?"

Sarah looked up in exasperation. "Mother, please!"

"Sorry, dear," Mary said with a smile. "I'll leave you alone."

Sarah grabbed a brush and began washing the breakfast dishes. She stacked them on the table and then she scrubbed all the pots and pans and propped them against the fireplace to dry.

Mary watched her daughter with amusement. "Sarah, you certainly are busy. What's the hurry?"

"I was wondering, do you think I could go visit Andy and Nathan today? They don't live very far away."

"I thought you might be asking me that," Mary replied. "Of course you can go visit your friends, but promise me you won't go any farther around the harbor. I don't want you anywhere near those men out at Whiskey Point."

Sarah ran across the room and hugged her mother. "Thank you, Mother. I'll be careful, I promise."

She went to her bedroom, brushed her hair, and put on a clean summer dress. After straightening her hair one more time, she skipped across the living room toward the front door.

"Don't forget what I told you about Whiskey Point," her mother said.

"I'll be careful."

Sarah ran down the front path and headed along the lane curving around the harbor. In the distance she could already see the *Emma Rose*, anchored near shore. She had been thinking all week about her sail across the harbor and how kind Andy and Nathan had been to her. She couldn't wait to see her new friends. Her heart was light for the first time since she had arrived on the island.

Andy and Nathan were busy working on shore, building racks to dry fishing nets. Ian and Patrick had abandoned the hooks and lines, replacing them instead with nets that would be secured to poles driven into the lake bottom. Ian said they could increase their catch by using the nets provided with the *Emma Rose*, as long as they were set in a good place and checked every day.

Nathan glanced up and saw Sarah approaching. "Hey, Andy, look who's coming."

Andy looked up and saw her. "Hi, Sarah," he called. "We're over here."

"Hi," Sarah said with a smile, leaving the path to join them. She suddenly felt shy.

"We were going to try to find you this afternoon," Nathan said. "All we have to do is hang these nets on the rack to dry, and then we're done."

"Still want to show us around the harbor?" Andy asked.

"Yes, if you want me to," Sarah said, feeling a bit more at ease.

She sat down on a log and watched as the two boys finished hanging nets. She had never met anyone who had just arrived from a foreign country. They both had the same Irish accent and yet they were so different from each other. Andy was more outgoing and seemed to always take the lead, and yet it was Nathan who seemed to be confident in his own quiet way. Together, they both were so intriguing compared to the Mormon boys she knew on Beaver Island.

"There," said Andy, hanging the end of the last net across the rack. "This net will be dry by evening if the sun stays out." He turned to Sarah. "We're ready. Where should we start?"

"Let's go back to the village." Sarah stood up and started back along the path with Andy and Nathan following. They passed several log cabins and a couple of fishing boats floating quietly near the shore. The bay was calm and hardly a ripple disturbed the sandy beaches. Overhead, branches of pine trees swayed gently in a light summer breeze.

"This is a great harbor," Nathan said. "Our boat has barely moved since we anchored."

"Did you really name it Paradise Bay?" Sarah asked.

"Actually, we did," Andy said. "I think it was Nathan's father who came up with the name. He said the bay reminded him of Ireland."

"My father sort of of took it from you, didn't he?"

"I think anyone would call it Paradise Bay. Look at the color of that water."

They all stopped and looked out at the harbor. The water was a shimmering deep blue and in the shallow areas along the shore it glowed with a brilliant turquoise color. A single puffy cloud hovered high in the sky as if it were moored over the island and reluctant to ever leave.

"It's a lot better than the harbor on Mackinac Island," Nathan remarked.

Farther around the harbor, Sarah pointed out some of the new houses and buildings. "There's Johnson's store, built last winter. He's building a dock this summer. Mr. Humphrey owns the lumber mill beyond the temple and he wants to build another one on the north side of the harbor. My father's going to build a school and a building for a newspaper this fall."

"Is that the whole town?" Andy asked, recalling the bustling waterfront on Mackinac Island.

"It's all new," Sarah replied. "The first settlers came over just last summer, and we moved here this spring."

"Where did you come from?" Nathan asked.

"We lived in Voree, Wisconsin for a year. My parents tried to start a farm, but my father wasn't much of a farmer. He joined the Mormon Church and then he discovered Beaver Island and decided to start a Mormon mission here. A lot of people from Voree are moving here."

"What do you do for fun around here?" Andy asked.

"I go to the North Beach," Sarah said.

"Where's that?"

"I'll show you." Sarah turned off the path and stepped into the woods, pushing aside the underbrush.

"Hey, wait for us! Where are you going?"

"To the North Beach. It's my secret place. No one ever goes there except me. C'mon, I'll show you the way."

Sarah jumped behind a crooked old oak tree and raced away through a grove of majestic pines. Andy and Nathan ran after her, trying to keep up, but Sarah knew this part of the forest well. She ran around a stand of birch trees and across a meadow, her long legs whisking through the grass. Just as Andy and Nathan came out of the woods behind her, Sarah jumped over a steep bluff and landed in soft sand, whooping with joy. She kept running all the way down to the beach, kicked off her shoes, and waded out into the cool water of Lake Michigan.

Andy and Nathan stood at the top of the bluff, panting for air. Sarah looked back at them and laughed. "What took you so long?" she shouted, splashing the water with her hands.

Andy jumped off the bluff, landed with a thud, and rolled down the steep slope. Nathan followed close behind him, plowing up a cascade of sand. They ran down to the beach just as Sarah came out of the water.

"You almost lost us, Sarah," Andy said, catching his breath.

"You're just too slow," Sarah replied with a smile.

"This is a beautiful beach," Nathan said. "Our shores back in Ireland are all rocky."

"Let's go down to that point," Sarah said. "I'll show you the other islands."

She put on her shoes and they all headed down the beach, kicking the sand and picking up small stones and shells. They soon reached a long sandy point, covered with grass and pebbles. A flock of seagulls squawked and took flight. On the horizon a group of islands gleamed in the midday sun.

"We call that one Garden Island," Sarah said. "A tribe of Indians lives over there. They come into the harbor sometimes."

"Real Indians?" Andy asked. "Do they wear war paint?"

"No, they're really nice. Sometimes the chief comes to see my father."

"What are the rest of those islands called?" Nathan asked.

"I'm not sure. I don't think they even have names."

"Let's go around the point. I want to see what's over there," Andy said.

"I can't go too far. That way goes back around toward Whiskey Point. I'll be in trouble if I even go near that place alone."

"But you're not alone, you're with us. Come on. We'll just go a little way."

This time Andy and Nathan went ahead, with Sarah following behind. They climbed up a low sand dune, making a trail through the tall grass. On the other side of the dune they saw another long sandy shoreline stretching into the distance.

"Hey, look," Nathan said, "there's someone else on the beach."

"Who is it?" Sarah asked, still climbing up the sand dune.

"I think it's your father, Sarah," Andy said.

"Oh, no, don't let him see me!" she exclaimed, dropping down low in the grass.

Andy and Nathan both crouched down so they were out of sight. Carefully they raised their heads above the grass and peered at the figure in the distance.

"Look, there's someone with him," Nathan said. "It looks like a girl."

Sarah crawled up next to them and raised her head for a look.

"Who's that with your father, Sarah?" Andy asked.

"I think her name is Elvira Field. Father says she's a schoolteacher. They must be talking about the school he wants to build this fall."

"Yeah, then how come he's got his arm around her?" Andy asked.

Nathan jabbed his friend in the ribs with his elbow. "Come on," he said, "I think we better get out of here."

They crawled back through the grass, slid down the dune, and quickly walked back the way they had come. No one said much. Nathan tried to skip a few stones without much success. Soon they reached the path where they had jumped down to the beach earlier in the day. They climbed the bluff and walked back through the woods to the harbor.

"I better go home," Sarah said. "My father might come back along this path. He doesn't know I'm out. He'll be angry with me."

"But all we did was go for a walk on the beach," Andy said.

"I know, but I went near Whiskey Point, and no one was with me."

"We were with you."

"No, I mean an adult, a Mormon, someone who…" Sarah was getting flustered. "Someone who can watch me. I like to get away. That's why I sneak through the woods to the North Beach, just so I can have some time alone."

Andy and Nathan both looked at her with curiosity.

"I'm sorry. It's not your fault. I really had a fun time today."

"We can meet again next week," Andy suggested.

"I don't know…"

"Listen, Sarah, your father knows us. It will be all right."

"Do you think so?"

"Sure. Next time we'll just walk the other way on the beach, away from Whiskey Point."

"That would be safer…"

"And we'll come to your house so you don't have to walk over here alone."

"That's a good idea. I'll take you to my secret berry patch. No one knows about it but me." She gave them both a smile and turned and headed for home. Andy and Nathan watched her leave and then headed back toward the *Emma Rose*.

"Wait," Sarah said, calling back to them. "My father promised that we could go to school together in the fall. Then we'll be able to see each other every day."

"That's true, he did say that," Andy replied. "We'll see you next week, Sarah."

Sarah skipped down the path, happy again and thinking about how wonderful her new friends were. They were so much fun to be with and she could not help thinking how handsome they both were. Andy had a wild and disheveled look about him that matched his free spirit, and Nathan had a quiet look and demeanor that made her think she could always depend on him. Everything would be all right now now that she had some friends, she thought as she approached her house.

"So, what did you think about Sarah's father and the schoolteacher?" Andy asked Nathan as they returned to the *Emma Rose*.

"About the same thing you did," Nathan said. "It looked fishy to me, the way he had his arm around her."

"Me, too," Andy replied. "Maybe that's why he doesn't want Sarah going to Whiskey Point."

Nathan shrugged. "Guess we better see if those nets are dry. We've got to get them coiled and loaded on the boat. We're supposed to go out fishing early tomorrow morning."

Andy and Nathan spent most of the summer out on the *Emma Rose*, checking nets in the morning and hauling in fish in the afternoon. It was hard work in the hot sun, but at the end of each day they returned to the harbor with a full catch. Even then the work was not done, for Ian and Patrick insisted that the fish be packed in salt immediately to keep them fresh. The only break usually came in the middle of the day. This was a lazy time when they ate lunch, dozed, and watched over the nets while the *Emma Rose* rocked gently in the waves, tied off to a net stake.

"Father, did you ever find out what a Mormon is?" Nathan asked one day.

"Actually, I did," Patrick replied. "When I went out to Cable's Store I asked Alva Cable about them. He says they came here from Wisconsin, but most of them are originally from Illinois."

"They're different than the other Americans we've met," Nathan said.

"Well, they do have their own customs, that's for sure. I guess you'd call them a church or a religion."

"Is it like our church back in Ireland?"

"Not really. The Mormons follow one leader. They believe he is a prophet sent from the Lord to give them direction."

"Who is that?" Nathan asked.

"According to Alva Cable, it was originally a man named Joseph Smith, but he was murdered a couple of years ago. Now there are two men who claim to be prophets. One of them, a man named Brigham Young, led a wagon train out west to Utah territory to start a Mormon commune. The other one, James Strang—"

"Sarah's father?"

"Yep, Sarah's father. He came to Beaver Island to start his own Mormon commune."

"Is he really a prophet?"

"The people who live here seem to think so."

"Are they going to make us leave the island if we don't join their church?" Nathan asked.

"Whatever gave you that idea?"

"I don't know. They just seem so serious about everything."

"Well, they are serious," Patrick replied, "but don't you worry about it. We have just as much right to be here as they do."

CHAPTER 4:

Winter Chill

As summer ended, strong winds kept the *Emma Rose* off the lake for days at a time. Ian and Patrick began constructing a log cabin near the crude dock they had built in the spring. It was hard work, but they knew that they could not live on the boat when winter arrived. One of the Mormon men lent them several saws and axes to cut trees and shape logs for the cabin.

"We need to make a trip to Mackinac Island," Patrick said. "Now that Alva Cable is buying our fish, we can get enough supplies to make it through the winter. We could also use a decent set of carpenter tools."

"That's a good idea," Ian replied. "We can buy everything we need at the Mackinac Fish Company and we'll get some more fishing gear, too."

"I think we should look for a good wagon and a team of horses next year," Patrick suggested. "Then we can haul our own barrels and maybe even start a freight hauling business on the side. We won't have to rely completely on fishing for our livelihood."

"I thought you didn't want to stay here."

"The fishing is better here, but we can't go fishing every day. These storms set us back, and we can't fish at all in the winter. If we get a wagon, maybe the boys would like to be in charge of it."

Nathan had been listening idly to their conversation, and now he really started to pay attention. "Can I take care of the horses, Father?"

"Of course you can, as long as you feed and water them every day," Patrick replied.

"Can I ride them?"

"Sure, but we'll get draft horses to haul heavy loads, so they probably won't be very exciting to ride."

"I've got to tell Andy!" Nathan hurried to the stern of the *Emma Rose*, where Andy was watching the fishing nets strung out behind the boat.

"You were right about those two boys," Ian remarked.

"How so?" Patrick asked.

"They've adjusted perfectly to this country. I'm not sure they even remember Ireland."

"Oh, they remember Ireland all right. I know I do."

"You know, if we go to Mackinac Island, we'll be able to send some letters home."

"I never thought of that," Patrick said. "All the more reason to go. As soon as we finish the cabin and the lake freezes over, we'll talk to Alva and plan a trip across the ice."

One day in October, the wind was again too strong for the *Emma Rose* to venture out on the lake. The boat was anchored safely, but whitecaps could be seen at the harbor entrance, and a powerful wind was blowing through the trees overhead. Ian and Patrick and the two boys went back to work on the log cabin. They finished raising the rafters and began nailing planks across them. Patrick was down on the ground cutting and splitting cedar shingles to make a sturdy waterproof roof. He was just getting ready to split another shingle when Sarah Strang came running up the path.

"Sarah! What brings you over here in the middle of the day?"

Sarah stopped, panting for breath. She had such a look of despair on her face that Patrick put down his axe and hurried over to her. "What's the matter?" he asked.

"We're leaving the island," she replied, holding back her tears.

Both boys dropped their tools and looked down at her in surprise.

"For good?" Patrick asked.

"No, just for the winter."

"Where are you going?"

"My father decided to go on a mission to New York. He says he needs more converts to bring back to the island. My mother doesn't want to stay here all winter with three kids and a baby, so we're going with him."

By this time Andy and Nathan had climbed down from the rafters.

"When will you be back?" Andy asked.

"In the spring, but that means we won't be able to go to school together."

"I'm so sorry, Sarah," Andy said, reaching out for her hand. "When did you find out?"

"My father's been talking about it for a while. They decided last night and told me this morning. We're going to live with my grandparents in Buffalo while father goes east to find people to join his church."

Everyone was silent for a minute while Sarah dried her tears.

Patrick knew how attached the three friends had become over the summer. "Sarah, why don't you have lunch with us?" he asked. "We were just getting to take a break anyway."

"Thank you. I would like that," Sarah said.

Patrick went inside the unfinished cabin, bustled around for a few minutes, and came back out with bread, pork, apples and berries.

Ian, who had been listening from the top of a ladder, climbed down and joined them. "I have an idea," he said. "We were planning on building a second cabin this winter, but we don't really need to do it right away. How about if we build a schoolhouse instead? Then next year you can all start school together in a new school building, instead of crowding into someone's cabin. How does that sound?"

"That's a long time from now," Andy said.

"I know, but it's the best we can do," Ian replied. "I'll go see Sarah's father this afternoon. He can tell me where he wants to build it and we'll plan it before you leave. How does that sound?"

The idea of a new schoolhouse cheered everyone up. While they ate lunch, they talked about what the school should look like and how they could all help finish the classrooms in the spring. Sarah thought she could bring some school supplies back with her from Buffalo. Andy and Nathan wanted a bell so they could mount it on a post in the schoolyard.

Ian went to visit James Strang that afternoon and together the two men selected a site for a new schoolhouse north of Johnson's Store.

"You are a most generous man, Ian McGuire," Strang said. "I assure you that I will be back in the spring with a boatload of converts to our faith, and their children will fill our schoolhouse. We will have Irish and Mormon children sitting side by side and learning together."

"We'll need a schoolteacher for our new school," Ian said.

"I will provide a schoolteacher," Strang replied. "In fact I already have one in mind who will be perfect for the job, if she will accept my proposition."

A week later, Sarah and her family gathered in front of Johnson's Store and watched the steamer *Oneida* pull up to the dock. Andy and Nathan had arrived early to help them carry their luggage. Tobias and Gurdon Humphrey, Oren Whipple, and many of the Mormon brethren came down to witness the departure of their leader and prophet.

James Strang and his wife Mary and the baby filed across the gangplank and boarded the *Oneida*. Nettie and Billy skipped along after them. Sarah turned to Andy and Nathan and gave them each a hug. Her heart was pounding when she put her arms around Andy, and she could barely meet his gaze.

"I'll see you in the spring," she whispered, pressing her head against his chest.

"I'll be waiting for you," Andy said, putting his arms around her.

The ship's whistle blew and Sarah hurried on board at the last moment. Andy and Nathan picked up the gangplank and pulled it back on the dock.

The huge paddlewheels of the *Oneida* bit into the water with a gurgle and a splash. A puff of black smoke rose from the stack and the boat pulled away from the dock. James Strang was standing on the bow, waving to his people. Sarah ran up beside him and waved to her friends. Andy and Nathan both waved as long as they could see her. When the boat was halfway across the harbor, they finally stopped waving and trudged back to resume work on their log cabin.

———

After a few weeks the cabin was finished. The cracks between the logs were chinked with flat rocks and clay and Patrick fabricated a stout wooden door. Ian nailed the last few shingles along the ridge of the roof to keep out the wind and rain.

There was a chill in the air and soon it became too cold to live on the sailboat much longer. The temperature dropped below freezing almost every night. Ian and Patrick worked inside the cabin, building shelves along one wall and a sleeping loft in the rafters. Andy and Nathan began the job of moving everything off the *Emma Rose* for the winter. As they were unloading a pile of blankets, they saw Tobias and Gurdon Humphrey and Oren Whipple walking along the path on their way to Cable's store.

"Greetings, boys" Tobias said. "I see that you're getting ready for winter. That's a fine cabin you've built."

"Thank you, sir," Nathan said. "We're moving in today."

"It gets mighty cold here in the winter. Lots of snow, too."

"It doesn't snow much in Ireland. Just a lot of cold rain," Andy said.

Gurdon pointed out at the *Emma Rose*. "What are you going to do with your boat?"

"Tie it to the dock with some extra lines. We'll have two bow lines and a stern line to shore."

"But what about the ice?" Tobias asked.

"My father thinks it will be all right. We'll be right here to keep an eye on it."

"Andy, the ice here gets very thick," Tobias said. "It will crush the hull of your boat if you leave it in the water this winter. You have to get the boat up on shore. I'd better go talk to your father."

"Yeah, your father must be pretty dumb if he doesn't know that," Gurdon said.

"My father's not dumb. We always left our boat in the water in Ireland, even in the winter."

"This ain't Ireland. It's Lake Michigan, and it freezes solid."

"Now, Gurdon, let's be nice," Tobias said, patting his son on the back. "Why don't you and Oren head on out to Whiskey Point? I'll be along in a minute."

Tobias went up to the cabin to talk to Ian and Patrick. Gurdon and Oren turned and walked away, laughing and snickering. Andy glared at Gurdon and almost started after him.

Nathan grabbed him by the arm. "Andy, where are you going?"

"I'm going to get that fat tub of lard. He can't call my father dumb."

"Don't worry about it. He's just a jerk. Come on, let's get the boat unloaded."

"He'd better not do it again. Next time I'll have to teach him a lesson."

"I think he's spoiled," Nathan said. "He never has to do any work."

"The other kid is just a scrawny chicken. He always hides behind Gurdon, did you ever notice that?"

"Oren? Maybe he's just shy."

"Oh, sure," Andy said, rolling his eyes.

A few minutes later Tobias came out of the cabin, gave the boys a wave, and headed toward Whiskey Point. Ian and Patrick came down to the dock a few minutes later to help carry the blankets.

"Listen, boys," Ian said, "Tobias just explained to us what ice can do to a boat in the winter. He says when the ice gets thick enough it can push in the planks at the waterline and crush the hull."

"I guess we've still got a lot to learn about the Great Lakes," Patrick said.

"The boat will sink if we leave it in the water all winter," Ian said. "We've got to build a ramp and get it out of the water quickly, before the harbor starts to freeze. We can use those logs left over from the cabin."

For the next several days, they worked from morning to dusk to build a ramp for the *Emma Rose*. They had to smooth the shoreline, dig a sloped trench, and roll two heavy logs in the trench so they extended into the lake. When they were finished Andy and Nathan pulled in the boat until the bow was nestled between the two logs.

"Now what do we do?" Andy asked.

"I'm not sure," Ian said. "The boat weighs a ton. Somehow we've got to slide it up those logs and get it out of the water."

"If there was a tide here, we could just wait until high tide and float the boat on the ramp," Nathan said.

"Well, there's no tide, so we're going to have to figure out something else."

"It's getting dark," Patrick said. "Let's stop for the night. We'll figure it out in the morning."

After they had a late supper, Ian and Patrick sat at the table and tried to come up with a way to get the boat out of the water. They thought of using ropes, pulleys, and levers in different ways, but nothing seemed strong enough for the job. Andy and Nathan finally got bored listening to them and went up to bed in the loft.

The next morning there was a loud commotion outside. Nathan peeked out a window and saw about a dozen Mormon farmers approaching the cabin and leading a large team of oxen.

"Come on!" Nathan yelled. "We're going to get the boat out of the water."

Everyone looked out the window, quickly got dressed, and hurried outside to greet the farmers. Nathan ran over to look at the oxen. He had never seen such large animals.

"Here we are, bright and early," Tobias Humphrey said. "Someone noticed you finished your boat ramp and figured you might need some help. Word travels fast on Beaver Island."

"I guess it does," Patrick said. "Good morning to you all."

"Those are some fine animals you've got," Ian said.

"Yes, they are. They belong to Wingfield Watson, right over there."

A portly man with a full beard and a jovial smile stood near the oxen, his hand resting on their harness.

"Wingfield?" asked Ian. "That's an interesting name."

"That it is, sir, and I'm proud to have it. It's my mother's maiden name."

"We sure appreciate you bringing your team of oxen. They look very strong."

"This is how we pull our boats out of the water. They do all the work and we guide the boat and keep it from tipping over."

"Can we pet them?" Nathan asked.

"Sure, son," Wingfield replied. "Just stay away from their hooves."

"Do they have names?" Ian asked.

"You betcha," he said. "The one on the left is named Wingfield and the one on the right is named Watson."

"You named them after yourself? How come?"

"So I can remember their names," he said with a hearty laugh. "They know exactly who I am and I know exactly who they are. Makes sense, don't it?"

"I guess so," Ian said, not quite sure what to think of that idea.

"All right, men, let's get to work. We'll have this boat out in no time," Tobias said.

Several of the men tied a strong rope around the boat and hitched it to a harness between the oxen.

"Here we go!" Tobias shouted "Six men on a side."

The men lined up on each side of the boat and Wingfield stood in front of the oxen holding a line tied to their harness.

"Pull!" he commanded in a loud voice. "Pull!"

The two strong animals dug in, the rope went taut, and the boat started to move slowly up the ramp inch by inch. The men guided the boat on both sides, and when it started to wobble they kept it upright with their shoulders. When the boat was completely out of the water one of the men grabbed a thick piece of firewood and wedged it under the keel.

"In the spring, you knock that wood out and the boat will slide back into the water with just a little persuasion," he said.

"All we needed was some muscle," Ian said. "Thank you all for coming over."

"You're quite welcome," Tobias replied "That's how we do things in our Mormon community. We heard about your offer to build a school and we all want to help with that, too."

Everyone shook hands and Ian and Patrick went over and admired the team of oxen.

"We got them for plowing fields," Wingfield said, "but they're good for hauling timber and wagons. They're very strong."

"They're solid animals, that's for sure," Ian said, slapping one of the oxen on the shoulder.

"Why don't you all come inside for coffee and bread?" Patrick asked. "We can talk about the new school."

"That's a good idea," Wingfield said. "It's cold out here."

The men piled inside the tiny log cabin and took their coats off. Ian threw a log on the fire while Patrick sliced a loaf of bread and heated up a pot of coffee. Andy and Nathan climbed up in the loft and leaned over the edge, listening to the men's conversation.

"James Strang showed me a good location," Ian said. "We pounded some stakes in the ground."

"He told us it would be a one-room school, but I think it should be bigger," Tobias said. "Everyone in this room has children, and more families will be moving here next summer."

"Let's build two classrooms with an entryway and a woodstove in the middle," another man said.

"That's a great idea," Tobias replied. "I've got a woodstove I would be willing to donate."

Ian took out a piece of of paper and a pencil and began to make sketches. Everyone crowded around the table to watch and make suggestions.

"Sarah would be glad to see this," Nathan whispered to Andy.

"Yeah, she would," Andy replied. "I wonder when she's coming back."

"I don't think she really knew for sure. Sometime in the spring."

"Maybe the school will be done by then. Won't she be surprised!"

Soon the men agreed on a plan, and they promised to meet the following week to start building. Wingfield said he would bring the oxen to haul heavy logs. The men put on their coats, shook hands again, and headed out the door and back toward their farms.

"Thanks again for the help," Ian called, waving as they departed. "We'll see you next week."

Ian and Patrick looked over at the *Emma Rose*, now sitting on dry land. The boat looked much bigger out of the water.

"We'd better get some more timbers and prop up the sides. I'd hate to see her fall over," Patrick said.

"This'll be a good time to inspect the planks in the hull. Now we can see what kind of shape this boat is in," Ian replied.

The following week the men met at the site for the new schoolhouse. All of them had built their own log homes, so it didn't take them long to get started on the school. In three days they laid a stone foundation and positioned the first tier of logs. By the end of the week they had completed walls of notched timbers and were ready to install the rafters and roof beams. After three weeks the roof was completed and a plank floor was installed. The cast iron wood stove donated by Tobias Humphrey was positioned on flat stones in the center of the entryway.

"This'll keep those kids warm," Tobias remarked.

"It'll keep us warm, too," Ian replied. "Now we've got all winter to finish off the inside."

The next day several of the Mormon women brought over fresh pastries and cider to celebrate the first fire in the wood stove. Without James Strang on the island there was no one to make a speech, so everyone just milled around and admired the building. Alva Cable and several of the men from Whiskey Point arrived with a box containing a brass school bell.

"It's been on a back shelf for over a year," he said. "I knew I bought it for a good reason. We can put it on a post in the front yard."

The Mormons all admired the bell and thanked Alva for donating it. They promised to erect a stout cedar pole to hold the new bell.

By late afternoon the men had secured a window and a door in the new building. They were just in time. That night an early winter storm blew in from the west and hit the island with a blast of cold air and a blanket of deep snow. The new school was buried, the village was buried, and in a few days the harbor was covered with ice.

The island and its inhabitants were frozen in for the winter.

In January Ian and Patrick began to build a second log cabin just to the west of the first one. Work proceeded slowly because of frequent winter storms. The men were used to rain and windy weather back in Ireland, but they were not used to the bitter cold and snow of northern Michigan. By February Lake Michigan was frozen all the way to the horizon. Except for occasional jumbles of jagged ice near the shore, the lake was a flat plain of smooth ice and snow.

One day, Ian came back from Cable's store and announced that he had made arrangements to travel with Alva Cable to Mackinac Island. Alva made the trip several times each winter to buy provisions for his store.

"I'll bring back salted pork, bacon, sugar, flour, coffee, and any apples and vegetables I can get my hands on," Ian said.

"We also need a decent set of woodworking tools and some fishing gear for next season," Patrick reminded him.

Alva used a dogsled and a team of eight dogs to travel across the ice. On the morning of departure, Ian met him at the store and together they hauled out the sled. The dogs, seeing the two men and the sled, all began barking wildly and pulling on their chains. To Ian, who had never handled dogs before, it was a chaotic scene.

"Are you sure you can control these animals?" he asked.

"Oh, yeah, once we get them tied to the harness they'll settle right down. You'll see."

Ian was not at all convinced as they struggled with the dogs, but as soon as Alva attached the harness all the animals sat down on their haunches and stared at him, waiting for his command.

"They just want to run," Alva said. "That's what they live for."

"Do they know the way?" Ian asked.

"Oh, sure. We're just along for the ride. Our only job is to watch out for open water and steer around it."

"What!" Ian cried, "You didn't say anything about open water."

"Hop on," Alva called. "As soon as I release this brake, we'll be off. These dogs are ready to go!"

Against his better judgement, Ian climbed on the back of the sled. Alva released a metal bar wedged in the ice and instantly the sled jerked forward and the dogs took off running. "Hang on, Ian!" Alva shouted. "We'll be there in no time."

Ian needed no further advice. He held on with a desperate grip as the sled careened across the frozen slick surface of Lake Michigan.

Patrick, along with Andy and Nathan, had hiked out to Whiskey Point to see them off. As they watched, the dogsled receded in the distance towards Mackinac Island until it was just a speck on the horizon.

"It makes me nervous, watching them go out on the lake like that," Andy said, keeping his eye on the sled.

"Don't worry," Patrick said, "Alva has made the trip many times and the Indians have been walking across the ice for years. Let's go back to the cabin. I'll make pancakes for breakfast."

Four days later, Alva and Ian returned, cold and hungry, but otherwise in good spirits. On the return trip they had walked on either side of the sled, for the sled itself was completely loaded down with boxes of freight.

"It always takes a lot longer with all of this weight," Alva said. "The dogs are worn out. They deserve a rest."

Patrick borrowed a toboggan and the two boys loaded it up with provisions and dragged it across the harbor. Patrick and Ian trudged through the snow after them.

"How was your first dogsled ride?" Patrick asked.

Ian laughed. "It's a lot different than sailing across the lake in the *Emma Rose*. The trip was cold and fast. You should see those dogs run."

"Did it bother you to be traveling on ice on top of the lake?"

"Not much. One time I saw some open water off to the south. That made me nervous, but Alva knows what he's doing. He says the place to watch is the crossing from the mainland to Mackinac Island because of currents through the straits. Sometimes the ice breaks up, and he says it can happen very fast."

"That's not a pleasant thought," Patrick said.

"No it isn't," Ian replied. "But listen, I've got some good news."

"Did we get any mail?" Patrick asked hopefully.

"No, but on my way to the Post Office I passed the government Land Office. I was curious about land on Beaver Island, so I went inside and talked to the agent for quite a while."

"Well, what did he say?"

"He said that Alva Cable owns twenty acres of land on Whiskey Point and James Strang bought thirty acres where his house and the temple are located. The rest of the land on the island is up for grabs."

"What do you mean, up for grabs?"

"I mean the government owns the land. The island has never been settled until now, so the land is still owned by the United States government."

"So Strang doesn't own the land where he said we could build our cabin?"

"No, we do."

"What do you mean, we do?"

"We do. I bought the land."

"You did what? Good God, Ian! We can't afford to buy land."

"Sure we can. The land agent explained it all to me. All I had to do was sign an affidavit that we live on the property and we're improving it by building a house and a farm or some other type of business. The agent said that fishing counted as a business as long as the land was on the lake."

"How much land did you get?"

"Twenty acres. Ten acres for each of us. I had to pay a fee of a dollar an acre, so it only cost me twenty dollars. Look here, I even got deeds, signed and notarized by the government land agent."

Ian pulled out two official-looking certificates, one for each piece of property, and showed them to Patrick. Patrick looked them over carefully and held them up to the sunlight to examine the signatures.

"These look real, but——"

"What's the matter," Ian asked.

"Ian, you knew I wanted to stay on Mackinac Island. Why didn't you wait until you got back to ask me about this before you spent our money on land?"

"How could I? We won't be making another trip to Mackinac Island this winter, and it was too good a deal to pass up."

"Yeah, just like when you bought those boat tickets in New York."

"Oh, come on, Patrick, don't bring that up again. This is land, real land. Neither one of us has ever owned land before. I thought you'd be excited."

"Owning land is fine, but on Beaver Island? There isn't even a school here for the boys to attend."

"What are you talking about? We just built a school."

"Yeah, at a spot picked out by James Strang, just north of the Mormon temple."

"So?"

"You mark my words, that will be a Mormon school and Strang will find a Mormon teacher to teach our kids."

"But he said——"

"I know exactly what he said. He said that the school was for everyone, but I think he wants to create his own commune, and the rest of us will just be guests. You've heard how he talks about bringing more people here."

"This island is huge," Ian said. "It's a lot bigger than Mackinac Island. There's already an Irish settlement out on Whiskey Point, and that's where we sell our fish."

Patrick sighed. "Maybe you're right, Ian. I've just got a bad feeling about these Mormons."

"I'll tell you what," Ian replied, "if they try to take over the whole island, we'll just sell out to them at a profit and move back to Mackinac. How does that sound?"

"That sounds better," Patrick said. "I just hope it doesn't come to that."

By this time they had reached the frozen shore in front of their cabins. Andy and Nathan had already pulled the toboggan between the buildings and were unloading supplies.

"Do you mind if I tell them about the land?" Ian asked.

"You bought it," Patrick replied. "Go ahead."

At first Andy and Nathan didn't seem too excited about the land, perhaps because the idea of actually owning property was foreign to them. Ian finally reminded them of their friend Barrie back in Ireland who owned several acres of land on the Barrow River. Barrie had a house for his family, a big barn full of livestock, and even a boathouse on the river.

"So we can do anything we want on our land?" Andy asked.

"Yep, we can do most anything, as long as we don't bother anyone else. We'll have both cabins finished before long and next fall we'll finish the dock and build a shed to store fishing gear. After that we'll build a barn."

"Can we get another cow, like Hannah?" Nathan asked.

"Maybe someday," Patrick replied.

"How about a pair of oxen, like Wingfield and Watson?" Andy asked.

"I think they're a little big," Patrick said with a laugh. "Say, speaking of Wingfield Watson, we had a little excitement here while you were gone, Ian."

"How so?"

"On Saturday one of the men from Whiskey Point got drunk and decided to attend a Mormon worship service over at the temple. He made a lot of noise during the sermon, so they threw him out. When the service was over and everyone was outside, he jumped out from behind a tree, dropped his pants, and exposed his backside to the entire congregation. Wingfield Watson chased him off with a stick."

Ian burst out laughing. "How did you hear about this?" he asked.

"The rest of it isn't so funny. Yesterday Mrs. Watson went out to Whiskey Point to buy some flour and mail a letter. Turns out the same man was watching Alva's store while Alva was gone with you to Mackinac Island. He refused to sell her any flour and he cussed at her and tore up her letter. She came by here in tears, so I calmed her down and walked her home."

"What did Wingfield do? I'll bet he's mad as a hornet."

"Nothing yet. He wanted to take his oxen out there and tear the store down, but Tobias and some of the other men talked him out of it. But Wingfield won't forget. As you can imagine, relations aren't too good between the Mormons and the men at Whiskey Point right now."

"Alva told me there was an altercation last month when some Mormon woodcutters were chased off for cutting trees on government land."

"I guess we cut a few trees from government land ourselves, didn't we?"

"We did at first, but it's our land now. We bought it fair and square."

Patrick sighed. "And here we are, halfway around the harbor and right between the Mormons and Whiskey Point. We're in the middle of it now."

CHAPTER 5:

Independence Day

The first boats to appear in the spring were sidewheelers and the new propeller boats, stopping to take on wood to power their steam engines. All winter the Mormons had been cutting wood, hauling it to Saint James, and stacking it on Johnson's dock. Now they were selling wood to the steamboats and making a good profit for their efforts.

As the weather improved, smaller boats arrived in the harbor, mostly fishing boats from Mackinac Island. The fishermen anchored near Whiskey Point and congregated at Alva Cable's store where they could sell fish and buy provisions at one location. In the evening they gathered in the back room for a drink of whiskey and a game of poker.

One sunny afternoon in April, another steamboat pulled into the harbor. This boat, instead of approaching the dock silently, let off a blast on its steam whistle as it crossed the harbor. The noise announced the return of the *Oneida* with James Strang and his family on board, along with a group of new converts to the Mormon Church. The passengers had listened to Strang preach in cities on the east coast during the winter. They were so moved by his sermons and promises of free land, prosperity, and religious freedom that they packed up their belongings and followed him to northern Michigan. Now they stood at the rails of the *Oneida* eagerly looking at their new home for the first time.

Andy and Nathan were patching some fishing nets when they heard the whistle. They both looked up at the same time.

"Is that the *Oneida?*" Andy asked.

"I'm not sure," Nathan replied. "Let's go see."

They ran down to the shore where Ian and Patrick were nailing planks on the dock.

"That's the *Oneida*, all right," Andy said. "Father, can we go down to the boat dock?"

"What for? Do you have those nets finished yet?"

"We're almost done. Sarah Strang might be on the *Oneida*."

"How do you know?"

"She said she would be."

"Oh, I see," Ian said, unconvinced. "Yeah, run along, but don't be disappointed if she's not on board today. You need to get those nets done."

"Don't worry, we will."

Andy and Nathan headed toward the village. As they approached the boat dock, they could see the *Oneida* slow almost to a stop. A large group of Mormons had already gathered on the dock, the men cheering and waving their hats. James Strang stood on the bow with his arms lifted high, just as he had done on the bow of the *Emma Rose* almost a year ago. The *Oneida* maneuvered close to the dock and a sailor threw a line to one of the Mormon men.

"Look," Andy shouted, "there's Sarah on the stern. Can you see her?"

Sure enough, Sarah Strang was standing alone on the stern, shielding her eyes from the sun and looking around the harbor.

"I see her!" Nathan said.

Both boys started to run along the path. Sarah saw them and waved frantically with both arms. Andy and Nathan made their way out the dock, weaving through the crowd. Everyone was cheering and looking up at James Strang. From his pulpit on the bow Strang began to make a speech to his brethren, but the two boys ignored him as they made their way back to the stern of the *Oneida*.

Sarah appeared at a hatch on the lower level. "Andy! Nathan!" she called, waving and smiling at them. She climbed out the hatch and jumped across the gap between the boat and the dock. Andy grabbed her arm to keep her from falling backwards.

"Are you crazy? You almost fell in the lake!" Andy cried.

"Thanks for catching me," Sarah said, recovering her balance.

Nathan came up from behind to join them. The three friends were reunited at last.

"I thought we'd never make it back to the island. We waited all spring for my father to get back from New York. I was so bored I couldn't stand it any more."

"Well, you haven't missed anything around here," Andy said, still holding her arm.

"Yeah, it's been pretty quiet," Nathan said. Sarah looked more grown-up after being away all winter. For the first time Nathan noticed how pretty she was.

By this time James Strang had finished his speech. The crowd surged forward to greet the new arrivals to the island. The gangplank dropped and Sarah's mother appeared among the passengers, holding Hattie and closely followed by Nettie and Billy.

"Hello, Mrs. Strang," Andy called. "May we help you with your luggage?"

"Hello, boys. How are you? Yes, I could use some help."

Andy and Nathan made their way through the crowd, helped Sarah's mother and the children off the boat, and then grabbed all of their suitcases and bags.

"We'll carry them up to your house for you," Nathan said.

"Thank you so much," Mary said. "It's been a long journey. The children are very tired."

Andy and Nathan led the way through the crowd and headed toward the Strang house. Sarah walked behind them with the two younger children, and Mary followed with Hattie. James Strang had disembarked and was telling the crowd about his success as a missionary during the winter. The audience listened in rapt attention, grateful for the return of their leader.

James Strang was back on the island, but he didn't stay long. During April and May he was preoccupied with assigning land and finding temporary housing for the new arrivals to the island. He spent his days staking out property, and in the evening he worked at the Mormon temple. He was so busy that he seldom was home, and Sarah only saw him early in the morning. When he did come home, he either went straight to bed or worked on his sermons by candlelight.

Later in the month, after the new settlers had been provided for, Strang made an announcement from the pulpit in the unfinished temple.

"My brothers and sisters, our brethren in Wisconsin have appeared to me in a vision. They have called out to me and I have heard their supplications. I will go to them and tend to their needs. I shall return with the truly faithful so that they also may share in our blessings and prosperity here on Beaver Island. Upon my return, I will call for a church conference to unite our two communities, safe from our oppressors. Our strength will grow in numbers as we gather on this island to set forth the tenets of our church. On July 8 we shall celebrate the organization of our kingdom in a ceremony that I shall reveal to you only on that day. We will establish a kingdom of the Lord and banish all non-believers from this island."

After the sermon the congregation filed out of the temple, greeting each other in the aisles. They all agreed that this was one of the most powerful sermons that James Strang had ever delivered. That afternoon, Sarah hurried home to get her father's things together. She washed his clothing, hung it out to dry, pressed his shirts and packed his suitcase. Strang planned to depart in the morning on the *Oneida*, bound for Wisconsin.

Sarah's mother was upset that he was leaving again. She had finally resigned herself to living on Beaver Island, but after spending a long winter alone with the children in Buffalo, she was hoping that her husband would stay home with his family.

"James, must you go? We've only been home a few weeks."

"Mary, you know I must serve my people. It is my duty."

"But your own children hardly know you."

"They will know me upon my return, I assure you. After the conference in July they will know me as a king and a prophet of the Lord."

"They just want a father—"

"Mary, I am not convinced that you fully appreciate the magnitude of the work I am doing. Our children will know me as a father of men."

Mary sighed and retreated to the kitchen, where she busied herself with putting away the dishes from the evening meal.

Early the next morning, Sarah walked down to the boat dock with her father. The *Oneida* was ready to depart, its stacks belching black smoke into the sky.

"Sarah, I want you to watch your mother while I am gone. I fear that she has been morose. Does she seem sad while I am away?"

"Sometimes."

"When I return, we shall spend more time together, I promise. I want you to share my vision for this island."

"Yes, Father."

Strang gave Sarah a hug and kissed her on the forehead.

"You are my first child and I love you very much."

"I love you too, father. Don't worry, I'll take care of mother and the children."

Strang picked up his suitcase and clambered aboard the Oneida.

"Goodbye, Sarah. I'll be back in two weeks," he called from the gangplank.

Sarah waved and watched as the *Oneida* pulled away from the dock. She had always been very close to her father, but somehow it was different this year. He seemed distant and preoccupied. Perhaps he was simply burdened with the task of caring for all of the new converts to the church. She tried to understand, but like her mother, she wished he would spend more time with his family.

When Sarah returned home, she found that her mother had gone back to bed. Hattie was playing by herself in the corner and Nettie and Billy were squabbling again. Sarah sighed and went into the kitchen to wash the breakfast dishes.

In a couple of days, Mary cheered up and took charge of the household again. Freed of having to help her husband every day at the temple, she was able to spend more time with the children. Sarah usually took care of the baby in the morning. In the afternoons, Mary sent her to Johnson's Store or allowed her to walk around the harbor to visit Andy and Nathan, warning her each time to stay away from Whiskey Point.

Sarah was elated to be back on the island. Every day she walked down to the harbor and looked for the mast of the *Emma Rose*. Sometimes Andy and Nathan were out fishing, but the lake could be rough in May, so the boys were often home, working around the dock or repairing nets. She found herself thinking more and more of Andy, and she often daydreamed about him while she was completing her chores around the house. Andy had changed over the winter, and he was now a lanky young man, brown from the sun and strong from handling fishing nets. Sarah was still a young girl, but she too had changed over the winter, and she found herself drawn to Andy in ways that she did not yet understand.

Sometimes on Sundays the three friends returned to North Beach. When they reached the shore they headed west, away from Whiskey Point and toward Sarah's secret berry patch. Although the berries were not yet ripe, they always stopped and sat on the grass overlooking Lake Michigan. Andy and Nathan told Sarah stories about their home in Ireland and about their voyage across the ocean. She laughed when they told her about their arrival in New York and about how Andy's father threw John Smith off the pier for taking their money.

"Andy, I can't believe your father threw a man off the dock."

"Well, he was mad. What else can I say?"

"Yes, but five minutes after you got off the boat? I'm surprised you weren't all arrested."

"At least we got our money back," Nathan remarked.

"We escaped," Andy said, "and they're still looking for us. That's why we're hiding out in your berry patch."

Sarah and Nathan both laughed. Sarah picked up a pine cone and bounced it off Andy's head.

In early July of 1850, the schooner *J.C. Spencer* sailed into the harbor, loaded with passengers from Wisconsin. It seemed that the entire village of Voree was on board. Just like the converts from New York, everyone crowded the rails of the *Spencer*, eagerly looking at Beaver Island for the first time. This time, however, James Strang was not standing in his usual place on the bow.

Sarah saw the *Spencer* entering the harbor when she stepped outside to hang up some laundry.

"Mother," she shouted, running into the house, "A new boat is in the harbor. Maybe father is on it."

Mary came outside and looked out at the *Spencer*. "I think you're right, Sarah. I see some of our friends from Voree on the bow."

"But I don't see father."

"He's probably in the ship's cabin. There's so many people on board I don't think you could see him anyway."

"Can we go down to the dock?"

"Of course we can. Help me get the children and we'll all go down together."

Sarah called to Nettie and Billy to come outside and Mary went in the house and picked up the baby. They all walked down to the boat dock to join the gathering crowd. Everyone was waiting expectantly to meet the new arrivals.

The *Spencer* slowed as it approached the shore. Two sailors threw out lines and the boat was soon tied securely to the dock. After a few moments the side hatches were opened, a gangplank was lowered, and passengers began to stream off the boat. Many of the people waiting on the dock had just moved from Wisconsin the previous year, so they welcomed old friends with smiles and handshakes. Mary saw some neighbors from Voree and hurried over to greet them.

Soon the last of the passengers were off the boat. Sarah approached one of the sailors by the gangplank. "Excuse me," she asked, "do you know if my father James Strang is on board?"

"Do you mean King Strang? Sure, he's still up in the cabin with his prime ministers," the sailor said with a grin.

Another sailor, standing nearby, burst out laughing. "Hey, don't be giving away his majesty's secrets."

Sarah had no idea what they were talking about, so she jumped on board the *Spencer* and ran across the deck to the cabin door. Inside she saw her father sitting at a crowded table, deep in conversation. She quietly entered the cabin and closed the door behind her with a click of the latch. The group at the table looked up, startled at the sound.

Strang stood up to greet his daughter. "Sarah! How did you get on board?"

Sarah came across the cabin to her father and Strang put his arms around her and gave her a kiss on the forehead.

"Gentlemen, this is my oldest child, Sarah. She is the love of my life."

"Everyone's waiting for you on the dock, Father."

"Yes, yes, I know. I must make my appearance. But first, I want you to meet my imperial council. This is George Adams, soon to be my prime minister. You remember Mr. Adams from Voree, don't you, Sarah?"

"Yes, sir." Sarah curtsied politely. George Adams was a tall and distinguished-looking man. Sarah's mother said he had been an actor in New York. He was accompanied by a beautiful and well-dressed woman who looked out of place in the cabin of the *Spencer*.

"Hello, Sarah," Adams said. "I am delighted to see you again. I would like you to meet my wife Louisa, recently of Boston. We were married this winter."

Louisa swept forward and graciously took Sarah's hand. "I'm delighted to meet you, Sarah. George has told me so much about you and your family. We must get together soon."

James Strang stepped forward and continued with the introductions. "This is Percival Graham, whom you must also remember from Wisconsin. He has agreed to serve as president of the quorum of the apostles."

"How do you do?" Sarah curtsied again, wondering what a quorum was.

"Hello, young lady. I'm very pleased to meet you," Mr. Graham said, standing and tipping his hat to her.

A third man was standing behind George Adams. He was a rough-looking character with a handlebar mustache and dark, piercing eyes.

"And this is Butch Jenkins, from Chicago," Strang said. "I hired him to be our new town marshall."

"Hello, Mr. Jenkins," Sarah said.

"Hello," Jenkins replied. His eyes did not meet Sarah's. He seemed to focus his gaze somewhere beyond her left shoulder.

Strang rose from his chair and picked up his suitcase. "Shall we go, gentlemen?" he asked. "We have much work to do. Sarah, will you lead the way?"

Sarah took her father's hand and they walked together out of the cabin. As soon as the crowd waiting on the dock saw Strang, they burst into cheers. Strang walked to the rail of the ship and waved his hat to the crowd, but this time he did not make a speech. Instead, he turned and spoke to George Adams, who was standing by his side.

"George, you'll look after the freight?" he asked above the din of the crowd.

"Yeah," Adams replied. "Those boxes are heavy. I'll have to get some of the men on the dock to give me a hand."

"Just be sure to get someone you trust. We don't want word to get out."

"What did you bring, Father?" Sarah asked.

Strang pointed at two wooden crates and a trunk strapped to the deck of the ship with heavy ropes.

"What's in them?"

"The small box is a printing press. We're going to set it up in the print shop and start a newspaper. That's what we need to make this a civilized community, don't you think, Sarah?"

"Can I help? I'm a good speller and I know everyone on the island. "

"Of course you can, my dear. I have someone in mind to run the newspaper, if she accepts my offer. I'm sure she would be glad to have your help."

"What's in the big box, father?"

"Ah, that I cannot tell you," replied Strang, patting her head. "You will know soon enough, I assure you, as will everyone else in Saint James."

"Not to mention Whiskey Point," George Adams added.

"Ah, well spoken. Well spoken indeed, Brother Adams. Now, shall we go, Sarah? I wish to see Mary and the children."

Sarah took one last look at the crate, her curiosity aroused. Whatever it was, it must be good, or why would her father wish to keep it a secret? Maybe it was something for the new schoolhouse. It might be a piano, or perhaps an organ for the temple. Some of the brethren had been wishing for an organ so they could have music at church services. Her father was certainly full of surprises, Sarah thought. She held his hand and together they walked down the gangplank.

Mary was waiting in the crowd along with Nettie and Billy. Hattie had grown restless and was starting to squirm in Mary's arms.

"James, here we are!" Mary called, trying to raise her voice above the crowd.

Strang heard her voice and headed her way, shaking hands with his admirers as he shouldered his way through the crowd. When he finally reached Mary, he embraced her and gave her a kiss on the forehead.

"James, the children are so happy to have you home. Now we can all spend some time together."

"I'm glad to be back, Mary. Where are the children? Ah, here they are, right behind me. Nettie, give me a hug. Billy, have you caught any fish while I was away? We'll go fishing soon, I promise. Mary, how is the baby? Crying again, I see."

Sarah caught up with them in the crowd and took the baby from her mother. Hattie stopped crying and snuggled in her arms. Nettie and Billy each grabbed their father by his legs, and Strang laughed and almost fell over backwards.

"I had a good trip, Mary. As you can see, many of the brethren from Voree have returned with me to live on the island, so now I will stay home and we can live together as a family once again."

"I'm so glad, James," Mary said, giving her husband a hug.

Strang looked across the heads of the crowd and saw Percival Graham walking toward the print shop.

"Mary, I brought a printing press from Voree. We're going to start our own newspaper. I must go and see that it is safely delivered to the print shop. I'll be home for dinner and I'll tell you all about it. We're going to build a kingdom, right here on Beaver Island!"

"That's wonderful, James—"

Strang disentangled himself from Nettie and Billy and started after Graham.

"Oh, and please set an extra plate this evening. I'll have a guest for everyone to meet." Strang disappeared into the crowd and left his family standing on the dock.

"I'm glad Father's home," Nettie said, pulling at her mother's sleeve.

"We're all glad, Nettie," Mary replied.

"Do you really think he'll take me fishing this time?" Billy asked.

"I'm sure he will, Billy," Mary said.

"Oh, boy! I know some great spots right here in the harbor."

"Let's head for home now, children."

Sarah looked around and saw that the crowd was dispersing. Over by the *Spencer,* she noticed that George Adams and several other men were sliding the wooden boxes down the gangplank.

"Mother, could you take Hattie?" Sarah asked. "I'll be home in a few minutes."

"All right, Sarah, but don't be long. I'll need some help with dinner."

Sarah handed Hattie back to her mother and walked over to the side of the dock. George Adams was standing by the gangplank as the men began to load the first box on a wagon.

"Hi, Mr. Adams," Sarah said.

"Hello, Sarah," Adams said. "Still here, are you?"

"I'm just curious about the boxes. They look heavy."

"They are heavy. You should have seen us trying to load them on the boat in Milwaukee."

"Is this one the printing press?"

"Yes, it is. I believe it is the only printing press in northern Michigan. We're going to set it up in the print shop and I'll be there every day to keep an eye on it."

"What's in the other box, Mr. Adams?"

Mr. Adams laughed. "My dear child, if I were to tell you I would be giving away a secret entrusted to me by your father. You would not want me to do that now, would you?

"But I won't tell anyone."

Adams got down on his knees so that his eyes were level with hers and he reached out and took her hand.

"I won't tell you what's in the box, but I will tell you this, Sarah. In your father's eyes, you are a princess. Who knows, someday soon you may be a real princess."

Sarah blushed. Except for her mother and father, George Adams was the only adult on the island that ever really spoke with her. Most of the brethren were too preoccupied with church activities or planting crops to worry much about talking to children.

"I cross my heart. I really won't tell anyone, Mr. Adams."

Adams glanced around and his voice took on a conspiratorial tone. "Sarah, soon we will demonstrate the glory of our new kingdom on Beaver Island. The first box, as you already know, contains a printing press. We will start a newspaper and with the power of the written word we will spread news to the world about the true Mormon kingdom right here on Beaver Island. The second box...Well, I really cannot tell you, Sarah. But your father tells me that you have some new friends, sons of gentile fishermen. Is that true?"

"Do you mean Andy and Nathan?"

"Ah, yes. Andy and Nathan! Sarah, if you bring them down here to the boat dock two days from now I promise that you will be the first to know what's in the second box."

"When should we be here?" Sarah asked.

"Early in the morning. But let's just let this be our little secret, shall we?"

"Sure," Sarah said. "I won't tell anyone, I promise."

"That's my girl," Adams said with a smile, releasing her hand.

"I better catch up with my family. Thanks, Mr. Adams."

"Goodbye, Sarah," he said, watching how graceful she was as she ran toward shore. He wondered what James Strang had in store for her in the next few years.

Dinner in the Strang household was always served at six o'clock. James Strang insisted on it. He said it was the one time of day they could all be together as a family. Promptly at six he arrived at the front door with a dinner guest at his side.

"Mary, you remember Elvira Field, don't you? She happened to be on the boat with us, so I took the liberty of asking her to join us for dinner. I hope you don't mind."

"Not at all," Mary replied. "Hello, Elvira. Welcome back to the island. Did your parents return with you?"

"Hello, Mrs. Strang. No, not yet. They'll be coming up as soon as they sell our farm in Voree."

"So, you're here alone?"

"Yes, for a short time. They'll be here in a few weeks."

"Well, in that case you can stay with us until your parents arrive," Mary said. "We have an extra cot we can set up in the sewing room for you. We can't have you staying alone somewhere; it isn't safe for a single girl. Will that be all right, James?"

"Of course, Mary," Strang replied. "Anything you say. I'd be delighted to have Elvira stay with us for a few days."

"Why, just last month one of our neighbors was accosted at Whiskey Point when she went to get her mail. Women just aren't safe on this island anymore."

"It does seem to be a problem," Strang agreed. "Those Irish—"

"Dinner's ready!" Sarah announced, coming into the room with a bowl of stew. She stopped, startled to see a guest by the table. She knew Elvira, but she had not seen her since last summer when the Field family first came to visit the island. Sarah remembered when she and Andy and Nathan had seen her on North Beach with her father. At that time Elvira had long black hair, but now her hair was cut very short, giving her an almost boyish look.

"Sarah, do you remember Elvira Field?" Mary asked.

"Yes, I do. Hello, Elvira."

"Hello, Sarah. It's nice to see you again."

"Shall we eat?" Strang said. "I'm starving and that stew smells delicious."

Strang sat down at the head of the table and invited Elvira to sit at his side. During the meal Strang regaled the family with tales of his exploits in the East during the winter. He told them how he and his secretary Charles Douglass had traveled to New York and Philadelphia. He described auditoriums packed with people who had come to hear him speak. While Sarah listened, she glanced across the table at Elvira. Her short hair barely covered her ears. It was parted neatly on one side and cropped straight across her forehead. Were it not for her fair complexion and soulful brown eyes, Elvira could almost have passed as a young man, Sarah thought. A bookkeeper perhaps, or a clerk in Johnson's Store. Sarah wondered why Elvira had changed so much over the winter.

After dinner Strang announced that he and Elvira were returning to the print shop to finish unpacking the printing press.

"We won't be gone long," he said. "It's been a long day and the conference starts tomorrow."

Sarah excused herself from the table and began to clear the dishes. Elvira pushed back her chair and picked up a stack of dirty plates to carry to the wash basin.

"Thank you very much for the dinner, Mrs. Strang," she said. "The stew was delicious."

Mary smiled at Elvira's kind words. It occurred to Sarah that she had not seen her mother smile in a long time.

"Now we must go," Strang said. "Coming, Elvira?"

"Sure. Just let me carry out these plates," Elvira said.

"Sarah, would you like to come along?" Strang asked. "You can help unpack the printing press. Elvira will show you how to set the letters for our first newspaper. She's going to write an article about the Mormon conference."

"May I go, Mother?"

"Of course, dear. I'll get the children to help with the rest of the dishes. Just be sure that someone escorts you home. It'll be dark soon."

"Don't worry about it, Mary," Strang said. "I'll bring her home with me."

The print shop building was almost complete. The first floor contained a large room in the front and two smaller rooms in the back. A stairway led to the second floor, where an unfinished room would soon be James Strang's new office. Earlier in the day, George Adams and Percival Graham had hoisted the printing press up on the porch and positioned it in the center of the front room.

"This press has traveled all the way across Lake Michigan on the deck of a ship," Strang said, looking it over carefully. "We had a couple of rough days. Elvira, why don't you check those small boxes? I want to make sure nothing was damaged."

"Everything's here, James," Elvira replied. "All of the letters are still in their trays, and none of the ink spilled."

"The press appears to be in good shape, too. What do you think, Elvira? Do you think we'll be able to print a special edition in time for the conference?"

"It'll only be one page, but we can do it."

"I think I'll name the paper the *Northern Islander*. How does that sound?"

"That sounds perfect, James."

Sarah had been examining the metal letters and turning them over in her hands, and she asked Elvira how they were transformed into written words.

"It's easy," Elvira said. "You just set the letters in these trays in the right order and slide the trays into the slots in the press. You have to be careful not to get the letters in backwards. It takes a while to set up a whole page but you'll get the hang of it in no time."

"Sarah, since you are going to be helping Elvira on the paper, how would you like to work on the very first article?" Strang asked.

"Can I, Father?" Sarah asked, excited about the idea of being a newspaper reporter.

"Of course you can. Now here's what I want you to do. Tomorrow, I want you to meet your friends Andy and Nathan and ask them to walk with you out to Whiskey Point. Tell them you need to check our mail."

"But Mother won't let me go to Whiskey Point."

Strang put his arm around Sarah's shoulders. "We'll just let this be our little secret. You'll be safe if you are with your friends, won't you?"

"Yes, but——"

"Now, when you are out there, I want you to look around and listen and remember everything you see and hear. I noticed that a lot of fishing boats have come into the harbor and they're all anchored near Whiskey Point. There are a lot of men out there and they just seem to be milling around. I'm afraid they are planning some mischief and they might try to to disrupt our conference."

"They wouldn't do that, would they, Father?"

"I am quite sure they would, my dear. They do not like us because we are Mormon. They want this island for themselves, but we have consecrated this land in the name of our Lord. They are welcome to join us, but we will chase them away if they try to usurp our will. Now, after you get the mail I want you to come straight back here and report to Elvira. She'll take notes, and then she'll write an article for the newspaper. Do you think you can do that, Sarah?"

"I think so," Sarah said.

"Just be sure to stay close to Andy and Nathan and you'll be fine. No one will harm you. And don't forget that this is our secret. Now, shall we head for home?"

The next morning, Sarah left the house early, telling her mother that she was going to the print shop, which was only partly true. She walked in that direction until she was out of sight and then she slipped into the woods, circling around to North Beach. She walked down the shore about a mile and cut back into the woods again, coming out behind Andy's cabin.

Andy and Nathan were out on the dock, packing barrels of fish with salt and nailing on the lids. Sarah saw a chance to surprise them, so she tiptoed around the cabin and hid behind a large tree.

"Hey!" she said in a loud voice.

Both boys jumped, startled. "Sarah! What are you doing here? Jeez, you scared us."

"Good," she said with an impish smile. "I wanted to."

"But how did you get here?"

"I came through the woods. I'm going out to Whiskey Point to check for father's mail."

"But I thought you weren't allowed to go there by yourself," Andy said.

"Father was busy today, so he sent me. He said you would walk out there with me."

"After you scared us like that? I don't think so," Andy said with a smirk.

"Really?"

"Nah, just kidding. We're sick of these dead fish anyway. You're more fun."

"Than a dead fish?"

"Yeah, most of the time."

"Maybe I'll just go with Nathan then," Sarah said. "C'mon, Nathan."

She grabbed Nathan by the arm and marched down the path.

"Hey, wait up," called Andy.

"Try to catch me," Sarah replied, letting go of Nathan's arm and running ahead.

The two boys chased her all the way to a field near Whiskey Point, where they collapsed, laughing together in the grass. Across the harbor they could see the Mormon temple, the print shop, and several buildings clustered around the dock. Sarah could even see her own house just beyond the temple. She felt a pang of guilt at the lie she had told her mother, but remembered that Elvira was waiting for her report.

"Look at all the boats," Nathan said. "I've never seen so many boats in the harbor."

Indeed, there was a cluster of fishing boats surrounding Whiskey Point. Some of them were anchored offshore and others were pulled up on the rocky beach. There was a large crowd of men in front of Cable's Store and tents were set up on the grass behind the store. The smell of cooked bacon from a breakfast meal lingered in the air.

Sarah looked around the crowd, trying to see a familiar face so she could tell Elvira who was here. She hardly recognized anyone.

"Who are all these men?" she whispered to Andy.

"I know a few of them from the fishing grounds," Andy replied, "but I think most of these boats sailed over here yesterday from Mackinac Island."

"Why are they all here?"

"I don't know, but I'm sure we'll find out before we leave. Let's go get your mail."

"Oh, yeah, I almost forgot."

Andy started to weave through the crowd, with Sarah following and Nathan in the rear. All of the men were talking loudly and there seemed to be a commotion on the front steps of Cable's Store.

Andy finally saw a familiar face, an older man who was a friend of his father. The man saw Andy and smiled and waved.

"What's everyone doing here?" Andy asked.

"Today's the Fourth of July! You know, Independence Day. The day the United States broke free from England. We're here to celebrate."

"What are you going to do?"

"Well, you're just in time, Andy. Yesterday we cut down a cedar tree and put up a flagpole. See it there in front of the store? We're just about to raise the flag."

"And that's not all," piped up a man standing next to him. "We came to fish. The fishing's better here. We're going to move over from Mackinac Island and set our nets around Beaver Island. We'll catch every fish in the lake!"

"Yeah, if we can get rid of those damned Mormons," said a third man. "They're taking over the place. We should run them off the island, that's what I say."

A loud voice shouted out above the noise of the crowd. It was Alva Cable, who was standing on a barrel in front of his store. "Gentlemen, may I have your attention! We're going to raise the flag."

Everyone quieted down and looked toward the flagpole. Two men unrolled an American flag and held it up for the crowd to see. Amidst a scattering of applause, they tied it to a rope and raised it to the top of the flagpole.

Alva spoke again. "Men, today is Independence Day, the day the United States was founded. This is the day we declared our independence from England. This is the day we declared our freedom from tyranny." The men all cheered and clapped, and several of them threw their hats in the air. They pressed forward, and Sarah lost sight of Andy and Nathan in the jostling crowd.

Alva raised his hands to get the men's attention. "One more thing, men. I've got a barrel of whiskey out behind the store. This one's on the house."

The men laughed and cheered again and surged toward Cable's store for a free drink. Lost in the crowd, Sarah searched frantically for Andy and Nathan. As she looked for them, a grizzled man reached out and pinched her.

"Ouch!" she exclaimed with surprise. The man put his arms around her and roughly pulled her close to him. "Leave me alone," Sarah cried, struggling in his grasp.

Andy appeared in the crowd and saw what was happening. "Hey, leave her alone! What do you want, mister?"

"You're too young to know what I want, sonny boy. A pretty young Mormon girl should know what it's like to be with a real man."

"Let her go, mister," Andy said, grabbing the man's arm.

"Piss off, boy."

A bearded fisherman in the crowd saw what was happening and grabbed the man by the throat with one burly arm and lifted him off the ground. "You heard what the boy said, Jack Bonner. Leave the lady alone," the fisherman said with a salty Irish accent.

"Damn you, git yer hands off me!"

"Yer drunk. It's mighty early in the day to be drunk. I think you need to sleep it off. Maybe this will help."

The fisherman pulled back his fist and punched Bonner squarely on the nose, sending him sprawling in the dirt. He was out cold, his legs twitching. A slime of blood and spittle drooled across his face.

"I'm sorry about that, miss," the fisherman said, tipping his hat. "You'd best head fer home. This ain't no place for a young lady. There's gonna be a lot of drinkin' here today."

Andy took Sarah by the arm, and Nathan joined him, taking Sarah's other arm. They squeezed through a group of men on the porch, went inside the store, and slammed the door behind them. The door immediately opened again and Alva came charging in.

"Sarah! Are you all right?"

"I'm f-fine," Sarah said hesitantly

"He didn't hurt her," Andy said. "We just want to get the mail and get out of here."

"Where's your father, Sarah?"

"He sent me today. I came with Andy and Nathan."

"Well, these men are going to get rowdy. It's Independence Day. I'll get your mail for you and you'd better go home."

Cable went into the back room, returned with a parcel stuffed full of envelopes, and handed it to Sarah.

"Was that Jack Bonner?" Andy asked. "I heard that fisherman call him Jack Bonner."

"It sure was," Alva replied, "He's one of the best fishermen around here, but every time he comes to town he gets drunk. Why, do you know him?"

"Yeah, I m-mean no," Andy stuttered, "but I've heard of him."

"Well, there won't be any more whiskey for him, that's for sure. Now, you boys will walk Sarah all the way home, won't you?"

"Yes, sir."

"Thank you, Mr. Cable," Sarah said, brushing her sleeve. "I'll be fine."

"I know you will, Sarah," Alva replied. "I just want to get you away from this crowd and home safely."

Alva opened the door, took Sarah's hand, and elbowed his way through the men on the porch. Andy and Nathan followed until they made it to the back of the crowd.

"Are you sure you're all right, Sarah?" Alva asked.

"Yes, I'm perfectly fine. Where did you get the flag, Mr. Cable?"

"I ordered it last fall, all the way from Detroit, just so we could have a flag at the entrance to the harbor. Ain't it a beaut?"

"It's very pretty," Sarah replied. "We should get one for the school."

They all looked up at the flag, flying proudly above the rustic store and the entrance to Paradise Bay.

Another man was now standing on the barrel in front of the store and making a speech. "I say this is a free country and I say that this will be a free island as soon as we get those damned Mormons out of here. They're cutting down our trees and catching our fish. I say we round them up and put them on a boat and send them packing, back to where they came from. Then we'll have this island to ourselves."

The man picked up a bottle, took a long swig, and promptly fell backwards off the barrel, provoking a laugh and jeers from the crowd.

"Don't worry about him," Alva said. "He's just another drunk."

"He can't get up. He's trying, but he can't get up," Nathan said.

"Well, that's probably for the best. We've heard enough out of him. Andy and Nathan, you take Sarah straight home now, you hear?"

"We will, we promise."

Just before they entered the woods along the shore, Nathan turned and looked back at the crowd. "That man still can't get up. He must be really drunk."

Elvira was waiting for Sarah at the print shop. She proceeded to interrogate her about what she had seen at Whiskey Point. At first Sarah told her about the Independence Day celebration and the new flag at the harbor entrance, but Elvira was persistent and kept asking her other questions. Sarah then told her about the free barrel of whiskey behind the store, the drunken men, and the threats against the Mormons.

"What kind of threats?"

"Some of the men said they wanted to chase us off the island."

"Why?"

"Mostly they said they wanted to take over the fishing grounds. One man said they would catch every fish in the lake."

"Did you recognize any of the men?"

"No, not really, except for Mr. Cable."

"Well, if you didn't recognize them, where do you think they were from?"

"I don't know."

"Do you think they were from Mackinac Island?"

"Maybe. Andy thought some of them were from Mackinac Island."

"Do you think they came over here to cause trouble?"

"I'm not sure. They were celebrating Independence Day and they raised an American flag, but a lot of them were drinking too much. They said they wanted to take over the whole island."

"Sarah, you seem a little distraught. Is there anything else you'd like to tell me?" Elvira asked.

"Not really."

"Sarah...?"

"Well, there was one man who kind of grabbed me."

"Was he drunk?"

"I think so."

"Did you hear his name?"

"I think I heard someone call him Jack Bonner."

"Hmm. I don't know that name. I'll have to ask around."

"Please don't tell anyone, Elvira."

"Don't worry, Sarah. I'll be discreet."

Sarah stood up. "Can I go now? My mother will be angry if she finds out I went to Whiskey Point."

"Sure, Sarah. You've been a great help. I can see you're going to make a good newspaper reporter."

Sarah smiled at the compliment, but she was annoyed with all the probing questions. She hurried out the door and ran for home. She had been gone a very long time.

CHAPTER 6:

Coronation of the King

The following morning, Sarah cooked breakfast, cleaned the dishes, and helped her mother straighten up the house. As she worked, she wondered if Elvira had finished the article. She was excited about seeing her words in print in a real newspaper.

"Mother, may I go down to the print shop? I promised Elvira I would help her today."

"Of course, dear. Did they get the printing press set up yet?"

"I think so. Elvira was working on it all day yesterday. She said she was going to print a special edition of the newspaper today."

"Already? Why so soon?"

"Father wants to have the paper out so people can read about the church conference."

"Well, that makes sense. You run along, and say hello to Elvira for me."

"I will, Mother," Sarah said. She grabbed her shawl and bolted out the door.

"And don't forget to bring me a copy," Mary called.

Elvira was bustling around the office of the print shop when Sarah arrived.

"Sarah! You're just in time! I just printed the first batch of papers. It's only one page, but it will get bigger when we have more time."

"Did you write our article?" Sarah asked with excitement.

"I sure did. I stayed up late and finished it last night. It's right at the top of the page. Here, take a look."

Elvira grabbed the top page from a stack of papers and handed it to Sarah. Sarah sat down at her father's desk and began to read.

Angry Mob Threatens Mormon Conference

Yesterday a mob of men from Mackinac Island gathered at Whiskey Point and threatened to disrupt the Mormon conference beginning today on this island. Using a celebration of Independence Day as a cover and raising an American flag as a cynical display of patriotism, the gang plotted to attack the Mormon community. The ringleaders, not content to sell whiskey to the Indians, provided free whiskey to all men who would join them.

Brandishing guns and knives, these men —

Sarah put down the newspaper and looked up at Elvira. "I didn't see any guns and knives," she said.

"I know," Elvira replied, "but other people have. I heard about it from other sources."

"But there weren't any—"

"Sarah, your own father has reported seeing men with guns and knives on Whiskey Point many times."

"They were just celebrating Independence Day, but some of them made speeches and threatened to make us leave the island," Sarah admitted. "They were all drinking and I even saw a fight.

"That's what I mean," Elvira said. "It may have appeared to be a patriotic celebration, but my job as a reporter is to gather facts from as many sources as possible. Sometimes things are not what they seem from only one point of view, and only an experienced reporter can see the whole truth."

Sarah was crestfallen. "I tried to tell you everything I saw," She said.

"Don't worry," Elvira replied. "You'll get the hang of it. This was only your first assignment. You're going to be a good reporter."

Sarah put down the newspaper and walked slowly out of the print shop. She was very confused. She shuddered at the thought of the horrible man who had grabbed her. Maybe Elvira was right; after all, she was older and seemed to know a lot about reporting.

Sarah looked up and noticed a group of men huddled on the dock in front of Johnson's Store. Suddenly, as if on cue, they broke out of their huddle and ran back toward shore.

BOOM! A huge explosion rocked the harbor and a cloud of smoke engulfed the dock. Sarah jumped in shock and Elvira came running out of the print shop.

"They did it! They did it!" she yelled.

"Did what?" Sarah's heart was pounding. She had heard loud guns before, but she'd never heard anything this loud. Her ears were still ringing.

"The cannon! They fired the cannon! Look at all the smoke."

"What cannon? There's no cannon on the island."

"Oh, yes there is. It came over on the boat with the printing press."

The second wooden box! Sarah had forgotten all about it.

"C'mon, let's go down there," Elvira said. "They're probably going to shoot it off again."

Sarah and Elvira hurried toward the dock. As they approached, the group of men gathered near the cannon again and then ran back toward shore.

BOOM! Another loud explosion broke the serenity of the harbor and another cloud of smoke rose above the dock. Far out in the harbor, off the end of Whiskey Point, a splash could be seen where a cannonball hit the water. The men all ran back to the cannon and began to re-load it. Sarah could see George Adams picking up another cannonball.

"Raise the barrel higher," Adams shouted to the men. "I want to put a shot right off the end of their dock."

Two men raised the barrel so that it pointed higher into the sky. Adams stuffed the cannonball into the barrel and another man rammed it in with a long rod.

Sarah and Elvira joined a crowd of Mormons converging on the dock. They had all heard the explosions echo through the village. James Strang arrived with Mary and a few moments later Butch Jenkins and Louisa Adams joined them at the front of the crowd.

Andy and Nathan came running out on the dock and hurried over to Sarah. "What's going on?" they both asked at once. They were out of breath after running half way around the harbor.

"They're shooting a cannon. They brought it over on the boat."

"What for?" Andy asked.

"I don't know," Sarah replied. "It's really loud."

"They're doing it to scare those fishermen out on Whiskey Point," Elvira said.

"But my father's out there today!" Andy cried.

James Strang came up behind them. "Don't worry, son" he said, "we're just going to scare them so they'll leave us alone."

"Why don't you just go and talk to them? You don't have to shoot at them."

"I'm afraid the talking days are over. We cannot abide any more threats to our community. George, make sure you don't hit anything out there."

"Don't worry, James, I'm just going to aim for the dock."

"The dock!" Andy yelled. "What if someone's on it?"

Adams prepared to light the fuse on the cannon. Andy ran forward and grabbed his arm.

"Don't fire! My father's out there!"

"Get back, kid, you don't belong here."

Adams pushed Andy away. Nathan came running forward to help his friend, but Butch Jenkins and two other men grabbed the boys and restrained them.

Adams lit the fuse. A third cannonball arced across the harbor and landed with a splash between two fishing boats moored off the end of the dock. Men could be seen running from Cable's Store to their boats. One boat had already raised its sail and was heading out of the harbor.

"There, did you see that?" Adams shouted with glee. "Now they know we can hit them any time we want."

Andy was so mad that all he could do was snarl and struggle with the men who held him. "Whatcha have to do that for?" he shouted.

"Get those two kids outta here," sneered Adams. "Get 'em off this dock and send 'em home."

The men holding Andy and Nathan began to drag them away.

"Wait," Strang said. "I've got a better idea. Keep them here for a while and we'll send them home with a message."

"Good idea," Adams agreed.

Strang climbed up on top of a barrel, raised his arm for silence, and addressed the crowd.

"My fellow Mormons, we came to this island in peace. We came to build homes, raise our families, and live in harmony with our fellow man. We wish harm to no one. But we will no longer stand idly by while our lives are threatened and our women are accosted. I wish everyone to understand that we will defend ourselves against these attacks.

"You all have seen with your own eyes the activities that take place on Whiskey Point. You have watched with alarm the so-called celebrations, which I say are just another name for drunkenness and depravity. I myself have learned that yesterday a mob was formed with the sole intention of driving us off this island. Let our cannon be a warning to all who threaten us: Cable's Store is the meeting place of these scoundrels. Cable's Store has provided them with whiskey and weapons and a place to plan their dastardly deeds. I proclaim to you today that if any Mormon is attacked we will blast this den of heathens into splinters and we will raze every building on Whiskey Point. If anyone tries to disrupt our conference they will be captured and put in chains and I will be the judge and jury—"

"And I will be the executioner!" Adams shouted, waving a copy of the *Northern Islander*.

"Those are strong words," said a man standing in the front row. "How do you know they're going to attack us?"

"What's yer proof, Brother James," shouted a man from the back of the crowd.

"Yeah, what's yer proof," shouted another.

Strang reached down and grabbed the newspaper from Adams' grasp.

"Since you asked, I'll show you my proof. It's all right here in the first edition of the *Northern Islander*. Listen to this: 'Yesterday a mob of men from Mackinac Island gathered at Whiskey Point and threatened to disrupt the Mormon conference. The gang plotted to attack the Mormon community.'

Need I say more, gentlemen? If you would only read your own newspaper you would know that we will never be safe as long as these gentiles are living among us."

"What newspaper? We don't have a newspaper."

"Oh, yes, you do. They're right up at the print shop. First edition, hot off the press! Go and get one and then you'll know what I'm talking about."

"I go to Cable's Store every week for groceries," said the man in the front of the crowd. "I've never had any trouble."

"You still don't believe me?" Strang asked. "Who do you suppose the ringleader is? Who do you suppose is inciting the gentiles to attack us?"

"Who? Who is it?" shouted several men in the crowd.

"It's Black Jack Bonner, that's who. He was seen out at Whiskey Point yesterday, and he's there today, plotting against us. You all remember Black Jack. We ran him off the island for drunkenness, lechery, and abominations against our women, and now he's back with his henchmen and he wants revenge!"

Strang and Adams had worked the crowd into a frenzy. Andy and Nathan were shoved aside by several men pushing their way forward to listen to Strang and Adams. Andy turned around to look for Sarah, but she had disappeared.

"Hey, Nathan, where's Sarah?"

"I don't know. She was here a minute ago."

"I saw her running up the dock," Elvira said. "She must have gone home."

"She didn't go home," Andy said, "but I think I know where she went. C'mon, Nathan." Andy squeezed through the crowd and ran toward shore with Nathan following behind.

"Where'd she go?" Nathan asked, catching up with him.

"I'll bet she went to her secret berry batch."

"Why would...." Nathan paused for a moment. "Yeah, I think you're right."

The two boys ran along the shore and turned into the woods on the trail to the North Beach. They were quickly engulfed by the silence of the forest, and the noise and commotion on the dock suddenly seemed a long way away. Andy followed the trail and soon they came to a clearing in the trees. Sarah was sitting on a log with her back to them. She had her chin cupped in her hands and she was staring out at the berry patch.

"Hi, Sarah," Andy said, coming up behind her.

Sarah looked around at them and then turned back to stare at the berry patch.

"What's the matter?" Andy asked.

"I don't know what I did wrong," Sarah muttered, not looking up.

"What do you mean?"

"I just wanted to help with the newspaper. I wanted to be a writer."

Andy and Nathan sat down on the log on either side of Sarah.

"They said I could help on the newspaper. They showed me how the printing press worked and said I could be a reporter someday."

"Who did?" Andy asked.

"My father and Elvira."

"So? That's good, isn't it? You like to write."

"Do you remember yesterday when we went to Whiskey Point? My father said I could go with you even though I'm not supposed to be out there. He said he wanted me to get the mail. Elvira told me I could help with her first article in the newspaper. All I had to do was see what was going on at Whiskey Point and tell her all about it."

"What did you tell her?" Nathan asked.

"Nothing! All I told her was that there was an Independence Day celebration and a lot of drinking. Then she started asking me all these questions. She asked me if anyone threatened the Mormons. She asked me lots and lots of questions. She wouldn't stop. She kept asking me if they wanted to attack us."

"Did you help her write the article?"

"No! I just went home. I would never write those things. She got it all wrong!"

"The headline said, 'Angry Mob threatens Mormons'," Andy said.

"I know! I didn't mean that at all. She just wrote what she wanted to, and my father believes her, because he doesn't even know what I really said to

Elvira. Now they're shooting off cannons and talking about executing people. It's all my fault."

"Sarah, it's not your fault. You didn't know what she was going to write."

"Maybe you can explain it to your father and Elvira can write another article saying what really happened," Nathan offered.

Sarah laughed bitterly. "After that speech he gave a few minutes ago? I don't think so."

"Maybe my father can talk to them and straighten things out," Andy said. "They're friends, especially after your father saw the new schoolhouse."

"Yeah, and my father is pretty good about calming people down," Nathan added.

"That may work," Sarah said, "but I'm never working at that stupid paper again."

Andy and Nathan were silent for a moment. They didn't know what else to say.

"Sarah, what do want to do when you grow up?" Nathan finally asked.

"What? Why are asking me that now?"

"I'm serious. What do you want to do?"

"I don't know. Maybe be a schoolteacher or something like that."

"Wouldn't working at that paper help you to become a teacher?" Nathan asked.

"How? By learning how to tell lies?"

"No, by learning how to write. If you were working there the stories would be better. There are a lot of fishermen here who just mind their own business, but they don't have a newspaper. Maybe you could tell their story, too."

"I know there are, but what about Elvira? She might change my story again."

"I know she's a little weird, but maybe she just made a mistake. After all, it's only the first issue of the paper."

Sarah sighed. "I suppose I could try. I just don't want to hear that cannon go off again."

"Neither do we," Nathan said. "But we think you'll be a good writer."

"All right, I'll try, but I don't know if it will work."

"C'mon, Sarah, we'll walk you home," Andy said.

"Thanks. I feel better now. I need to help my mother today anyway."

The three friends stood up and walked through the woods, back toward the harbor.

"Say, Sarah," Andy asked, "you didn't say much to Elvira about Jack Bonner, did you?"

"Yeah, I did tell her some. That man was really drunk and he grabbed me. Elvira kept asking me about him, over and over."

"Uh-oh."

"Why? What's wrong?"

"Jack Bonner is my father's cousin."

The next day the Mormon conference began. The population of the island had tripled in the last few days with the arrival of several passenger boats. Many of the brethren had come to join the church and were moving to the island with their families. In the morning, the new converts filed into the temple and took a holy covenant. Placing their hands on a wooden cross, they swore allegiance to the Mormon Church and to James Strang as their prophet and spiritual leader.

In the afternoon, twelve church elders were selected and ordained as apostles of the Mormon Church of Beaver Island. These men were hand-picked by James Strang and George Adams because of their loyalty to Strang. The elders immediately retired to the privacy of the print shop for a secret meeting. Percival Graham and Elvira Field stood on the front porch and politely turned away all curious visitors.

Earlier in the day, Adams had appointed several men to guard the cannon. Guards were also posted at the doors of the temple. Adams had been relentless in his accusations against the gentiles on Whiskey Point, warning that they might attack at any moment, even though only a few boats remained in the harbor.

It was clear to the new arrivals that something momentous was about to occur. They had seen the special edition of the *Northern Islander* and they had heard the cannon blasts. Many of them had heard Strang's warnings about the gentiles on Whiskey Point. Those who had traveled north on the *Spencer* told of closed-door meetings in the captain's quarters with Butch Jenkins guarding the door armed with a brace of pistols.

～～

The next day the sun rose over Paradise Bay with a heavenly glow. Sarah was up early and out in her yard, drawing water from a well for breakfast and the daily laundry. She lowered a bucket, watched it fill, and began to haul it to the surface with a stout rope.

A hand appeared next to hers on the rope. "Here, Sarah, let me help you."

Sarah turned to see her father standing beside her. He took the rope from her and hauled the bucket to the surface.

"This bucket is mighty heavy, my child. Do you do this every morning?"

"I usually get three or four buckets. There's always a lot of laundry because Mother likes to keep the baby's clothes clean."

"Couldn't Billy help you? He's strong enough."

"Sometimes he does."

"Ah, that's good," Strang said. "Well, this morning I will help you."

Strang rolled up his sleeves, leaned over the well, and quickly hauled four buckets of water to the surface.

"There," he said with satisfaction. "A little manual labor is the best way to start the day, I always say."

"Where are you going today, Father?" Sarah asked.

"Back to the temple. Today is the most important day of the conference."

"Are all of those people going to stay here on the island?"

"Most of them are. They took the covenant and now they are true members of the Mormon Church. I suppose I must set aside some land for them."

"What's happening today at the temple?"

"Ah, today you and your mother and all of the brethren are in for a big surprise."

Strang sat down on a bench near the well and beckoned Sarah to sit beside him. "You may as well be the first to know, Sarah. Yesterday the quorum of the apostles elected me spiritual leader of the Mormon Church."

"But you already are the leader, Father."

"Yes, but they have given me a new title. This morning I shall be crowned King of the Mormon Church."

Sarah gasped. "King? Can you be a king?"

"That is the wish of the quorum. They felt that the church needed a strong leader because of the threats from the gentiles at Whiskey Point. At first I tried to dissuade them, but some of our new believers are weak and they must be protected, like sheep. Only a king can do that. Now I will be both their spiritual leader and their king."

"But how do you become a king? I thought kings were just in old countries."

"That's true, but this is America and here you can be anything you want to be. George Adams is in charge of the whole affair. Even I don't know what he has planned but I am sure that it will be a grand event for all to see. Everyone on the island is invited."

Sarah was still unsure of the idea. Her own father, a king! It was hard to imagine.

"Can my friends come, too?" she asked.

"Of course they can, and they can bring anyone they want. I want everyone on the island to become a Mormon."

"Can I go and tell them after my chores are finished?"

"Sure, but let's carry this water in first. Here, I'll help you."

Strang picked up the buckets and carried them to the back porch where a pile of soiled laundry covered the steps.

"Well, I'm off to the temple," Strang said, dropping the buckets.

"Bye, Father." Sarah watched him as he opened the gate and strode away.

"Ten o'clock," he called. "Don't be late."

"I won't." Sarah turned back to the laundry. She sorted it in piles and carried two more buckets of water inside to heat on the stove. She then set the table for breakfast and poured milk for the children, who were just getting out of bed.

Mary came bustling into the kitchen. "Good morning, Sarah. You're up early today."

"The sun came in my window. I couldn't sleep."

"Look what Wingfield Watson gave us yesterday. A dozen fresh eggs."

"That was nice of him," Sarah said. "I'll get the frying pan."

Sarah grabbed the pan and in no time she was frying four eggs over the wood stove. Nettie and Billy came into the room rubbing the sleep from their eyes. The children sat down and Sarah served a breakfast of eggs, bread, and milk.

"Guess what?" Sarah said, "Father's going to be crowned king today."

"King!" exclaimed Billy.

"King of what?" asked Mary, putting down the pitcher of milk and placing her hands on her hips.

"The Mormon Church of Beaver Island."

"He's King of Beaver Island!" shouted Billy, jumping down from his chair and running around the table.

"Oh, for heaven's sake," Mary said. "That's the most ridiculous thing I ever heard."

Nettie jumped down from her chair and chased Billy off into the other room.

"He said to come to the temple at ten o'clock," Sarah said.

"For what? A marching band and a coronation?"

"Um, he did say there'd be a coronation. Mr. Adams is in charge."

"I suppose that makes me queen of all of these dirty dishes."

"I'm sorry, Mother. I'll help you." Sarah was surprised at her mother's sarcasm. She cleared the table and poured some hot water into a pan. Together they washed the dishes and set them out to dry, and then they went outside and washed dirty clothes and hung them on a line tied between two trees.

"Can I go down to Andy's?" Sarah asked. "I want to see if Andy and Nathan want to come to the temple with me."

"I suppose so," Mary replied, staring at the dripping laundry.

Sarah could see that her mother was upset. She had to admit that the idea of her father being crowned a king was a little strange, but it was also exciting. The island was crowded with newcomers, and they would soon be converging on the temple for the coronation. It would be the biggest event of the year.

"I'll meet you at the temple, Mother. We'll save you a seat."

"I'm not sure I'll be there, Sarah."

"But you have to—"

"Oh, never mind," Mary said, picking up the clothes basket. "I'll be there with the children, not that anyone will notice."

Sarah hurried away, wondering why her mother was being so cross with her. At least Andy and Nathan will want to go to the coronation. But as she got close to Andy's house, she looked out and saw the *Emma Rose* sailing across the harbor. To her dismay, she could see Andy and Nathan on the bow. They were going out to pull nets, so they would not return until dusk. Disappointed, Sarah turned around and walked back toward the village. She would have to attend the coronation by herself if her mother didn't show up. Maybe later she would stop by the print shop. She didn't feel like going back home.

By the time Sarah made it to the temple everyone was already seated and latecomers were standing along the walls and across the back of the building. She could not see her mother anywhere in the crowd. She finally managed to find one empty seat in the back row.

A stage had been erected across the front of the temple and a red curtain hung from the rafters. Twelve empty chairs were lined up in front of the curtain. It was quiet in the temple, and the crowd was waiting with anticipation. At precisely ten o'clock the curtain parted and George Adams appeared. He was wearing a dark suit with a white shirt and tie and a black top hat. In his left hand he carried a silver cane. With a flourish of the cane, he addressed the crowd.

"My brothers and sisters, we are gathered here today to witness a momentous occasion. We are here to consummate our faith and our allegiance to the Mormon Church. You have all taken the covenant, you have all attended the services, and you have all borne witness to the birth of the true Mormon Church here on Beaver Island. You may know of other deceived members of our church who have headed west to the Utah territory with Brigham Young, known by all to be a false prophet. You, my friends, chose to head north, by wagon and by boat. Your travels and your sacrifices have led you here, and we welcome you all. Today, in this temple, you are about to witness the crowning of the true prophet, the imperial primate, the true king of the Mormon Church. But first, my brethren, I invite you to greet our new disciples, the Quorum of the Apostles, chosen from our own membership. I invite you to feast your eyes upon them as they enter this house of worship."

George Adams raised his cane high in the air and pointed to the rear of the temple. Everyone in the audience turned to look. From behind the log walls, twelve men dressed in colorful robes filed solemnly into the temple. Each man stopped briefly in front of George Adams, bowed, and took a seat on the stage, facing the audience.

"Ladies and gentlemen, I present to you the Quorum of the Apostles. These twelve men, in their infinite wisdom, and with the guidance and blessing of the Lord, have met in prayer and have chosen our leader. And now, as duly appointed Prime Minister, and without further ado, I give you the Imperial Primate of the true Mormon Church, James Jesse Strang!"

With another flourish of his cane, Adams pulled aside the curtain. He raised his arm and pointed, directing everyone's gaze to the center of the stage.

Seated in a high chair covered with gold cloth was James Strang. His shoulders were adorned with a scarlet robe decorated with gold trim. In his right hand he held an ornamented scepter made of carved wood. Adams got down on one knee, lowered his head, and kissed Strang's left hand. He then rose again, stepped to one side, and bowed his head.

Strang rose, holding his scepter with both hands. He looked out at the crowd, smiled, and began to speak in a quiet, self-effacing voice.

"My brethren, you all know me as an elder of the Mormon Church. You traveled with me to Wisconsin and now you have followed me to Beaver Island. We have all shared hunger, fatigue and danger in our search for a better life and a place to practice our faith. We have all banded together to protect one another from those who wish to destroy us. I have watched you as you have started families of your own. I have watched your children grow and at the same time I have watched your faith in the Lord grow."

Strang captivated the audience with his intimate conversation. Now his voice rose and filled the temple.

"Now I must tell you what you do not know about me. I am a descendant of the House of David of Israel. Through the ancient lineage of David and through a revelation from God, I have been called to the church. I have been ordained by a host of angels to serve as your Imperial Primate and King on this earth until such time as we are all called to serve in Heaven. I shall be your leader and your King!"

Strang stood before his people and George Adams came forward. "The imperial crown, please!" he called in a booming voice.

Louisa Adams, dressed in an exotic costume of flowing robes, came down the aisle carrying a tray covered with a white cloth. When she reached the stage Adams flung aside the cloth and revealed a silver crown. He lifted it and held it high for all to see. He then placed the crown on Strang's head and announced, "I pronounce you King James the First."

Adams stepped aside and beckoned the audience to stand. "Ladies and gentlemen, I now present to you for your edification our new king, King James the First. Long live King James, son of David and King of the Mormons!"

The crowd repeated the cheer. "Long live King James!"

"Raise the royal flags!" Adams commanded.

Two men, standing on each side of the stage, raised red flags and held them high. King Strang stepped down from the stage and walked solemnly down the center aisle, followed in procession by the Quorum of the Apostles.

"Fire the royal salute!" Adams shouted from the stage.

Outside, the cannon fired with a blast, attended by Butch Jenkins and two Mormon men. Sarah jumped at the sound of the cannon and cowered behind her bench in the back row. The coronation of King James the First was over. The reign of King James over Beaver Island had just begun. The smell of gunpowder drifted into the temple.

Sarah had not seen her mother anywhere in the congregation. Her father was standing outside the temple, surrounded by his apostles. Not seeing any familiar faces, Sarah squeezed through the crowd and headed for home. When she arrived, she found her mother sitting at a table, looking a bit out of breath.

"Did you see the ceremony, Mother?" Sarah asked. "I didn't see you there."

"Yes, I did," Her mother answered. "I was sitting against the side wall with the children. We left early."

"Why?" Sarah asked.

"I had to get the baby home," she answered curtly.

It was clear to Sarah that her mother did not want to talk about the coronation. Then Billy and Nettie came in and tried to play king and queen with the dining room chairs. Mary shouted at them and chased them outside with a broom. That was enough for Sarah. She went back out the door and sat on the front step. Her eyes wandered to the harbor, looking for the *Emma Rose*, but Andy and Nathan were still out fishing. With nowhere else to go, she got up and wandered over to the print shop. Everyone was still at the temple, so the building was empty. Elvira would be back soon and anxious to prepare another special edition of the *Northern Islander*, Sarah thought. The coronation of a king would be a fine sequel to her first article.

Sarah had never been in the print shop alone. The printing press stood in the middle of the room and a tray of printing letters rested on a table. In the corner of the room several copies of the *Northern Islander* were stacked on a trunk. Sarah picked up a copy. Sure enough, there was the offending headline: 'Angry Mob Threatens Mormon Conference'. Sarah swept them aside, watching in guilty satisfaction as they fluttered to the floor. She grabbed the last remaining copy, wadded it up, and tossed it over her shoulder.

Underneath the papers, Sarah noticed the words 'Charles Douglass, New York City' written across the top of the trunk. Her father had mentioned Charles Douglass as a secretary who had accompanied him during his mission travels. Sarah wondered what his trunk was doing here on Beaver Island. She walked across the room and peeked out the window. The crowd was still gathered in front of the temple. There was no sign of her father or Elvira Field. She turned back to the trunk, intent on solving the mystery.

The latch was not locked. Sarah lifted the lid and peered inside. She picked up a black umbrella and a man's winter coat. Beneath the coat there were several men's shirts and ties, neatly stacked along one side. On the other side were some books, a pile of loose papers, and a leather binder. Sarah picked up the binder and opened it. It contained several photographs, the kind she knew were taken in studios cropping up in cities on the east coast. The first photograph was of a group of men she did not know. They looked like church elders. She set it aside and picked up the next photograph, not prepared for what she was about to see.

"Oh, my!" Sarah exclaimed.

The second photograph was of Elvira Field. She had the same short hair, but she was wearing the coat that Sarah had just removed from the trunk. Sarah squinted at the picture in the dim light and carried it over to the window. Yes, there was no doubt about it; the photograph was of Elvira, dressed as a man. With a shirt and tie and a somber expression, she looked just like a young law clerk.

"What is going on here?" Sarah asked aloud. With short hair, a square jaw, and dark eyebrows, Elvira could easily pass as a man, yet Sarah knew her as an attractive young woman who was staying as a guest in her home. Looking intently at the photograph, Sarah could not be sure. Was Elvira a man or a woman?

Sarah closed the binder and placed it carefully back in the trunk. She peeked out the window and saw that the crowd around the temple was beginning to disperse. It was time to leave. She put the coat and umbrella back in the trunk, closed the lid and picked up the wayward copies of the *Northern Islander*. Checking again at the window, she slipped out the front door and scurried around the back side of the building so no one would see her.

⁓

That night, Sarah couldn't sleep. Her room was stuffy, even with an open window. She lay in bed staring into the darkness, confused and overwhelmed by the events of the day. She was still awake when her father and Elvira finally returned home. They muttered a few whispered words before her father went upstairs and Elvira retired to her bedroom.

The wall between Sarah's room and Elvira's room was made of rough pine with knotholes and cracks between the boards. Sarah heard Elvira strike a match and she saw the light of a candle shining through the cracks. Curious, she crossed the room on silent feet and peered through one of the knotholes.

Elvira was sitting at a table next to her bed and writing in a diary. After a few moments she closed the diary and put it in a drawer. She then raised her arms, pulled her blouse off over her head, and reached for her nightgown. Her heart pounding, Sarah watched Elvira undress. In the flickering light of the candle she caught a glimpse of pale curving flesh. She turned away and scurried back to the safety of her own bed.

So that's it, Sarah thought. Elvira is a woman. But she is also Charles Douglass, a woman disguised as a man, a man who spent the entire winter with her father on the east coast. She rolled over and pulled the covers over her head. But her eyes were drawn back to the knothole.

Elvira had hung her blouse over the back of a chair. She was naked from the waist up and facing away from Sarah. She turned and blew out the candle with a quick puff. A brief glimpse was all that Sarah needed. From the back she could have been mistaken. From the front there was no doubt about it. Elvira was a woman.

Sarah again retreated to her own bed. After her heart stopped pounding, she pondered over the contents of the trunk. Could she be the first to know that Elvira Field was also Charles Douglass? Why would Elvira dress and act like a man, and how could she have deceived everyone all winter? Sarah had no answers, but she shuddered at the thoughts swirling in her mind. She buried her head in her pillow and tried to go to sleep.

Sarah slept late the next morning. When she finally awoke the sunshine was already streaming through her window. She closed the curtains, feeling as if she had just been aroused from a bad dream. Her head was still swimming from the photograph she had seen of Elvira in the trunk. A dim memory nagged at her, a memory of a trunk tied to the deck of the *Spencer* next to the printing press and the cannon. Was that the same trunk?

Sarah opened her bedroom door and stood motionless on the threshold, her heart pounding again. She was terrified of confronting her father, but she was also furious with him. Last fall he had taken the entire family off the island for the winter, leaving them in Buffalo while he traveled on to New York City, supposedly to recruit new members for the church. Somewhere along the way he must have met up with Elvira and disguised her as a man, passing her off as his personal secretary. Together they had travelled up and down the east coast all winter, staying together at night and extolling the virtues of the Mormon Church during the day. With that final thought, Sarah took a deep breath and stepped into the hall.

She could hear her father's voice in the parlor. He was talking rapidly and pacing back and forth. He was practicing his sermon for next week.

"My brothers and sisters, thou hast followed thy king to this consecrated holy land. Thou hast braved death on the waters. Thou hast braved starvation in the winter. Thou hast suffered the persecution of your fellow men, the gentiles. Now ye shall join me and together we shall consecrate this land. We shall take what is rightfully ours and we shall build a community of the Lord. We shall be free forever from the wrath of our enemies. As your king, I have heard the words of the Lord. The Lord has commanded me, James Jesse Strang, to be your leader."

Sarah grasped the front of her nightgown with both hands and twisted it into a knot. "Father?" she said, her voice breaking.

King Strang looked up at her. "Not now, Sarah. I am busy."

He paused for a moment, and continued his sermon.

"The Lord hath commanded me to be your leader. Thou art destined for the army of the Lord. With the torch of the Lord thou shall light up this land. On this island, and on these waters, and on this country thou shall wield the sword of the Lord. Thou shall lay waste to towns and villages. Thou shall go forth and tread down the wicked, the sinful, and all of the unbelievers. Yea, thou shall even go to foreign lands. There shall thou wield the sword with the vengeance of a destroying angel. And thou and thy brethren shall dash to pieces the kingdoms of this world and rule them with a rod of iron. And thou shall consecrate their dominion to your king and to the Lord of the whole earth."

Strang stopped for a moment and began scribbling notes on a pad of paper.

"Where are mother and the children?" Sarah asked.

"I sent them outside. Please, Sarah, I cannot concentrate with all these interruptions," Strang said with irritation.

"Father, I need to talk to you about Elvira."

"I told you I am busy. I must finish this sermon."

"I found out about her. I know she dressed up like a man. I know she's Charles Douglass."

King Strang looked up at her with surprise, his mouth agape. For once in his life, he was speechless. Silence reigned in the dining room, but not for long.

"Come, Sarah. Come and sit on my lap." Strang smiled and held out his hands to his daughter. After some hesitation, Sarah padded across the room in her bare feet, but she did not sit on his lap. She remained standing in front of him with her arms crossed.

"Sarah, my darling, you are my first daughter. On the day that you were born, it was as if all of the angels of heaven shined their lights upon you. It was as if all the firmaments on high looked down upon me and blessed me from the heavens. I never have felt such joy as the joy I felt when our Father delivered you to this earth."

But Sarah would not be distracted. Ignoring his remarks, she asked him again: "Father, why did Elvira dress up like a man?"

Again James Strang was silent, humbled by his own daughter.

CHAPTER 7:
A School for the Island

The next day, Elvira moved out of the Strang household. She was up at dawn, packing her bags and straightening up Mary's sewing room. After a quick breakfast, she politely thanked Mary for her hospitality and loaded her bags on a wagon. James Strang came out to help her and together they hauled the wagon off to the print shop.

Mary was somewhat taken aback at Elvira's hasty and unexpected departure. "Elvira is a fine young lady," she said. "She's very polite."

Sarah stared down at her plate and poked at her food.

"I wonder why she left so soon," Mary continued. "You don't suppose she was upset with us about anything, do you Sarah?"

"Um, no, I don't think so, Mother."

"Well then why did she leave?"

"I think she wants to be near the printing press to work on the newspaper," Sarah mumbled, still staring at her plate.

"But we live so close—"

"There's a room in the back of the print shop with a desk and a bed for her."

"Surely that can't be as comfortable as our house."

"Mother, she wants to write."

"That print shop is drafty. There are holes in the walls."

"It's summer...."

"I suppose you're right, Sarah, but I sure took a liking to her. Maybe she'll want to move back in with us if her parents don't arrive soon."

"Maybe." Sarah couldn't keep up the charade any longer. She stood up and began to clear the breakfast dishes.

King Strang, as he now called himself, spent most of his time at the print shop over the rest of the summer. In the mornings he held court in his office, conducting church business and meeting with the church apostles. In the afternoons, he rolled up his sleeves and worked on the unfinished temple with some of the men. Now that he was king of the church, it seemed that he had less time than ever to spend at home. He usually managed to come home for dinner, but he always went back to the print shop afterwards to help Elvira work on the *Northern Islander*. It was always late in the evening by the time he returned home.

After confronting him and listening to his earnest denials and ludicrous explanations, Sarah barely spoke to her father over the next few weeks. She was furious with him for his deceitful effort to hide Elvira's double identity. She kept busy helping her mother with the children, but she could not forget what she had seen inside the trunk. The image of the photograph of Elvira dressed as a man haunted her memory.

Finally, in an attempt to forget about the picture in the trunk, Sarah decided to take on a project. The new schoolhouse was scheduled to open in September, only a few weeks away. But the interior of the log building was still unfinished, so Sarah began to transform the empty rooms into classrooms. She started by hauling away scrap wood left by the carpenters and stacking firewood in the corner behind the wood stove. By evening, she was just finishing sweeping both classrooms and the entry room when she heard footsteps on the porch. She looked up and saw her father standing in the doorway.

"Hello, Sarah," he said.

"Father! What are you doing here?" Sarah was shocked to see him.

"Your mother said you've been working on the school. I've come to see what needs to be done."

"Well, I took out the scrap wood and swept up the sawdust and brought in firewood—"

"That's excellent, but why are you doing this all by yourself?"

"It's almost September, and I want the school to be ready. Somebody has to do it."

"Do you know what I think you need here most of all?"

"What?"

"You need some help."

"It is a lot of work..."

"Let's look around and you show me what needs to be done." King Strang stood up and walked to the center of the room. "Well?" he asked, looking back at Sarah and putting his hands on his hips.

"It's dark in here."

"You're exactly right. I'll get some men to put in more windows. And we should whitewash these walls; that will brighten things up. I know two young fellows who would be just right for the job. Now, what else do you need?"

In spite of herself Sarah smiled, getting into the spirit of his questions. "We need some pictures on the walls, and a map of America, and a globe..."

"Yes, yes, go on," Strang said.

"And a blackboard for the wall and an alphabet to go above it."

"Ah, I know just the person for that. Do you know Edith Watson, Wingfield Watson's wife?"

"Yes," Sarah replied, thinking of the rotund and jolly woman who often came by the house with a gift of fresh eggs.

"The Quorum of the Apostles has just selected her to be the first school-teacher on Beaver Island. I'm quite certain that she would love to help you decorate the school."

"Mrs. Watson's going to be our teacher? She's really nice."

"She is well qualified. She taught school back in Wisconsin."

"Do you think she'll be mad that I started working here by myself?"

Strang laughed. "I'm sure she'll be delighted. I'm going to see Wingfield tonight, so I'll ask Mrs. Watson if she can come by here tomorrow afternoon. Now, what else do you think we need?"

"Hmmm, I can't think of anything," Sarah said.

"Are you sure?"

"Pretty sure..."

"What about furniture? I don't see any furniture."

"Oh, I forgot about that."

"Perhaps some desks?"

"School desks, and we'll need some chairs, and a table along the wall, and a big desk for the teacher, and some bookshelves."

"Now you're talking," Strang said with a laugh. "That's a big order, but I'll see what I can do."

"Thank you, Father," Sarah said.

"That's enough work for one day," Strang said. "It's getting dark. Let's go home."

He walked out the front door. Sarah shut the door and quickly followed him.

"Sarah, there's something I want to talk to you about," Strang said without looking back to see if she was behind him. "It's about Elvira…."

Sarah's stomach tightened. She didn't want to talk about Elvira. She wasn't in the mood for another argument.

"She misses you," Strang said.

"She misses me? Why would she miss me?"

"She's lonely at the print shop. George Adams is off on a mission trip and she has no one to keep her company when I'm not there."

"What about Mrs. Adams? She's still here, isn't she? Can't Elvira talk to her?"

"Ahh, Louisa Adams," Strang said, stroking his beard. "I have forbidden Elvira from talking to her."

"Why? She's all alone too, if Mr. Adams is gone."

"Well, it's complicated. All I can tell you is that I have recently learned that Mrs. Adams is not what she appeared to be when she came here in June."

"Well, I don't want to work at the print shop and I don't want to be a reporter."

"But Sarah, Elvira still wants you to be a reporter, and so do I. We would like you to write an article for another special edition of the *Northern Islander*."

Sarah looked up. "Write an article? All by myself?"

"Yes. All by yourself."

"But Elvira changes my words."

"Sometime you have to change the words. That's what an editor does."

"But she changes the meaning of my words."

King Strang turned and looked at his daughter. "Sarah, I know that you and Elvira had a bit of a falling out over the Fourth of July article, but she means well, she really does. And she is devoted to our mission here on the island. Perhaps she was just trying to get the article to fit the page."

"She changed everything I said. Some of those men were drunk, and they did threaten us, but most of them were just celebrating. She made them seem like a gang of criminals."

"Well, perhaps she did get carried away," Strang allowed. "I'll tell you what I'll do. If you write the article I'll edit it myself, without Elvira. Then we'll go over it together and make sure it says exactly what you want to say. How does that sound?"

"What am I supposed to write about?" Sarah asked, not yet convinced.

"The new school," Strang said, pointing back at the unfinished building. "I think you should write about how the school was built by the Mormons and Irish fishermen. You should say that this will be the first school on Beaver Island and that all children are welcome to attend. Perhaps an interview with Mrs. Watson would be interesting. Of course, I'll leave that all up to you; it's your article. What do you say?"

"That sounds good. I guess I could do that."

Strang clapped his hands together. "That's excellent, Sarah. We'll make you a first-rate reporter."

The next afternoon, Sarah hurried over to the school building. She knew her father had a knack for getting things done quickly, but when she arrived, no one was there and everything looked the same. Disappointed, she picked up her broom and went inside to resume sweeping. But before she even got started, she heard voices outside. She quickly put down her broom and ran out on the front step.

"Hey there, young lady, we're lost. Do you know where we can find the new Beaver Island School?" It was Wingfield Watson with his wagon and team of oxen.

Sarah smiled and waved. "This is it! It's right here!" she called to him.

The wagon was full of furniture: chairs, tables, bookcases and a large wooden desk. Two men who Sarah recognized as carpenters from the temple rode on the back of the wagon, holding the furniture in place.

"We have a delivery for you. Where would you like it?" Wingfield asked.

"Where did you get everything?" Sarah asked in amazement.

"Word travels fast on Beaver Island. We asked for donations and before we knew it we had a full load."

Wingfield stopped the wagon in front of the school and tied the oxen to the school bell post. Sarah ran to the side of the wagon, reached through the railing, and slid her hand across the smooth wooden surface of the desk.

"That was Edith's school desk back in Wisconsin. We hauled it all the way up here to the island, and now I know why. She's going to be a teacher. Where is she, anyway? That's just like her, to be late on her first day of work."

"Yoo-hoo, yoo-hoo, here we are!"

Sarah and Wingfield looked down the lane and saw three figures approaching. Edith Watson bustled along, carrying a large wicker basket. King Strang strode briskly beside her with a box under each arm. Far behind them, Elvira Field trudged along, struggling with a wheelbarrow full of books.

"It's getting crowded around here," Sarah said to Wingfield.

"Do you think so? Look in the other direction."

Sarah turned and looked behind her. In the distance she saw Andy and Nathan, each carrying a bucket. She looked back at Mr. Watson for an explanation. Wingfield held out his hands and raised his eyebrows, feigning ignorance. They all waited until Andy and Nathan came up to the wagon and put down their buckets.

"Hi, Sarah," Andy said, smiling at her. "We're here to whitewash the walls."

Elvira was the last to arrive. She dropped her wheelbarrow with a thud. "Here they are," she said, catching her breath, "books for the new school library."

"Wingfield clapped his hands. "Well, we're all here. What are we waiting for? Let's get to work!"

Sarah ran back to the school and held open the door. She could not believe so many people had come to help.

Nathan came in first. "We'll start painting in the back," he said. "Then we won't get in anyone's way."

Andy came in with the second bucket and just smiled at Sarah. He didn't have to say anything as their eyes met.

The two carpenters struggled up the steps with the large wooden desk, with Edith Watson giving them instructions all the way.

"Be careful! Don't bump it on the door. Put it right in the middle of the room so the boys don't splash whitewash on it."

King Strang came in with a box of school supplies and he and Elvira carried books into the schoolhouse and piled them on the floor. Sarah cringed as Elvira passed close by, her arm brushing Sarah's sleeve.

"Sarah," Strang said, "why don't you and Elvira put the books on the shelves? Maybe you should alphabetize them."

Elvira crouched down on her knees at one side of the pile of books and began sorting. Reluctantly, Sarah knelt at the other side of the pile and began looking at the titles, many of which were new to her. They sorted the books in silence for a few moments until Elvira handed her a worn volume of poetry.

"Here, Sarah, you might like this one. I read it on the boat."

"Thank you," Sarah replied. "I'll look at it tonight."

Elvira pointed out some other interesting titles, and soon Sarah became engrossed in examining the books. She even picked out a couple more to take home.

By late afternoon, the work was almost done. "We'll come back tomorrow when the walls are dry and rearrange the furniture," Wingfield said.

"I'll come back, too," Mrs. Watson added. "Sarah and I can tack paper letters of the alphabet on the wall and we'll hang up a few pictures."

"Thank you, everyone," King Strang said. "Because of your efforts, we'll have the best schoolhouse in northern Michigan. Classes start in a week, and all the children on the island are welcome to attend."

"Thank you, Father," Sarah said. "I never expected to see so many people."

"You are most welcome," he replied, turning to look for Elvira, who was coming down the steps.

King Strang took Elvira by the arm. "Sarah, please tell your mother I'll be home later." He walked away with Elvira, heading back to the print shop and leaving Sarah standing on the school steps.

Sarah watched them walk away, involuntarily examining Elvira's figure. Even though she was wearing a baggy pair of men's work pants, it was still obvious that Elvira was a woman. Looking at her, Sarah was astounded that Elvira had been able to spend all winter disguised as a man without being discovered. Was it possible that no one else on the island knew the truth about Elvira Field and Charles Douglass?

Wingfield Watson called to his wife, breaking Sarah's thoughts. "Let's go, Edith. It'll be dark soon."

"I'm coming, I'm coming," Mrs. Watson called from the doorway. She walked to the wagon, followed by Andy and Nathan, who were both spattered with whitewash. As Wingfield started to untie the oxen from the post he glanced up at the school bell.

"There's just one thing missing here," he said. "They did a nice job putting the bell on top of this post, but they forgot to put a rope on it. You can't even ring the bell. We can fix that real quick."

He reached underneath the wagon seat and pulled out an old piece of rope. "Here, Andy, why don't you stand on the wagon and tie this rope to the bell."

Andy took the rope and hopped up on the back of the wagon. "I can't reach it," he said.

"Can you shinny up the pole?" Wingfield asked.

"Then I can't let go to tie it."

"Hmmm." Wingfield thought for a moment. "I know. Sarah, why don't you get up on Andy's shoulders? Then you can reach the bell and tie the rope to it. You can tie a knot, can't you, Sarah?"

"Sure," Sarah replied. "It's just like sewing."

Andy stooped down and Sarah climbed on his shoulders, grasping his neck and holding the rope in one hand. Andy grabbed her ankles and slowly stood up, wavering a little.

"Don't lose your balance," she giggled.

"I'll try not to," Andy said, planting his feet firmly on the wagon.

Sarah could feel the muscles tighten in Andy's neck. She squeezed her legs together for a better grip, reached upward with both hands, and awkwardly tied the rope to the bell.

"There," she said. "I think I got it." She put both her hands on Andy's head, holding on tight to keep her balance.

"Coming down," Andy said.

He stooped down, lowered his head, and Sarah hopped off, catching Andy's hand to keep from falling. She almost made it but she stumbled, sprawling in the hay on the bed of the wagon. They both burst out laughing.

"Good job!" Wingfield said. "Now you can ring that bell. Thanks for the help today, boys. Good night, Sarah."

"Thanks, Mr. Watson. Thanks, Mrs. Watson."

Wingfield helped Edith up on the wagon seat and then clambered up beside her. He slapped the reins, and the oxen plodded away down the lane, pulling the wagon and its two portly passengers.

"We're not going out fishing tomorrow, Sarah. Can you come over?" Andy asked.

Sarah felt out of breath, but she didn't know why. Andy had done all the work lifting her. She looked at him and then looked away, taking a deep breath. "I really can't," she said. "School's only a week away and I have to get ready."

"But that's a whole week. We have plenty of time," Andy said.

"Yes, but I have to write my article."

Andy and Nathan looked at each other and then looked back at her. "Article? What article?" Andy asked.

"My article for the newspaper."

"I thought you were done writing for the newspaper."

"I was, but—"

"Well, what's your article about?"

"You'll see," Sarah said, throwing them both a coy glance over her shoulder as she skipped away.

Sarah went straight home and started writing. She stayed up late, working by candlelight, and finally finished writing long after everyone else had gone to bed. In the morning, she took her completed article to the print shop and presented it to her father. King Strang tilted back in his chair and began reading. He stroked his beard and nodded in approval as he turned the pages.

August, 1850
New School Opens on Beaver Island

A new school building has been completed over the summer and will be open for classes in September. This school will far surpass in size and quality any school in northern Michigan, including the school on Mackinac Island.

"All children of school age will be allowed to attend, regardless of church affiliation," according to King Strang, leader of the Mormon Church.

Mrs. Edith Watson has agreed to serve as the first schoolteacher at the new school. Mrs. Watson was a teacher in Wisconsin before moving to Beaver Island. She is already hard at work preparing her lessons and she looks forward to the opportunity to teach our young people. Classes will be taught in reading, writing and arithmetic, as well as penmanship and history.

Special thanks are given to Wingfield Watson for the generous use of his team and wagon, Tobias Humphrey for donating the woodstove, Alva Cable for donating the school bell, and Ian McGuire, Patrick O'Donnell and all the other men who designed and built the schoolhouse. Thanks are also due to all of our generous friends and neighbors who provided furniture and school supplies and who helped prepare the classrooms for the first day of classes.

The successful completion of the Beaver Island School is an example of what can be accomplished when everyone in a community cooperates and works together. The staff of the *Northern Islander* predicts that within a year the children of Beaver Island will have the best education in all of northern Michigan.

By Sarah Strang

"Do you like it, Father?" Sarah asked when he finished reading.

"It is excellent, Sarah. Well done! You have a good introduction, background information, detail, human interest, and even a quote," Strang said. "I think this is good enough for the front page of the *Northern Islander*. We will print it this weekend, just before the first day of school on Monday.

"You wouldn't change anything?" Sarah asked.

"Only a couple of things. First, I would describe Mrs. Watson as a Mormon teacher, not just a teacher."

"But why would that matter? You said the school was for everyone."

"So I did. But Mrs. Watson is a member of our Mormon church and she taught in a Mormon school."

"I don't see what difference that makes. She's just going to teach us reading and writing and numbers. Those are the same for everyone, aren't they?"

"Well, yes, I suppose they are the same for everyone, but——"

"So I should just call her a teacher, right?"

Strang laughed. "Sarah, you are stubborn and tenacious, just like me. You're going to make a fine Mormon princess someday."

Sarah laughed too, but she was not sure she liked the idea of being a Mormon princess.

"Now," Strang continued, "you forgot one other thing. You forgot to mention how you took it upon yourself to clean up the classrooms and get them ready for the first day of school."

"But that would be bragging."

"Ah, well, you can't be modest in this church business. No one would ever listen to you."

"I really would prefer to leave that part out."

"As you wish," he said. "A promise is a promise. We shall print the article exactly the way you have written it."

King Strang was as good as his word. On Friday, Sarah's article was printed on the front page of the *Northern Islander*. Elvira printed extra copies and stacked them on the porch of the print shop. She delivered a stack of papers to the Mormon temple and Johnson's Store and she even took some extra copies over to Sarah's house.

"I knew you'd make a good reporter," Elvira said when Sarah opened the door. "Here's your first headline. You should keep a copy in a safe place."

"Thank you, Elvira," Sarah said, pleased at the compliment. She almost invited her in, but she hesitated, uncomfortable with the charade and fearful that her mother had somehow discovered why Elvira had moved out of the house so abruptly.

Elvira seemed to sense Sarah's discomfort and turned to leave. "I've got to get back to the print shop," she said. "Your father wants to start printing regular weekly editions by the end of the year, so I've got a lot of work to do."

The following Monday was the first day of school. Promptly at 8 o'clock Mrs. Watson rang the school bell and all of the children filed into the schoolhouse, taking seats on benches donated by island families. Sarah sat between Andy and Nathan, as she had wanted to do for so long. Gurdon Humphrey and Oren Whipple were the last to arrive and sat in the back row.

As soon as Mrs. Watson entered there was silence in the room. She walked to the front of the room and turned to face the students. "Good morning, class," she said. "Welcome to the first day of school. I will ring the bell every morning and I expect you all to be in your seats by the time I come inside to take attendance. If you are tardy you shall have to stay after class for an extra assignment. Is that clear to everyone?"

No one said a word, so Mrs. Watson continued. "We have two classrooms, so by the end of the day I will divide you into two groups. The younger students will remain here and the older students will move to the other classroom. Meanwhile, this morning I will take attendance and pass out pencils and paper. Then I will introduce the students whose families are new to the island. We have a large class, so I will expect your attention at all times. Now, shall we begin?"

Mrs. Watson maintained discipline in the classroom, but after school there was plenty of room for mischief in the schoolyard. It didn't take long for trouble to start. When Andy and Nathan came down the steps they saw Gurdon and Oren cornering two younger Irish boys.

"This here is a Mormon school," Gurdon said to the boys, who were cowering behind the bell pole. "We just let you Irish in because we want to. We might even let a few Indians in, if they shut up and sit on the floor."

"Yeah, and they're not even real Americans," piped up Oren.

"That's right, and neither are you, Irish," Gurdon added.

Andy looked at the two boys and saw the fear in their eyes. It was the same fear he had seen in Ireland, on the *Dunbrody* crossing the Atlantic Ocean, and on faces of immigrants at the docks in New York. "Why don't you leave them alone, Gurdon?"

Gurdon turned around and glared at Andy. "Well, lookee here, it's another Irish, and he don't know when to shut up either."

"Aww, c'mon, Gurdon, it's the first day of school."

"Yeah, it is, and I want these worms to know who's in charge here."

"We all know you're the biggest kid in the school. Why do you have to pick on them?"

"Maybe I should pick on you instead."

"I don't want any trouble with you, Gurdon."

"Then you should just shut up, McGuire, like I told you before."

Nathan and Sarah came up behind Andy. "Come on, Andy, let's go. He's not worth it," Nathan whispered.

Sarah put her arm around Andy's arm and led him away, but not before Andy turned and sneered at Gurdon.

"Hey, Sarah, why don't you stick with your own kind?" Gurdon called. "You're Mormon, not Irish, like these scum."

"Let's get out of here," Sarah said, putting her other arm around Nathan's arm. She pulled both of the boys across the schoolyard and shuttled them out the front gate, prattling cheerfully about the first day of school until both boys forgot about Gurdon and Oren.

After a few days, classes in the schoolhouse settled into a routine. Every morning at eight o'clock Mrs. Watson rang the school bell. The children scrambled inside at the first chime, while the older students lingered outside as long as possible before filing in and taking their seats.

Although Mrs. Watson was a strict disciplinarian, she proved to be a favorite with the younger children. She soon earned the respect of the older students by recruiting them to help her run the classroom. Sarah taught the small children reading and writing. Oren, who was good with numbers, helped with addition and subtraction. Nathan taught geography by telling stories about Ireland, the Atlantic Ocean, and New York. At the end of the day Sarah cleaned the blackboard and Andy and Gurdon swept the floors and stacked firewood. Mrs. Watson warned the boys that when winter arrived they would also be shoveling snow from the front steps.

At first, Andy had trouble paying attention in class. He was used to working on boats, not sitting in a classroom. After a few weeks he became an attentive student when a topic interested him. Like Nathan, he loved geography and he especially loved maps and stories about the oceans of the world.

Gurdon, already known as a troublemaker, became a good student under Mrs. Watson's tutelage. He liked reading and history, and he especially liked to read about the history of the Mormon Church. As time went by, he asked Sarah about some of the Mormon doctrines. Occasionally she responded by discussing reading assignments with him during recess.

As for Sarah, she loved going to school. Every day she was waiting on the front steps before Mrs. Watson rang the bell. She always sat between Andy and Nathan with her books open, ready to begin her studies.

Gurdon's improved behavior under Mrs. Watson's watchful eye didn't fool Andy or Nathan. Gurdon still bullied the younger students in the school yard, and Andy was the only one who would stand up to him. When class was in session they glared at each other, but since they were responsible for keeping the wood stove burning they managed to keep the peace, at least while Mrs. Watson was around.

However, away from the school yard it was another matter.

CHAPTER 8:

Trouble Begins

The following week Gurdon Humphrey arrived at school early and sat at the desk directly in front of Sarah, who was reviewing her lesson for the day. After dumping his books, he turned around and put his elbow on her desk.

"Hi, Sarah," he said. "Have you read any good books lately?"

Sarah involuntarily leaned back in her chair, surprised by Gurdon's early intrusion into her thoughts. "Um, good morning, Gurdon. Actually, no, I haven't."

"I was just thinking that we could study together sometime."

"Yes, perhaps we could."

Andy and Nathan arrived at the door at the back of the classroom. They were late, and when they hurried to their seats they saw Gurdon leaning over Sarah's desk. Sarah gave Andy a pleading look to rescue her, but Mrs. Watson chastised the two boys for being tardy, ordered Gurdon to quiet down and immediately started class.

All day Gurdon kept turning around and talking to Sarah. He asked her about schoolwork, made bad jokes, and tried to engage her in conversation. On several occasions, Mrs. Watson had to ask him to be quiet and face the front of the class.

At the end of the day Sarah was the first to stand up and head for the door. Andy took her cue and immediately joined her at the back of the classroom. They started to leave, but Mrs. Watson called Sarah back.

"Sarah, aren't you going to clean the blackboards today?"

"Oh, yes, I'm sorry, Mrs. Watson, I forgot."

Sarah hurried to the front of the classroom, with Andy right behind her.

"I'll just wait here," Andy said, taking a seat in the front row.

Gurdon, seeing them together, picked up his books and stomped to the back of the room, slamming the door on his way out. Oren was waiting for him at the bell pole, grinning and snickering.

"What are you laughing about?" Gurdon snarled at his friend.

Over the next few weeks Gurdon sat near Sarah almost every day, abandoning Oren in the back of the room. Gurdon tried to win her favor in every way he could, asking her about books she was reading or about class assignments. He often asked about her father, King Strang. He seemed to be particularly interested in the activities of the Mormon Church. Gurdon acted the perfect gentleman, but Sarah still tried to stay away from him and as close to Andy as possible. For his part, Andy kept his eye on Gurdon and tried to maintain his composure, especially in the classroom.

One day the *Emma Rose* brought in the biggest catch of the season, so Andy and Nathan both had to miss school. They were needed to clean and pack fish, fill barrels, and seal the lids before the catch spoiled. Ian said this catch alone would make them enough money to survive the winter, so he wanted to get the barrels out to Whiskey Point right away.

Sarah attended school alone that day. Gurdon took the seat on her left, the seat usually occupied by Andy. Oren summoned up his courage and sat on her right, in Nathan's seat. Sarah endured a long day without her friends, but she concentrated on her studies, helped the small children with their letters, and even shared a passage in a history book with Gurdon, who looked over her shoulder as she read aloud to him.

At the end of the day, Sarah stayed behind to clean the blackboards. She deliberately took her time, hoping that Gurdon and Oren were not loitering in the school yard. When she was finished, she grabbed her jacket and headed for the door. Just as she reached for the knob, the door swung open and there stood Gurdon with a load of firewood in his arms.

"Hi, Sarah," he said. "I didn't realize you were still here."

"Hi, Gurdon. I was just leaving. See you tomorrow."

"Let me stack this firewood and I'll walk you home."

"I'll be fine. It's only a short way," Sarah replied, edging for the door.

Gurdon dumped the firewood on the floor. "But we're going in the same direction. You wouldn't want me to just walk behind you by myself, would you?"

Sarah was trapped. Mrs. Watson was gone and the room was empty.

"No, I guess not..."

Gurdon opened the door for her and walked with her down the porch steps.

"What do you think about that history stuff you read to me?" he asked.

"It was good. I've read it before..."

They walked along in awkward silence. Sarah didn't feel like talking.

"Do you like Mrs. Watson?"

"She's all right. Sometimes she's a little strict."

"Sarah, I was wondering..." Gurdon began.

Sarah cringed, waiting for him to ask about Andy.

"I was wondering how it feels to have a king for a father?"

Relieved that the question wasn't too personal, Sarah answered, "Not much different than anyone else. He isn't really a king, you know."

"Sure he is. He's King Strang, king of the Mormon Church."

"I know, but it's not like he's the King of England or anything like that. He's just a regular person. Just ask my mother."

"Yeah, but he's still a king. My pa says he's a saint, too."

Sarah laughed. "He might be a king, but he's no saint. I'm quite sure of that."

"If he's a king then that makes you a princess, don't it?" Gurdon asked.

Sarah was silent, not enamored with the idea of Gurdon thinking of her as a princess.

Not getting a response, Gurdon changed the subject. "My father has a lot of books."

"Really?" Sarah asked, now mildly interested in the conversation.

"Yeah, in fact he has a whole library."

"What kind of books does he have?"

"All kinds. Every kind you could think of. I don't even have time to look at them all," Gurdon answered.

"Well, where does he keep them?" Sarah asked.

"In our house. They cover a whole wall next to the fireplace. Would you like to see them?"

"Oh, no, maybe some other time. I have to get home to help my mother."

"But we're almost to my house. My pa's probably in there right now reading a book. He's rich, so he has lots of time to read."

Reassured by the presence of an adult in the house, Sarah considered Gurdon's invitation. There weren't many books on the island, and she was curious to see Mr. Humphrey's library.

"C'mon, I'll show you," Gurdon said.

"All right," Sarah said, "but just for a minute."

They reached the gate in front of Gurdon's house and Gurdon held it open. Sarah looked up at the Humphrey house. She had passed by every day on her way to school, but she had never realized how big it was. It had a large front porch and finished wood siding, not like the log cabins that most of the islanders lived in. Mr. Humphrey had made money in the lumber industry on the mainland and now he was cutting timber on Beaver Island. He also owned a schooner to carry his lumber to Milwaukee once a week.

Gurdon walked behind Sarah, giving her time to take in the wide sidewalk leading to the stately home. She walked up the porch steps and Gurdon hurried past her and opened the front door. Sarah peered into the dim interior and saw a grandfather clock, a rich tapestry hanging on a wall, and a curved stairway leading to the upper rooms. She gingerly crossed the threshold and stepped inside Gurdon's house.

As Sarah entered the front hall of the Humphrey residence, Andy and Nathan were standing ankle-deep in fish guts sloshing around in the bilge water of the *Emma Rose*. They were cleaning the last of the fish from yesterday's record catch. Earlier in the day the boat had been floating low in the water, weighed down by the biggest pile of fish they had ever seen. The dock was lined from one end to the other with wooden barrels. Patrick was filling a barrel with fish while Ian wheeled another barrel out to the end of the dock.

"That should be the last one, Ian. Do you have any more salt?" Patrick asked.

"A little, but it's almost gone. I hope there's enough to preserve these fish before they get to market," Ian replied.

Nathan picked up the last fish from the bottom of the boat and tossed it up to his father. "That's all the fish. We're going to rinse off. We stink."

"You sure do," Patrick said with a laugh. "Why don't you get some dry clothes and then we'll roll these barrels up on shore."

Nathan and Andy climbed wearily out of the boat and put down their knives. Their hands were covered with slime, and bloody fragments of fish guts clung to their clothes. After rinsing off in the shallow water near the beach, they stripped and ran up to the house to change into dry clothes.

"That's the best catch we've ever had," Ian said. "Fourteen barrels."

"Where's your cousin, Ian?" Patrick asked. "He should have been here by now."

"I don't know. I hope he shows up soon. I'd sure like to get these barrels loaded and hauled away. It's been a long day."

"Well, let's get these lids nailed on. He'll be along soon."

Andy and Nathan came back down to the dock just as Ian nailed on the last lid. He tipped the barrel over on its side and rolled it a few feet, pushing it with his foot.

"C'mon," he said, "let's get these barrels up by the road."

They each got behind a barrel and rolled it along the dock. The rest of the barrels were lined up in a row along the road.

"How are we going to get all these barrels out to Whiskey Point?" Andy asked. "There's no one to haul them."

"Oh, yes there is," Ian replied. "I think I hear him coming now, if he doesn't kill himself before he gets here."

They all looked down the road in the direction of Whiskey Point. Beyond the trees they heard a clatter of hooves and the sound of someone shouting.

"Who is it?" Andy asked, standing on a stump so he could get a better view.

"You'll see."

Around the corner came a man riding on Alva Cable's wagon. It was Jack Bonner. Two horses were straining in their harnesses to pull the wagon as Bonner slapped their backs with the reins.

"How many barrels did' ja git?" Jack shouted. "Charlie Booth got twelve last June."

"We beat him. We got fourteen," Ian shouted as the wagon went past.

"Whoa there, whoa," Jack shouted at the horses. "How do you stop this thing?"

Seeing that the wagon was not going to stop, Nathan ran along the side of the nearest horse, grabbed the harness, and gently slowed the frightened animal. Both horses finally came to a stop, wild-eyed and wheezing.

"That's no way to treat these horses, Jack," Patrick snapped.

"Hey, I was in a hurry."

"You're late. We expected you an hour ago."

"No matter," Ian said. "Let's just get these barrels loaded."

Patrick walked the horses in a wide circle until the wagon was turned around and facing back toward Whiskey Point. Andy and Nathan walked beside the horses and talked to them gently to calm them down.

"What are their names?" Andy asked.

"That one's Guy, and the one with the white spot is Lois," Jack said, climbing down from the wagon. "I'm watching them while Alva visits his nephew down at Cable Bay. They're talking about opening a new store down there."

"They're hot and sweaty," Ian said to the boys. "Why don't you brush them down while we load the barrels?"

Andy and Nathan grabbed two brushes from the back of the wagon and began to brush the horses, stroking them and talking to them while they worked. The three men went to the back of the wagon and began to load barrels, rolling them one by one up a wooden ramp until the wagon was full.

"That's about all the wagon can handle," Ian said, rolling one last barrel in place. "It'll take four trips to haul all of them to Whiskey Point. Boys, why don't you ride with Jack. You can learn how to handle the horses. Maybe Jack can learn something, too."

"Ha, ha!" Jack laughed. "Good joke, McGuire. I can make them go. I just can't make them stop."

"Just make sure you take it easy. You've got a lot of weight on that wagon."

"Don't worry, we will."

"C'mon, Andy, climb on," Nathan said. Both of the boys hopped up on the wagon seat.

"Roll the barrels off right near the dock." Ian said. "There's a boat coming to pick them up in a couple of days."

Jack climbed up and sat in the middle. He picked up the reins and proceeded to tell the boys how to use them to control the horses. He shook the reins once and the horses began to pull.

Ian and Patrick watched the wagon depart. "He's a wild one, that cousin of yours," Patrick said.

"Yeah, he is. But look at him, teaching those boys how to use the reins. Maybe they'll be able to settle him down."

Patrick laughed. "But who's going to settle the boys down?"

"Good point," Ian said with a wry smile.

Sarah was enthralled with the books in Mr. Humphrey's library. "Gurdon, this is a wonderful collection," she exclaimed, picking up a volume and turning it over in her hands. "Most of them are classics. Where did you ever get them?"

"My pa bought them all from some old guy who was almost dead. He brought everything up here on our boat. He even brought a piano."

"You have a piano? Can I see it?"

"Sure. It's right behind you under the stairs. It's the only one on the island."

Sarah walked over to the piano and lifted a cloth off the ivory keyboard. She was impressed that the Humphreys had so many fine possessions in their home.

"Who plays it, Gurdon?"

"Um, no one. My pa brought it for my ma before she died."

Sarah put her hand on Gurdon's sleeve. "I'm so sorry, Gurdon."

"That was a long time ago. I don't really remember her."

"Still, it must be hard for you."

"She died in Illinois. We moved to Wisconsin, and then we came here."

"Your father must be very lonely."

"He works all the time," Gurdon said, dismissing the subject. "Would you like to play the piano?"

"I don't know how to play, but I always wanted to learn," Sarah said. "Do you mind if I sit down and try it?"

"Sure, go ahead. You can come over and play it anytime. No one ever uses it."

"Thank you, Gurdon. I would like that."

Gurdon pulled out the piano bench for her. Sarah sat down and gently placed her hands on the keyboard. Gurdon sat next to her. "Go ahead," he said. "Try it."

Sarah ran her fingers along the keyboard and delicately pressed a few of the keys. A trio of clear notes floated into the air.

"This is wonderful, Gurdon. It makes a beautiful sound."

"My mother played it every evening."

"You must miss her very much."

Gurdon squirmed around on the bench and inched towards her. "Sarah, I was wondering..."

"Yes, Gurdon?"

"I was wondering if we...I mean you and I, I mean, if we could become engaged."

"What?" Sarah asked, looking at him incredulously.

"You know, engaged. So we could be married, I mean, someday."

"Gurdon, I'm only fourteen years old!"

"I know, but you'll be fifteen next summer, and I'll be seventeen.

"But I haven't even finished school yet," Sarah protested.

"You don't need school. A lot of Mormon girls get married when they are fifteen."

Sarah stood up from the piano bench. She was shocked at Gurdon's outrageous proposal and now she was getting angry. "Sure, when their parents make them get married."

"Just think, Sarah. Your father is King Strang, king of the Mormons, and my father is the richest man on the island. It would be perfect."

Sarah couldn't believe what she was hearing. "I don't see anything perfect about it at all," she said, walking toward the door.

Gurdon hurried across the room and stood in front of her.

"But we would be rich and famous. We could have a big house, even bigger than this one."

"I don't want to be rich and famous. I just want to go home," Sarah said, her voice trembling.

"But won't you just think about it? We have lots of time. I know you'll want to after you think about it."

"Gurdon, I—"

"What?"

"I have... I already have a suitor," Sarah blurted out without thinking. Her heart was pounding. She had to get away from this awful house and this awful person. How could he even think of such a thing?

Gurdon remained, standing in front of her, but Sarah could wait no longer. She scurried around him before he could even move, threw open the front door, jumped off the porch, and ran across the lawn. Forgetting about the open gate, she jumped over the fence and ran down the path toward home without looking back.

The next day in school, Gurdon took his usual seat in the back of the room next to Oren. He ignored Sarah completely, and he resumed his earlier behavior of disrupting the class with sarcastic remarks and spitballs aimed at the blackboard. In the schoolyard, he bullied and abused the younger students, cornering them every chance he could.

On several occasions both Andy and Nathan grumbled to Sarah about Gurdon's renewed belligerence. After a rough start at the beginning of the school year, he had become a reasonably well-behaved student. But something had happened to cause Gurdon to revert to his old ways. Andy thought it was a rebellion against his strict Mormon upbringing. They finally concluded that he was just a bully, plain and simple. Of course Sarah knew the real reason for Gurdon's behavior, but she was terrified that Andy would find out about his proposal to her, even though she had refused him. She didn't want any more trouble between Andy and Gurdon, especially in the school yard.

Two weeks passed, and Alva Cable still had not returned from Cable Bay. Nathan came out to Whiskey Point every day to help Jack Bonner feed and water the horses. He spent time brushing and talking quietly to them, so the animals soon were compliant and responsive to his commands. Before long Nathan was harnessing them and he became proficient at driving the wagon.

One Friday afternoon in October Nathan hitched the horses to the wagon. He was going to pick up new barrels in Saint James and deliver them out to Whiskey Point. Even though Cable's Store was still closed, the few fishermen who remained were still using Alva's dock to unload their catch and pack the fish in barrels. After making several trips, Nathan went back to Saint James for a final load. This was his last trip of the day, and he and Andy had planned an afternoon of fishing from shore at one of the inland lakes.

As Nathan left the village, he saw Sarah on the road ahead, walking to town on her way to Johnson's Store. She usually did some shopping on Friday and Nathan had been hoping to see her. After another week of enduring the friction between Andy and Gurdon in the classroom, he wanted to be with Sarah alone. She always had a special smile for him, and at times Nathan even imagined that she cared for him in some small way.

"Hey, Sarah," he called out, "Hop on and I'll give you a ride."

Sarah turned and smiled when she saw him. "Hi, Nathan. I'd love to. Is this your last load today?"

"Yep." Nathan always felt a little tongue-tied around Sarah.

Sarah patted both of the horses and hopped up on the wagon seat. She was wearing a fall dress with a shawl over her shoulders and a white bonnet tied loosely around her hair. Nathan could not help noticing how pretty she was in the afternoon sunshine.

"Giddyup, Guy! Giddyup, Lois!" He snapped the reins sharply and the horses started off at a brisk walk.

As they rode around the harbor, Nathan and Sarah saw Gurdon Humphrey and Oren Whipple walking behind a row of fishing nets hung out to dry. As usual, Gurdon was talking loudly and waving his arms and Oren was listening to every word and following one step behind.

"Oh, oh," Sarah said. "Here come a couple of troublemakers."

"Oren always picks on my horses," Nathan replied.

They rode on, looking straight ahead and ignoring the two boys, who had stopped to throw rocks at a squirrel.

"Here we are," Nathan said, stopping in front of his house. "I wonder if Andy is around anywhere. I haven't seen him today."

Sarah stood up in her seat and looked for Andy. Her hair spilled out of her bonnet as she stood and she brushed it back with a careless wave of her hand. "Let's see if we can find him," she said. "Yes, there he is! He's down on the dock."

Sarah jumped off the wagon and ran out the dock without looking back, leaving Nathan sitting alone on the wagon. He watched with envy as Sarah approached Andy and took his hand. Sighing, he tied the horses to a stump and gave them each an apple.

Andy had just cast off the dock lines to the *Emma Rose*. His father and Patrick were going to check out a new fishing location on the far side of Whiskey Point.

"See you tonight, son," Ian called out. "We'll be back in a couple of hours."

"Good luck!" Andy said. "We'll meet you when you get back."

The wind caught the main sail of the *Emma Rose*. Ian grabbed the tiller, Patrick tightened the lines, and soon they were sailing away. Andy and Sarah walked back up the dock and Nathan came down to join them. Behind him, Nathan noticed that Gurdon and Oren had approached the wagon and were standing next to the horses. Gurdon was tossing a rock from one hand to the other.

"Hey, McGuire," Gurdon called out, "not going fishing today?"

Andy was silent. Nathan could see that he was in no mood to deal with Gurdon Humphrey. Oren picked up a stick and began poking one of the horses.

"What's the matter," Gurdon asked, "are you afraid of the water?"

"No, I'm not afraid of the water," Andy said in a low voice.

"Maybe he can't swim," chirped Oren, continuing to poke at the horse.

Nathan glared at him. Oren took a step behind Gurdon and let the stick fall from his hand.

Gurdon sauntered down the dock, with Oren following behind. They stopped when they were about ten feet from Andy and Nathan. Gurdon tossed the rock up in the air and caught it with his other hand.

Nathan looked over at Andy. Andy's face was red and both of his fists were clenched. "Oh, great," Nathan thought. "This looks like trouble."

"What's the matter, McGuire," Gurdon sneered, "are those fish too hard for you to catch? Those are Mormon fish, you know."

"They sure are," chimed in Oren.

"They are not!" Andy said.

Nathan reached over and put a hand on Andy's arm.

"Why don't you go back to Ireland, McGuire, and maybe you can handle some of those little Irish fish. Maybe your pa could even catch some of those fish with his little Irish boat. *Emma Rose!* What kind of a name is that? What a stupid name for a boat."

At that, Sarah took three steps across the dock and slapped Gurdon hard across the cheek. "It's his mother's name. Now you stop it! Stop it right now!" she cried.

"Ow! Hey, that hurt!" Gurdon looked at her in shock and surprise. His cheek turned red from the slap and then his whole face turned a deep crimson color. He took a step toward Sarah, and then he stopped. An evil grin came across his face and he looked straight at Andy.

"What's the matter, McGuire? Do you need a Mormon girl to do your dirty work for you?"

That was enough for Andy. He snarled once, threw Nathan's hand away from his arm, and charged across the dock toward Gurdon. Gurdon put his arms up and turned to run away, his eyes suddenly wide with fear. He started to run and stumbled on the rough dock, falling and hitting his head on the hard wooden planks.

Andy was all over him in a second with both fists swinging. Gurdon lashed out with both of his feet, waving his arms wildly. Andy swung hard and hit Gurdon in the temple and then hit him again just below his left eye. Gurdon kicked out hard with both feet and managed to cuff Andy a few times with his fists, but he could not recover from his early fall. Andy drew back his fist and hit Gurdon square on the nose. Gurdon cried out in pain, and blood spurted from both nostrils. He pulled his arms up and tried to protect his face but Andy kept hitting him, again and again. In his rage he swung both fists wildly, and Gurdon could only curl up in a ball to protect himself.

"Andy, stop it! You're going to kill him!" Sarah cried. She ran past Nathan and grabbed Andy in a futile attempt to stop him. Andy was still swinging as Sarah wrapped her arms around his neck and tried to drag him away.

Nathan and Oren looked at each other across the melee. Without a word they both charged forward. They picked up Sarah and pulled her off Andy's back, dumping her in the weeds by the edge of the dock. Then they grabbed Andy by his arms and with a mighty heave lifted him up and threw him over backwards onto the dock. Andy fell hard on the wooden planks and lay there, stunned.

Gurdon was still squirming in the dirt and hollering in rage. Oren hurried over to him and pulled out a rag to stop the blood streaming from Gurdon's nose.

"I'll get you, you Irish bastard," Gurdon screamed. "I'll tell my father and his lumberjacks will take care of you for good!"

Oren stood up and let his friend holler. Oren had lost a shoe, his shirt was torn and somehow he had gotten a bloody lip in the tustle. By this time Nathan was helping Andy to his feet. Sarah was still sitting in the weeds behind them, staring incredulously at Andy.

Oren stooped down and picked up Sarah's bonnet, which had come off in the scuffle and was lying crumpled in the grass. He marched straight between Andy and Nathan and stood before Sarah. "Here's your bonnet," he said.

Sarah stood up and took the bonnet. "Thank you, Oren."

Oren turned and walked between Andy and Nathan again. Then he turned around and looked between them, directly at Sarah. "I'm sorry, Sarah. I'm sorry you had to see this."

Oren glared at Andy and Nathan and then turned and walked back to his blubbering friend. He put his arm around Gurdon's waist and helped him to his feet. The two of them limped away, leaving Oren's shoe lying in the dirt.

When they reached the road, Gurdon turned one last time and shouted, "I'll get you, McGuire. Our lumberjacks are going to get you."

Nathan took a deep breath. He glanced at Andy and then he stared at Gurdon and Oren. Skinny little Oren was doing his best to support his larger friend as they hobbled along, while Gurdon continued to holler and curse. Suddenly Nathan realized that he was wrong about those two. Oren wasn't a coward at all. He wasn't afraid of either Andy or Nathan. It was Gurdon who was the coward.

"I had him, Nathan," Andy said, flexing his fists. "Why did you pull me off?"

"Because you wouldn't stop. Like Sarah said, you were going to kill him."

Nathan looked over at his friend and realized that the feud between Andy and Gurdon wasn't over. It was only beginning.

CHAPTER 9:
The King is Arrested

Trouble was also brewing among the leading members of the Mormon Church. In August George Adams had departed on a mission to Ohio to recruit new members. While he was away his wife Louisa managed to wear out her welcome on Beaver Island, especially among the Mormon wives. Always a fancy dresser, she had attracted the attention of the island men as she shopped at Johnson's Store or strolled down to the boat dock. In September she was seen in the company of several lumberjacks on the south side of town. Some folks said she was playing poker with them in a lumber shanty. Others said there was more going on in the shanty than just a game of poker. It didn't really matter; the idea of Louisa playing cards with the men while her husband was away was enough to lead to her downfall.

The end came in October. Elvira caught Louisa with Butch Jenkins in the print shop. Elvira had been away for most of the day, working at the temple and running errands for King Strang. She came back to the print shop late in the afternoon, looking forward to a short nap and a quiet evening of writing for the *Northern Islander*. As soon as Elvira opened the door she realized she was not alone. From the stairway to the upper room she could hear the sound of giggling and whispered voices.

"Who's here?" she asked. Without thinking, she hurried up the stairs to see who had invaded her privacy. When she reached the landing she saw Louisa and Butch Jenkins in bed, covered with only a blanket. Louisa's fancy dress was draped over a chair.

Startled, Louisa sat up and pulled the blanket to her chin. "Elvira! You're home early. We were just——"

Elvira didn't wait to hear the rest of Louisa's answer. "I know what you're doing," she cried. "This is King Strang's room!" She scrambled down the stairs to her own bedroom and slammed the door.

A week later George Adams returned to the island from Ohio. He was immediately summoned by King Strang. Strang didn't waste any time. "George, your wife has been excommunicated from the church. She must leave the island immediately."

"What!" Adams cried. "What has she done?"

"She has been accused of consorting with men, debauchery, and prostitution."

"You lie!" Adams shouted.

"It's not me, George. It's the Quorum of the Apostles. They have heard the evidence and they have voted to excommunicate her."

"They all lie! Louisa is my wife and I'll not hear of it, from you or anyone else."

"I have heard from reliable sources that she is not a lady of high society from Boston, as you led me to believe. She is merely a common prostitute. The quorum has voted and their vote is final. She must leave the island. I remind you that prostitution is a capital offense, punishable by hanging."

Adams was dumbfounded. His hands clenched the air and his faced turned red. He finally sputtered, "I have been away on a mission for your church, raising money and seeking converts, and this is how you treat me?"

"Perhaps you were also seeking pleasures of your own," Strang said calmly. "I'm doing you a favor, George. If she leaves now, I promise no harm will come to her. Since you choose to question my veracity, I require you to leave with her. You are hereby expelled from the church."

Adams pulled a pouch from beneath his shirt and shook it in Strang's face. "You see this? This is all the money I raised on *your* mission. I'm keeping it, you bastard! I'm keeping every penny. Damn you! Damn you and damn your church, *King Strang*." Adams stormed out the door, slamming it behind him and shaking the entire building.

Butch Jenkins sauntered out of a back room and leaned against the wall. "That went well," he remarked.

Strang sighed. "Butch, I hired you to be the town marshall. In the future I would advise you to conduct your personal affairs with more discretion."

The very next morning, George and Louisa Adams were seen boarding a boat at Johnson's dock. George Adams took one last look at Beaver Island, shook his fist in the air, and disappeared into the passenger cabin.

If King Strang thought he had rid Beaver Island of a troublesome couple by excommunicating George and Louisa Adams, he was mistaken. The Adams' did leave the island, but they didn't go far. They settled on Mackinac Island, home to most of the fishermen who had hastily departed Beaver Island on Independence Day. George Adams was quick to find a sympathetic audience and he proceeded to denounce the Mormon Church and King Strang.

"He is no king," Adams said to anyone who would listen. "He is an imposter." Forgetting his own role in the coronation ceremony, he ridiculed Strang as a false prophet wearing a paper crown. "He claims to speak the word of God, but he is nothing but a villain and a scoundrel. I have seen his treachery and heard his lies."

Encouraged by the crowds who came to hear him, Adams went even further. He approached the sheriff of Mackinac Island and persuaded him to arrest Strang for threatening his wife. A week later, Adams and the sheriff and a posse sailed to Beaver Island to apprehend him. The sheriff carried a warrant charging Strang with threatening the life of Louisa Adams and forcing her to leave the island against her will.

Sarah was the first to see George Adams arrive at the boat dock. She hurried to the print shop to tell her father.

"I saw George Adams," she said. "He's down at the boat dock."

Strang jumped up from his chair and peered out the window. "It's Adams all right," he said, closing the curtains. "He's brought the new sheriff and a posse, but they'll not catch me."

Strang locked the door and grabbed his coat. In his most recent sermon he had condemned Adams as traitor to the church and a thief for making off with the pouch of money collected during his mission trip. He was not about to be arrested in his own office by a former lieutenant and a gang of malcontent fishermen.

"What are you going to do, Father?" Sarah asked.

He turned to her with fire in his eyes. "Tell your mother I'm going to Mackinac Island. Tobias Humphrey will take me on his schooner. I'll meet these scoundrels on their own turf."

With that final remark, King Strang slipped out the back door and vanished into the forest.

The disappearance of King Strang caused great consternation within the island community, particularly since George Adams had arrived that very same day with the sheriff and a posse. The Mormons knew Adams had been excommunicated and there was bad blood between Adams and Strang. They feared Adams had returned for revenge. Some even suspected foul play.

It wasn't long before word of King Strang came from Mackinac Island. Two fishermen arrived at Cable's Store and announced that he had been arrested and was standing trial for threatening Louisa Adams. Details were sketchy, but it appeared that he would be released on a technicality and would soon return to Beaver Island. Alva Cable, who had returned to his store, immediately located Percival Graham and together they went to notify Mary.

"Thank God he's all right," Mary sighed, collapsing in a chair. "That man Adams has a terrible temper. I don't know what James ever saw in him."

"At first he truly believed in our work," Graham said, "and he possesses great speaking skills. That's why James made him his prime minister. But you're right, Mary, he does have a temper."

Mary nodded. "Ever since he came back to the island with Louisa he's caused trouble."

"Well, let's just be thankful that James is fine and will be returning to us soon," Graham replied.

Sure enough, a few days later Tobias Humphrey's schooner sailed into the harbor with King Strang standing at the bow, none the worse for his brief incarceration in the Mackinac Island jail.

As the year 1850 came to a close and the first ice appeared in the harbor, it seemed that peace had returned to Beaver Island. Most of the fishermen had departed and the Mormons were preparing for cold weather. Wingfield Watson and his team of oxen were busy hauling firewood and delivering it to homes and businesses around the harbor. Every afternoon he stopped to pick up Mrs. Watson at the school. He always had a smile and a wave to Sarah and the other students as they came out of the classroom. Andy and Nathan came out to greet the two oxen, Wingfield and Watson, who snorted and stomped their feet in the snow.

"How much do they weigh?" Nathan asked, patting the shoulder of one of the beasts.

"I'm not sure," Wingfield replied, "but they can haul tons of lumber."

"I'd like to have my own team of oxen someday."

"Well, you'd better start with horses," Wingfield replied with a hearty laugh. "These fellows will eat you out of house and home."

Mrs. Watson soon came out and climbed on the wagon next to her husband. Wingfield cracked his whip and the oxen headed for home, ready for a meal and a night of rest in their stable.

As for King Strang, he settled back into his daily routine. In the mornings he tended to church business. In the afternoons he worked on the *Northern Islander* with Elvira. Together they were preparing to expand the paper. Strang wanted the *Northern Islander* to become a regular newspaper, published and distributed once a week.

"It will be the first and only newspaper in northern Michigan," he said. "I want to send copies to Mackinac Island. Perhaps then they will learn to respect our little community here on Beaver Island."

The first enlarged edition was printed in early December. By this time Elvira had mastered the printing press and was able to print the newspaper by herself. Every Thursday a stack of papers appeared on the porch of the print shop. Even though winter was rapidly closing in, Strang delivered several copies to every boat sailing to Mackinac Island. Since most of the articles extolled the virtues of the Mormons, he wanted to be sure the message was received by George and Louisa Adams and their cohorts.

Although the charges against Strang had been dismissed, he soon faced another challenge from a man named Eri James Moore, a close ally of George Adams. Moore and his wife had left the island at about the same time as Adams, and they also resided on Mackinac Island. The Moores had built up a prosperous farm on Beaver Island, but after several years of toil they decided that Mormon life was not for them. They left their house and belongings behind them, but when Moore returned to collect his property he found that it had all been consecrated by the Mormon Church. Moore confronted Strang, who replied that his property now belonged to the church.

Moore left the island the next day, angry but not defeated. He wrote to the governor of Michigan, asking for protection from Strang because of numerous threats made against him. He also demanded compensation from Strang for the property taken from him.

Together on Mackinac Island, Eri Moore and George Adams made a formidable pair. Moore possessed the talent of the written word and Adams possessed the oratory skills to ignite passions against the Mormons. Together they contacted state and federal authorities, accusing the Mormons of crimes ranging from theft of property to counterfeiting, arson and piracy. The charges caught the attention of a Detroit newspaper, and the paper wrote a scathing article about the Mormon kingdom on Beaver Island. King Strang soon heard of it, but he was icebound on the island for the winter. All he could do was vow to arrest Adams and Moore if they ever set foot on Beaver Island again.

In February, Butch Jenkins stomped into the print shop, knocking the snow off his boots. "Eri Moore is on Garden Island," he announced.

"Are you sure?" Strang said, jumping to his feet.

"Yep," Jenkins replied. "I heard it from some hunters. They said he was selling whiskey to the Indians."

"Now's our chance," Strang said. "Butch, get a posse together. Take a constable with you and arrest him. We'll give him a trial right here. A few nights in our jail will teach him a lesson."

In just a few hours Jenkins had assembled a posse of ten men. Several of them were armed, and they all dressed warmly for the march across the ice to Garden Island. While they were gathering, Strang and Percival Graham prepared a warrant for the arrest of Eri Moore.

"It's against state law to sell whiskey to the Indians," Strang told Jenkins, "and it's also against Mormon law. We'll teach him to slander us."

Strang watched from his window as the posse departed. After they had set out across the harbor ice, he returned to his writing, satisfied that he would soon have Moore in his grasp. But the next day the posse returned, cold and empty handed.

"What happened?" he asked, meeting them on the porch.

"There were too many of them," Jenkins replied.

"But you were armed. You had guns."

"The Indians surrounded them. We couldn't even get close."

Strang sighed. "Well, I guess that was to be expected. If Moore is providing them with whiskey, they're certainly going to protect him."

"It's not worth anybody getting killed," Graham remarked.

"Not unless it's Eri Moore," Jenkins retorted.

"All right, Butch, there'll always be another day," Strang said, dismissing him.

After Jenkins and his men departed, Strang and Graham sat down to resume their work.

"James, I'm worried about Butch Jenkins. He's a rough character. He could cause a lot of trouble for us."

"I know what you mean, Percival, but with these constant threats against us, we need a few rough characters on our side."

"Let's just hope he stays on our side," Graham replied.

That night Strang stayed up alone to complete the final draft of an article for the *Northern Islander*. Frustrated by the events of the day, he tore up the last page and threw it on the fire. Taking a new sheet of paper, he wrote a new conclusion to his article:

'These men will continue to harass and slander us. They wish to destroy us and drive us from our blessed island. They will never let up until they have driven us to extinction. But they shall not succeed. We shall rise up against them and defeat them as sure as God is our master. Our will shall be unyielding and our power shall have the strength of iron. We will crush them into dust and consecrate all that they possess unto the name of the Lord. As your king, I promise you that we are ready for their attacks and we will respond without mercy. No outsider will ever force us to surrender our island home.'

Two days later the article was printed in the *Northern Islander* and delivered across the ice to Mackinac Island. The article soon found its way into the hands of George Adams and Eri Moore. King Strang had no way of knowing the effect his words had on the two men and on the plans they would make over the winter.

———

In the spring of 1851 Percival Graham stopped by to visit Ian and Patrick. It was a windy day so the two men had decided to stay on shore to prepare their nets for the approaching season.

"Hello, Percival," Ian called, waving at the approaching figure.

"Good morning, gentlemen. It's breezy today, isn't it?"

Patrick put down his tools and shook Graham's hand. "Too rough to go out fishing, that's for sure. At least we'll have a chance to get these nets ready. What brings you out this way?"

"I'm on my way out to Cable's Store to get the mail for King Strang. I never saw anyone get so much mail. He has quite a following."

"He sure does," Patrick agreed.

"There seems to be no limit to the faithful. But I must say I hope they stop coming to the island in such numbers. There isn't enough land for them. They didn't even have time to build decent houses last year before winter set in."

"Don't worry, another Michigan winter will keep them away," Ian said.

"That's for sure," Graham said. "Say, I also came here on an errand."

"What would that be?" Ian asked.

"It's about the school. It has been open for eight months now."

"So it has. Our two boys are learning a lot."

"King Strang has opened the school to all students. He values learning greatly, and he wants every child to have an education."

"So do we. Andy and Nathan wouldn't have gotten any kind of education back in Ireland, the way things were."

"We're glad to have you here with us," Percival said. "Now, you know we hired Edith Watson last fall to be the school teacher."

"We hear she's doing a good job," Patrick replied.

"And there are books and other expenses to run the school."

"Yes?"

"The Quorum of the Apostles has voted to impose a tax to pay Mrs. Watson and to support the school"

"That's certainly fair. We need a good school and a teacher. How much?" Patrick asked.

"Twenty dollars a year for each household."

"That seems high," Ian said.

"Perhaps it does, but King Strang would like to buy textbooks, and we expect there will be a lot more students next year if our missionary work goes well this winter. We might even need another teacher."

"Sure, Percival, that's fine," Patrick said. "We'd be glad to support the school. We just sold a boatload of fish, so I can pay you right now."

Patrick reached in his pocket and gave Graham several gold coins. Graham pulled out a ledger and a pencil and carefully recorded the transaction.

"Thank you, gentlemen. We appreciate your support. I'll be on my way now. I've a few more stops to make before I get to Cable's Store."

Graham put away his ledger and headed toward Whiskey Point.

"That school seems to be drawing the islanders together," Patrick said. "Perhaps there won't be any more trouble between the Mormons and the Irish."

"You could be right, Patrick," Ian replied. "But there's one thing I don't like."

"What's that?"

"We never got a chance to vote on these new taxes. The decision was made by the Mormon apostles, or whatever they call themselves. We ought to have a say in it, too."

"You're right, Ian. I never thought of that," Patrick said, stroking his chin.

The two men went back to work on the fishing nets, patching holes and splicing frayed ropes. When they were done, they hung the nets up and began to clean out the boat.

Just as they were finishing for the day, they heard several shouts coming from the direction of Whiskey Point. Looking up, they saw Percival Graham running toward them with two men in hot pursuit. The men caught up with him, swung him around, and knocked him down in the dirt. They both started kicking him, and he yelled for help. One of the men pulled out a club and began beating him. Graham raised his arms over his head but he could not protect himself from the assault.

Ian picked up a stick and ran as fast as he could, shouting at the two men. The men looked up, took a few more swings and ran away, disappearing into the woods.

When Ian and Patrick reached Graham, he was lying on the path with his face in the dirt. Blood was flowing from the back of his head and running down his neck. Patrick pulled out a handkerchief and pressed in into the wound to stop the bleeding.

"Let's turn him over," Patrick said. "We've got to see if he's bleeding anywhere else."

The two men carefully lifted Graham up by the shoulders and rolled him over. His face was covered with angry red welts from the beating and he had another cut above his left eye.

Just at that moment, Alva Cable came running along the path from Whiskey Point.

"What's going on? I heard shouting."

"It's Percival. Two men beat him up."

"My God!" Alva exclaimed, looking down at Graham. "Who did this?"

"We don't know," Patrick said. "They ran off into the trees."

"What can I do to help?"

"Run and get some water so we can clean him up. There's a bucket by the well and some towels on the clothesline. We'll try to get him over to our house," Ian said.

Alva ran off to the well as Ian and Patrick tried to lift Graham.

"Aughh!" Graham cried.

"Put him down," Ian said. "There's something else wrong with him."

"I think his arm's broken. Look how it's bent," Patrick said.

"You're right, it is broken! We're going to have to set it right here."

Alva returned with a pail of water and a towel.

"I'll use my stick as a splint," Ian said. "Alva, tear that towel into strips."

Patrick took a scrap of the towel, dipped it into the cold water, and wiped off Graham's face. His eyelids fluttered, and soon the cold water brought him around.

"What happened?" he asked weakly.

"You got attacked," Patrick said.

"Percival, you have a broken arm. I have to put a splint on it. This might hurt," Ian said.

"All right, go ahead," Graham said.

Ian held the stick along Graham's arm and tied it to the stick with strips of towel. Graham cried out again, this time kicking his feet in the dirt.

"All done," Ian said. "I did it fast."

"Oh God," Graham moaned, "That hurts! Don't touch it again."

"We won't," Patrick said. "Now let's get you cleaned up." He poured some more water on a rag and wiped Graham's face again.

"You have a lot of cuts and bruises, Percival. I'd like to wash the back of your head with some hot water. Can you make it to the house?"

"I think so," Graham replied, breathing deeply.

He slowly got to his feet and walked to the cabin, with Alva holding his good arm and steadying him. Once inside the house, Alva guided him to a chair while Patrick put a pan of water on the stove.

"Who did this to you?" Ian asked. "We couldn't see who they were."

"Hoy."

"Who?"

"Hoy. James Hoy. James Hoy and Oliver Renfrew."

"They live in a shack out near Whiskey Point," Alva said. "They make pretty good fish barrels, at least when they're sober."

"I stopped there before I came out to your place, Alva," Percival said, grimacing in pain. "I asked them for money for the school. They cursed me and ran me off with sticks. Said they didn't have any kids and even if they did they wouldn't send them to a damn Mormon school."

"They must have hidden in the trees and ambushed you on your way back," Alva said.

"I saw them coming and tried to run, but they were too fast for me."

"Here," Patrick said. "I've got some hot water. Let me clean up your head."

Patrick gently parted Graham's hair, revealing a long cut in his scalp. He dabbed at it with a rag soaked in hot water to clean up the wound.

"That's quite a cut, but it's not too deep. I think you'll be all right, Percival. Here, just hold this rag for a minute, and I'll tie it around your chin. How does it feel?"

"Fine. It's the arm that hurts."

"How about if I walk you home? Are you up to it?" Patrick asked.

"Thank you. I'll be sure to tell King Strang of your good deed today."

Patrick helped Graham to his feet.

"Listen," Alva said," I'd better get back to the store. Those two rascals are probably ransacking the place right now."

"I'd better go with you," Ian said. "They might come after you, too."

"I doubt it, but I'd appreciate the company, anyway."

Patrick and Percival headed off toward Saint James and Ian went inside to grab his coat. When he came back out, Alva was watching Patrick and Percival walk slowly away.

"He sure took a beating," Ian said.

"Yes, he did, and there'll be hell to pay for this," Alva replied.

"What do you mean?"

"What I mean is, they're going to blame me."

"But you helped us, and he said he would tell King Strang about it."

"I'm not worried about Strang. I'm worried about Butch Jenkins."

"Why Jenkins?"

"You remember last summer when they shot that cannon across the harbor and aimed it at my dock?"

"Yeah, I do."

"Hoy and Renfrew had their boat moored to the dock that day. They had to scramble to save it. Ever since then they've been threatening to get Jenkins. I've had a few harsh words with Jenkins myself about that cannon."

"I don't blame you."

"One time Hoy and Renfrew were drunk and they threatened to kill him. Somehow Jenkins heard about it. He thinks I put them up to it. I quit selling them whiskey after that, but the damage was done."

"What are you going to do, Alva?"

"Jenkins would love an excuse to get the cannon out again and blast away at me, so I think I'd better lay low for awhile. I'll go and stay with my nephew James down at Cable Bay. He's opening a new store there this spring."

"But what about your store here?"

"I'll just have to see how things go this summer. I've sold down my inventory, so there isn't much left. A lot of the fishermen got scared off by these Mormons and they're going to fish elsewhere. That won't be good for my business."

"Is there anything we can do to help?" Ian asked.

"Actually, there is, Ian. I can't do much to protect my buildings, but if you could look after my horses and wagon while I'm gone, I'd sure appreciate it."

"We'd be glad to. We've been thinking about buying a team ourselves."

"Is that a fact?"

"Yeah, the boys keep asking about it, and we could haul freight when the weather's bad. You can't count on fishing all the time."

"That's a good point. You could pick up freight over at the Mormon dock. There's more of them arriving every day and you seem to get along with them pretty well."

"We've managed to stay out of trouble so far," Ian said.

⁓

King Strang was furious when he heard about what happened to Percival Graham. He immediately summoned Butch Jenkins. Jenkins arrived just as the Strang family was sitting down to dinner.

"Who did this?" Strang demanded.

"It was James Hoy and Oliver Renfrew," Jenkins replied. "We already searched their house but they must have gone into hiding."

"I want their house torched. Burn it to the ground," Strang ordered. "Then I want you to raise a posse and search the island. When you find them, bring them to me. We'll give them a trial and then we'll hang them for attempted murder. I want to see their necks stretched from a rope and their boots twitching in the air."

Sarah, who was seated between Billy and Nettie, was appalled at her father's outburst. She picked up the baby and quickly led the children to another room.

"Surely they didn't mean to kill him," Mary said, coming over from the fireplace.

"Of course they did!" Strang shouted. "They want to exterminate us. They'll probably come after me next." Strang was pounding his fist on the table. His face had turned red and the veins in his forehead were bulging.

"James, calm down," Mary said, coming over to his side. "I'm worried about your heart."

"I won't calm down until these men are captured."

"All right, James. Butch will catch them. I'm sure he can handle it."

"Yes, ma'am, I know just what to do," Jenkins replied. He had already been inching toward the door and he was glad to leave.

"Sarah," Mary called, "please bring me some water."

By the time Sarah came into the room Strang was back in his chair. Mary soaked a rag and held it against his forehead. Strang had settled down, but his hands were still tightly clenched on the edge of the table. Before too long he relaxed a bit and Mary persuaded him to retire for the evening.

"You need your rest, James," she said. "You've been working much too hard."

The next day Strang was up early to join in the search for Hoy and Renfrew. He was in much better spirits and had forgotten all about his threat of a double hanging.

"We'll find them, Mary, I promise you that."

"Just promise me you'll bring them back for a fair trial, James."

"Thirty lashes should be enough to take care of those two. After that we'll put them on a boat and send them away. There'll be no more assaults against Mormons on this island."

Strang left the house and joined Jenkins and his posse at the boat dock. Across the harbor smoke was rising behind the trees. It was Hoy and Renfrew's house. Jenkins had set it afire during the night.

"Good work, Butch," Strang said.

The posse searched the northern half of the island for several days but there was no sign of Hoy and Renfrew. King Strang was frustrated, but he had other duties back at the print shop, so he returned home after instructing Jenkins to continue the search.

A few days later Strang had troubles of his own. In the early morning hours of May 24, 1851 the navy vessel *U.S.S. Michigan* pulled quietly into the harbor. The *Michigan* was the only warship on the Great Lakes and it represented the force of the United States government.

On board were a U.S. district attorney from Detroit and a contingent of U.S. marshals. Their mission was to arrest King Strang on charges of defiance of the government of the United States, counterfeiting, and unlawful occupancy of federal land. By early afternoon the marshals found Strang and arrested him and several other Mormons. They were taken on board the *Michigan,* where the district attorney read the charges against them. The ship's captain promptly pulled anchor and steamed away to Detroit, where they would be put on trial. The vengeance of George Adams and Eri James Moore had finally caught up with King Strang.

Before Mary and Sarah could reach the dock, the *Michigan* was halfway across the harbor. Sarah was frightened to see her father arrested and hauled away, but Mary was more resigned.

"He wanted this," Mary said. "We talked about it several times. Now he can exonerate himself in a court of law. He'll be able to confront those men and expose their lies."

"How long will he be gone?" Sarah asked.

"Probably a month or two. Don't worry, Sarah, the court will find him innocent and he'll be home soon."

But Sarah was still worried. There was enough trouble on the island already. Now she had to see her father arrested and taken away on a warship. And who would keep the peace while he was away?

CHAPTER 10:

Shootout at Cable Bay

A few weeks after King Strang was arrested, a fishing boat left a message at the post office for Ian and Patrick. It was from Alva Cable. He said he had decided to stay at Cable Bay and close his store on Whiskey Point.

"What do you think, Patrick?" Ian asked after reading the message. "Do you think the Mormons scared him off?"

"I don't know if they scared him off, but they scared most of the fishermen off and those men were his best customers. After they left, his business on Whiskey Point dried up."

"Listen to this. He asks if we would be willing to load up supplies from his store and deliver it to Cable Bay."

"That sounds like a lot of work," Patrick replied. "We've got to get our fishing nets set for the season."

"Aye, but he says he'll sell us his horses and wagon at a bargain price in exchange for making the trip. He needs the merchandise for his new store."

"Ian, we still have to get those nets in. We'll lose our best fishing spot if we don't get out on the lake soon."

"I've got an idea," Ian said. "Let's wait for a windy day when we can't go out anyway. We'll go to Alva's store and load his supplies, and then we'll let the boys take the wagon."

"All the way to Cable Bay? That's miles away. There's nothing but a logging trail through the forest."

"I know, but the boys are good with the wagon, and Alva will look after them when they get there."

"That's true," Patrick said, pondering the idea. "Well, we were talking about buying that wagon anyway. We might as well do it now and save some money."

"Good, then it's settled. We'll talk to the boys tonight and see if they think they can handle the trip by themselves."

"Are you kidding?" Patrick replied with a laugh. "For them it will be an adventure."

Sure enough, Andy and Nathan were estatic at the prospect of traveling alone all the way to the south end of the island.

"First you're going to have to help us load the wagon," Ian reminded them.

"And don't forget to stay on the trail," Patrick added. "It's a long way down there."

After school the next day, Andy and Nathan met Sarah on the front porch of the school and told her about their upcoming trip.

"Guess what?" Andy said. "We're taking the wagon all the way to the other end of the island this weekend."

"By yourselves?" Sarah asked.

"Sure. Why not?"

"But you've never even been there before."

"So what? We know the way," Andy replied.

"That's an awful long way. When will you be back?"

"We'll leave early Saturday, drop the stuff off, spend the night, and come back on Sunday."

Nathan glanced inside the school while they were talking. He noticed that Oren Whipple was lurking behind the woodstove, eavesdropping on their conversation.

"C'mon," Nathan said in a low voice. "Let's head for home." He walked down the porch steps and across the schoolyard and motioned for Andy and Sarah to follow him.

"Mr. Cable had a lot of stuff in the store," Sarah said. "Who's going to help you?"

"A lot of fishermen are taking their boats there now. I'm sure someone will be around to give us a hand."

As they left the schoolyard, Oren peeked out the door. When they were well out of sight, he jumped off the porch and ran in the other direction, straight to Gurdon Humphrey's house. He found Gurdon in his room and told him what he had heard. Together they rushed into the library where Gurdon's father was talking to Butch Jenkins.

"Gurdon! Can't you see I'm busy? What do you want?"

"Oren knows where Alva Cable is!" Gurdon exclaimed.

Both men jumped to their feet. "Where is he?" they asked in unison.

Gurdon grabbed Oren by the arm and dragged him forward.

"Tell us what you know, young man," Jenkins said.

"H-he's at the south end. He's going to open a new store there."

"So that's it!" Humphrey exclaimed. "They're abandoning Whiskey Point and they're going to take over the south end of the island."

"Who's with him, Oren?" Jenkins asked.

"N-no one," stuttered Oren. "I mean, I don't know."

"James Hoy and Oliver Renfrew must be there. They're probably staying with the Bennett brothers. Jack Bonner's probably there also."

"Who're the Bennett brothers?" Gurdon asked.

"They're friends of Jack Bonner's. They're a couple of thieves and pirates, but we've never been able catch them in the act," Jenkins said.

"We may not be able to get the Bennetts yet, but we can sure bring in Hoy and Renfrew. They almost killed Percival Graham," Humphrey said.

"I'll form another posse! I'll get as many men as I can. We'll need weapons and a stout hanging rope," Jenkins said. He was pacing back and forth and could barely contain his excitement.

"Take it easy, Butch," Humphrey said. "We don't want a lynch mob."

"They're guilty! We'll hang them from the nearest tree!"

"No, Butch. We're not hanging anybody. We're going to arrest them and bring them back to Saint James for a trial. Now make sure you notify the sheriff. We want to make this official."

"All right then, we'll hang them after the trial. We've got to get these vermin off the island."

Jenkins threw on his coat and stomped out the door, slamming it behind him.

"I suppose I'd better go with them," Humphrey sighed. "With King Strang gone, someone's got to preserve order on this island."

"Can we go, Pa?" Gurdon asked. "We found out where they were."

Humphrey paused for a moment, considering his son's request.

"I suppose you both can go, as long as the sheriff goes, too. We have to arrest those two men in accordance with the law. You might as well learn how justice is served on Beaver Island."

It was still dark on Saturday morning when Nathan brought Guy and Lois out of the stable and strapped them in their harnesses. Andy joined them, carrying a sack of food for the trip to Cable Bay. They climbed up on the wagon, yawning and rubbing their hands together to keep warm.

"Giddyup, Guy. Giddyup, Lois," Nathan commanded, slapping the reins across the horses' backs.

The wagon creaked and groaned and moved slowly forward. Nathan slapped the reins again. The horses pulled harder and the wagon picked up speed.

"This is going to be a long trip," Andy said, stretching in his seat. "We've got a heavy load back there."

"I'm glad we started early," Nathan replied. "I just hope the trail is in good shape."

They rode in silence around the harbor, passing the school, the print shop, and finally the Mormon temple. Then they headed south on a straight dirt lane called the King's Highway, passing smaller homes and several Mormon farms as the sun began to rise in the east.

"How far does this road go before it turns into a trail?" Andy asked.

"I don't know. The Mormons were working on it last summer."

Except for some rough areas and a few deep puddles, the road turned out to be in decent shape. They had to stop to pull a few branches out of the way, and once they got stuck in a mud puddle, but for the most part they made good progress. By noon the road had dwindled to a narrow trail and they were traveling along a high bluff near the east shore of the island. The area had been logged recently, so they could look out and see a wide expanse of Lake Michigan.

"Look," Nathan said, "there's a boat out there."

"I see it," Andy replied. "That's one of Tobias Humphrey's schooners, probably heading to the mainland with a load of lumber."

"He's sailing pretty close to shore, "Nathan said. "Shouldn't he be farther out if he's heading to the mainland?"

"You'd think so," Andy replied.

"There are a lot of people on board, and I don't see any lumber. I wonder where they're going."

"Who knows?" Andy said, settling back into his seat. "They're probably off on some church mission."

After about a mile the trail dropped back into the forest, and they lost sight of the schooner. After crossing a small stream, they stopped the wagon for a while to water the horses before continuing on their journey. Finally, late in the afternoon, they arrived at Cable Bay. The new village was nothing but a lumber camp carved out of the edge of the forest. In a clearing near the lake a sawmill belched out smoke and steam. In front of the mill a crude dock made of logs and boulders jutted out into the lake. Some men were stacking cordwood on the dock, hoping to sell it to a passing steamboat. Several log cabins were scattered across a grassy field, separated only by tree stumps and dirt paths.

On the side of the road leading into the camp there was a new building with a covered front porch. A sign above the porch read "Cable's Store: Provisions and Hardware".

Andy and Nathan both saw the sign at the same time. "We made it!" Andy shouted. "There's Alva Cable's new store!"

"I was beginning to wonder," Nathan said with relief. "That was a long trip."

Nathan pulled the horses up to a hitching post in front of the store. He tied the horses, and Andy ran down to the lake to fill a bucket with drinking water. Alva saw them and came out the front door to welcome them.

"Well, look who's here," he said with a big smile on his face. "I didn't expect to see you two. Where's Ian and Patrick?"

"Hello, Mr. Cable," Nathan said. "They couldn't come. They had to get their nets out so they wouldn't lose their favorite fishing spot."

"That's a long journey for you. How did it go?"

"Pretty well. We got stuck a couple of times."

"Ah, you're lucky. A month ago that trail was nothing but mud all the way to town."

Alva went to the front of the wagon and gave Guy and Lois each a pat on the head. "I sure missed these horses. Looks like you've been taking good care of them."

"Yes sir. We built a stable for them."

"That's good. They look real healthy."

"We'll feed and water them and then we'll unload the wagon," Nathan said.

"You boys go ahead and take care of the horses. I've got a couple of men working out back who can unload the wagon. Walter! Charlie!" Alva called. "We've got some visitors. Come and give us a hand."

Two men emerged from the back of the building. Andy and Nathan recognized them as fishermen who had worked out of Saint James last summer. As soon as they were done with the horses they pitched in and helped Walter and Charlie unload crates and carry them into the store.

"Now I've got some merchandise to sell," Alva said with satisfaction as he moved boxes around and placed them on shelves.

With everyone working, it didn't take long to unload the wagon. The entire floor was covered with boxes. Walter and Charlie pushed them aside so there was a narrow aisle to the back of the store.

"That's enough for today," Alva finally said. "You boys have had a long day. Why don't you stay here tonight? I've got some bunks in the back room."

Andy and Nathan were both worn out after the long day of travel. "We'd be glad to stay," Andy said. "Thank you very much."

"You must be hungry," Walter said. "The Bennett brothers cooked a big pot of fish stew today. Why don't you come over for some supper?"

"Sure," they both said at once. "We're starving."

"I'm going put away a few of these boxes," Alva said. "You boys run along and get some grub."

"We'll be back soon," Andy replied.

Andy and Nathan went with Walter and Charlie over to the Bennett's cabin, which was down near the dock. Smoke curled from the chimney and the aroma of fish stew and fresh bread filled the air. Walter knocked and, without waiting for an answer, opened the door and went in. The boys followed him, ducking their heads as they entered. Inside the cabin, four men were standing around a cook stove, watching the stew boil.

"Hey, Walter. Hey, Charlie," one of the men said. "I see you've brought some company."

"Aye, we have, and they're hungry. These boys just brought a wagonload of provisions for Alva's store. You all remember Andy McGuire and Nathan O'Donnell."

"Sure we do. Welcome, boys. That's a long trip, ain't it?"

"Yes, sir," Andy said, "but we didn't have any trouble."

"How's fishin' in Saint James?"

"It's too soon to tell. There aren't not many boats in the harbor yet."

"There probably won't be, with all those damn Mormons around."

"Well, boys," Walter said, "This here's Tom Bennett, his brother Sam, and James Hoy and Oliver Renfrew."

"You're just in time," Tom said. "Grab a bowl and a plate. We've got whitefish stew and fresh bread. After you eat you can give us all the news from Saint James."

Andy and Nathan each took a bowl and Tom ladled out the hot stew. After they sat down he placed a loaf of bread on the table between them and cut it in half. Andy and Nathan were famished from their long trip and they dug in, tearing off chunks of bread and dipping it into the stew. After they each had three helpings they finally pushed their bowls away. The entire loaf of bread had vanished.

"See, I told you they were hungry," Walter said, pushing away his own bowl.

"Exactly how much food did you boys bring with you?" Tom asked.

"Not much," Andy admitted.

"I thought so," he said with a laugh. "I never saw anyone eat so fast. So tell us, how are things in Saint James?"

"Pretty good," Andy replied. "Everyone's glad that spring is finally here."

"Yeah, so are we. What about Cable's store on Whiskey Point?"

"It's still there, but it's empty."

"I'm surprised the Mormons didn't take it over by now. They will soon, I'll wager."

"What about Percival Graham? How's he?" piped up James Hoy.

"The man who got beat up?" Nathan asked.

"Aye."

"He's fine now. He had a broken arm and a cut on his head."

Nathan thought he heard a sigh of relief coming from somewhere in the back of the room.

"Are there a lot of fishermen coming back to the harbor?"

"No, not too many, but it's still too early for—"

Walter, who was standing near the open door, suddenly interrupted the conversation. "Hey, there's a boat sailing into the bay."

"Who is it?" Tom asked.

"I don't know. I don't recognize it."

All of the men stood up and crowded around the door.

"It doesn't look like a fishing boat," commented one of the men.

"It looks like a lumber schooner to me," added another.

Andy nudged Nathan and whispered in his ear. "Do you think it's the boat we saw earlier today?"

"I don't know," whispered Nathan. "Let's go look."

The two boys crept up behind the men and peered around them to get a glimpse of the boat. One of the men stepped aside, giving them a view.

"It is," Nathan said. "It's the same boat."

"Should we tell them?"

"I guess so."

"We know whose boat that is," Andy announced. "It's Tobias Humphrey's. We saw it on our way down here today."

"Tobias Humphrey?" Tom asked. "What's he want with us?"

"There's a lot of men on that boat," someone observed.

"There sure are. Do you recognize any of them?"

"I think I see Butch Jenkins on the bow. Who's that next to him?"

"That's the Mormon constable! That's Constable Chambers!"

"This means trouble, men," Tom said. "Looks like a posse to me."

"They're going to be at the dock in a minute. What're we going to do?" asked Walter.

"Close that door right now," Tom ordered. "Sam, go close that window."

The two men jumped. Walter pushed everyone back inside and slammed the door. Sam Bennett closed and latched the window.

"Why would they be sending a posse all the way down here?" Walter asked.

"I have no idea. We didn't pay our taxes to the Mormons last year. They were mad, but they're not going to send out a posse just for that," Tom said.

"We never broke no laws in Saint James, unless you count having a nip or two o' the whiskey," James Hoy added.

"That's not it, either," Tom said. "Everyone on the island takes a nip, except maybe King Strang, and he probably does too. Andy, what did you say about Percival Graham a few minutes ago? You said he got beat up?"

"Yeah, a couple of weeks ago, right near my house. Nathan and I were in school."

"Who did it?"

"We don't know. No one would tell us."

"James, didn't you and Oliver have some kind of an argument with Graham?" Tom asked.

"Yeah, we did. He kept coming around asking for taxes. We finally got sick of him and ran him off."

"Did you beat him up?"

"Ah, we may have roughed him up a little, just enough to keep him from bothering us."

"My father helped Mr. Graham," Nathan said. "I saw a bunch of bloody rags when I got home from school."

"Damn!" Tom exclaimed. "Roughed him up a little, eh? I'd say you did more than rough him up."

"He had it coming—"

"Listen," Tom said, "there's a posse at our dock. They're going to arrest you both and charge you with assault or attempted murder. With Butch Jenkins along, they may even try to lynch you. He's crazy enough to do it."

"What'll we do now?" James asked.

"You and Oliver both have to get out of here, fast. Go hide in the woods until this blows over. Sam, open the window in the back room for them. Bust it out if you have to. Just get them out of here. Then we'll see if we can fend off this posse."

Sam quickly led Hoy and Renfrew to the back room and pried open the window. The two men climbed on a chair, squirmed through the narrow opening, and scurried off into the woods.

By now Humphrey's boat was tied up to the dock. Two sailors lowered the sails and secured them to the mast. The rest of the men clambered off the boat and milled around on the dock. Tom Bennett peeked out the window and watched them. The men were all standing in a group, apparently engaged in an animated conversation about their next course of action. One of the men finally broke away from the group and strode toward the cabin.

"Here comes Constable Chambers," Tom said, quickly closing and latching the window. "He's coming alone. Best I should go out and talk to him, one on one. Walter, you and Charlie keep an eye on those two boys."

Tom opened the front door and walked out to meet the constable, pulling the corners of his mouth back into a toothy smile. "Constable Chambers, welcome to Cable Bay! What brings you all the way down to this end of the island?"

"Good day, Thomas Bennett," the constable replied in a formal tone. "I'm lookin' for you and your brother Sam."

"Sam is indisposed at the moment, but I'm sure I can speak for him. Now, if it's about those taxes—"

"It ain't about your taxes, Thomas. I'm lookin' for two criminals and I have reason to believe that you may be harboring them."

"And who might those two criminals be, constable?" Tom asked.

"Oliver Renfrew and James Hoy."

"Ah, yes, I've heard of them. What might they be charged with, if I may ask?"

"Attempted murder on the person of Percival Graham."

"Attempted murder! That's a serious charge. Are you sure?"

"I'm sure. Do you know where they are, Thomas?"

"Well now, I reckon I've seen them around once or twice, but, no, I can't say that I know exactly where they are at this moment. They could be any-where on the island, for all I know."

"I'm going to have to search your cabin, Thomas."

"You're not searching my cabin, constable. Not with all those Mormons standing on my dock."

"I came down here to find those two men and take them back to Saint James for a trial, and that's what I intend to do."

"You brought a lot of men down here with you," Tom said, looking down at the group standing on the dock. "Is that a posse you brought with you?"

"Yes, it's a posse. We're looking for two dangerous criminals."

"How do I know it's not a lynch mob?"

"It's not a lynch mob, Thomas, it's a sworn posse. I swore them in myself. Now, I have to search your cabin for those two fugitives."

"Do you have a warrant?"

"I'm the constable——"

"You came all the way down here with a posse of Mormons and didn't bother to get a warrant? Go back and get a warrant if you want to search my cabin. We're part of the United States of America at this end of the island. This ain't the Kingdom of Saint James."

"It's all the same——"

"It ain't all the same," Tom said, his voice rising in anger. "Those Mormons chased us away from Whiskey Point last summer. We moved all the way down here and they're still after us. Look at 'em! They're all over my dock. They can't take over the whole damned island."

Tom stalked back to the door of the cabin. He turned and shouted at the men. "No one is searching my cabin. Get off my dock, all of you. You're tres-passing." Then he went inside the cabin and slammed the door.

"You told them what fer, brother," Sam said, pumping the air with his fist. "They won't hang around here for long."

Tom slumped against the back of the door, closing his eyes in the dim light and taking several weary breaths. "God, I hope not," he said.

Walter was at the window, peering through a crack. "Yer right, Sam. Chambers is going back to the boat. They're all getting in. Maybe they'll leave us alone this time."

"I wouldn't count on it, Walter," Tom said.

The Bennett's had always been at odds with the Mormons. Tom and Sam were some of the earliest Irish fishermen to settle on Beaver Island. Unfortunately, they had built their first cabin on prime farmland only a short distance from the site of the Mormon temple. It wasn't long before the Mormons were after them for taxes and eventually for possession of their land. One day the Mormons simply took over the land while Tom and Sam were out fishing. The Bennett's realized that a struggle to keep their cabin would be useless, so they moved to the south end of the island.

"Wait a minute," Walter exclaimed, still looking out the window. "They all got in the boat, but one of them just got back on the dock. It looks like he's got a gun."

"What's he doing?" Sam asked, crowding up behind Walter.

"He's waving his arms in the air. It looks like he's yelling."

"Is it the constable?"

"Nope. It's Butch Jenkins."

"That crazy bastard! He's a hothead, that's for sure."

"Hey, they're all getting off the boat! They're back on the dock!" Walter exclaimed.

"All of 'em?"

"Yeah, all of 'em. They've got rifles and pistols. Here they come!"

Everyone in the cabin jumped at once. Walter closed and latched the window. Tom ran to the door, locked it, and wedged a chair under the latch. Sam ran to a corner and grabbed a shotgun hanging on the wall. Andy and Nathan clambered over the table, sending dirty dishes crashing to the floor.

Tom jerked around at the sound of the dishes. "Damn! This is no place for boys! Out the back window, both of you! Run!"

"Where do we go?" Nathan asked, cowering behind the table.

"Hide in the woods. I don't care. Just git!"

Frightened by the chaos in the room and Tom's sharp commands, the boys scrambled to the back of the cabin. Nathan went first, climbing on the chair and diving out the window. Andy followed, taking one last look around the room. The last thing he saw was Sam Bennett holding the shotgun in one hand and pulling the chair away from the front door.

They both landed in a pile of sawdust behind the cabin. Shaking off the dust, they ran across a field and into a thick cluster of trees, well out of sight of the cabin. They could hear men shouting but could not make out any words. Then they heard a single gun shot, followed by an explosion of gunshots that seemed to come from all directions. The sound reached them in a roar that lasted several seconds and then tapered off into a series of lethal pops. Then there was silence.

The two boys had instinctively dropped to the ground. "Andy, what's happening?" Nathan gasped, grabbing him by the arm.

Andy looked at Nathan, his eyes wild with fear. "I don't know, but it can't be good."

"What are we going to do?" Nathan asked, his voice shaking.

"Shh. Listen."

Nathan was still. All he could hear was his own pulsing heart. "I don't hear anything," he finally said.

"I don't either," Andy replied, "but we can't go back there, that's for sure."

"How are we going to get home?"

"Let's cut through the woods in a big circle and see if we can come out near the store. Maybe we can get to the wagon."

"All right, but let's go slow and stay hidden. I don't want to see any of those Mormons. They're all crazy."

The two boys eased back into the woods, ducking under trees and treading gingerly through the brush and leaves. They stopped every few feet, listening. The forest embraced them, closing in with silence. Overhead, a thick canopy of branches blocked out the sunlight. They crossed a small stream, thick with cedar trees, and then they swung in a wide circle through an open stand of birch trees, hoping to come out behind the store.

In the distance they heard a crashing noise in the underbrush. The sound got louder, and it was followed by a deep rumbling sound. A voice shouted, "Stop! Stop!"

"What's that?" Andy asked, standing on a stump in an effort to see through the trees.

"I don't know, but you'd better get down," Nathan replied. "It could be anybody." He reached up and grabbed Andy by the belt, yanking him to the ground.

The crashing sound got louder, and they both raised their heads and peered through the trees. They were astonished to see Guy and Lois charging through the brush with the wagon careening along behind them. The churning wagon wheels were crushing bushes and knocking over saplings, springing them over and snapping them back. A lone figure stood in the wagon seat clinging to the reins, desperately trying to stop the horses as they charged through the trees.

"It's a runaway!" Andy shouted. "The horses have panicked!"

They both jumped up and ran after Guy and Lois, trying to grab the reins. The wagon bounced away from them and suddenly crashed to a halt, wedged between two stands of birch trees. The horses were pulled up short, rearing against their harnesses. The figure perched on the wagon went sailing through the air and landed on the ground with a sickening thump.

Andy and Nathan caught up with Guy and Lois. The horses were both still thrashing in their harnesses. The boys stroked their necks and talked softly to them until the frightened animals calmed down and finally stood still and lowered their heads. They were breathing hard and covered in sweat.

On the other side of the wagon a prone body lay on the ground, half buried in the leaves.

"Who is it?" Nathan asked.

"I don't know, but we'd better go help him," Andy said.

They hurried around to the other side of the wagon and approached the still figure.

"It's Oren Whipple!" Andy exclaimed. "What's he doing here?"

"There's a jug of water behind the seat," Nathan said. He grabbed the jug, pulled out the cork, and poured water on Oren's face.

Oren sputtered and coughed and spat out the water. He opened his eyes and a momentary look of terror came over his face.

"Don't hurt me," he cried, curling away from them.

"Oren, it's Andy and Nathan. We're not going to hurt you," Andy said. "Here, take a drink."

Andy held the jug and tilted it while Oren took a long drink. He immediately started coughing again.

"Don't choke," Nathan said. "Why don't you try to sit up?"

The boys lifted Oren up by the arms and propped him against a tree.

"Are you hurt?" Andy asked. "Does anything feel broken?"

"I-I don't think so," Oren replied with a tremor in his voice.

"Here, take another drink of water."

Oren took the jug, tilted it to his mouth and swallowed deeply. When Nathan took the jug back, Oren sighed and took several deep breaths.

"Can you tell us what happened, Oren?" Andy asked.

"They shot him!" he blurted out. "They killed him!"

"Shot who?" Andy and Nathan both asked in unison.

"Tom Bennett. They shot him dead."

"Oh, my God! Are you sure?"

"I'm sure, because they tried to take the wagon but I took it instead and then the horses started to run and——"

"Wait, Oren!" Andy cried. "You're not making sense. Here, have another drink."

Oren took the jug again and took a long swig, letting the jug fall between his legs. He closed his eyes for a moment and leaned back, looking up at the sky.

"Now, can you start from the beginning and tell us what happened?"

"I just came because Gurdon wanted to. His father said we needed to see justice being served."

"Oren, we were inside the cabin. We saw the boat come in and we heard the constable. When the men came up from the dock with guns we jumped out a back window and hid in the woods. Do you know what happened in the cabin after that?"

"Yes."

"Can you tell us? If Tom Bennett got killed and you know how it happened, you have to tell someone."

"When everyone got out of the boat again, the constable told Gurdon and me to stay put, but we didn't. We snuck over by the sawmill to watch."

"What did you see?"

"Everyone had guns and they surrounded the cabin. Sam Bennett came out on the porch. He was really mad. He was swearing and yelling and telling everyone to get off his property. He had a shotgun, but he was holding it straight up, not pointing it at anyone. Butch Jenkins said something to him that I couldn't hear. Sam swore at him and started to lower the gun. Tom Bennett ran out on the porch and tried to grab the gun from his brother, but it went off and shot a hole in the roof. Butch Jenkins fired at him and then everyone else started shooting. There was a big cloud of smoke and we couldn't see much for a minute."

"Then what happened, Oren?"

"All of the men ran into the cabin. They brought out two other men and tied them up. Sam Bennett was hurt. They shot part of his hand off and he was bleeding real bad. Tom Bennett was just lying there on the porch. All I could see was his boots. Then they dragged him outside and down on the grass. His head bounced on the porch steps. I got scared and ran away and hid behind your wagon. I could hear the men arguing. They wanted to take his body back to Saint James on the boat, but Mr. Humphrey wouldn't let them. So they were trying to figure out what to do, and then Butch Jenkins saw your wagon."

"Then what happened?" Nathan asked.

"A bunch of the men came to get the wagon—"

"They killed Tom Bennett and they were going to steal our wagon to carry his body?" Andy asked in amazement. "I can't believe it. Those dirty—"

"Wait, Andy," Nathan said. "What happened next, Oren?"

"I saw them coming so I untied the horses and jumped up on the seat. I grabbed the reins and shook them, and the horses took off running. We were going pretty fast, so the men couldn't catch us. They were yelling and running after me."

"Why didn't you just let them have the wagon?"

"I don't know. It happened so fast I didn't even think about it. Those men killed Tom Bennett. I couldn't let them take the wagon, too."

Andy and Nathan looked at each other with amazement. Oren Whipple, the skinny kid who always hid behind Gurdon Humphrey and who would never talk to anyone, had just confounded a gang of armed killers, struggled with a pair of runaway horses, and survived a headlong catapult through the trees.

"How far did you ride through the woods?" Nathan asked.

"A long way. We came across a field and the horses picked up a trail and followed it. They slowed down for a while but then something scared them and they started to gallop. When the trail petered out they just charged through the trees. I couldn't stop them."

"Do you think those men can find us here?" Nathan asked.

"I don't think so. They must have turned back."

"Yeah, we're pretty far back in the woods."

"But they'll be looking for us soon," Andy said. "I think we better get out of here tonight. Oren, do you think you can find that old trail?"

"It's must be behind us, back across that field."

"If we can get to it then we can probably find the main road and ride out of here, as long as no one spots us," Andy said. "Otherwise we're trapped and they'll catch us for sure."

"But it'll be dark soon," Nathan said.

"That's all the better. No one will see us, and the horses can follow the road in the dark."

"All right then," Nathan said, "but first we have to get the wagon out of these trees."

The three boys each grabbed a corner of the wagon and pushed and heaved until they finally freed it from the birch trees and turned it around. Then they walked in front of the horses, picking their way across the field through the juniper bushes until they came to a faint trail.

"This is it," Oren said. "This is where we were."

"Let's keep leading the horses," Andy said. "This isn't much of a trail."

Along the way they moved some logs and brush so the wagon could pass. Several times they had to duck down and steer the horses underneath low hanging branches. The sun began to set behind them and the shadows deepened in the woods. Oren went ahead to scout the trail, while Andy and Nathan led the horses, carefully picking their way.

"There's the main trail," Oren whispered. "Right up ahead in that clearing."

Nathan moved one more log out of the way and they soon had both horses and the wagon back on smooth ground. So far, no one had heard or seen them.

"This trail goes right past Cable Bay," Nathan said. "We just better hope those men aren't waiting for us."

"I think we'd better ride on the wagon," Andy said. "If we see anyone we can outrun them."

They all climbed up on the seat of the wagon. Nathan took the reins and coaxed the horses into a slow walk. The wheels of the wagon turned silently in the sand and the boys huddled together, watching and listening.

The entrance to the village was deserted and the dark outline of the sawmill blocked the view of Bennett's cabin. As they passed behind Cable's store they could see a bonfire on the shore, flickering orange light between dark vertical shadows.

"There they are," Oren whispered. "They're all standing around the fire. I think we're safe."

"Not yet," Andy replied. "We need to get up the road a ways."

They rode on in silence, leaving Cable Bay behind them. Nathan handled the reins gently, keeping the horses at a quiet and steady pace. After about twenty minutes, he slapped the reins firmly, and the horses picked up speed. All three boys glanced back one more time and saw only darkness. They had made their escape and were on their way home at last.

"It's going to be a long ride in the dark," Andy said.

"Cold, too," Nathan replied. "I wish we had a couple of blankets. How about you, Oren? That was quite a spill you took back there in the woods."

"I'm all right," Oren replied. "Pretty hungry, though."

"When did you last eat?"

"Breakfast."

"Nathan, didn't we have a loaf of bread left over from this morning?" Andy asked.

"Yeah, but it probably fell out of the wagon."

"I'll go look." Andy climbed in the back of the wagon and searched around in the dark for the bread. "I found it!" he exclaimed. "It was wedged underneath the seat." He hopped back up, tore off a big chunk of bread, and handed it to Oren.

"Thanks for rescuing our wagon," Andy said.

"Yeah, thanks, Oren," Nathan said.

"Um, that's all right," Oren replied, tearing off a chunk of bread and stuffing it in his mouth.

"You took quite a chance, taking off through the woods. Have you ever worked around horses before?" Nathan asked.

"Nope."

"Do you think you'll get in trouble when those men get back to town?"

"Nope. Mostly they just leave me alone 'cause I don't say much."

"Well, if anyone gives you a hard time, you let us know and we'll explain what happened."

Guy and Lois were able to follow the trail even though darkness had closed in. Nathan didn't have to do much to steer the horses. He just kept a loose hand on the reins. Sometimes the boys dozed and sometimes they got out and walked behind the wagon to try to stay warm. The moon came out and cast a dim light on the trail ahead. Several times they heard owls in the woods and once a pack of coyotes started howling. After riding for most of the night they finally reached the outskirts of Saint James just before dawn.

Oren lived with his parents on a small farm on the King's Highway just behind the village. Nathan stopped the wagon in front of Oren's house, a neat log cabin set deep in the trees away from the road. Smoke was curling from the chimney and a dog began to bark.

"Here we are," Nathan said.

Oren climbed off the wagon. Nathan could see that he was shivering from the cold.

"Thanks again, Oren. You'd better go inside and get warmed up."

"Yeah, thanks, Oren," Andy said. "See you in school."

Oren opened the gate. "Thanks for the bread," he said.

Nathan slapped the reins and the horses started up again, heading toward home.

"He's a tough little kid," Andy remarked.

"He sure is," Nathan replied. "It's a good thing he didn't get hurt when he went flying off that wagon."

"Yeah, well, he may still get hurt when those men get back to town. We'd better keep an eye out for him."

The morning sun was just rising in the east when the wagon reached the Mormon temple. The harbor was still quiet but Andy and Nathan could see a couple of men already out on Johnson's dock, ready to start another day of work. A steamer was tied to pilings at the end of the dock, waiting to take on a load of firewood.

"Guy and Lois have had a long trip," Nathan said. "We should brush them down and get them some food and water. I'll take the wagon straight to the stable."

"After we feed them I'll be ready for some breakfast myself," Andy replied.

As Andy and Nathan pulled up to the stable, Ian and Patrick came out to greet them, wondering why they were home so early.

CHAPTER 11:

Consequences

Later that day two boats sailed into Paradise Bay. The first was Tobias Humphrey's schooner returning from Cable Bay with the Mormon posse. The second was the Bennett's fishing boat. Butch Jenkins and Constable Chambers were sitting in the stern with Jenkins at the helm. Walter and Charlie were in the bow, tied together as prisoners. Sam Bennett was huddled behind them, his injured hand wrapped in a sheet. The body of his brother Thomas lay in the bilge, wrapped in burlap.

The two boats sailed across the harbor, tacking against a west wind. By the time they tied up at Johnson's dock a crowd had gathered to greet them. At first everyone was loud and boisterous, celebrating the return of the Mormon posse, but when they saw the injured man and the covered body in Bennett's boat they quieted down and waited with uncertainty.

Percival Graham had seen the boats come in and hurried down to the dock. He pushed his way through the crowd and stood on the edge of the dock, surveying the men in the boats.

"Was it a good trip? All safe and accounted for?" he asked.

"All but one," Constable Chambers replied.

"And who might that be?"

"An Irishman. Thomas Bennett. He resisted arrest."

"Tom Bennett! He was a good man. What happened?"

"He pulled a gun on us."

"Did you have to kill him?"

"You heard the constable," Jenkins interjected. "He pulled a gun on us and we let him have it. We should have plugged the rest of them, too."

"Lord, I was afraid it would come to this," Graham said, almost to himself. "Well, let's get him out of the boat. We're going to have to examine him for cause of death and prepare a coroner's report. King Strang is still off the island, and he's going to want to know exactly what happened. What about these other men?"

"We've got two prisoners," Constable Chambers said. "They didn't take up arms against us so I'll let them go if they can post bail. Sam Bennett there is injured. He's going to need Doc Johnson to sew up his hand."

"It's your fault, you bastard," Bennett growled, staring furiously at Jenkins.

"I'll shoot your other hand if you don't shut up," Jenkins snarled.

"That's enough, Butch," Constable Chambers said. "He's my prisoner, not yours, and I'm taking him to a doctor right now."

"He'll be nothing but trouble, you mark my words."

"I'll be the judge of that. Get up, Bennett. Let's get that hand taken care of before it gets infected."

Sam Bennett struggled to his feet and climbed up on the dock, immediately falling to his knees from pain and loss of blood. Constable Chambers took him by the arm, helped him to his feet, and led him away.

"C'mon, men, let's get this body out of the boat," Jenkins said.

Several of the men climbed down in the boat and lifted the wrapped body of Thomas Bennett up on the dock.

"Put him in a wheelbarrow and take him to Doc Johnson's for an exam. He'll write a coroner's report. This is all legal." Jenkins said to the crowd. "We'll make it legal."

Percival Graham watched in silence as the body was loaded in a wheelbarrow and carted away.

"Butch, where are James Hoy and Oliver Renfrew?" he finally asked.

"They got away. We think they ran off in the woods."

"Aren't they the ones you went to arrest?"

"Don't worry, we'll catch them. They can't stay away forever."

"But you killed an innocent man!"

Jenkins glared at Graham. "Percival, sometimes I don't think you have the stomach for what we are trying to do on this island."

"Exactly what are you trying to do, Butch?"

"We're trying to build a kingdom."

"Surely we can build a kingdom and still get along with our neighbors. These Irish fishermen may not follow our faith, but they work hard and they mean us no harm."

"We must purge this island of those who would plot against us," Jenkins replied. "Don't you remember the cannon? That's why we brought the cannon, to purge the island of all gentiles so we could live in peace."

Graham paused, trying to conjure up a response to this contradictory statement. He had grown weary of the conflict and turmoil on the island, and now a man had been shot dead.

"Perhaps you're right, Butch," he finally said. "Perhaps I don't have the stomach for this."

On Monday after school, everyone in the schoolyard was talking about the shootout at Cable Bay. Gurdon Humphrey was the center of attention because he had been a part of the posse, or so he said. He stood near the bell post while the younger kids crowded around to listen to his exploits.

"The gentiles locked that cabin up like a fortress, but we had them surrounded. We knew they were armed, so we spread out and took our positions. One of them finally came out the door and started shouting at the constable. At first we thought he was going to surrender, but then we saw he had a shotgun. We were ready for him. He only got off one shot and then we let him have it."

Sarah came out the door of the school and saw the crowd listening to Gurdon at the flagpole. She gave them a wide berth as she crossed the schoolyard, but she could still hear snippets of Gurdon's embellished oration. Andy and Nathan were waiting for her by the road.

"Did you hear him?" she hissed. "I think it's horrible—"

"He sounds like a one-man posse, that's for sure," Andy said.

"It's not just that," Sarah continued, her voice rising in anger. "A man was killed, and Gurdon's bragging about it. He thinks he's a hero. Look at all those little kids admiring him. I can't believe there was a gunfight on Beaver Island. It's disgusting."

"Yeah, Gurdon is disgusting, wouldn't you agree, Nathan?" Andy said with a grin.

"Andy, that's not funny. You both were right there. You could have been killed! I can't believe your father let you go down there alone. I don't know what's happening to this island. It used to be such a peaceful place."

"Aw, we were gone before anything happened," Andy said, chastened by Sarah's rebuke.

"Yeah, we spent most of the day unloading freight at Alva Cable's new store," Nathan said.

"But you were there at Bennett's cabin. You told me this morning—"

"Only for a few minutes. We were gone out the back before the shooting started."

"But you were so close," Sarah said, her voice trembling. "I don't know what I would do if anything ever happened to either of you. You're my best friends and I worry about you all the time. I would just die if anything ever happened to either one of you..."

Andy and Nathan were both embarrassed at Sarah's emotional outburst. They stood for a moment in awkward silence. In the distance Gurdon was still exalting his exploits to the crowd around the flagpole.

"I'm going home now. I have homework to do," Sarah finally said, breaking the silence.

Both of the boys jumped. "We'll walk you home," they said.

Sarah did not wait for them. Andy and Nathan ran along the road to catch up with her.

"I can't believe it, Andy. Gurdon is bragging and you're making jokes."

"I'm sorry, Sarah," Andy said.

"Things were strange enough here this weekend, and then there's a gunfight and you're both in the middle of it. You could have been hurt or killed."

"Why, what happened here?" Nathan asked.

Sarah stopped. "Didn't you hear?"

"We were gone Saturday and we slept all day Sunday."

"You remember Elvira Field, don't you?"

"Sure," Andy said. "She writes the newspaper for your father."

"We haven't seen her around all spring," Nathan said. "What happened to her?"

"She has a baby. I just found about it from Mrs. Watson."

"But she's not even married—"

"She had the baby over a month ago. She's been keeping it secret in the back of the print shop."

"So why keep it a secret? Who's the father?"

"I—I don't know," Sarah stammered.

Andy and Nathan both shrugged. They didn't seem very interested. Sarah suddenly regretted mentioning anything about Elvira and her baby. She had been planning to tell them the baby's name but she now realized that it would mean nothing to them. Sarah alone knew about the trunk in the print shop and the photograph of Elvira, dressed as a man named Charles Douglass. And now Elvira had a baby and she had named it after her secret identity. She had named her baby Charles. Charles James. It was too much for Sarah to explain to them, so she decided not to try.

They had reached the gate in front of Sarah's house. Sarah could see her mother in the side yard, hanging out laundry. Billy and Nettie were chasing each other around the vegetable garden, laughing and shouting at each other.

"I have to help my mother," Sarah said.

"Don't worry, Sarah," Nathan replied. "We won't be going back to Cable Bay for awhile."

"Yeah," Andy added. "No more gunfights for us. C'mon, Nathan, let's go home."

"Whew!" Andy exclaimed as they walked back toward the school. "Girls are too much for me. First she's upset about a gunfight and then she's worried about a baby in the print shop. I'm going to stick with fishing."

"Me, too," Nathan said.

"Nathan, do you remember two summers ago when we first met Sarah and we went for a walk on North Beach?" Andy asked.

"Yeah, I remember," Nathan replied.

"We saw Sarah's father on the beach with someone. Wasn't that Elvira Field?"

"I don't know. That was a long time ago. She was pretty young then."

"Yeah, she was, but if it was her, she's two years older now. Old enough to have a baby."

"Hmm. You're right. Maybe Sarah knows something we don't know."

Andy and Nathan passed the schoolyard. It was empty now. Gurdon Humphrey was gone and the school kids had all headed for home.

"Gurdon must have finished his speech," Nathan remarked.

"Yeah, I'm sure he's a big hero now," Andy replied.

<hr />

Sarah closed the gate behind her and walked across the lawn toward her mother. Mary was clutching a handful of clothespins and struggling with a sheet blowing in the wind. Sarah grabbed a corner and pinned it up.

"Hi, Sarah," Mary said. "How was school today?"

"Hi, Mother. Math was boring, but we spent a lot of time on geography and writing."

"Those are your favorite subjects, aren't they?"

"Yes, they are. I learned that Beaver Island is almost half way between the Equator and the North Pole."

"That makes sense. We get all four seasons here."

"Gurdon Humphrey was bragging about the shootout at Cable Bay after school."

"Gurdon was at Cable Bay?"

"Yes, he went with the posse with his father."

"I can't believe Mr. Humphrey would take his son down there. He must have known that there could be trouble."

"Gurdon says the Bennetts started it," Sarah said, not mentioning that Andy and Nathan were also at Cable Bay.

"That wouldn't surprise me, but some of those men in the posse are just looking for trouble, if you ask me. Especially that Butch Jenkins. He frightens me, the way he talks sometimes. He says the most horrible things. I just wish your father would get back from Detroit so he can take care of these problems," Mary sighed.

"Have you heard anything? When is he coming home?"

"Soon, I hope. We surely do need him here. First those men beat up Brother Graham and now another man is dead. I just don't know what's going to become of us."

"What do you mean, Mother?"

"I don't know if I, uh, we can stay on this island. We may have to leave if things get much worse."

"Leave Beaver Island? But I have friends here. Andy and Nathan—"

"I know, dear. I know you don't want to leave your friends. It's just that our men and the Irish fishermen have got to stop fighting if we are all going to live here in peace."

"Elvira Field says the Irish want to chase us off the island and steal everything we own."

"Elvira Field? When did she say that?"

"I read it in the *Northern Islander*."

"Oh, I don't even read that paper anymore. It's just a bunch of gossip."

"But you liked my article about the school, didn't you?"

"Of course I did, dear. Your article was very good. I wish she would write more articles like yours, instead of attacking the Irish all the time."

"I'm sorry, Mother. She does do that a lot."

"Tell me, Sarah, what do you know about Elvira?"

"Um, nothing," Sarah said, her face turning red.

"Nothing at all?"

"She just works at the print shop."

"I see. I was just wondering if you had heard anything else about her."

Sarah looked away, and her mother was silent for a moment. Finally she said, "I'm sure your father will be home soon, and he'll sort this all out."

Mary put down the laundry basket and put her arms around her daughter, holding her for a very long time.

It was a busy week at the fishing dock. The crew of the *Emma Rose* pulled nets and harvested fish from dawn to dusk. Every day they came back to the harbor with a full load of whitefish and lake trout. As soon as the boat reached the dock, Andy and Nathan rolled out more empty barrels. Ian and Patrick tossed the gutted fish on the dock and they all packed the barrels, filled them with salt, and nailed down the lids. It was grueling work, but it was satisfying to see the full barrels lined up along the shore.

"They're still paying top dollar for our fish," Ian said with satisfaction. "The more barrels we pack, the more money we make."

"The nets will probably be full again by the time we go back out tomorrow," Patrick replied.

"We're going to get rich, if this work doesn't kill us first."

"Sure, but we've got all winter to rest up."

"No fair!" Nathan cried. "We have to go to school in the winter."

Ian and Patrick both laughed. "Actually, boys, we're going to be pretty busy this winter," Ian said. "Wingfield Watson stopped by last week. He's organizing a crew to build a lighthouse out on Whiskey Point and we volunteered to help. He says that King Strang has been trying to raise money from Washington for a brick tower and a keeper's quarters. In the meantime, Wingfield wants to put up a wooden tower with a light on top for everyone to see."

"It could take years to get money from Washington," Patrick added. "One of these days someone's going to miss the harbor entrance and run aground."

"We've got the same crew that built the school," Ian said. "Some of the fishermen are going to help, and Wingfield's bringing his wagon and oxen to drag timbers. No one on the island wants to see a shipwreck. It'll be Mormon and Irish men, working together, just like before."

Later in the week, Andy and Nathan took another load of salted fish out to Whiskey Point. While they were gone, Ian and Patrick washed down the *Emma Rose* and prepared the fishing gear for another day on the lake.

Just as they were coiling the last of the ropes, Ian noticed someone loitering between the cabins. "Hey, Patrick," he called, "who's that up by your house?"

"I'm not sure," Patrick said, standing up in the stern of the boat. "Why, it's Butch Jenkins."

"Butch Jenkins? What's he want? He never comes around here."

"I don't know, but he sees us."

"Well, we'd better go talk to him. Now we'll never get our work done." Ian wiped off his hands with a rag and both men climbed up on the dock and walked up to the cabins.

Jenkins came down to greet them. "How are you gentlemen today?"

"Very well, thank you," Patrick replied.

"It looks like the fishing has been good, or do they just jump into your boat?"

"Yeah, it's been a good summer so far."

"I've heard that all the Irish fishermen are making record catches this year."

"So are we. The cooper shop can't make enough barrels for us, and we're almost out of salt."

"I hear they're paying you top dollar for every barrel."

"So far they are," Ian said. "We just hope it lasts."

"What brings you around to this side of the harbor, Butch?" Patrick asked.

"I'm here on business," Jenkins said. "I came to talk to you about your taxes."

"I thought Percival Graham took care of that. We paid him twenty dollars last year."

"Well, he's gone now."

"Gone? What do you mean, gone?"

"Gone off the island. He was excommunicated from the church by the Quorum of the Apostles."

Ian and Patrick looked at each other in dismay.

"Excommunicated! Why?"

"That's private church business."

"Where did he go?"

"I have no idea. We put him on a boat."

"Just like that?"

"Just like that. He was either with us or against us, and he chose to be against us."

Ian and Patrick were speechless. Percival Graham and Wingfield Watson were just about their only Mormon friends on the island. It was hard to believe that Percival had just vanished.

"Now, about those taxes—"

"We'll pay you as soon as we get paid for our fish," Ian snapped.

"It's all right, Ian," Patrick said. "Butch, we paid last year and we'll be glad to pay this year. Our boys are learning a lot at school. Just give us a couple of days and we'll have the money. I'll bring it to you myself."

"The Quorum of the Apostles has decided to raise taxes for everyone on the island," Jenkins continued. "Expenses have been high this year. There's the school and Mrs. Watson, and work on the King's highway, and we need a new shipping pier and a lighthouse at Whiskey Point. Of course the Mormon temple still isn't finished—"

"Wait a minute," Ian interrupted. "Stop right there. We'll pay for the school and the roads and all that, but we shouldn't have to pay for the temple."

"But it's all part of the taxes, Ian. Everyone has to pay."

"Butch, we helped build the school and we're going to help build a new lighthouse this winter, but we don't have to pay for your church."

"Like I said, it's all part of the taxes. Everyone has to pay."

"But we're not Mormons!" Ian was starting to get angry.

"You live here, don't you?"

"Since when do you have to be a Mormon to live here?"

"This island is a Mormon kingdom. We'll let you live here, but you have to pay your taxes, just like everyone else."

"What do you mean, you'll *let* us live here? This is a free country."

"Let me put it this way, Ian. It would be better for both of you if you converted to Mormonism and gave allegiance to the king."

"Damn your hide, Jenkins! We're not bowing down to any more kings. We had enough of that crap back in Ireland."

"You're either with us or against us, just like Percival Graham," Jenkins said. "It's your choice."

"Is that a threat?" Ian shouted, rolling up his sleeves.

Patrick, who had been listening to the conversation with increasing alarm, realized that he was going to have to intervene or there was going to be a fight.

"Listen," he said, stepping between the two men, "how about if I talk to King Strang. He'll be back soon. I'm sure we can work this all out."

"It's too late for that," snarled Jenkins. "You're just like the rest of them. The king gives you land and you stab him in the back."

"Give us land! No one gave us land. We bought it."

Patrick put his hand on Ian's arm to restrain him. "Butch, we'll pay our fair share of the taxes, just like last year. Let's just wait until we can sit down with King Strang and we'll talk it over with him."

It was too late. Jenkins had turned his back and was already striding away. He raised his arm and shook his fist in the air without looking back.

"That son of a bitch!" Ian cursed. "We're not paying him anything."

Patrick still had his hand on his friend's arm. "Ian, he's a hothead, we all know that. Don't you be a hothead too."

"They don't own this island!"

"I know, I know. It's a difficult—"

"I'm sick of this. I'm gonna go finish cleaning out the boat," Ian said, stalking away.

Patrick could see that there was no use in talking to Ian until he calmed down, so he let him go back to work. At that moment, Andy and Nathan appeared with the wagon, returning from another delivery to Whiskey Point. They waved as they came to the clearing in front of the cabins. "We're back," Nathan hollered. "The horses were tired, so we decided to walk."

"They've worked hard, haven't they?" Patrick said. "I think we're just about done for the day, so they can take a rest."

Out on the *Emma Rose*, they could hear Ian cursing and throwing things around inside the boat. "What's wrong with him?" Andy asked.

"He'll calm down in a few minutes. Butch Jenkins came by to see us while you were gone."

"Oh, that explains it," Nathan said. "He could make anybody mad."

CHAPTER 12:
The King's Triumphant Return

In early July King Strang arrived back on the island aboard the *Wisconsin* with a contingent of loyal followers. This time the *Wisconsin* circled the harbor before docking, making a fanfare of Strang's return. By the time the boat tied up at the dock, he had made his way to the bow to address the crowd gathered below him.

"My friends, I am pleased to announce that I have been acquitted of all charges against me. Just two days ago a jury found me innocent and instructed the court to release me. The Detroit newspapers have praised the court for conducting a fair trial without bias of any kind. And my accusers? They have been humiliated and exposed as liars for all the world to see. Let them crawl away like worms and suffer eternal damnation. Never again shall we suffer such indignity and persecution. A new day has arrived on Beaver Island. We are now free to practice our faith without fear of reprisal. Together we shall——"

Butch Jenkins, who had come aboard the *Wisconsin*, interrupted Strang's speech. Strang listened to Jenkins for a moment and then turned back to the crowd. "My brothers and sisters, I have only been back on the island for a few minutes and already I am in demand. I must leave you and attend to important business."

Strang hurried down the gangplank with Jenkins at his side. Several island men approached with greetings and salutations, but Strang waved them off and hurried away to the print shop.

On Saturday the log pews in the Mormon temple were packed with parishioners attending the morning service. Everyone had heard that King

Strang was back on the island, and they all were anxious to hear his sermon. All week rumors about the shootout at Cable Bay had been circulating from household to household. The Mormons expected their king to tell them the true tale of events from the other end of the island.

But Strang had other matters on his mind. After the first hymn, he stood and made his way to the pulpit. Pausing for a moment to look at his notes, he began his sermon.

"My brethren, I bring you news from our community in Wisconsin. I am happy to report that our brothers and sisters in Voree are growing in the Mormon faith. They send you their greetings, and many more of them will be making the journey to join us here on Beaver Island. In the next few weeks I will be working to see that all of our new brethren will be provided with a free inheritance of land, as was also provided to each of you. This land, given from God through the efforts of your king, will provide sustenance to the faithful, to those who work hard, live in peace, and grow and multiply.

"It is with great humility that I report to you that our efforts in Voree have not been without tribulation. Our brethren suffer from poverty and prejudice because of their faith. They cannot afford to buy land for their homes and farms. Land speculators have taken advantage of them by charging exorbitant prices. Many of the men have followed false prophets or have left the faith completely, leaving the womenfolk to fend for themselves. There are simply not enough men to build homes, work the farms and raise families. The women cannot afford the land and they cannot find suitable and faithful husbands.

"My friends, I have pondered these problems through lonely travels and many sleepless nights. I confess to you that I despaired of a solution until an angel of the Lord called upon me in my darkest hour. In a vision the angel appeared before me and spoke as I lay prostrate on a humble bed of straw. When I awoke, my despair had miraculously vanished. My path was clear before me. While the image of the angel was fresh in my mind, I took pen in hand and applied my thoughts to paper. The words of the angel have thus become permanent and sacred tenets of our church, and I shall now impart them to you.

"Firstly, for those faithful citizens who have the courage to travel to Beaver Island, we shall continue to offer a generous inheritance of land, given freely by our church. In exchange, we shall be blessed with new neighbors, new homes, and new farms. Our brothers and sisters will share in the bounty of this land and of our faith and brotherhood.

"Secondly, in the words of the angel, we shall provide for the single women who have joined us, for those who have been widowed or abandoned, and for those who cannot find a suitor. We shall provide each and every woman with a home to raise a family. We shall provide her with a husband, and though the husband may be required to take more than one wife, he shall provide equally for her, raise her children, and love her as she shall love him. We shall adopt the doctrine of spiritual wifery."

Sarah was sitting in the front row with her mother. She had not seen her father since his return to the island. He stopped by the house once to see Mary and the children, but he had been spending the rest of his time at the print shop with Elvira Field.

Ever since Sarah had learned that Elvira had a baby, she had been trying to fathom why Elvira still lived alone at the print shop and why she had been hiding her baby all spring. Sarah had finally come to the realization that her own father must be the baby's father. It was the only possibility that made any sense. They had been together during the previous winter, traveling in the east while Sarah and Mary waited patiently in Buffalo with the other children. They had also been together last summer when Elvira helped George Adams organize the king's coronation. For the rest of the summer King Strang had spent many evenings alone with Elvira at the print shop setting up the printing press and preparing the *Northern Islander* for publication.

Sarah had long ago accepted the fact that Elvira had traveled with her father disguised as Charles Douglass. But now Elvira was starting to venture out of the print shop with her baby. Worse, by naming her baby Charles, Elvira seemed to be inviting discovery. If anyone made the connection, it would not be long before gossip spread to every household on the island. Sarah was terrified of what would happen to her family if Elvira's secret was discovered.

King Strang continued his sermon: "Let all who stand before me today hear my words. It is our duty as Mormons to be fruitful and multiply so that our names are not lost in the dust in generations to come. As you marry, gentlemen, you shall not dismiss one wife to take another. You shall not take a multitude of wives in disproportion to your wealth and inheritance. Most importantly, you shall not take any wife whom you do not love, or does not love you. This love is the covenant of our faith. It does not arise from the flesh, but rather from the spirit."

Strang paused, and then he continued. "My brothers and sisters, today I am proud to introduce to you to my first spiritual wife. Her name is Elvira Field. You shall know her as Elvira Field Strang. She will be a member of my household along with my beloved wife Mary. I shall love them both equally as a covenant of my faith."

King Strang finished the rest of his sermon and took a seat. The choir began to sing a hymn and the congregation sat in shocked silence. All eyes were upon Mary Strang.

Earlier in the service, Andy had quietly entered the temple and taken a seat in the back row. He had rowed alone across the harbor and left his boat on the beach. Like many others, he wanted to hear what Strang had to say about the shootout at Cable Bay. Disappointed that King Strang did not even mention it, Andy slipped out the rear door when the service was over and headed back to his boat. He was just about to climb aboard when he heard a voice calling to him.

"Andy! Wait for me!" Sarah appeared at the edge of the field below the temple and ran toward him along the beach

"Sarah!" Andy stopped and held the boat at the water's edge.

"Didn't you see me? I was in the front row," Sarah gasped, out of breath.

"I looked, but I couldn't find you. There were too many people in there," Andy replied.

"I know! I think everyone in Saint James is in the temple. I had to get out of there. I snuck out a side door and that's when I saw you."

"After what happened last weekend at Cable Bay I wasn't sure how welcome I would be in the temple, so I left early."

"You've never come to a Mormon service before, Andy. Did you come to look for me?"

"No, I just wanted to hear what your father had to say about the shootout."

"Oh," Sarah said, sounding disappointed.

"No, wait," Andy quickly said. "I didn't mean that. I mean, I did come to hear your father, but I also hoped that—I wanted to—I mean, I was sort of looking for you."

"Sort of?" Sarah asked.

"Yeah. No, I mean more than sort of."

Sarah smiled at him, amused at his embarrassment.

"Would you like a ride home in my boat?" Andy asked.

"Andy, I can't. You wouldn't believe what happened in church. My father—"

Andy stepped out and reached for her hand. "Come on," he said. "I'll row."

Sarah took his hand. Hesitating, she glanced back at the crowd gathering in front of the church.

"Here, you can sit in the stern," Andy said.

Sarah could feel the warmth of Andy's skin and the firmness of his arm, grown strong from pulling fishing nets. She looked at him, their eyes met, and she felt an irresistible glow inside her. This one glance was all it took for her to see that everything would be different between them now. She could see it in his eyes. She kicked off her shoes and, holding her church dress around her knees, stepped into the boat.

Andy pushed the boat away from shore. Now that he was on the water, he was in control, and he moved gracefully from the bow to a plank across the center of the boat. He grabbed both oars and spun the boat around. By the look on his face, he appeared to be focusing solely on piloting the boat, but Sarah knew better.

"I've never gone home from church in a boat before," she said, taking a deep breath and trying to keep her composure.

"Do you like it?" Andy asked.

"Oh, yes, the view is much better and I don't have to stay any longer inside that stuffy temple."

"We used to go to church all the time back in Ireland."

"What did you think of our service today?"

"It was all right. I liked the music."

"What about my father's sermon?"

"It was all right."

"Only all right?"

"I was expecting him to talk about what happened at Cable Bay, instead of all that stuff about wives."

Sarah decided that she really didn't want to talk about her father's sermon. She just wanted to be alone with Andy in his boat, watch him row across Paradise Bay, and forget about what she had just heard in the temple. She leaned over the edge of the boat and gently caressed the surface of the water with her fingers. A clear ripple escaped from each fingertip and drifted away, fanning out and growing stronger, as if in delightful escape.

"Andy, do you remember when we first met?"

"Sure," Andy replied. "It was out at Whiskey Point. We just arrived on Beaver Island and the *Emma Rose* was full of fish."

"You and Nathan were hiding in the cabin and peeking out the porthole at me."

"Yeah, Nathan's kind of shy and we'd never met an American girl before."

"You let me steer the boat all the way across the harbor," Sarah said.

"You did pretty well for your first time at the helm."

"I was terrified! I thought I was going to wreck your boat."

"You did fine."

"That's because you were helping me steer."

"Naw, you could have done it yourself. It's not that hard."

Sarah splashed her hand against the surface of the water and sent the ripples scattering. She sat up in the boat and put her hands back on her knees, turning to face Andy.

"So, do you like American girls?" she asked.

"You're the only one I know," Andy replied.

"Do you like me?"

Andy's face turned a crimson red color and he stopped rowing. "Yes," he said. "Yes, I do like you, Sarah."

"I like you too, Andy."

"Sarah, I was wondering...do you think maybe I could see you next Sunday?"

"Sure," Sarah said. "We always do."

"No, I mean just you and me, alone. Maybe we could go for another boat ride."

"But everyone would see us together. People would start talking."

"For taking a boat ride?" Andy asked. "Who cares? Everyone talks too much on this island anyway."

"I have a better idea," Sarah said. "I'll make a picnic basket and we can go to North Beach for a picnic. We can pick berries at our secret berry patch."

"Alone together on North Beach? Now that might make people talk," Andy said with a grin.

"I don't care. Anyway, maybe it's time I actually did something to make people talk," Sarah replied. She turned red as soon as the words left her mouth, embarrassed at the impropriety of her remark.

Andy looked at her in surprise, and then he eased her discomfort by quickly changing the subject. "Look at the temple, Sarah. I've never seen so many people. What are they doing?"

Sarah looked across the water toward the temple and saw that the Mormon parishioners were still gathered on the lawn in front of the main entrance. "They're talking," she replied. "That's what they always do after church."

"Sure," Andy said with a grin, "they're probably talking about us right now."

As they watched, a woman broke away from the crowd and walked down to the beach alone. She had a shawl draped over her shoulders and a bonnet covering her head. She paused at the water's edge and gazed out at the lake and then turned and walked away from the temple, her head lowered.

"Sarah, isn't that your mother?" Andy asked.

"I don't know. Let me look." Sarah stood up and gazed at the lone figure on the beach. "Yes, I think it is. I recognize her shawl."

"Where is she going?"

"I don't know, probably home," Sarah said, still standing in the stern of the boat. Suddenly she smacked the palm of her hand on her forehead. "Oh, my God, what am I doing here? Andy, I need to go. Please take me to shore right now."

"What for?"

"Can't you see she needs me? Please hurry!"

"All right, but sit down before you tip the boat over."

Sarah sat down on the board with a thump and Andy spun the boat around and rowed toward the beach.

"I can't believe I've been so stupid and selfish."

"Sarah, what are you talking about?"

"Andy, I can't explain right now," Sarah said, her voice starting to break. "All I've been thinking about all summer is you and me together and now there's this strange thing with Elvira Field, and my mother's all alone. Didn't you hear my father's sermon? He's marrying Elvira and my mother didn't even know about it until today. No one has even talked to her and now she's all alone. Please hurry, Andy!"

Andy pulled harder on the oars and the boat surged forward. The moment the bow touched the beach Sarah stood up, put a hand on Andy's shoulder, and stepped out of the boat.

"Thank you, Andy. I'm really sorry. I hope you understand."

"Sarah, I know you're upset, but I really want to see you next Sunday. Do you think we can still go to North Beach for a picnic?"

Sarah stopped, with one foot in the water and one still in the boat. "Of course we can, Andy. I promise. I really want to see you too. Don't worry, everything will be all right by then."

Sarah still had her hand on Andy's shoulder. She bent forward and kissed him lightly on the cheek, and then she turned and ran down the beach.

Andy was stunned. He watched her go, his hands still locked on the oars. Sarah's dress fluttered in the breeze and her feet kicked up wet sand as she ran. She was the most beautiful girl he had ever seen. He looked down and saw her footprint in the sand, a round heel and five dainty toes.

Andy had no idea what it felt like to be in love. He only knew that Sarah was in his mind all the time. When he closed his eyes he saw her, and when he dreamed at night he dreamed of her. When he was with her he felt a warmth and comfort that he had never felt before. Sarah had been his first friend on Beaver Island, a gangly, awkward girl, and now she was growing into a young woman, more beautiful every day. Andy watched until Sarah reached her mother. He raised his hand and touched his cheek where Sarah had kissed him. Still watching her, he pushed the boat off the beach and began rowing slowly across the harbor, lost in his dreams.

CHAPTER 13:

Romance on North Beach

On Sunday Andy was up early. He had been thinking all week about his rendezvous with Sarah. A few days ago he had been confident that she would respond to his affections. Now he was not so certain. A couple of times he had even thought about not going at all, but then Sarah would not understand. After all, she had seemed eager to meet him. The sight of Sarah's mother had shattered a moment between them that he could not forget. The look in her eyes, the touch of her hand on his arm, and the brief unexpected kiss was more than he could ever have hoped for.

Andy stepped quietly out the front door and took a deep breath of warm summer air. Closing the door behind him, he ran down to the beach and plunged in with a splash. The icy chill gave way to an exhilarating coolness as he ducked his head in the water. After a quick rinse, he climbed up on the dock and headed back to the cabin, feeling clean for the first time after a week of catching and gutting fish.

After putting on his cleanest clothes, Andy slipped out the door again and started down the path toward the village. As he passed Nathan's house, Nathan saw him and came out on the front doorstep.

"Hi, Andy, where are you going?"

"Oh, just into town."

"Want to go fishing? I hear the perch are biting on the inland lakes."

"Naw, I've had enough of fishing this week. Thanks, anyway."

"Yeah, you're right. I'm pretty sick of it myself. You mind if I come along?"

"Um, actually, I was just going to see Sarah for a few minutes. I'll be back soon. Maybe we can go out to Whiskey Point or something."

All summer the three of them had met at least once a week in the school yard and walked around the harbor or along the beach. Something in Andy's expression made Nathan realize that he was not to be included on this day. "That's all right," he said. "I've got to take care of the horses and clean the barn today anyway."

"I'll see you later then," Andy said.

Nathan watched sadly as Andy walked away and then he turned and headed back to the barn to tend to the horses.

Sarah was waiting for Andy at the schoolhouse. She was wearing a colorful gingham dress and holding a wicker picnic basket. Her hair was braided and tied with a white bow. When she saw Andy approaching, she straightened her dress around her knees, brushed her hair back with both hands, and took a deep breath.

"Sorry I'm late," Andy said. He was surprised by how young and vulnerable Sarah appeared, sitting by herself with the empty school building behind her. For some reason, Andy had a momentary thought that someday he was going to have to protect her.

"Did you catch a lot of fish this week?" Sarah asked. "I've been watching you go out on the *Emma Rose* every morning."

"Oh, yeah, we caught a ton of fish. The lake's been calm, so we've been pulling nets every day."

"I wasn't sure you were coming today, so I've just been waiting here."

"I wasn't sure you would be coming, either." Andy sat down on the steps beside her.

"I'm really sorry about last week, Andy."

"What for?"

"You were so nice to give me a boat ride, but I made you row me to shore and then I ran away."

"That's all right. You were upset."

"It's just that my mother really needed me. She found out in front of everyone that my father had married another woman. No one was even talking to her and she was walking home alone. I felt awful for her."

"How is she?" Andy asked, not knowing what else to say.

"She's fine now, I think. She said she was going to leave the island, but I talked her out of it."

"How did you—"

"It was the kids. I told her that no one would be able to take care of Billy and Nettie and especially the baby."

"What did she say to that?"

"She wanted to take all of us with her back to Wisconsin to live with her parents, but she knows my father would never permit it."

"So she's trapped here?"

"That's what she said, but I told her it might not be so bad. She loves being a mother and she doesn't really care about the church all that much. This way she can stay at home with us and my father can worry about the church and stay over at the print shop."

"That's a strange notion," Andy said. "I don't think my mother would have done that."

"Some of the other Mormons have more than one wife."

"I know, but that doesn't make it fair."

"It isn't fair. That's why she wants to leave the island."

"What about you, Sarah?" Andy asked. "Would you leave the island with her?"

"Me? Oh, no, I don't think so."

"Why not?"

"Because I...I like it here, and because...I would miss you too much."

"I would miss you, too, Sarah," Andy said, turning towards her. "You were the first person I met here. I can't even imagine being on Beaver Island without you."

Their eyes met and Andy reached out his hand and placed it over Sarah's hand. It was if they were back in the rowboat again and surrounded by water, except that now they were surrounded only by their growing love, a love that was blind to the conflicts swirling around them.

"Let's get out of here," Andy finally said, breaking the spell between them.

"Where do you want to go?" Sarah asked.

"To the secret berry patch."

"All right. You lead the way."

"Here, let me carry the picnic basket."

Andy picked up the basket and together they walked behind the school and into the forest. The leafy canopy above them transformed the sunlight into emerald beams of light that beckoned them deeper and deeper into the woods. They walked together, absorbing the magical moment and leaving their thoughts and worries far behind them. After passing through a stand of pine trees, they came upon a field sprinkled with clusters of white birch. A grassy meadow sloped away from the trees and ended abruptly in a high bluff overlooking Lake Michigan. From this height the lake made a brilliant panorama, sparkling with a thousand tiny reflected suns. Across a wide strait of water they could see the rolling hills of Garden Island.

"Isn't it beautiful?" Sarah asked.

"When we first came here we named it Orla Island after my Aunt Orla, Nathan's mother."

"Yes, I remember."

"I've heard there's an ancient Indian burial ground over there."

"That sounds mysterious. We should go there sometime and go exploring."

'We will, I promise." Andy said. "As soon as I get my own boat, we'll go. Maybe we'll even stay overnight."

"That sounds scary," Sarah said with a shudder. "I don't know if I want to do that."

Andy laughed. "Don't worry, we'll start a big fire on the beach. That'll keep the spirits away."

"You would protect me, wouldn't you, Andy?" Sarah asked, putting her head on his shoulder.

"Of course I would," Andy replied, putting his arm around her.

A cloud briefly crossed Sarah's brow. "I'm sorry, Andy. This is such a small island. I worry about all the fighting. It just gets worse and worse and there just doesn't seem to be anyway to get away from it."

"I know," Andy said. "A few days ago my father almost got in a fight with Butch Jenkins. That guy is a troublemaker."

"What happened?"

"Jenkins came around to collect taxes. I don't know exactly what he said, but Nathan's father had to get between the two of them."

"I see him a lot at the print shop when he comes to talk to my father. Sometimes they get all worked up and they talk really loud."

"What do they talk about?" Andy asked.

"I don't know. Religion, mostly. They want more Mormons to move here."

"My father says the Mormons want to take over the whole island," Andy said.

"I've heard them talk about that," Sarah replied, "but I don't think they'll ever do it."

"Don't you remember when they shot the cannon at Whiskey Point? I heard that was all Butch Jenkins' idea."

"Maybe you're right, Andy. I do know that he doesn't like the Irish fishermen," Sarah said. "I just wish everyone would get along."

"Well, look at this way, Sarah. A few years ago there was nothing on this island but dirt and trees. Now there's a new village and lots of people living here, thanks to your father. I was starving in Ireland, and now we own our own land and we have a house and a boat and two horses."

"That's true," she replied. "Thanks for making me feel better, Andy."

They both looked out over the water at Garden Island. A freshening breeze from the west raised lines of whitecaps across the lake. Several seagulls coasted overhead, riding the wind with spreading wings.

"Do you want to go down to the lake?" Andy asked.

"Sure. The water should be warm today," Sarah said. "Want to race?"

Before Andy could reply, Sarah jumped down the bluff, landed with a pounce in the sand, and raced toward the beach. Andy jumped, momentarily lost his balance, and chased after her.

"No fair!" he shouted. "I've got to carry this picnic basket."

"I win!" Sarah said, laughing and slipping off her shoes to test the water with her bare toes.

"What's in this basket, anyway? It's heavy."

"Just our picnic lunch."

Andy put the basket down, took off his shoes, and stepped into the water. "You're right, Sarah, it is warm." He knelt down, dipped his hands in the water and playfully splashed her.

Sarah shrieked, splashed him in return, and ran back up on the beach. She watched Andy as he waded further out into the lake. He was wet to the waist and splashing water over his head. She laughed at his joyful antics, and suddenly she realized she was in love with him. She had known it ever since their rowboat ride, but she had not quite been able to give in to her feelings. But now it was there, surrounding her and filling her with wonder.

Andy turned back and churned his way through the water up to the beach. He was still laughing and splashing, trying to get Sarah wet. She stood motionless on the beach, adoring him from a distance.

"The water's fine," he said, standing before her in knee-deep water.

"You're getting drenched, Andy McGuire," she said. "Come in and get warm."

Andy shook his head, spraying water from his hair, and wiped his face on his sleeve. "Why are you staring at me? Am I wet?" he asked.

"Yes," Sarah replied. "Yes, you're very wet."

"Don't worry. I'll dry out in the sun."

"I know, but right now you're soaked."

"Want to go to the berry patch? I'm hungry."

"Yes, I do," she replied.

Andy picked up the picnic basket and together they walked down the beach, occasionally picking up stones or examining a shell in the shallow water. When they reached the trail up to the berry patch, Andy took the lead, holding Sarah's hand as they climbed up the bluff. In a clearing at the top, they found a tangle of blackberry bushes, sharp with thorns and plump with new berries. They skirted around the brambles, arriving at a grassy area of high ground with a view of the lake.

"Here's a good spot," Andy said, motioning to a patch of grass in the shade of a large birch tree. He put down the picnic basket. "I'll go collect some berries."

"Don't be long," Sarah said.

Andy went back to the berry patch and began picking. He soon filled both of his shirt pockets and scooped a few extra berries into his hands. When he returned, Sarah had spread a blanket on the grass and was busy arranging dishes and silverware.

"You brought dishes? No wonder the basket was heavy."

"Of course," she said, looking up at him with a smile. "This is a special picnic."

"Why is it special?"

"You'll see. Now just sit down here next to me. I've got everything right here."

Sarah took the berries from Andy and poured them into a cup. Then she pulled out a fresh loaf of bread, a jar of homemade jam, a block of cheese, apples, pears, a flask of apple juice, and a sweet pudding cake for dessert.

"Sarah! You did all this yourself this morning?"

"Actually my mother helped me bake the cake, but it's a secret. Don't tell my father because he'll be mad."

"Why?"

"Well for one thing, he doesn't know where I am. Even worse, we're here all alone. We don't even have an escort."

"Does that bother you?"

"No, but it would sure bother him."

"Why, doesn't he like me?"

"I think he likes you a lot, Andy, but..."

"But what?"

"Well, I think he wishes you were a Mormon."

"I could become a Mormon if it would make you happy."

Sarah looked at him with surprise. "That's very sweet of you, Andy, but I don't think you'd make a very good Mormon."

Andy looked at her with mock indignation. "I beg your pardon?"

"Don't be hurt," she said, touching his arm. "It's just that there are so many rules."

"Hmmm, maybe you're right. Our church back in Ireland didn't have very many rules, except that they made you sit still for a long time on Sundays. I'm not too good at sitting still."

"I noticed, especially in school. Anyway, you were just a kid back then."

"Yeah, that seems like a long time ago," Andy said, looking out at the lake.

"Do you miss Ireland?" Sarah asked.

"Yeah, sometimes, but I like it here, too. Beaver Island reminds me of Ireland."

"Do you ever miss your mother?"

Andy sighed, looked down at his hands, and then looked into Sarah's eyes. "I miss her all the time. She used to tuck me in at night. She always asked me to think of something nice that happened each day, and then we said our prayers."

"I'm so sorry, Andy," Sarah said, placing her hand back on his arm.

"I probably wouldn't even be alive today if it wasn't for her. When the potato crop went bad, everyone just stayed indoors and they all got sick. My mother said it was because of poisoned air. She made us sleep outside even when it was cold. She made my father go fishing every day so we had fresh food, even in the winter. He got sick himself once, but he didn't die."

"I'm glad. He brought you here."

"I'm glad, too, but I sure miss my mother. Maybe I would settle down if she were still alive."

Sarah laughed. "I doubt that, but perhaps I could help."

"You already have, Sarah," he said, putting his hand over her hand. "Nathan asked me to go fishing with him today, but I've been waiting all week just to have a picnic with you."

Sarah blushed. She was feeling nervous again, just like she had in the rowboat. She pulled her hand away and began to fuss with the dishes. "Oh, my, I almost forgot about our picnic! We'd better eat before the ants get it all."

She placed the plates and glasses on the blanket and then proceeded to fumble with the silverware, scattering forks and spoons in the sand while Andy watched, making her even more nervous.

"You could help me, you know," she said with exasperation.

"Sorry," he said. "I'll go rinse off the silverware."

Andy scooped the silverware out of the sand and ran down to the beach. Sarah watched him for a moment, took a deep breath, and pulled the loaf of bread out of the picnic basket, taking care not to drop it in the sand. She cut two slices and smothered them with jam, setting them aside. While she waited for Andy to return, she scooped a dab of the succulent preserve on her finger and raised it to her lips, stealing a taste of the meal to come.

After their picnic, Andy and Sarah lay together on the blanket and watched the mid-day sun sparkling on the lake. Several white clouds congregated over Garden Island and the sun painted crimson shadows on the water beneath them. To the north, a distant range of thunderheads marched quietly across the sky.

Andy cut the pudding cake for dessert and placed a slice on each plate. Sarah dished out the fresh berries and sprinkled them on the cake.

"Mmmm. This is delicious," Andy said, taking a bite. "Your mother is a good cook."

"Yes, she is," Sarah agreed. "She's good at everything. I don't know what I would ever do without her."

"She doesn't seem to like it here, does she?"

"Not really. She liked our farm in Wisconsin."

"Do your parents still own it?" Andy asked.

"Yes, but nobody takes care of it. It's probably all weeds by now."

"That's too bad. Crops don't grow here. The soil is too sandy."

"Nothing grows here but trees."

"Yeah, and those aren't going to last long, the way the lumberjacks cut them down."

"Andy, what do you think is going to happen to the island?" Sarah asked, turning to look at him.

"There won't be any trees left. The island will be bare."

"No, I mean, between the Mormons and the Irish."

"Oh, that. I don't really know."

"Why did those men have to beat up Percival Graham?"

"He was trying to collect taxes. Knowing who did it, they were probably drunk."

"My father hates drinking. He says it brings out the worst in people. That's why he doesn't like the fishermen out at Whiskey Point."

"They do drink a lot, but mostly they just want to fish. These islands have the best fishing in Lake Michigan."

"Why don't they just fish around some of the other islands?"

"Because Beaver Island has the best harbor in the lakes and the steamers stop here to buy their catch. The steamers also buy wood from the Mormons, so it helps everybody."

"My father wants to turn Saint James into a Mormon kingdom."

"He can't do that. Everyone should be able to live here."

"I know, but that's what he says he wants to do."

"We had English kings telling us what to do in Ireland, and all they did was steal from us. My father lost everything. That's why we came here after my mother died."

"But don't you think the Mormons should have a safe place to live?"

"Sure they should, but they don't need to be shooting cannons across the harbor, and they sure didn't need to kill Tom Bennett."

"They say it was an accident and he should have surrendered peacefully."

"He had about ten bullets in him. That was no accident."

Sarah sighed and picked up a handful of sand, watching it funnel through her fingers into the grass. "I'm just afraid that something else bad is going to happen. Why is it so hard for people to live together?"

"It's the adults," Andy replied. "They don't even try to get to know each other, so they just fight. We're the next generation. We won't be like that."

"But Andy, you got in a fight with Gurdon Humphrey. You beat him up really bad and Nathan and I had to pull you off."

"I didn't beat him up because he's a Mormon. I beat him up because he's a jerk."

Sarah giggled. "I know, but I was just saying that—"

Andy came over to Sarah and put his arms around her. "Don't worry, Sarah. Everything's going to be fine."

"But what's going to happen to us?" Sarah asked, warming in his embrace.

"Like I said, we'll be fine. The older people, the Irish and the Mormons, are just going to have to solve their own problems. We're young and free, so we can do whatever we want. We're going to build a town here, and soon there will be a hundred steamboats in the harbor every day."

"Do you really think so?"

"Sure, and I'm going to have a fleet of fishing boats and I'm going to build you a house."

"You are?" Sarah asked.

"Yep. We'll have a horse and buggy, too."

Sarah looked up at him. "Does that mean we're going to be together?"

"Of course we are," Andy replied, holding her close. "I can't even think of life without you on Beaver Island. We'll always be together." He looked at her and gently brushed a wisp of hair off her forehead. "I love you, Sarah."

Sarah wrapped her arms around him and looked up into his eyes, overwhelmed by the intensity of his expression. She had only an instant of doubt: Andy was impulsive and he had a temper, she knew that. But he was carefree and fun and so full of life. She knew what he said was true. They would always be together.

"I love you, too, Andy," she whispered.

CHAPTER 14:

Sarah's Lament

For the rest of the summer Sarah and Andy were inseparable. Every evening after the *Emma Rose* came in from the fishing grounds and after his work was done, Andy came straight over to Sarah's house. Sarah always watched for the boat to return to the harbor, and she waited for him.

They took walks around the harbor, sat on the front porch, or helped Mary with the children. Andy soon became a favorite of Billy Strang, who was growing up fast and was weary of playing with his sister. They often played catch or tag in the front yard until dusk. Sometimes Andy and Sarah took the children down to the schoolyard to play.

As for King Strang, he seldom came to the house, except for brief visits to see the children. He spent most of time at the print shop with Elvira.

When she wasn't with Andy, Sarah divided her time between helping her mother and working at the print shop. She had become adept at setting up the letters on the printing press, so she did most of the preparation work while Elvira wrote articles. Whenever Sarah had a chance, she wrote articles and even some poetry, but they were seldom published. King Strang personally reviewed and selected the news material, and he preferred to print Mormon propaganda or articles that were critical of his foes.

King Strang and Elvira often left the print shop, leaving Sarah to look after Elvira's baby. At first Sarah did not mind, but she soon became frustrated with the extra responsibility. Their absences became longer and longer, and one day they were gone all afternoon. When they finally returned, the baby was crying and Sarah was still busy setting letters for the printing press.

"Sarah, why isn't Elvira's article ready for printing?" her father asked. "The paper has to be out tomorrow."

"It was too long to fit on one page," she said in exasperation. "I had to take out some parts."

"You can't cut her article. Our readers need to know the truth and she has a lot to say."

Sarah lost her temper. "If she has so much to say, then why can't she stay here and take care of her own baby?"

"Sarah! That's enough! We were doing important work at the temple."

"I can't hold her baby and set these letters at the same time. It's impossible."

"Sarah, you are being disrespectful to Elvira. Now stop it."

"I don't care! It's almost September and school starts in two days. I'm supposed to help Mrs. Watson teach this year. I'll bet you didn't even know that."

"I won't hear anymore talk like that. Obviously you can't handle the work here, so we'll finish it ourselves."

"You don't even know how to do it. No one knows but me."

Her father glared at her and pointed at the door. "Go home, right now!"

"You don't even care about us anymore." Sarah marched out the door and slammed it shut behind her. She burst into tears and ran for home.

There was no paper the next day.

On Monday morning Mrs. Watson stood in the damp grass in front of the school and pulled on the bell rope. The peals of the bell rang across the harbor, announcing the beginning of the 1851 school year and inviting all of the island children to a new year of classes. Sarah and Andy and Nathan were the first to arrive.

"Good morning, Mrs. Watson," Sarah said.

"Good morning! Welcome back to school!" Mrs. Watson said with a grand smile. "Here, you two young men ring this bell. Sarah, you come inside with me. We have to get ready for class."

Mrs. Watson put her arm around Sarah's shoulder and led her to the schoolhouse. Sarah peeked around and saw Andy and Nathan standing idly by the bell post. She pointed up at the bell and gestured to them to pull the rope.

Mrs. Watson squeezed Sarah's shoulder. "Boys!" she exclaimed. "They can't even follow the simplest instructions, can they, dear?"

Sarah smiled up at her. "No, they can't," she agreed.

"Well, we'll teach them a thing or two this year, won't we?"

The bell finally started to ring again. Children of all ages congregated in the schoolyard, laughing and greeting each other. Mrs. Watson went out on the porch steps and waved her handkerchief. All of the children lined up and filed into the classroom. Andy and Nathan were still ringing the bell until Mrs. Watson clapped her hands for them to come in also.

Mrs. Watson greeted the children and made a few remarks about rules in the classroom and subjects to be studied, and then she introduced the new students. There were a lot of them, mostly Mormon. Many families had moved to the island over the summer.

"Now, class, I want you to divide up. Grades one through six shall go in the other room with Sarah Strang, and the older students shall remain here with me. Everyone please find a seat." Mrs. Watson clapped her hands in a commanding manner and all of the students scattered between the two classrooms.

Sarah looked at Mrs. Watson, seeking guidance. She had never been in charge of an entire class before and she was a little nervous.

"Don't worry," Mrs. Watson said. "I'm going to get this group started on a reading assignment and then I'll be over to help you. Just keep them occupied for a few minutes."

"There sure are more kids this year," Sarah said, looking from one room to the other.

"Yes, there are. It's a good thing the men thought to build two classrooms. We're going to have to build an addition if this keeps up."

Sarah quickly learned how to handle a classroom of young students. She found that it wasn't really all that different than babysitting, especially with the first and second graders. She really had no idea how to teach, but fortunately Mrs. Watson moved back and forth between the two rooms and tried to spend most of her time with the younger students. Soon Sarah was able lead the class in a recitation of the alphabet as she pointed to each letter printed on the blackboard.

In a few weeks Sarah was comfortable standing in front of the class and working with the children. One day she had a particularly good day of teaching. She left the classroom early to meet Andy and Nathan out by the bell post. Sarah was proud of her progress as a teacher and she was anxious to see them.

"Hi, Sarah!" they both said as she came down the front steps carrying a stack of books.

"Hi, Andy. Hi, Nathan."

"How was your day today, Miss Strang?" asked Andy, putting his arm around her.

"It went very well, Mr. McGuire," Sarah replied. "We're already learning a new set of words from lesson five. How was your day?"

"Gurdon Humphrey found a dead mouse and pinned it to the wall. Other than that, it was pretty boring," Nathan said.

"Ugh!"

"Want to see it?" Andy asked. "It's still hanging there."

"I think I'd rather not, but I would be pleased if you both would walk me home."

"Gladly, Miss," Andy replied gallantly, bowing and holding out his hand to her.

Sarah took Andy's hand and Nathan carried her books. As they walked, a few fall leaves scurried in the wind around their feet. Andy squeezed Sarah's hand and held it tight.

"I filled the back of our wagon with hay," Nathan said. "Maybe we can all go for a hayride around the harbor sometime this fall."

"That would be wonderful, Nathan," Sarah said.

"Nathan has been working with the horses every day," Andy said. "He's got them really well trained."

"It took a while," Nathan replied. "I walk them and I brush them down and talk to them, so they know me pretty well."

"We'd love to go, Nathan," Sarah said."

"I still have barrels to haul, but after the fishing season is over we can go anytime."

By then they had completed the short walk to the gate in front of Sarah's house. A gust of wind swirled through the tree above them and showered them with leaves.

"We'll see you tomorrow," Andy said.

"'Bye, Andy. Thanks for carrying my books, Nathan," Sarah said, letting go of Andy's hand and opening the gate. She watched the boys as they walked away and she couldn't help thinking how lucky she was. She had friends, she was teaching school, and, as if life were not good enough, she was in love with Andy.

Sarah picked up a handful of red maple leaves and sorted them into a colorful bouquet. She took one last look down the path. Andy must have read her mind, for he turned and waved to her. She smiled and held up her bouquet for him, and then skipped up the path to the front door, clutching her leaves. She was as happy as she had ever been on the island. She had no way of knowing that her life was about to plunge into turmoil.

Sarah opened the front door and saw that the house was quiet and dark, which seemed odd to her at this time of day. She shut the door behind her and put the leaves on a table. At first she thought no one was home, but then she heard the sound of muffled sobbing coming from a bedroom. She hurried down the hall and saw her mother kneeling at the side of her bed, her head buried in a pillow.

"Mother! What's wrong?"

"Sarah! Thank God you're here."

Sarah kneeled next to her mother and put arm around her. "What's wrong?"

"It's awful. It's just awful," Mary said between sobs.

"What's awful?"

"Your father has ordered me to leave the island."

"Leave the island! Why?"

"It's horrible. I can't believe he would accuse me of such a thing."

"What, Mother? What did he accuse you of?"

"He says I tried to kill Elvira's baby."

"What! You would never do such a thing. I can't believe he would say that!"

"I've been taking care of that baby every day since you went back to school, just like he told me to."

"What happened?"

"I made a mistake. I—"

"What happened, Mother?" Sarah asked, shaking Mary's shoulder. "Please tell me."

"He told me yesterday that I didn't need to come over to the print shop, that they were going to stay there and they would take care of little Charlie. He was talking about next week, but I thought he meant this week, so I stayed home today. I was confused."

"Was Elvira there with Charlie at the print shop?"

"No. She went over to the temple this morning to be with James."

"Why didn't she wait for you before she left the baby alone?"

"I don't know. I guess she thought I would be there in a few minutes."

"That's ridiculous. You never leave a baby, even for a minute. You taught me that."

"I know. I tried to tell them that and your father said it was still my fault."

"Oh, no," Sarah said in disbelief. "Is Charlie all right?"

"Yes, thank God," Mary said. "Elvira came back at noon and found him out of his crib on the floor, cold and crying."

"But it's her baby. She never should have left the print shop."

"It doesn't matter now," Mary said in despair. "It's too late. Your father says it's my fault and I have to leave the island."

"But where are you going to go? What about our family?"

Mary took a deep breath and looked up at Sarah with tears in her eyes. "I'm going back to Voree to live at our farm. I still have some friends there."

"Are you sure? Maybe we could find somewhere else to live here."

"No, I'm leaving. I refuse to watch that hussy's baby while she waltzes around the island with my husband. I've been humiliated enough."

Sarah could feel her mother's body trembling. "Wait here," she said. "I'll be right back."

Sarah went out to the pantry and opened the cupboard. Standing on a stool, she reached to the back of the top shelf and pulled out a bottle of brandy. She blew the dust off the bottle, pulled out the cork, filled a glass, and carried glass and bottle back into the bedroom.

"Here, Mother, drink this. It'll calm your nerves."

Mary was sitting on the edge of the bed. She had stopped crying and she was drying her eyes. "Sarah, where did you ever find this? I thought your father threw it away a long time ago."

"I hid it. I don't know why. Here, take a sip."

Mary sipped the brandy. She grimaced at the unfamiliar pungent taste, and then she tilted the glass and took a long drink. Sarah watched her in silence and held her mother's hand until she stopped trembling. "I'm going with you," she said firmly.

The brandy soon took effect and Mary shook off her melancholy. She was composed now and she squeezed her daughter's hand.

"Sarah, your father wants me to take the three younger children with me and he wants you to stay here to keep house for him."

Sarah looked at her in amazement. "I don't care what he wants. I'm still going with you."

"But what about Andy? You've been seeing him all summer."

Sarah hesitated. "I'll ask him to come with us," she finally said.

"He's a nice boy and I can tell he's very fond of you," Mary said, "but I would hate to see you ask him to leave his father."

"Mother, I can't let you leave. What would I do without you?"

"Frankly, Sarah, I don't think your father would let you get on the boat with me. He would figure out a way to separate us at the dock."

"Then I'll sneak away later. I'll get on a different boat."

"But how would you travel alone?"

"I'm old enough. You could meet me in Milwaukee."

"But don't you want to see how things work out with Andy? I can tell that you care very much for him. You seem so perfect for each other."

"I don't know, Mother. I'm so confused right now."

"I have an idea," Mary said. "I'll give you some money and if things get worse here after I leave you can just get on the boat. As long as you are quiet about it, no one will even notice. I hate to have you travel alone, so you can bring Andy if you want to. I have friends in Milwaukee. They can meet you and bring you to Voree. It isn't very far."

"Are you sure?"

"I just want you to be happy, Sarah."

"But are you ever coming back?"

"Not while Elvira is here. But next summer you can come to see me in Voree. By June you'll have spent a whole year teaching school, and you'll be qualified to get a job as a teacher anywhere."

"Can I at least think about it?" Sarah asked.

"Of course you can, dear. I know it will be a long winter, but I'll write and we'll be back together soon." Mary reached under the bed and pulled out a purse. She took out two twenty dollar gold pieces and wrapped them in a handkerchief. "Take these. Hide them where your father can't find them. You can use them to travel, any time you like. There's one for you and one for Andy."

"That's a lot of money, Mother."

"It's easily enough to get both of you to Voree, with plenty to spare."

"Thank you, Mother. I'll hide them in a safe place."

"Oh, one other thing, Sarah, I wouldn't give this to Andy, at least for a while. Your father would be very angry if he found out. He could make trouble for Andy. He might even send someone after him. There are some bad men here on the island."

"I know, Mother. We'll be careful."

"I worry about both of you. I know it sounds strange, but I have a feeling that something terrible is going to happen on this island. I can feel it inside. I just don't know what it will be."

"We'll be fine—"

Mary grabbed her daughter by both shoulders and looked her in the eyes. "Promise me, Sarah, if you are frightened or if anyone threatens you in any way, you get on the first boat you can and you get away from this island. Do you promise?"

"Yes, I promise."

Mary squeezed Sarah's hands around the two coins. "Hide these carefully. They will get you off the island."

"I will, Mother."

Two weeks later, Mary Strang boarded the *Louisville* with Billy, Nettie and baby Hattie. Andy and Nathan carried their luggage. Mrs. Watson and

Wingfield came down to the dock to see them off, as did many of the Mormon women.

Sarah hugged her mother and tried to keep a brave face. Although she had often been separated from her father when he traveled, she had never been away from her mother, even for one night.

"Goodbye, Sarah," Mary said. "I'll see you in the spring, I promise."

Sarah's lower lip trembled as she tried to keep from crying. "Goodbye, Mother. I love you."

"I love you too, Sarah. If you have any problems at all, you talk to Mrs. Watson and she will help you."

The captain of the *Louisville* blew a loud blast on the ship's whistle. Two sailors coiled the dock lines at the bow and stern and threw them on the deck. Mary tore herself away from Sarah's grasp and boarded the boat. Sarah gave Billy and Nettie each a hug and kissed the baby on the forehead. Mrs. Watson grabbed Sarah by the waist and held her back. "Watch out, Sarah. The boat is pulling away."

Sarah stepped back and stood on the edge of the dock with Mrs. Watson still holding her. She watched and waved as the boat pulled away and headed toward the open lake. Her mother waved with one hand and disappeared into the ship's cabin with the baby in her arms. Billy and Nettie ran to the stern of the boat and waved and shouted. A puff of black smoke belched from the stack of the *Louisville* as it began to pick up speed.

King Strang was not present to witness the departure of his first wife.

The first week was the hardest for Sarah. She stayed home alone, and it was terribly quiet without her family. Andy walked her home every day after school and often stayed to study. Mrs. Watson stopped by each evening and they worked together at the kitchen table on lesson plans for the next day of classes. But no matter who was there with her in the evening, she dreaded the long nights alone.

The following week, King Strang and Elvira Field Strang moved back into the house.

"The print shop is too small for us," Strang said.

"We can't keep it warm with the cold weather coming," Elvira said.

In the custom of the times, Strang took the largest bedroom for himself and Elvira moved back into the sewing room, where she had previously resided. She removed Mary's sewing table and replaced it with a baby crib for little Charlie.

"We shall turn the front parlor into a meeting room where all Mormons will be welcome," King Strang said. He brought in several more chairs and arranged the furniture in a circle. All of Mary's books were replaced with Mormon writings and publications. The latest editions of the *Northern Islander* were placed on a table in the center of the room.

With Mary and the children gone from the island, there were no longer any constraints on King Strang. He converted the dining room into an office for himself and Elvira took over the children's bedroom for her office. Almost every evening Butch Jenkins came to the house and made himself at home in the parlor. Tobias Humphrey and other members of the church council frequently stopped in for a visit. The men sat in the parlor and discussed church affairs, often until late at night.

Sarah's bedroom was directly across the hall from the parlor. At first she listened with curiosity to their conversations, but soon she became bored with the incessant droning. After a time the noise became annoying to her, for she was required to rise early to prepare breakfast and get to school on time. She eventually hung a blanket over the door to muffle the sounds from the other room.

Butch Jenkins spoke in a loud voice when he had a captive audience. He spent most of his time lamenting the injustices inflicted upon the Mormons from just about everyone in the outside world. He was particularly hard on the Irish, warning of their evil intent to eradicate the Mormons from Beaver Island by force if necessary. Sarah could hear every word he said, even when she covered her ears with a pillow.

Now that he had access to the house, Jenkins took a particular interest in Sarah, peering in her bedroom to say hello or ask about her progress at school. One night, Sarah was in the back room washing dishes after the evening meal. She could hear the resonating voices of several men in the parlor, apparently engaged in debate of a particularly contentious issue. She leaned over the washbasin to scrub the bottom of a blackened stew pot. Reaching up for a rag, she was startled to see Jenkins standing in the doorway and gazing at her.

"Hello, Sarah," he said.

"Mr. Jenkins! You scared me."

"I'm sorry," he said, walking toward her. "I didn't mean to frighten you."

"It's just that I didn't expect to see anyone back here in the wash room," Sarah said, wiping her hands with the rag.

"How is school coming along these days, Sarah?"

"It keeps me busy. I have a lot of homework to do after I finish these dishes." Sarah turned her attention back to the dirty pot in the basin.

"Doesn't Elvira ever help you with this women's work?"

Sarah stopped scrubbing for a moment. That question had also occurred to her, but she had never raised the issue for fear of angering her father.

"No, she's too busy taking care of her baby," Sarah replied. She resumed scrubbing, bending over the basin and scraping her fingernails on the blackened bottom of the pan.

"Here, let me help you," Jenkins said.

He reached around her shoulders, took both of her hands in his, and guided them into the soapy water. Lowering his head, he nuzzled her hair with his chin until he was almost touching her cheek. Sarah cringed at the smell of his humid breath and curled her shoulders inward in a futile effort to withdraw from him. He pressed his thighs against her from behind and pushed forward, pinning her to the edge of the basin.

"No, please, I can do it myself," Sarah gasped.

"You're a beautiful girl, Sarah," he said, breathing into her ear. "You're going to make someone a fine Mormon wife someday."

"No!" she cried with a shudder. "Please let go of me."

"I just want to help you, Sarah," he said, sliding his soapy hands up and down her arms.

Sarah jerked her hands out of the water, splashing both of them with suds. Jenkins loosened his grip momentarily and Sarah managed to slither out of his grasp.

"I don't want to be a Mormon wife," she cried.

"Sarah, I care about you very much. I think that you—"

"I have to go do my homework now." Sarah scurried across the kitchen and down the hall to the parlor. She was about to retreat to her bedroom when her father spoke sharply to her.

"Sarah, you are being rude! Come and say goodnight to these gentlemen."

The men were all staring at her from their comfortable parlor chairs. Sarah curtsied stiffly and gave them an empty smile. She could feel soapy water running down her arms and dripping on the floor.

"Good night," she said, her lips quivering and her stomach churning with nausea.

Escaping the men's gaze, Sarah closed her bedroom door. A haze of vertigo overcame her and she slumped to the floor. She huddled behind the door for a long time, waiting for the last visitor to depart for the evening. Then, rising in the darkness, she pushed her bed against the door. Putting on her nightgown, she crawled under the covers and waited in vain for the trembling to stop.

Sarah was tired and withdrawn at school the next day. She was impatient with the children and could not concentrate on her own studies. She wanted the day to end but dreaded the thought of going home. Finally the last class of the day ended and she excused the students.

Andy was waiting for her at the bell post. "Are you all right, Sarah?" he asked. "You look pale."

"I'm fine."

"Are you sure? You were awfully quiet today."

"I'm just really tired, Andy. I didn't get much sleep last night. There are too many people at my house all the time."

"C'mon," Andy said, taking her hand, "I'll walk you home."

They walked together out of the schoolyard and turned toward Sarah's house. Andy kicked at the crisp leaves on the ground, making them scatter in the wind. He picked up a handful of red maple leaves and handed her the brightest one.

"Here, this should cheer you up."

"Thank you, Andy. It's beautiful. I'll press it in the pages of my diary."

"You have a diary? What does it say?"

Sarah squeezed his hand and smiled at him. "I'm not telling you. It's a secret."

They reached the fence in front of Sarah's house and Sarah opened the gate.

"It doesn't look like anyone's home," Andy remarked.

"That's good," replied Sarah. "I want you to come in for a few minutes."

"What for?"

Sarah put her arms around Andy and pulled him close. "You'll see. Just follow me."

Once they were inside the house, she closed and latched the front door and lowered the curtains in the parlor.

"Sarah, what if someone comes home? We'll get in really big trouble."

"Don't worry. I'll keep a watch out the window."

"I thought you were tired."

"Andy, I want you to install a latch on my bedroom door. Do you think you can do that?"

"Right now?"

"Yes, if you would, please."

"I suppose so. Are you worried about something?"

"I'll tell you later, I promise. What do you need?"

"Tools and some pieces of wood, I guess."

"My father's tool chest is in the woodshed. Please hurry, before anyone comes home."

"All right, I'll see what I can do."

Andy found the toolbox and a few scraps of wood. He crafted two brackets and installed them on either side of the door and then he trimmed a larger board to fit firmly in the brackets, preventing the door from opening into Sarah's bedroom. Sarah tried it out, and Andy could not make the door budge from the outside. It was crude, but it would keep out any intruders.

After Andy replaced the tools and left for home, Sarah checked his handiwork again and then she inspected the latch on her window. She wanted to make sure it was locked, but she also wanted to make sure that she could open it quickly if she needed to escape.

King Strang came home at dinnertime. For once he was alone.

"Where's Elvira?" Sarah asked.

"She's working late on an article for the *Northern Islander*. She'll be along shortly."

Sarah took a deep breath. She had kept her distance from her father ever since Mary and the children left the island. She missed her mother terribly. For King Strang's part, he was completely absorbed in his relationship with Elvira. Sarah didn't quite know how to begin or even what she was going to say.

"Father…"

"Yes?"

"Father, I'm tired."

"Why? Haven't you been able to sleep?"

"No. It's hard to sleep. It's too noisy around here."

"Have we been keeping you awake with our evening meetings?"

"My bedroom is right next to the parlor."

"Would you like to move into a different room?"

"No, I like my room."

"Perhaps I could ask our church brethren to go home earlier."

"I think we should have our parlor back, like it was before."

"I need the parlor. How about if we have our meetings just twice a week, and I'll send everyone home at nine o'clock."

"That would be better. But do you think we could also put a lock on the front door?"

"A lock? What for?"

"Just to be safe."

Strang laughed. "Sarah, I'm the King of Beaver Island. No one's going to come in here and bother us. We're perfectly safe."

"It's just that I'm home alone a lot, and I get nervous."

"Afraid of the dark, are we?" Strang said. "Sarah, if you want me to, I'll have a latch installed on the front door, and on the back door, too. How does that sound?"

"Thank you, Father." Sarah was glad that she had summoned the courage to talk to him about her fears. It was only much later that she regretted not having the courage to tell him about Butch Jenkins.

It wasn't long before the last of the maple leaves fell from the trees and scattered before the wind. Ice began to appear along the quiet edges of the harbor. The fishing boats returned with the last of the fall catch and the fishermen strung their nets out to dry in the waning sun.

The *Emma Rose* was tied to the dock, quietly bumping against the pilings. As they did each fall, Ian and Patrick unloaded the boat and hauled everything to the barn for storage. It wasn't long before Wingfield Watson appeared with his team of oxen and a crew of willing helpers. In just a couple of hours the *Emma Rose* was on dry land, nestled for the winter in her bed of timbers.

After the boat was secure, the men all met in Patrick's cabin to discuss construction of the new lighthouse. "We can start next week," Ian said. "We've got plenty of time before winter sets in."

"It only needs to be a temporary tower," Wingfield said. "King Strang has persuaded the government to build a brick lighthouse on Whiskey Point in a couple of years."

"That's excellent," Patrick said. "The harbor will be a lot safer with a real lighthouse at the entrance."

"If we all pitch in we can have it done in no time, just like we did with the school," Wingfield added.

A few days later, Ian and Patrick were putting away the last of the fishing gear when they saw a group of men approaching from the direction of the village of Saint James.

"Were we supposed to start working on the lighthouse today?" Ian asked.

"I don't think so," Patrick answered.

"Well then, who is that?"

"That's King Strang in front. I can tell by his top hat."

"You're right, Patrick, and that's Butch Jenkins and Tobias Humphrey with him. Who are those two big fellas in the back?"

"They're lumberjacks who work for Tobias. I don't know their names, but I've heard they're pretty rough characters," Patrick said.

"I wonder what they want."

"I don't know, but I have a pretty good idea."

Ian and Patrick put down their fishing gear and walked up to the cabins. When they reached the front porch of Ian's cabin, King Strang came around the corner, followed by his entourage.

"Greetings, gentlemen," King Strang said.

"Hello," Ian said. "What brings you out this way?"

Strang ignored the question and turned to address his followers. "Men, these are the two gentlemen who saved us when we first came to Beaver Island. They were in the harbor on the occasion of our first feast of the temple, and they provided us with a boatload of fresh fish, free of charge and without hesitation. Indeed, they provided our brethren with sustenance throughout the entire summer." Strang turned to face Ian and Patrick. "For this, gentlemen, I am eternally grateful."

Ian and Patrick both shook the king's hand. "Thank you," Ian said. "That was quite a while ago."

"Nevertheless, on behalf of my congregation, I express our gratitude. Now, today, gentlemen, we come here on business."

"How may we help you?" Patrick asked.

"If it's about our taxes——" Ian began.

"Ah, yes, I have heard that there was an incident, a slight misunderstanding, if you will."

"Here is our position," Ian said. "We are glad to pay our share to support the school and the roads. We just don't think that we should have to pay for the construction of the Mormon temple."

"Gentlemen, the taxes are collected for the benefit of everyone on the island. Surely you can understand that."

"But we're not Mormon. We haven't been inside a church since we left Ireland."

"You may recall that on our very first meeting I invited you to join our congregation. That invitation is still open."

"Thank you, but we're not interested."

"You must realize by now that this island is to become a Mormon kingdom. I have proclaimed it."

"Isn't it worth anything that we helped build the school?" Patrick asked. "It was designed right on my kitchen table."

"Ah, you have a point, my good man. That should be worth something, wouldn't you say, Butch?" Strang said, turning to address Jenkins, who was glowering in the background.

"So we don't have to pay the full amount?" Ian asked.

King Strang waved his hand, dismissing the entire issue. "Gentlemen, we digress. I shall let my lieutenants handle this trifling affair as they see fit. Actually, I have come today on another matter."

"What would that be?"

"You all know Tobias Humphrey. Perhaps you have seen his sawmill across the harbor?"

"Sure we do," Patrick said. "Hello, Tobias."

"So you must know that his sawmill is the largest employer on the island," Strang continued.

"All Mormons, I reckon," Ian said.

Strang ignored the jab. "Now, Tobias has a problem. You see, he wants buy one of those new steam-powered saws so he can cut more lumber. It will be the first one in northern Michigan. The problem is that the water is too shallow on the south side of the harbor."

"The lumber boats cannot get to my dock," Tobias said.

"Tobias had his men take depth soundings all around the harbor," Strang said. "They found that the deepest water is located here along the north shore. Tobias wants to build a new sawmill where the lumber boats can load cargo."

"Where exactly on the north shore do you want to build?" Ian asked.

"Right here," Strang replied.

"Are you joking? This is our land. We built two cabins, a barn and a dock here."

"Ian, I am here today to consecrate this land for the church."

"Consecrate? What the hell does that mean?"

"It means that I am giving this land to the church for the benefit of the entire congregation."

"You can't do that. We own this land!"

"No, you don't. The church owns this land and the church needs it for a sawmill."

Patrick stepped in. "Wait a minute, King Strang. Ian bought this land from the United States government, fair and square."

"That's impossible. All of the land on this island belongs to the church."

"I beg to differ," Ian said. "The first winter we were here, I went by dog-sled over to the government land office on Mackinac Island. I bought twenty acres of land and paid for it in cash. We each own ten acres."

"I don't believe it."

"Patrick, go and get the deeds and we'll show them."

Patrick ran inside his cabin and came back with two pieces of yellow paper. "See, they're signed and stamped by the United States government."

Strang took the two documents and huddled with Butch Jenkins and Tobias Humphrey. They inspected the signatures and ran their fingers over the embossed stamp of the land office, mumbling to each other and glancing back at Ian.

"These are forgeries," Jenkins proclaimed.

"Well, if they are forgeries, then King Strang doesn't own any land here either, because he has thirty acres recorded in the land office himself. His name is right next to ours on the list. I saw it myself," Ian said.

Strang returned to the huddle with the other men. After a lengthy conversation, he came back over to Ian and Patrick.

"Now see here: Even after I gave you this land and invited you to join our church, you went behind my back to Mackinac Island to obtain these worthless pieces of paper. I do believe that Butch is correct; these deeds are forgeries."

"They are not! We paid for them—"

Strang held up his hand for silence. "However, under the circumstances, I am inclined to give you both a reprieve."

"A reprieve! From what?"

"We continue to be grateful to both of you for your contributions to this community. In consideration of your efforts to build the school and of your expected work on the new lighthouse this winter, I shall allow you to stay in your houses for now."

"Well, that's mighty big of you," Ian said sarcastically. "Then what happens?"

"Then the church will consecrate this land and Tobias Humphrey will build a saw mill here."

"He'll do no such thing. We own this land. We just showed you the deeds"

Tobias spoke up. "Ian, we only need about half the land, just enough to build a dock and a loading area."

"Yeah, and what about my house?"

"I regret to say that your house will have to be torn down to make way for the steam engine. However, I will gladly pay you a fair price for the barn. We'll be cutting a lot of wood, so we can use it for storage."

"And the land?"

"As King Strang said before, the land will be consecrated by the church. We bear you no ill will; in fact, we wish you would join us in worship. Every weekend we pray for you."

Ian and Patrick looked at each other, dumbfounded at the audacity of this statement. They could not believe what they were hearing. They were being robbed of their property and of everything they had worked so hard to build, and the robbers were praying for them.

Butch Jenkins, who had been mostly silent up until now, stepped forward. "By next summer, this whole island will be a Mormon kingdom. You would do well to join us now, before it is too late."

A few moments ago, Ian had been incredulous, but now he was getting angry.

"What if we don't?" Ian asked.

"Then we will torch your house and allow you to watch it burn before we run you off the island."

"I've had enough of your threats, Jenkins. I'm telling you right now that I will shoot anyone who touches my house."

The two lumberjacks stepped forward, brandishing wooden clubs that they had been hiding inside their overcoats. Ian grabbed a shovel that had been leaning against the house and pointed it at them.

"Gentlemen, gentlemen, there's no need to resort to violence," King Strang said graciously, gliding between the antagonists. "I'm sure that we can work this out amicably."

"I don't think so," said Jenkins. "Not anymore."

"Now, Butch, please stand back and call off your men. I'll handle this."

Jenkins backed off and stood between the two lumberjacks, who slowly lowered their clubs. King Strang addressed Ian and Patrick.

"Gentlemen, I apologize for the behavior of these men. As you can see, their loyalty to the kingdom is such that they would do anything for me. Sometimes I must control their enthusiasm."

"So it would appear," Patrick said, holding his ground next to Ian.

"Today we shall retire," Strang said, "but we will return, I assure you. Your property deeds are not valid and we must consecrate this land for the church. Perhaps you will be lucky and I can persuade Tobias to move your house to a better location."

"That's not bloody likely," Ian said.

"We shall see. In the meantime, you may stay until further notice. Good day, gentlemen."

King Strang turned and marched away, beckoning to his men. Butch Jenkins and Tobias Humphrey followed quickly behind him. One of the lumberjacks walked over to Ian's cabin, pulled out a piece of charcoal, and drew a large X on the front door. Both lumberjacks then departed without a word.

Ian and Patrick were silent for a moment, staring at the X.

"I don't like the looks of that," Ian said.

"What are we going to do?" Patrick asked.

"We're going to protect our homes. That's all we can do. If that doesn't work, we're going to have to leave the island."

"We can't leave the island. Look at everything we've built here. Anyway, it's almost winter. We just pulled the boat out of the water."

"I know. We'd have to abandon everything if we left now. Listen, Patrick, I have an idea."

"I hope it's a good one."

"Let's go ahead and build the lighthouse out on Whiskey Point with Wingfield Watson and his men. We were going to do that anyway."

"Then what?"

"I have a feeling that Strang will change his tune after we build the lighthouse, and Tobias Humphrey is a practical man; there's no reason why he can't move his sawmill a hundred feet to the west and stay off my property."

"What about Jenkins and his thugs?"

"That's a problem," Ian admitted. "He's nothing but trouble. The first thing I'm going to do is wipe that cross off my door. They're not touching my house, now or ever. I'll see to that."

Nathan and Andy came home from school late in the afternoon and found their fathers sitting at the table in Ian's house, deep in discussion.

"What's going on?" Andy asked, tossing his hat in a chair.

"We had a visit today from King Strang and some of his friends," Ian replied. He proceeded to tell them the whole story, leaving out the part of the altercation with Butch Jenkins.

"We're not leaving the island, are we?" Andy asked with a worried look.

"No, we have too much invested here. But Patrick and I have been talking and we just made a decision. This winter, after the lake freezes, one of us is going to make a trip to the mainland to look at some other harbors near the fishing grounds. That way, if things ever get dicey with the Mormons, we can leave quickly on the *Emma Rose*."

"What about the wagon and the horses?" Nathan asked.

"We'll figure out a way take them if we can, but we may have to sell them," Patrick said.

A look of such anguish came over Nathan's face that Patrick came over and put his arm around his son. "Don't worry," he said. "This is all just a precaution. I'm sure that everything will work out. We won't sell the horses unless we absolutely have to."

After a few more assurances, Patrick and Nathan finally departed for their own cabin next door. Ian and Andy went inside and Ian threw another log on the fire and filled the teakettle with fresh water.

"Andy," he said, "I have to ask you something. You're courting Sarah Strang, aren't you?"

"Yeah," Andy mumbled. He thought he knew what was coming next.

"I notice that you go over to her house a lot after school."

"Yeah, when she's not working or planning her lessons."

"She's a fine girl. I think the world of her."

Andy didn't respond, so Ian forged ahead with his speech.

"Andy, I just want you to be on your best behavior when you're over at Strang's house."

"I will. I always am."

"Be very careful about what you say, especially if King Strang is around. He is a very powerful man."

"Do you really think he wants to chase us off the island, Father?"

Ian paused for a moment, choosing his words carefully. "I think he wants a kingdom so he can have control of this island. I also think he is influenced by people around him. Take Tobias Humphrey; he just wants to make money. And Butch Jenkins wants power. Money and power, that's what the Mormon religion is all about on Beaver Island."

"If we mind our own business won't they just leave us alone?"

"I wish it were that simple, son. I don't know if you've noticed, but we're vastly outnumbered here. Most of the Irish folks have already moved away, but not us. It's going to take more than a few threats to chase us away."

After dinner Andy tried to do his homework at the kitchen table, but he couldn't concentrate. He didn't really care about King Strang and his men. Sarah was all that really mattered to him. Sometimes he just wished they could start a new life together far away from Beaver Island. He dreamed of building a boat of his own and sailing away with his hand upon hers on the tiller, just as they had done on the *Emma Rose*.

Just before dark Nathan went out to the barn to take care of Guy and Lois. Earlier in the evening his father had explained to him the gravity of their situation. Although it was Ian's house that was in jeopardy, Patrick wanted them all to stick together. They had come across the ocean, purchased the *Emma Rose*, and made a fresh start in America. He did not want to give all that up to a few of King Strang's thugs hiding behind the Mormon religion.

Nathan filled a bucket and fed and watered the horses. He loved to stand between them and stroke their manes while they nuzzled his pockets, looking for a treat. He thought about what his father had said about sticking together. Even though they all wanted to stay on Beaver Island, it was clear that their position was going to be difficult. Nathan was frightened about what the future would bring. To escape his fears, he found solace in the company of his strong and patient companions.

Nathan's thoughts turned to Sarah. He had finally become resigned to seeing Sarah and Andy together every day. They always tried to include him, but he sensed that they often wanted to be alone. He knew how much Andy cared for Sarah, and he could see the growing love between them. At the same time he felt a deep emptiness and longing in his own heart. Nathan was too young to understand his feelings, but he too was in love with Sarah Strang.

CHAPTER 15:

Land Grab

Even Ian was surprised at how well his gamble paid off. Over the winter Ian, Patrick, Wingfield Watson, and several Mormon men built a tower on Whiskey Point to guide boats into the harbor. It was a crude structure, but it would suffice until a permanent lighthouse could be built. In the spring, Irish fishing boats and larger vessels bringing settlers and hauling lumber all cruised safely past Whiskey Point and entered Paradise Bay. King Strang said nothing more about building a sawmill on Ian's property and Butch Jenkins' threats were apparently forgotten.

Four years passed, and by the fall of 1855 the village of Saint James had grown and prospered. Converts to the Mormon faith continued to move to the island with a promise of free land. New shops lined the main street and every week farmers came to town to buy provisions and sell produce. Fishing remained an important source of income and lumber schooners sailed in and out of the harbor almost every day.

As for King Strang, he had not been idle since his trial and acquittal in Detroit. Capitalizing on the prosperity of the island, he worked tirelessly to recruit new followers and expand his kingdom. As busy as he was, he still found time to fully embrace the doctrine of spiritual wifery. Elvira, always by his side, remained his primary wife. In 1852 he married Betsy McNutt, an older woman who took over cooking and household duties. When Betsy moved in, Elvira moved into Strang's bedroom at the top of the stairs. By 1855, Strang's attention turned to younger women. In July he married Sara Wright, a seventeen year old island girl. In October he married Sarah's cousin Phoebe, who had just turned nineteen. The Strang household became crowded with four wives all living under the same roof. Indeed, Strang was obliged to build a large addition to accommodate all of his wives.

Sarah turned seventeen in July. She was still teaching at the school under the tutelage of Mrs. Watson. She now had her own desk and spent most of her time teaching and grading papers. Almost every day after class she went around the harbor to spend time with Andy. Although she had grown accustomed to Elvira and Betsy at home, the addition of two girls her own age to her father's harem was too much for Sarah, so she simply stayed away.

As for Andy and Nathan, they had completed school and were now fishing full time on the *Emma Rose*. After work, Andy spent as much time as he could with Sarah. By this time they were regarded as a couple, having been together for the last four years. Nathan had recently acquired a second wagon to haul freight arriving at the boat dock. He was even building a sleigh to haul freight in the winter.

Ian and Patrick were the only Irish fishermen still living permanently on the island. Although they lived in the midst of the Mormon kingdom, they had done well. The *Emma Rose* was still a solid vessel and they sold all the fish they could catch. They were able to move freely around the island, but they were always on their guard. They both remembered well the ominous X scrawled on Ian's door.

So far they had managed to stay in the good graces of King Strang and the Mormons. But that was about to change.

— ~ —

A few weeks after the first snowfall, Nathan went to Saint James to get an axle on his new wagon repaired. The blacksmith's shop was located next to Johnson's Store, with only a narrow alley separating the two buildings. While the blacksmith was working, Nathan waited on the front porch. A north wind whistled around the building so he retreated to the alley, wishing he had worn a heavier coat. As he waited, two men came out of Johnson's Store, slamming the door behind them.

"Are you sure you want to do this, James?" the first man asked.

"I am quite sure. I want her to be strong in the Mormon faith, but I fear she has slipped from the fold."

"Well, I must tell you that I am humbled and honored. I will treat her well, I give you my word."

"I'm quite sure that you will. That's why I chose you, Tobias. Now, about the money..."

Curious, Nathan peeked around the corner of the store. The two men on the porch were none other than King Strang and Tobias Humphrey. They sat down on a bench with their backs to Nathan and began to speak in earnest. Nathan pulled his head back quickly, but he remained in his hiding place, listening in astonishment to what the two men were saying. He could hardly believe what he was hearing.

The men stood up and clumped across the porch and down the steps, stopping directly in front of the alley. Nathan ducked behind a rain barrel, terrified that they would see him.

"My men will start cutting trees next week, and I'll make the first payment at the end of the month," Humphrey said.

"Excellent," replied King Strang. "You'll have your sawmill by next summer, Tobias."

The two men shook hands and went their separate ways. Nathan remained behind the rain barrel until he was sure they were gone. Then he crept to the back of the alley, dashed across an open field behind Johnson's Store, and disappeared into the woods. He had forgotten all about his wagon in the blacksmith's shop.

Andy was out by the barn chopping firewood when Nathan emerged from the forest. He looked up, startled. "Nathan! Where did you come from?"

"Andy," Nathan said, "I have to talk to you right now."

"Sure, just catch your breath for a minute."

"This is important," Nathan said. "You have to listen to me."

Andy put down his axe. "I'm listening."

Nathan took a deep breath. He did not know where to begin. "Let's go in the barn."

Andy dutifully followed him. Nathan closed the door and sat down on a bale of hay near the horse stable.

"What's the matter?" Andy asked.

"Look, I was over at the blacksmith shop and I overheard King Strang and Tobias Humphrey talking on the front porch of the store."

"So what did they say?" Andy asked, straddling a second bale of hay.

"They made a secret deal," Nathan said, taking a deep breath. "King Strang is going to consecrate all the timber on the entire island in the name of the Mormon Church. Tobias Humphrey will hire Mormons to cut trees and haul them to his sawmill. Humphrey will pay Strang for the timber and sell it in Chicago. King Strang is going to make a fortune."

"Well, that doesn't surprise me," Andy said. "That will give all the work to the Mormons and run the woodcutters out of business, not that there's very many of them left."

"Exactly," Nathan replied. "King Strang told Humphrey he'll use the money for the Mormon Church, but he'll just keep most of it for himself."

"But why would Humphrey pay Strang for the timber when he can buy it directly from the woodcutters?" Andy asked. "I don't think he cares about the Mormons either way. He just wants to make money."

"Because King Strang is finally going to consecrate land on the north side of the harbor for Tobias' sawmill. That means they'll tear your house down."

"My father will never let that happen," Andy said.

"Maybe not, but it's a lot worse than that. There's more to the deal than just land and money," Nathan replied.

"They've already threatened to tear our house down. What could be worse than that?"

Nathan took a deep breath. "Andy, it's about Sarah."

Andy jerked around and grabbed Nathan's arm. "What? What about Sarah?"

"I might as well just tell you straight up. Part of the deal is that Sarah must marry Humphrey."

"What!" Andy shouted. "That fat chicken bastard! I beat him up once and I'll do it again. This time I'll finish the job. I'll pound his head in and

I'll throw him in the harbor. Sarah betrothed to marry Gurdon Humphrey! Never! I'll never let him touch her!"

Andy was so agitated that Nathan jumped up and pushed him off the bale of hay to stop his tirade. "Andy," he cried, "you've got it all wrong."

"How have I got it all wrong? That's what you just told me!" Andy hollered, furiously grasping for Nathan as he fell over backwards.

Nathan grabbed Andy by both shoulders and pinned him to the floor. "Listen to me, Andy. It's not Gurdon. It's Tobias, Gurdon's father. Sarah will marry Tobias Humphrey in the spring, by command of King Strang himself!"

Andy grasped at both of Nathan's arms and ripped them away, struggling to get up. Nathan restrained him, grabbing him around the waist. They thrashed around in the hay and finally he pinned Andy to the floor, holding him in a tight grip.

"Calm down, Andy," he gasped. "I don't want you taking off on me. That won't do any good."

Inexplicably, Andy went completely limp, but Nathan kept him in a tight hold to keep him from getting up.

"Does Sarah know?" Andy asked in a wooden voice.

"I don't think so. They said they want to keep it a secret until spring."

"I'm going to have to tell her."

"Yeah, I think you should. You have to stop them."

Nathan slowly released his grip on Andy and the two boys stood up, brushing the hay off their clothes.

"God, that's disgusting," Andy said. "Do you realize that Humphrey is probably three times as old as Sarah? What a pig."

"I don't know if you've noticed, but there are a lot of older men married to young girls on this island, and most of them are arranged marriages."

"Yeah, I've noticed. They're all disgusting."

"Not only that, but Gurdon will be Sarah's stepson." Nathan said. He instantly regretted his remark, fearing it would trigger Andy's temper again.

"No, he won't," Andy replied, "because it isn't going to happen."

"What're you going to do?"

"Sarah and I will just have to leave the island. The sooner the better."

"Andy, it's winter. All the boats are pulled out and there isn't enough ice to walk across to the mainland. We're stuck here until spring."

"Dammit, I didn't think of that," Andy said. "Well, we have to do something."

"Listen, Andy, you have all winter. They're not going to do anything right away, except maybe cut some wood. Why not just lay low until spring? Who knows, maybe they'll just forget the whole thing. The boats will be running by then, and you can leave if you have to."

"Maybe you're right," Andy said, "but I'm still going to warn Sarah."

"If you tell her, you'd better both swear to keep it a secret. If Strang or Humphrey find out that you know, they might just plan an early wedding. Not only that, they might even send Butch Jenkins to burn your house down. He'd be glad to do it, I'm sure."

"Since you put it that way, we'll keep it a secret, I promise."

"You'd better, or we'll all be in trouble." Nathan said with a worried look.

"Don't worry, we will," Andy said.

"Listen, I'd better go," Nathan said, suddenly remembering that his horses were still tied up at the blacksmith shop. "I have to pick up the wagon."

Nathan slipped out the back door and Andy picked up his axe. He grabbed a chunk of firewood and placed it on the chopping block. Raising the axe, he swung with all his might, severing the wood and sending two chunks flying through the air and clattering against the side of the barn.

It wasn't until later in the week that Andy finally had a chance to talk to Sarah. He waited for her by the bell post until all the students were gone and the playground was empty. In a few minutes, Mrs. Watson came out of the school and closed the door behind her.

"Hello, Andy. Are you waiting for Sarah again?" she asked. "It's mighty cold out here."

"Yes, ma'am," Andy replied.

"She's grading some papers. She'll be out in a minute."

Mrs. Watson paused for a moment before speaking again. "Sarah's a good girl. You'll watch out for her, won't you, Andy?"

"Yes, ma'am, I will," Andy said.

"I know you will. I just don't know what's going to happen on this island."

"No, Mum," Andy replied, wondering what she was talking about.

"Well, I'm off. Wingfield will be waiting for his supper. Goodnight, Andy."

"Goodnight, Mrs. Watson."

An hour later, Sarah and Andy were sitting in an empty classroom in the schoolhouse. Andy had closed and latched all the doors so that no one would intrude upon them. They were both seated on chairs behind the teacher's desk, their knees almost touching. The fire in the woodstove had burned down to a pile of glowing embers.

Andy told Sarah everything. He told her what Nathan had overheard at the blacksmith's shop. He told her about the lumber deal and about the new sawmill. Then, without mincing any words, he told her about the plan for Tobias Humphrey to take Sarah as his bride.

At first, Sarah didn't believe it. She didn't think her father would do such a thing. Maybe Nathan had heard it wrong, she thought. She remembered her encounter with Gurdon on the piano bench and his proposal to marry her. This was worse. This was much worse.

"What are we going to do?" Sarah asked, wiping a tear from her cheek.

"I think we should follow Nathan's advice," Andy replied. "We can't get off the island until spring. We're just going to have to keep it a secret. If they find out that we know they'll probably move up the wedding. Tobias Humphrey would insist on it."

"Are you sure about this, Andy? Are you really sure?"

"Sarah, I trust Nathan. If I didn't, I wouldn't be telling you this. He sat there and heard everything they said. He's not just spreading rumors."

Sarah slammed her fist on the desk in frustration. "I can't believe my father would do this to me."

"I was meaning to ask you about that, Sarah. Why would he? He seems to care about you."

"I don't know. We haven't been that close ever since Elvira came along. It didn't exactly help when they got married and she moved into the house. Now he's got three other wives. I hardly even talk to him."

"No, I suppose not. Do you think this was Elvira's idea?"

Sarah thought for a moment. "No, I don't think so. She's not like that."

"Then who?"

Sarah stood up and walked over to the window. She gazed out at the harbor and then looked back at Andy. "Ever since my mother left the island, my father has been obsessed with his church. Mother was the only one who could ever talk any sense into him. Now he does exactly what he wants. He made himself into a king, and he thinks everyone should bow down to him. He doesn't even care about me anymore."

Andy watched her, listening.

"My mother used to have talks with him after dinner. She always reminded him that his first duty was to look out for the people who left their homes and followed him to Beaver Island. He listened to her until Elvira came along. After that, he didn't listen at all, and mother just didn't seem to care anymore. Now he only listens to Elvira, Tobias Humphrey, and Butch Jenkins. But mostly, he listens to himself."

"I'm really sorry, Sarah," Andy said, taking her hand.

"My father has arranged other Mormon marriages on the island," Sarah continued. "I suppose in a way this one makes sense, too."

Andy looked at her, startled. "Makes sense! How could it possibly make sense?"

"Think about it, Andy. Tobias Humphrey doesn't have a wife and he's the richest man on the island. And me, I'm the daughter of King Strang, the most powerful man on the island. If you believe in arranged marriages, what could be better?"

Andy thought for a moment. "I guess when you put it that way, it is a perfect—"

"Yes, perfect for them. No one ever even asked me. It makes me sick to think about it."

Andy didn't know what to say, so he just squeezed her hand.

"Andy, I want to get off this island, and I want you to go with me."

"Where do you want to go?"

"To my mother, in Wisconsin. I'll teach school and you could get a job, maybe in Milwaukee."

"Are you sure you want to leave the island?"

"I'm positive. I don't want to stay here any more. My father married a woman who dressed up as a man and then he turned her into a queen. Now he wants me to marry an old goat with a fat bully for a son. I'm sorry, but I'm not marrying anyone on this island."

"Sarah—"

"What?" She was still agitated.

"I'm on this island. Would you marry me?"

All of Sarah's frustration and anger instantly melted. She did not have to marry Tobias Humphrey and live in his house, nor did she have to be a stepmother to Gurdon Humphrey and endure his leering glares. It was so easy. All she had to do was follow her heart and marry the person she truly loved. That person was Andy McGuire.

"Oh, yes, Andy. Yes!" She took his hands in hers and held them to her face and gazed into his eyes.

"I love you, Sarah."

"I love you, too, Andy."

"I don't care what anyone thinks, as long as we are together."

"I don't care, either. We can get away from all this. They can't hurt us, as long as we love each other."

Andy put his arms around her and held her close. "We have all winter, Sarah. We'll leave for Milwaukee on the first boat in the spring. We can get married in your mother's house. Would you like that?"

Sarah put her head on Andy's shoulder.

"That would be wonderful. I'm so happy, Andy." She wiped another tear from her cheek, but this time it was a tear of joy.

CHAPTER 16:
A Secret Plan

It was a winter of secrets on Beaver Island. The harbor froze in December as it always did. But this year, instead of freezing into a smooth sheet of glass on the first cold night, it froze into a confused jumble of jagged edges, driven together by contrary winds.

As winter closed in, Sarah busied herself with her teaching. She arrived early at the schoolhouse every day to go over her lesson plan. At the end of the day she cleaned blackboards, swept the floors, and spent time on her own studies. Mrs. Watson was pleased with her work and usually left Sarah alone to teach the younger children.

When she wasn't with Andy, Sarah's home life had settled into a routine. King Strang and Elvira spent much of their time at the print shop, so Sarah often ate dinner with Betsy, Sara, and Phoebe. After the meal she retired to her room to prepare lessons. She enjoyed this quiet time of the day. The evening meetings in the living room were a thing of the past. Even Elvira had demanded that the meetings be held elsewhere, so the men now gathered after dinner in the front office of the print shop.

One day, Sarah was working in her room when she heard a knock on her door. She looked up and was surprised to see Elvira in the hall, dusting snow off her coat.

"You're home early," Sarah said. "Where's my father?"

"He's still at the print shop. A bunch of men showed up while I was working on the newspaper. They'll talk all night. I couldn't get anything done so I came home," Elvira said, tossing her hat and gloves on a chair.

"Oh," Sarah replied, remembering her confrontation with her father about the men in the living room.

"They are so loud!" Elvira said, coming into Sarah's room. "It wouldn't be so bad if they weren't so loud." Elvira seemed to want to talk.

"I know," Sarah said. "I could never get my homework done when they came over here."

"How is your teaching job at the school going?" Elvira asked.

"I like it. The kids can be a handful on some days."

"Doesn't Mrs. Watson help you?"

"Yes, but she spends most of her time with the older students."

"Sarah, you could come back and help with the newspaper sometime, if you want to."

Sarah was surprised at this offer. She hadn't worked on the paper in a very long time. "I'm really too busy teaching right now," she replied.

"Sarah, there's something I want to ask you."

"Yes?"

"It's about Butch Jenkins."

Sarah froze in her chair, poised with a pencil in her hand.

"Do you know him well?" Elvira asked.

"Not really. I mean, just through my father."

"Has he ever been friendly to you?"

"Sure, he talks to me sometimes."

"Has he ever been too friendly?"

"I don't know what you mean," Sarah replied, digging her fingernails into the pencil.

"Well, he always seems to come around the print shop when James is gone. He talks to me and he won't go away."

"What does he talk about?" Sarah asked. She was thankful again that Andy had put a latch on her bedroom door.

"Nothing! He doesn't talk about anything. One time he put his arm around me and he wouldn't let go."

"I don't think you have too much to worry about, Elvira. He has a wife."

"I know, but how often do you see her?"

"Never," Sarah admitted.

"James says she was a prostitute from Boston."

"I heard that she was a widow."

"Maybe she's both. Maybe she killed her first husband. Maybe they killed him together and came to Beaver Island to hide out."

"That's pretty unlikely—"

"But it's possible. What am I supposed to do when James travels off the island? Butch might attack me."

Sarah realized that Elvira was even more frightened of Butch Jenkins than she was, but she had no intention of telling Elvira about her own encounter with him. She knew how fast rumors could spread around the island. Still, she felt some obligation to assuage Elvira's fears.

"Elvira, why don't we both watch out for each other?"

"What do you mean?" Elvira asked.

"When you're going to be alone at the print shop, you tell me, and when I'm home alone here, I'll tell you. If we check up on each other we'll both feel safer."

"I guess that would help some..."

"If he tries anything with either one of us, I'll tell Mrs. Watson and she'll send her husband after him."

Elvira laughed. "Wingfield Watson? He's the biggest man on the island. He must weigh two hundred pounds."

"You should have seen him when they built the school. He just picked up the logs and put them in place."

"He would take care of Butch Jenkins in a hurry!"

"He sure would, and he'd probably hook him up to his oxen and drag him around town."

Elvira reached out and touched Sarah's hand. "I feel safer already. We'll look out for each other."

Sarah felt safer too. She didn't want Butch Jenkins coming around again, especially when she was alone. Now all she had to worry about was Tobias Humphrey.

⁓

In April of 1856 the island came alive again. As soon as the harbor was free of ice, boats began to arrive. Some stopped to refuel with firewood and others brought freight and passengers to the island. Most of the new arrivals were converts to the Mormon Church recruited during mission trips. Some came seeking religious freedom and some came just to make a new start, but they all came because of the promise of free land offered by the church. As soon as they arrived they hauled their meager belongings to the print shop to pay homage to the king. Strang greeted them personally in his private office and welcomed them to the island. After a brief interview he dispensed a small tract of land to each family.

Those who chose to stay and build a home were compelled to join the Mormon Church and take a vow of allegiance to King Strang. If they refused, they soon found Beaver Island to be a very uncomfortable place. At first they heard strange noises in the night, and then they noticed footprints in their yard in the morning. Soon farm tools and even livestock began to disappear. Crops were silently destroyed in the night. Occasionally a barn mysteriously burned to the ground.

Meanwhile King Strang was basking in the glory of his growing church. Every Saturday he glorified the success of his kingdom from the pulpit in the temple. He told the story of a message from God delivered to him by angels and commanding him to seek out a safe haven from all of the evils of the world. He spoke of his vision to establish a kingdom on Beaver Island for all true believers. He told them of his calling to be their leader and he spoke of his appointment by angels to be the king of the true Mormon Church.

King Strang appeared to be oblivious to the mischief taking place at night. When someone did come to him to report a crime, he pleaded ignorance, claiming that there could be no crimes among the true believers of the church. If there was any illegal activity at all, he blamed enemies who were trying to destroy him. He always made a vague assurance that he was making every effort to drive the criminals off the island for good.

One day Ian and Patrick were working on the *Emma Rose* when King Strang paid them a surprise visit. This time they didn't see him coming.

"Good afternoon, gentlemen," he said, walking out the dock toward them. "Another successful day on the lake, I trust? You always seem to bring in the biggest load of fish."

Ian and Patrick looked up when they heard his voice. They put down their tools and stood on the deck of the boat.

"As you can see, I am here alone. No distractions, shall we say?"

"Hello, King Strang. How can we help you?" Patrick asked, wiping his brow with a dirty rag.

"Ah, I have just come to pay my respects. May I ask how you weathered another Michigan winter?"

"It was a long one, but we managed."

"Yes, it was," he agreed. "We had a lot of snow this year." Strang put his foot on the bow of the *Emma Rose* and then he looked back at the two log cabins nestled in the pine trees.

"Well," he finally said, "I can see that you are busy, so I won't waste your time with small talk. I came to see what your intentions are."

"Our intentions are to catch lots of fish," Ian said. "We're going to set two extra nets this year."

"I have no doubt that you will catch lots of fish. I am here today to try again to persuade you to join our island community and our church."

"We're already part of the island community," Ian said, "but with all due respect, we don't want to join your church," Ian said.

"But on Beaver Island, the community is the church. Don't you see, everyone must join the church. We are trying to build a kingdom here."

"Listen, we've heard that before and we're not interested. We just want to make a living and raise our boys in peace. We don't want any trouble."

"Nor do I. As you can see, I came here alone today."

"I was wondering about that. Where are your henchmen?"

Ignoring Ian's sarcasm, Strang continued. "I thought it would be most beneficial to speak to you gentlemen in private."

Ian softened a little. "King Strang, you've done a lot of good things on this island, but you can't force people to join your church."

"Most people join voluntarily, for the good of the community."

"Well, we helped build the school and after that we built the lighthouse, but we're not joining your church."

"Is that your final word?"

"Yes, it is."

"Very well. I must say that my persuasive abilities appear to be failing me today. Why, just this morning I was speaking with Tobias Humphrey about his sawmill. I should tell you that he remains adamant about building a mill here on the north side of the harbor."

"This is my land and I'm not moving. You can tell him that."

King Strang sighed. "It would be much better for you if you would simply join us. Since you refuse, you make my job more difficult. However, for your sake, I shall try again to persuade Tobias to build elsewhere."

"All right, you just do that."

"I should warn you, there are people on the island who would take this land by any means necessary. I have been able to protect you for several years now, but there is not much more I can do if you are not willing to join our church. Remember, my door is always open. We can discuss this further if you wish to pay me a visit. I would not wait too long. Good day, gentlemen."

Ian and Patrick watched King Strang as he walked up the path and headed back toward Saint James. "Hogwash," Ian said. "I'm not afraid of him or his thugs." He picked up his tools and went back to work on the *Emma Rose*.

The next morning, a large X, scrawled in charcoal, appeared on the front door of Ian's cabin. Patrick noticed it first. "Ian, did you see that?" he asked, pointing at the door.

"Damn," exclaimed Ian. "They didn't waste any time, that's for sure."

"Who put it there?"

"I've got a pretty good idea."

"You think King Strang did it?" Patrick asked.

"Naw, he's too smart for that, but I'm sure he knows all about it."

"This is the second time they've marked your house."

"Last time they gave me a reprieve. This time I think they mean business."

"What do you think they're going to do?"

"Tobias Humphrey still wants this land for his sawmill. I think they're either going to torch my house or run me off the island. Either way, Tobias gets the land."

"Ian, we have to fight back. We can't let them get away with this. We own this land."

"Don't worry, I'm not afraid of them, but we're going to have to guard the house, especially at night."

"But we have to set the fishing nets. That takes all four of us."

"I don't think they'll try anything for a few days. Let's take the boys and get the nets out right away. After that, one or two of us can stay on shore and guard the house."

"But we can't watch the house all summer."

"Oh, I imagine they'll show their hand soon enough."

Ian and Patrick spent the rest of the day preparing the nets and cutting stakes to secure the nets to the bottom of the lake. Andy and Nathan loaded the nets on the *Emma Rose*, along with buoys, anchors, and several coils of rope. It was still dark the next morning when they released the dock lines and headed out to the fishing grounds.

They had only been out on the water for a few hours when they saw a plume of smoke rising over the island. It billowed above the trees in a dark cloud and drifted away across the lake.

"Andy, pull up the anchor!" Ian shouted. "Nathan, raise the mainsail. Be quick about it!"

In no time the *Emma Rose* was churning through the water, straight on a course back to the harbor. Patrick was at the helm, watching the sail and coaxing all the speed he could out of the boat. Ian was staring at the island and trying to determine the origin of the cloud of smoke.

"It could be a brush fire," Patrick said.

"Maybe it's the sawdust at the lumber mill," Andy called from the bow. "It caught fire twice last year."

"We'll find out soon enough," Ian muttered.

By the time the *Emma Rose* passed Whiskey Point and entered the harbor, it was clear that the smoke was coming from Ian's cabin. As they approached their dock, flames could be seen flashing through the windows.

"Why isn't anyone trying to put it out?" Patrick asked with dismay.

"Are you kidding?" Ian replied. "There's no Irish left on the island and the Mormons sure aren't going to help. They started the damn thing."

"Maybe it was a chimney fire," suggested Patrick.

"Oh, come on. You saw the X on the door."

"What are we going to do?" Andy shouted from the bow.

"We'll try to put the fire out and salvage what we can. You boys grab those buckets. Whatever you do, don't go inside the house. It could collapse."

Just as the bow of the *Emma Rose* touched the dock, a fountain of flames burst through the cedar shingles on the roof and exploded in an eruption of heat and sparks.

Ian watched the fire and shook his head in resignation. "We can't save it now,"he said. Boys, dump those buckets on Patrick's house to keep it from catching fire. And stay away from those flames."

Andy and Nathan hauled their buckets up the hill and splashed water on the side on Patrick's cabin, stomping out embers on the scorched grass. The flames roared through the shingles and searing waves of heat kept all of them at a distance.

By evening the house was reduced to a pile of blackened timbers and glowing embers. As the sky darkened in the west, the last of the flames flickered out and died. Ian and Andy sat next to each other on a log, forlornly staring at the remnants of their home. Not a single person from Saint James had come to help them contain the fire.

"You can sleep in our loft tonight," Patrick said. "We've got extra quilts."

"Thanks for the offer," Ian replied, "but I'm going to sleep on the *Emma Rose*. There's no telling what they'll do next. If we lose the boat we're done for."

"I'm going to sleep in the barn and keep an eye on the horses," Nathan announced.

"You can't stay out there alone," Patrick protested. "What if someone decides to torch the barn?"

"I'll stay out there, too," Andy said. "We'll take shifts."

"All right, but be careful. I'll leave the window open and you holler if anyone comes around."

Nathan and Andy trudged off to the barn, carrying a couple of old blankets. They were exhausted and covered with soot. They sacked out in a pile of hay, covering up with the blankets to keep warm.

In the morning, a few wisps of smoke still rose from the ashes of the cabin. Andy and Nathan emerged from the barn, brushing hay and soot off their clothing. Ian was already busy digging a trench between the cabins and throwing dirt on the coals. Patrick was cooking breakfast and the boys could smell eggs and bacon through the open window. Soon they were all seated at the table while Patrick poured coffee. "You know, we never had supper last night," he remarked, trying to raise everyone's spirits.

"I think we were all a little distracted," Ian replied.

"What are we going to do now?" Andy asked with a worried look on his face. "We don't have a place to live."

"Well, son, I've been thinking. That wasn't much of a house anyway. We're going to build a new house, and we'll make it bigger. We'll put some real rooms upstairs, instead of just a sleeping loft."

"Aren't you worried about Tobias Humphrey?" Patrick asked. "He'll probably want to start building his sawmill now."

"No, I'm not worried, and I'll tell you why," Ian said. "After our last encounter with King Strang, I took the deed to my property and buried it in a jar. I can still prove that I own this land."

"But they told us the deeds were fake."

"That's their opinion. If I have to, I'll go over to Mackinac Island and bring back the federal marshal. I'll tell the marshal about all of the government land that King Strang has been giving away to anyone who agrees to join his church." Ian downed the last of his coffee and slammed the cup on the table. "No one is going to chase us off this island," he declared. "We're here to stay!"

The next few weeks were a time of suspense for Andy and Sarah. The school year ended without even a rumor of an engagement between Sarah and Tobias Humphrey. It had been almost six months since Nathan had overheard Humphrey and King Strang talking in front of Johnson's store. Perhaps

Nathan had been mistaken. Perhaps King Strang had changed his mind and called the deal off. It hardly seemed possible that such a story could be kept secret on the island for so long.

On a Saturday in June, the suspense ended abruptly. At the morning church service, King Strang gave his usual sermon, extolling the virtues of the Mormon colony on Beaver Island and condemning all those who would oppose him. The congregation, many of whom were new to the island, listened in rapt attention. They had never heard such a powerful speech or such a compelling speaker.

Sarah was late to the service. She slid into a back pew next to Elvira, who wagged her finger at Sarah and smiled. Through the entire winter they had helped each other avoid the unwanted advances of Butch Jenkins, who still seemed to be on the prowl. In the process they had become confidants and even friends, of sorts. When the men had their evening meetings at the print shop, Sarah and Elvira made a pot of tea, settled down at the dining room table, and caught up on all the latest island gossip. It was an unlikely friendship; perhaps it was only a friendship of necessity, but they had grown to enjoy each other's company. There were only two subjects that Sarah kept close to her heart. She never talked about her mother and how much she missed her; it was too painful. And she never told Elvira that she and Andy were engaged to be married. That was her secret to cherish.

After a lengthy sermon, King Strang took a seat behind the pulpit. The choir stood and proceeded to struggle through several monotonous songs. Two of the church elders passed a tray, collecting offerings for the church. The service was almost over, or so it seemed. But King Strang rose and stepped up to the pulpit again.

"My brethren," he began, "Today I have a special announcement to make." He paused for effect, and the congregation grew silent.

"As your spiritual leader," he continued, "I am often called upon by many of our brethren to serve as an intermediary in matters of the heart. I serve in this capacity with great joy and today it is a special honor. Today it is my great pleasure to announce the betrothal of my daughter Sarah Strang, teacher at the school and a princess in her own right, to Tobias Humphrey, owner of the sawmill and several schooners and employer of many of you in this congregation."

Sarah froze in her seat. A murmur floated above the congregation. Several of the women turned to look at Sarah, clucking like hens, their bonnets tied tightly around their faces.

Elvira reached out and put her hand on Sarah's sleeve. "I had no idea..." she whispered.

"This may come as a surprise to many of you, but I have been observing this couple for many months. They both are outstanding members of our community and true believers in our church. I admire and love them both and I know that they will soon learn to love each other. In time, they will bring forth a multitude of children, thereby improving the breed and building the next generation of our kingdom."

Sarah grasped Elvira's hand and shoved it off her arm. She jumped up from her seat and ran out the back door of the temple. She did not stop running until she reached the front of her own house. Looking out at the harbor for the *Emma Rose*, she saw that it was gone for the day, off to the fishing grounds. With nowhere else to go, she ran into her bedroom and slammed the door.

An hour later, King Strang walked up the front steps with Elvira on his arm.

"Sarah? Sarah, are you home?"

Sarah had been waiting for them. She burst out of her bedroom door. "How could you do this to me?" she snarled.

Taken back by Sarah's ferocity, Strang replied, "I thought you would be glad—"

You humiliated me in front of everyone, just like you did to my mother when you married Elvira!"

"I have some work to finish," Elvira said. "I think I'll go to the print shop." She slipped out the door and quickly closed it behind her.

"Sarah, you can't treat Elvira like that. You just chased her away."

"I don't care! I've never been so embarrassed in my life."

"I thought you would be happy to have everyone know about your engagement."

"Why didn't you ask me first? You can't tell me who I'm going to marry."

"Church doctrine requires a father to select a good husband for his daughters. It is my duty to find someone who can provide for you."

"Church doctrine! Who wrote the church doctrine? You did! You're just trying to control my life."

"No, I'm not. I would never do that—"

"I will never marry that man," Sarah declared. "He's old and fat and I can't stand him."

"Sarah, he's a good Mormon and he's the richest man on the island. He owns the lumber mill and three schooners and he has the biggest house in Saint James. I'm sure you would like him once you get to know him."

"Father, he's old! I'm still in school."

"Yes, I'll admit he is somewhat older. But look at me and Elvira. We do just fine."

Sarah restrained herself. She did not even want to talk about how he had abandoned her mother for a young woman who dressed up like a man.

"Listen," Strang said, "Why don't you just think about it for a while. It's not like being engaged really changes anything. You don't have to get married right away. Perhaps you would like to finish school first—"

"Then what exactly am I supposed to tell Andy?"

"Who?"

Sarah threw up her hands in frustration. "Andy! Andy McGuire, who walks me home from school every day."

"Oh, Andy McGuire, the Irish boy. Why, is he courting you?"

"Yes, as a matter of fact he is, if you haven't noticed by now."

"But he's a gentile. He's just a poor Irish boy."

"Father, Andy and I are engaged."

"What! You can't be engaged!"

"Yes, we can, and we are. He asked me to marry him last winter and I said yes."

"But you never told me!"

"We kept it a secret. I wanted to finish school first."

"My, my, this does complicate things, doesn't it?"

"Not for me it doesn't."

"Well, you're just going to have to give him your regrets."

Sarah stared at him in astonishment. "Regrets? I'm not going to give him my regrets. I'm going to marry him."

King Strang slumped down in a chair in the living room and wiped his brow with a handkerchief.

"Do you love him?" he asked.

Sarah was surprised at the personal nature of the question. "Yes, very much," she responded.

"Does he love you?"

"Yes, he does."

"What are his prospects? Does he have any?"

"Oh yes, he does, Father. He's a hard worker and he knows boats and he knows how to fish. Have you seen how many barrels of fish they send off the island every week?"

Strang wiped his brow again and threw the handkerchief in a corner. "It is clear that I have inadvertently caused you emotional distress due to circumstances beyond my knowledge. I would suggest that we address this matter tomorrow when you are not so distraught."

"Fine," Sarah said, "but I'm not marrying Tobias Humphrey, and that's final."

Strang pursed his lips together. "Stubborn, just like your mother," he said to himself.

Sarah stared at him.

"Well," Strang said, rising in his chair. "I was hoping to have you meet Tobias at his house this afternoon. He has purchased a rather expensive gift for you. I shall tell him that you are temporarily indisposed. He will be disappointed, of course."

"I'm sure he will. May I go now?" Sarah asked.

"Yes, you are dismissed," Strang said wearily with a wave of his hand. He slumped back into his chair and closed his eyes.

Sarah went into her bedroom, closed the door, and fastened the latch that Andy had installed. She pulled a small parcel from the bottom drawer of her dresser. Securing it in her blouse, she opened the window, climbed up on the windowsill, and dropped silently to the grass below. After listening for a moment to be sure her father had not heard her, she tiptoed around to the back of the house and disappeared into the woods.

Sarah knew every trail to the North Beach. This time, she took the faintest of the trails to make sure no one spotted her. When she reached the bluff overlooking the lake, she jumped to the sand below, ran along the shore, and crept silently through the woods to the back of the horse barn. She expected that someone was probably guarding Nathan's cabin. Sure enough, as she approached, she could see Patrick near the dock, repairing a fish net. When he turned away for a moment she slipped through a door into the cool recesses of the barn. After her eyes adjusted to the dark, she climbed to the loft and settled down on a bale of hay to wait for Andy to return.

Late in the afternoon the *Emma Rose* rounded Whiskey Point and sailed into Paradise Bay. Sarah watched through a crack in the wall and she noticed how beautiful the white sails of the *Emma Rose* looked against the blue water of the harbor. But directly below her she could also see the charred hulk of Andy's home. The stone chimney was still standing, a forlorn monument blackened with soot. An acrid burnt smell still emanated from the ashes.

When the *Emma Rose* reached the dock, Patrick caught the bow line and Nathan jumped on the dock with the stern line. They tied the boat securely to the dock, and the routine of cleaning and packing fish began. It seemed like hours before the last barrel was full and nailed shut.

Andy and Nathan washed up and walked to the barn. As soon as they opened the door, Sarah called to them from the top of the ladder.

"Sarah! What are you doing here?" Andy exclaimed.

"Shhh! I don't want anyone to know I'm here."

"Why not?"

"Andy, we really have to talk."

Andy and Nathan threw their fishing boots in a corner and climbed up to the loft.

"What is it, Sarah? What's the matter?"

"Nathan, do you remember last winter when you overheard my father talking to Tobias Humphrey outside Johnson's Store?"

"Of course I do. How could I forget that?"

Andy interrupted. "Why, what happened, Sarah?"

"I thought maybe he had forgotten about it by now, but he finally did it."

"Who did what?"

"My father. He arranged my engagement to Tobias Humphrey."

Andy jumped to his feet. "How do you know?"

"He announced it in church this morning."

"In church! Now everyone on the island will know."

"I'm sure they already do. I was supposed to meet Mr. Humphrey this afternoon, but I climbed out my bedroom window and ran away."

"Is there any chance your father will change his mind?"

"He says that Mr. Humphrey bought me an expensive gift."

"You're not going to accept it, are you?"

"Of course not! Don't be ridiculous."

"We're going to have to leave the island. I'm not letting you marry that old geezer."

"Andy, I think there might still be a chance. My father said that I didn't have to marry him right away. I think he might be having second thoughts about the arrangement."

"Why do you say that?"

"Because I told him all about you. He's so obsessed with his church that I don't think he ever even noticed us together. He acted surprised, and then he asked me a bunch of questions."

"What kind of questions?"

"Questions about us."

"Like what?"

"He asked me if I loved you."

"And..."

"I said yes, Andy."

Nathan had been standing at the top of the ladder and listening to the conversation. He wished now that he had gone straight home. If Andy and Sarah left the island, he would probably never see them again. If they found a way to stay on the island, he would see both of them every day, with each other. "Listen," he said, "I've got to go take care of the horses."

"All right, I'll see you later," Andy said, glancing over at him and then turning back to Sarah. "So what happened next?" he asked her.

"Nothing. I mean, he didn't say anything."

"Did he change his mind?"

"No...not really. But I think he might be considering it."

Andy detected a moment of hesitation in Sarah's response. The idea of Sarah married to Tobias Humphrey was so abhorrent to him that he could barely get his words out fast enough.

"Sarah, these are the same people that burned my house down. Humphrey wants to build his sawmill on the ashes where I used to live. He wants to use this barn to store his lumber. Now he wants you for his wife! Think about it, Sarah. A year from now you might be living in the biggest house on the island, but you'll be married to an old man and you'll be cooking breakfast every morning for Gurdon Humphrey. Do you want to take a chance on that?"

"Of course not. I don't want to even think about it."

"Then we have to get off the island right away. We'll go to your mother's house in Wisconsin, just like I promised."

Sarah brightened at the thought. "All right, Andy, I'll do whatever you say."

"We're going to have to figure out how to get away from here. I don't know if you've noticed, but Butch Jenkins has his men guarding the dock whenever a boat comes in or leaves the harbor. They're sure not going to let you and me get on a boat together. Sarah, can you climb in and out of your window at night without being caught?"

"I think so, as long as I'm quiet. I did it today."

"Good. Meet me tomorrow night in the schoolyard after the moon comes up."

"Are you serious?"

"Bring a duffle bag with everything you want to take with you."

"Andy, what are we going to do?"

"I'm going to hide our bags here in the barn. The *Louisville* comes once a week from Milwaukee, so it will be here again next Friday. We're going to leave on that boat. I just need to think of a way to do it without getting caught by Butch Jenkins and his men."

"But that's impossible," Sarah said. "They'll stop us for sure."

"Don't worry, I'll figure something out," Andy replied. "Listen, you'd better get back home before your father misses you. Meet me at the school-yard tomorrow night and I'll have a plan. Trust me, Sarah."

"I do, Andy." Sarah stood up and brushed the straw from her blouse.

"Sarah?"

"Yes…"

"I love you, too. More than ever." Andy took Sarah in his arms and embraced her. She put her head on his shoulder, feeling his strength. They held each other in silence for a long time.

"Don't worry," Andy finally said, "soon this will be over and we'll be together."

"Andy…"

"Mmm…" Andy was caressing her hair with his cheek.

"If anything happens to me, you'll come and rescue me, won't you?"

"Of course I will. But don't you worry; in a few days we'll be standing on the stern of the *Louisville,* looking back at Beaver Island."

Sarah put her arms around his neck and kissed him on the cheek. She turned to go and then she stopped.

"Oh, wait, Andy. Here, I want to give you something." Sarah reached inside her blouse, pulled out a handkerchief tied in a knot, and handed it to him.

"What is it?"

"Open it."

Andy untied the handkerchief and pulled out a shiny twenty dollar gold piece.

"What's this for, Sarah? This is a lot of money."

"My mother gave me two of them before she left. She said I should use them if I ever had to leave the island. She wanted me to be able to get away and travel to Wisconsin. I think she had a premonition that something bad was going to happen."

"Where's the other one?" Andy asked.

"I kept it, so we each have one. If we get separated, we can both make our way to Milwaukee and meet at her house in Voree."

"I don't want to take your money, Sarah. Why don't you just keep it?"

"But you might need it. Please take it, Andy." Sarah took Andy's hand and closed his fingers over the coin.

"All right, but I'll give it back to you as soon as we get to Milwaukee."

"Hide it in a safe place," Sarah whispered. "I'd better get home. I'll see you tomorrow night in the school yard." She kissed him on the cheek again, climbed down the ladder, and disappeared out the barn door.

Andy stared at the empty doorway. He stood alone in the loft, turning the gold coin over and over in his hand and thinking about how he could get them both safely aboard the *Louisville*.

The next day, a strong east wind blew whitecaps into the harbor, keeping the *Emma Rose* tied to the dock. Andy was thankful that he did not have to go out on the lake, for it gave him more time to think. He spent most of the day repairing fishing nets and making plans to escape the island. By late afternoon he had finally devised a way that he and Sarah could board the *Louisville* right under the noses of Butch Jenkins' guards. It was a bold idea, but he thought it might work. He just had to figure out the final details.

Ian had been out on the dock patching a sail on the *Emma Rose*. When he finished he came up to the wreckage of the cabin and threw a few logs on the glowing embers of a campfire. A black pot of fish stew rested on a makeshift grating of stones. In a few minutes the stew started to simmer and steam. Ian dished out two bowls of stew while Andy poked at the fire with a stick.

"You're awfully quiet, son. Is anything troubling you?"

"No, I'm fine," Andy replied.

"I was just wondering," Ian said.

Andy looked over at the ashes of his home. A few weeds had grown up amid the black rubble. "What's going to happen to the house, Father?"

"We're going to start rebuilding as soon as fishing season is over. Like I said, this time we'll build a real house, not just a log cabin. Patrick and I made some sketches yesterday. Tobias Humphrey isn't going to stop us, I'll tell you that."

"Oh," Andy said. Then he asked, "What time do you think the *Louisville* will be here on Friday?"

"Probably late in the morning. We're shipping thirty barrels of fish on the *Louisville*, so you and Nathan will have to start early. It'll take about four trips with the wagon to get them all down to the dock."

"We'll be ready," Andy said.

"If this wind calms down, I'd like to head out early tomorrow and pull a couple of nets. Maybe we can pack another ten barrels before Friday."

"I guess I'll turn in early, then," Andy said. "I'm kind of tired."

"This time next year, we'll both be sleeping in a new house. How does that sound?"

"That will be great," Andy said. "See you in the morning." He rinsed off his plate and headed for the barn. He was disturbed at the thought of leaving his father alone to build the new cabin, but he could see no other way to rescue Sarah from the clutches of Tobias Humphrey.

Darkness soon fell over the harbor, so Andy caught a few hours of sleep before his midnight rendezvous with Sarah. Shortly after the moon rose, he slipped quietly out of his cot and squeezed through an opening in the barn door, taking care not to waken Nathan, who was asleep near the horses.

Sarah was waiting for him when he reached the school yard. She was sitting on the front steps of the school, a shawl wrapped around her shoulders to fend off the night chill.

Andy took her hands in his and embraced her. "I missed you today, Sarah," he said, holding her close.

"I missed you too, Andy," she said. "This morning I was wondering if we're doing the right thing. I mean, we're both going to be leaving our beautiful island."

"I know, Sarah. I feel the same way. My father—"

"But now I'm sure," Sarah continued.

"What convinced you?" Andy asked.

"This afternoon I started to go down to the boat dock. I saw Tobias Humphrey and Gurdon down there. They were on one of the lumber schooners."

"Did they see you?"

"No. I ducked into Johnson's Store and watched them through the window. Mr. Humphrey was making his sailors load more lumber on the boat and Gurdon was throwing stones at a seagull."

"That sounds typical."

"I also saw Butch Jenkins and a couple of other men on the dock. They were just hanging around, not doing anything. I think you're right, Andy. I think they're guarding the dock."

Andy confirmed her suspicions. "There are a lot more of them around when a passenger boat comes in. At first I thought they were just greeting new arrivals to the island, but now they're sticking around and watching who leaves."

"Why would they do that?"

"I'm not sure. I think they're getting worried that some Mormons will try to leave the island. I do know one thing; they sure aren't going to allow the daughter of King Strang to get on a boat."

"So what are we going to do?"

"Here's my plan, so listen carefully. The *Louisville* will be here Friday and we have to ship several wagonloads of fish. Nathan and I will bring the wagon down to the dock and roll the barrels on the boat, just like we always do. I'm going to pack our duffel bags inside an empty barrel. It will look just like the rest of them.

Sarah was with him so far. "But what about me, Andy?"

"I want you to come over to the barn early in the morning, before the sun comes up. Nathan and I are going to fix one of the barrels so you can ride in it. We'll cut some air holes and put in some blankets for cushions. After you get in we'll attach the lid and load you on the wagon with the rest of the barrels."

Sarah stared at Andy in amazement. "Are you crazy? You want to put me inside a barrel?"

"It's only a short ride around the harbor," Andy replied. "I'll let you out as soon as the boat leaves the dock."

Sarah got to her feet and paced back and forth in front of the bell post. "I won't do it," she said.

"We'll make it comfortable and we'll cut a peephole so you can see. We'll only put the lid on with—"

"Andy, there's got to be another way to get me off the island. Couldn't your father just take us across on the *Emma Rose?*"

"I thought about that, and I'm sure he would be willing to do it, but he wouldn't be able to come back. They'd charge him with kidnapping."

"What about one of the other fishermen?"

"I don't know if you've noticed, but there aren't many of them around anymore. They're still out on the lake, but they won't come into the harbor."

Sarah shivered and pulled her shawl up around her neck. "Andy, if we leave, aren't you going to miss your father and Nathan and Patrick."

"Sure, I am, but I think they're going to have to move to the mainland soon. The fishing here won't last forever, and the Mormons will probably chase them away. I've already overheard Patrick and Nathan talking about moving to Wisconsin to start a farm."

"But what about your father?"

"Well, he's stubborn. He wants to rebuild our house, but I don't think Humphrey will let him. Before we leave I'm going to talk to him about joining us later."

"That would be wonderful, Andy. He could live near us and so could Nathan and Patrick. We would all be together again"

Sarah stopped pacing and thought for a moment. Then she turned to face Andy, her hands on her hips. "You have to leave the lid loose so I can get out on my own if anything happens."

"I'll just wedge it on with a couple of sticks. You'll be able to kick it out if you have to."

"And one more thing," Sarah continued.

"What?"

"You better not put any fish in that barrel."

Andy grinned. "I'll try not to." He stood up and put his arm around Sarah and held her close.

They both looked out at Paradise Bay, perhaps for the last time. The moon had risen over Whiskey Point and moonbeams were reflecting on the water, creating a sparkling triangle of light on the harbor.

CHAPTER 17:
Assassination of the King

In the morning the lake was calm so Andy went out fishing with his father and Nathan. They pulled only one net, but it was full of fish so Ian was sure they would be able to ship an additional ten barrels on the *Louisville*. Late in the afternoon, Nathan noticed a black smudge on the horizon, signaling the distant approach of a steamboat.

"That's not the *Louisville*, is it?" Andy asked in alarm. "It's not supposed to be here until Friday."

"No, the *Louisville* doesn't put out that much smoke," Ian replied. "None of the lake boats do."

"It looks like it's headed to Beaver Island."

"If it is, we'll know soon enough what kind of boat it is. Let's get this net back in the water, and we'll head for home."

Andy and Nathan pulled out the last of the fish and lowered the net. Ian raised the mainsail, grabbed the tiller and set a course for Saint James. An hour later, they sailed past Whiskey Point and into the harbor. Behind them, the black smudge on the horizon had turned into a billowing cloud of smoke. They could make out a smokestack, a black hull, and the white spray of churning water on either side of the hull.

"It's a sidewheeler!" Andy shouted from the bow. "A big one!"

"It's fast, too," Nathan said. "It sure caught up with us in a hurry."

"I think that might be the *Michigan*," Ian said. "It's been here before, but we missed it."

"What's the *Michigan*?" Andy asked.

"It's the only war ship on the Great Lakes. It's owned by the United States Navy."

"A war ship!" Andy said with excitement, standing on top of the cabin and hanging onto the mast. "That boat is huge. I wonder why it's coming here."

"Maybe they're going to tell Tobias Humphrey he can't have my property," Ian joked. "After all, I did pay my taxes."

Andy and Nathan both ran to the stern to watch the *Michigan* as it entered the harbor. It was the biggest boat they had ever seen on Lake Michigan. The powerful black hull plunged ahead through the water and two huge paddlewheels churned the lake into foam. The smokestack belched forth a plume of black smoke and a shower of fiery orange sparks. The ship's whistle let out a piercing shriek, announcing the ship's arrival to the people of Saint James.

"Can we go down to the dock and look at it?" Andy asked.

"No," Ian replied. "We've got to get these fish in barrels and salted down or they'll rot."

"Can we go after that?"

"It'll be pretty late. Why don't you go first thing in the morning. I'm sure they'll spend the night here."

"Awww..." Andy and Nathan said in unison.

"You'll be able to get closer then. They may even let you on board."

That thought cheered the boys up. As soon as they reached the dock they both set to work cleaning and packing fish, covering them with salt, and rolling barrels off the dock. Ian was right; it was almost dark by the time they finished. They all had a quick supper and Andy and Nathan headed to the barn for the night.

Andy was excited about seeing the *Michigan*, but it hadn't kept him from thinking about his approaching rendezvous with the *Louisville*. As soon as he went to bed he remembered that Friday was only two days away. He lay awake in the dark until he finally convinced himself that his escape plan would work. But he was still troubled by the thought of leaving his father. He loved and respected him more than any man. Andy knew that everything Ian had done since they left Ireland had been for his welfare and future. Tomorrow he would have to tell him that he and Sarah were leaving the island. Perhaps he could convince his father to finish out the fishing season and sail the *Emma Rose* to Milwaukee in the fall.

Andy also thought about Nathan. They had grown up together back in Ireland. They had survived the famine and crossed the ocean to a new country and a new life. Through it all, they had remained the closest of friends. Andy would miss him almost as much as he would miss his father.

Even worse, Andy was worried about Sarah. She was taking the greatest risk of all by following him. What if she was discovered in the barrel? Andy had no doubt that she would be dragged away and that a quick wedding to Tobias Humphrey would be her fate.

Andy lay on his cot in the darkness for a long time, warmed by his love for Sarah and distracted by his fears for her safety. Finally the hollow silence of the barn lulled him into a deep sleep.

As Andy slept, Sarah was reading by candlelight in her bedroom. She was trying to concentrate, but she couldn't keep her mind on her book. It didn't seem possible that she would be leaving her island home in a few days.

There was a knock on her bedroom door. "Sarah? Are you still awake?" It was her father.

"Yes, I am," she replied.

"May I come in?"

"Yes." Sarah got out of bed and unlatched the door.

"Reading again?" King Strang asked. "It's very late."

"It's a book from school."

"We have a lot of books at the print shop."

"I know. I've looked at most of them." Sarah noticed that her father seemed unusually subdued. Perhaps it's just the lateness of the hour, she thought.

"Sarah, I've been thinking…"

Sarah stiffened and closed her book.

"Have you changed your mind at all about your engagement to Tobias Humphrey?"

"He's three times older than I am. I don't even know him."

"He is a good Mormon. I think he will be a good husband for you."

"I already told you, father, I don't want to marry Tobias Humphrey."

"Are you sure? I just want what's best for you. I want you to be happy, Sarah."

Sarah tossed her book on the floor in frustration. "Father, I am happy. I'm happy with Andy. Haven't you seen us together? He already asked me to marry him, but you're telling me I have to marry an old man. Why do I have to marry an old man?"

"In the Mormon faith, the father traditionally arranges the marriage of the daughter."

"You already told me that, but I don't want to marry him. I want to marry Andy McGuire."

"Well, what shall I tell Tobias?"

"Tell him the engagement is off. Please, Father!"

King Strang stood up and walked over to the window. He opened it a few inches, letting in a breath of cool evening air.

"Your mother told me when she left the island that I was a selfish man. I must confess that it is true. I have been thinking only of myself. Through my own perseverance I have become the spiritual leader of the Mormon Church, but thus far the wealth I have longed for has eluded me. Perhaps I wanted to see you with Tobias only to strengthen my own position on the island."

"Father, we don't need riches…"

"You are absolutely correct, my dear," Strang said, turning back to Sarah. "We already have everything we need right here."

Strang opened the window all the way, allowing a gust of air to blow into the room.

"I have made a decision," he announced. "Tomorrow I shall summon Tobias Humphrey. I'll tell him you already have a suitor and I must call off the engagement. Of course, he will not be pleased—"

Sarah jumped up on her bed. "But I will! I'll be the happiest girl on Beaver Island. Oh, thank you, Father! I'll tell Andy—"

Strang whirled around and slammed the window shut behind him. "You'll do no such thing! You know how news travels on this island. You must allow me to speak to Tobias in private. No one must know until I have spoken to him, is that clear?"

Chastened but still joyful, Sarah sat still on the corner of her bed. "I promise, father. I won't tell anyone."

"Sarah, you must understand that I am placing myself in a most difficult position. Tobias Humphrey is a rich and powerful man. I have made promises and now I must go back on my word. I shall have to approach him in a manner that will allow him to retain his dignity. Perhaps I can persuade him that it is he who should break off the engagement. That would allow him to save face."

"I don't understand…"

"That's because you only see me as King Strang, the leader of the Mormons. You do not realize that there are powerful forces on this island that oppose me. Even within our own church there are people who regard me as a false prophet. Indeed, I have had premonitions that a day will come when my work will be done and I shall be obliged to leave the island."

"But, Father, you have done so much here."

"That is true. I have created civilization from a savage wilderness, but along the way I have made many jealous enemies."

"Please don't talk like that, Father. It upsets me."

"Do not despair, my child. I will stay until my work is done, I promise you that."

"You will be here a long time, Father."

"Ah, the optimism of youth!" Strang said. "Come, my dear, you must get to bed. I shall speak to Tobias Humphrey tomorrow and attend to your happiness."

Sarah climbed into bed and scrunched down under the covers.

"Goodnight, Sarah."

"Goodnight, Father. I love you."

"I love you too, Sarah."

King Strang blew out the candle and closed the door behind him. Sarah rolled over in her bed and hugged her pillow, as if it contained all the wonderful things the day had brought to her. She didn't fully understand what had made her father change his mind. All that mattered was that she would not have to marry Tobias Humphrey. She was free to marry Andy and they wouldn't have to leave the island after all. With this final joyous thought, Sarah drifted off to sleep.

Andy and Nathan were awake before dawn. They had a quick breakfast and hurried off to Saint James to see the *Michigan*. By the time they got to the village a crowd had already gathered on the dock, and there was also a large group of men standing in front of Johnson's Store.

"Where did all these people come from?" Nathan asked.

"I have no idea," Andy replied. "It's amazing how many people come out of the woods when a boat comes in."

"We're going to have to squeeze through this crowd if we want to see anything."

"You go ahead," Andy said. "I'm going to climb up on this woodpile to get a better view. I'll join you in a few minutes."

"All right. Meet me by the bow," Nathan replied. He left Andy and edged his way through the crowd to get closer to the ship.

Andy circled around to the back of the woodpile and climbed up the logs until he found a good vantage point. The *Michigan* was tied to the dock directly in front of him, with the harbor and Whiskey Point in the background.

The *Michigan* was an impressive vessel. It was the first iron-hulled ship on the Great Lakes. Two massive paddlewheels towered above the hull on each side, giving an impression of strength and stability. By treaty with the British government, the *Michigan* only carried one cannon, but this formidable weapon was prominently displayed on the forward deck. As Andy watched, a crew of sailors lowered a gangplank. They secured it to the dock and several armed marines marched down and took guard positions near the bow and stern.

Although the dock was piled with stacks of wood, there was plenty of room for spectators. From Andy's perch he could see several groups of Mormon farmers talking excitedly amongst themselves and looking in awe at the *Michigan*. Most of them had never seen a military vessel before, so this was quite an event for Beaver Island.

Andy looked around and saw a group of men making their way through the stacked logs. Leading the procession was King Strang himself, dressed in a fine robe and wearing a black top hat. He was accompanied by Tobias Humphrey, Butch Jenkins, and several men whom Andy recognized as leaders of the Mormon Church. They were headed for the *Michigan*, and they were clearly on a mission of some importance.

As Andy watched, several men came down from Johnson's Store and fell in line behind the king's entourage. Two of them, both wearing long over-coats, broke away from the group and ran behind a pile of logs on the far side of the dock. Andy lost sight of them until they reappeared in a narrow passage between the logs, directly across from him. They crept forward and peered around the log pile at King Strang and his followers.

Andy recognized both of the men. One of them was Thomas Bedford, one of the original Mormons to arrive on Beaver Island. He had been a loyal member of the Mormon Church until he became disenchanted with King Strang, calling him a false prophet and demanding that he give up his throne. For his transgression Bedford was strapped to a post and whipped in public.

He had never forgiven Strang for the pain and humiliation he had endured. The other man was Alexander Wentworth, a man of questionable background and a relative newcomer to the island. He was a fancy dresser with a reputation as a womanizer and with no apparent means of support.

As King Strang passed by, Bedford and Wentworth took off their overcoats and fell in step behind him. Andy saw that they had pistols stuck in their belts. To his horror, they pulled their weapons and aimed them directly at King Strang's head.

"King Strang!" he shouted. "Look out! They're going to kill you!"

Andy jumped to his feet and leaped off the woodpile, throwing his body against Strang and knocking him over. As they hit the ground, Andy heard two shots and felt a fiery blast slash across his shoulder. He fell on the dock, tangled with the king and rolling in the sawdust. Bedford and Wentworth were upon them in a second. Strang lay in the dirt, clutching his face with his hands. Andy reached through a cloud of smoke and grabbed Wentworth's pistol, yanking it from his grasp. Wentworth fell, then scrambled to his feet and ran away in the direction of the *Michigan*.

When Andy turned around, Bedford was clubbing King Strang in the head with the butt of his pistol. Before he could even move, he saw Butch Jenkins grab Bedford, spin him around and slug him in the jaw. Bedford dropped his pistol and fell to the ground, but before Jenkins could hit him again he stumbled to his feet and ran after Wentworth.

The dock was a scene of panic and bedlam. "Grab them! Don't let them get away!" Butch Jenkins shouted. He turned toward Andy and charged at him with a ferocious roar.

Andy dropped Wentworth's pistol and ran toward the *Michigan*, but instead of running up the gangplank behind Thomas Bedford, he veered away and darted between two piles of logs. Jenkins was right behind him but he was stopped by the marines and forced back at gunpoint.

Andy ran behind the logs stacked along the edge of the dock. Two other men came running after him, shouting at him to stop, but he was too fast. When he neared the shore, he jumped off the dock into a willow thicket and thrashed through the underbrush. The men jumped after him, but he burst out of the thicket and ran down the beach, leaving them tangled in the bushes.

Andy did not stop running until he reached the shelter of a thick grove of cedar trees on the south side of the harbor. He stumbled between the tree trunks and found a safe hiding place behind a fallen log. Looking back, he saw that the men had given up the chase and were returning to the boat dock. He collapsed in the weeds, his heart pounding and his mind racing in confusion. Everything had happened so quickly. In a few seconds, two of King Strang's own men had assaulted him in the middle of a crowd. Andy had tried to save him, but no one could survive shots like that at close range. With all the smoke and dust he could not be sure, but he had probably failed to save King Strang.

Andy had seen Bedford and Wentworth both make their escape to the *Michigan*. It was almost as if they had planned their getaway. Why had the guards let them run up the gangplank? Why had they stopped Butch Jenkins at gunpoint and forced him back to the dock? Most of all, why had Jenkins chased *him*? It didn't make sense. Andy was sure he had saved King Strang from the first shot by throwing him to the ground, but the second shot had probably killed him. Did Jenkins and those other men think he had something to do with the attack on the king?

Andy was bewildered and exhausted, but at least he had escaped. He crouched behind the log, hidden from view, and peered at the dock. The marines had marched back on the *Michigan* and two sailors were pulling up the gangplank. The Mormons were huddled on the dock, talking amongst themselves and shaking their fists in the air. One of them picked up a stone and hurled it at the *Michigan*. There was no sign of King Strang. Andy thought he must be hidden in the crowd of Mormons.

But where was Sarah? Andy had not seen her all morning. Surely she must have heard the gunshots. Andy watched the crowd carefully, thinking she may have come down to the dock after he escaped to the woods, but she was nowhere in sight.

It suddenly occurred to him that Sarah might be in danger. He was not sure why King Strang had been attacked, but if he was dead then Sarah was alone and vulnerable. He knew she was afraid of someone and had been for a long time, but she had never divulged his identity to Andy. He remembered the lock she had made him install on her bedroom door. Whoever it was, it must be someone who had frequent access to her house.

"Tobias Humphrey!" Andy jumped to his feet. Humphrey had spent many evenings at Strang's house. Had he accosted Sarah late at night when no one else was home? Was that why she was so frightened?

All winter Andy had assumed that Tobias Humphrey was going to bide his time until King Strang set a wedding date. Perhaps Strang had called off the wedding, or perhaps Humphrey's lust for Sarah had overcome him. With all of his money it would have been easy for Humphrey to arrange an attack on King Strang. He could have hired Bedford and Wentworth to do the job. That would draw suspicion away from him, and he would be free to have his way with Sarah. That all made sense, but how had Bedford and Wentworth been able to escape so easily to the safety of the *Michigan*?

Sarah did not hear the shots. She was several blocks away, in the back of her house scrubbing pots and pans. Today even this tedious job brought her pleasure, for she knew that soon her father would be telling Tobias the engagement was off. She could barely wait for him to return, for then she could tell Andy the wonderful news. There would be no need to pack their bags, no need hide in a fish barrel, no need to escape Beaver Island. They could be married and live on their island home forever. Her heart was full of love for Andy and for her father, who had changed so much in only one night.

When Sarah went out to the well to get water she noticed that a large crowd had gathered at the boat dock. Many of the men were shouting and shaking their fists, apparently at the *Michigan*. Some of them were even throwing stones and she could hear a metallic clink as the stones hit the iron sides of the steamship. Sarah put down her bucket and walked to the front of the house, wondering what was causing the ruckus. She soon had her answer.

A boy came running up the hill and stopped at the fence. "He's been attacked!" he shouted. "King Strang's been attacked!"

"What!" Sarah cried. "What happened?"

The boy turned and pointed. "Here they come now. They're bringing him here."

Sarah looked and saw a cluster of men coming up the hill and carrying a stretcher. Elvira was running ahead of them. Sarah opened the gate and started down the hill but Elvira waved her back.

"It's James!" Elvira called. "He's been shot!"

"Oh, my God!" Sarah exclaimed, starting forward again.

"It's bad, Sarah. Get some water. Quickly!"

Sarah ran back to the pump, grabbed a bucket of water and some clean rags, and hurried back into the house. By the time she reached the hall several men had crowded into a bedroom and were moving King Strang into a bed.

"Hurry, Sarah!" Elvira called. "We've got to stop the bleeding."

Sarah pushed her way through the crowd and was horrified to see her father covered with blood. She tossed a rag to Elvira and grabbed another rag from the bucket. Elvira immediately pressed her rag over a bleeding wound in King Strang's head.

"Elvira, what happened?" Sarah asked. "Who did this?"

"Two men shot him and ran on the *Michigan*. Andy tried to save him."

"But why——"

Elvira lifted her rag for a moment and blood gushed from the king's head. "Never mind! I need you to hold this rag. We've got to tie it off!"

Sarah took the rag and Elvira moved around to the other side of the stretcher, jostling with several of the men who were crowding around.

"Out! Out!" Elvira yelled. "We can't do anything with everyone standing in the way."

They all moved back and Sarah helped Elvira tie a neat knot in the rag. Elvira then took a smaller rag and wedged it under the knot.

"There," she said. "At least we have that under control."

The men were crowding in again, trying to see the king's injuries.

"Please," Sarah pleaded, "We need some privacy. Could you please wait in the other room?"

The men shuffled out and Elvira slammed the door behind them. "Thank God!" she said. "Now we can look him over and see where else he's hurt."

His heart still pounding, Andy climbed over the log and weaved back through the woods. He was not afraid of the men who had chased him. There were only two of them, and he knew he could outrun them. All he could think of was finding Sarah and rescuing her from Tobias Humphrey. Before he reached the dock, Andy cut through the beach grass in front of the Mormon temple. The building was empty and there was not a soul on the road leading to the dock. Even the sailors on the *Michigan* had gone below deck. It was as if the entire village had recoiled in shock and disappeared.

Andy circled around the temple and climbed the steep bank to the bluff overlooking the harbor. He approached King Strang's house and saw no one, but he heard the murmur of voices through an open window. "So that's where everyone is," he thought. They must have brought King Strang here and Sarah must be inside. Andy looked around the yard and down the street, but he could see no sign of his pursuers. He had been in Strang's house many times, so he reasoned he was safe from further pursuit.

He walked up the porch steps and knocked on the front door. A face appeared briefly in a window. Someone closed the curtains and slammed the window shut. Andy heard footsteps and the muffled sound of a door slamming, as if someone had gone out the back of the house.

Andy knocked again. The door flew open and there was Butch Jenkins.

"You!" Jenkins cried, lunging at Andy.

Andy turned and fled down the porch steps—right into the clutches of the two men who had chased him off the dock.

"Grab him! Don't let him get away!" Jenkins shouted.

"We've got him this time," one of the men said, wrenching Andy's arm behind his back.

"Let go of me!" Andy shouted, struggling to get free.

The two men grabbed Andy by both his arms and held him tight.

"Tie him up," Jenkins ordered. "We can't take any chances. He's a slippery one."

"Leave me alone! I didn't do anything."

Jenkins marched down the porch steps and slugged Andy in the stomach, making him bend over and gasp in pain. Then he grabbed him by the chin and forced his head up in the air. One of the men pulled Andy's arms behind him and tied his hands together with a stout rope.

"Let go of him," Jenkins said. "I'll deal with him now."

The two men released Andy. Jenkins pushed him and he fell backwards, landing in the dirt with a thud.

Jenkins towered over him. "Your plot to kill King Strang failed. Your two accomplices escaped, courtesy of the United States Navy. But we caught you, and we have our own laws here. Now you'd better talk, and fast."

"What accomplices?" Andy protested. "I tried to save the king!"

"Don't give me that crap. We all saw you jump on him."

"I was trying to save him! I saw Bedford and Wentworth pull their guns and I was trying to knock King Strang out of the way. Look, I even got shot myself." Andy rolled on his side and gestured with his chin to the red welt across his shoulder.

"Well, ain't that convenient," Jenkins sneered. "Too bad your partners ain't better shots. They might have got you instead."

"I'm telling you, they're not my partners."

"Don't lie to me. There were three of you and I want to know who put you up to this."

"No one!" Andy struggled to roll over and finally made it to a sitting position. Even though he was tied, the two men moved in and grabbed his arms again. "No one put me up to anything. I told you, I was trying to save the king."

"You'd better search him," Jenkins said. "He's probably got a weapon."

One of the men patted Andy down, looking for a knife. He put his hand in Andy's pocket and pulled out a handkerchief tied in a knot.

"Gimme that," Jenkins said, grabbing it. "Now what do we have here?" Jenkins turned the handkerchief over in his hand and examined it. "This is a mighty fine ladies handkerchief you've got here, boy. It has the initials 'M.S.' stitched in the corner. I don't suppose that stands for 'Mary Strang', now does it?"

Andy remained silent, knowing already that Jenkins was going to make the most of his new find. Jenkins untied the handkerchief and pulled out the twenty dollar gold piece, the one that Sarah had given to him several days ago. Jenkins held it up and examined it in the sunlight.

"You stole this from Mary Strang, King Strang's wife."

"I did not! Sarah gave it to me."

"So Sarah stole it from her own mother and gave it to you? That's just as bad, I'd say."

"She didn't steal it. Her mother gave it to her a long time ago and she gave it to me. It's just a loan. I'm going to pay her back."

"I don't believe it. You lie."

"It's true!"

"I'll tell you what I think is true," Jenkins said, reaching down and grabbing Andy by the neck. "I think you stole this money from Mary Strang so you could run away with her daughter. Then when you found out King Strang had promised her to someone else, you decided to to kill him, because that's the only way you would ever get the King's daughter for yourself. We've seen you following her around all winter like a little puppy, and everyone on the boat dock saw you jump on the king and hold him down. About the only thing you didn't do was pull the trigger. There are plenty of witnesses. I saw you holding a pistol, and now I have this coin and handkerchief as hard evidence. The only thing I don't know is how you got Bedford and Wentworth to help you."

Andy realized he was in serious trouble. "Where's my father?" he asked. "I want to see my father."

"I'm sure you'll be seeing your father soon enough," Jenkins replied with an evil grin.

"What do you want to do with him?" one of the men asked.

"Throw him in the jail for now. We'll give him a trial after the *Michigan* leaves."

"But the building's not finished yet."

"Is the blacksmith done with his work? Does the door on the cage lock?"

"Yes, but—"

"Then throw him in there. We'll let him sit for a few days and maybe he'll tell us the truth. I've got a pretty good idea, but I want to hear it from him."

Jenkins abruptly turned and went back inside the house, slamming the door behind him. The two men yanked Andy up off the ground.

"On your feet, boy."

"Where are you taking me?"

"Didn't you hear Butch? We're taking you to jail."

"But Beaver Island doesn't have a jail."

"If you hadn't been chasing girls all winter, you might have noticed we've been building one."

"Where is it?"

"It ain't far. Now shut up and get moving."

Andy stumbled along between the two men. When they reached the Mormon print shop, they cut through the weeds to the back of the building. Underneath a tree there was a cage made of iron bars. It was only about five feet high and it had a small hatch on one end. Someone had started to build a wooden enclosure, but the work was far from complete, and the cage was still exposed to the sun and rain.

"This is a jail?" Andy asked. "It looks more like a cage for animals."

"That's exactly what it is," replied one of the men. "A cage for animals. Now get in there."

They forced Andy to his knees and pushed him through the hatch. When he was inside, they slammed the hatch behind him and locked it with a heavy iron padlock.

"Now you stay right here."

"Yeah, and don't try to run away." Both men laughed and walked away without looking back.

For the first time in his life, Andy was terrified. He had known fear back in Ireland, but it was the fear of a hungry boy. Now he knew terror. With one act of bravery his life had been turned upside down, and now he was trapped in a cage, held by his worst enemies. Desperate to escape his prison, Andy rattled the latch, pried on the lock, and pulled on every iron bar in a futile attempt to find a way out, but he soon realized it was useless. The cage was solid.

Andy collapsed in a corner, exhausted and hoping that someone would find him soon. Sprawled in the dirt, he found that if he peered around the corner he had a glimpse of the boat dock and the *Michigan*. At least he could get some idea of what was going on in the harbor. Late in the afternoon, he saw a puff of black smoke rising from the *Michigan's* smokestack. The engines had been started and the paddlewheels began turning. Andy could hear the dull thud of each piston as the sound reverberated across the harbor. The ship backed away from the dock, turned slowly, and headed out of the harbor.

There go the two men who know I am innocent, Andy thought, and they are both murderers. Thomas Bedford hated King Strang and Alexander Wentworth had renounced the Mormon Church, so they both had a motive. But was it enough to want to kill? And why did they shoot King Strang in front of just about every Mormon on the island? Even if there was a conspiracy, and even if Tobias Humphrey was involved, it still didn't make sense to shoot the King on a crowded dock swarming with Mormons. Or did it?

When the sun went down Andy dozed fitfully and tried to sleep. There was nothing else he could do. Shortly after dark he was startled by a man crawling through the bushes. Andy recognized him as a Mormon farmer from the center of the island. He seldom came to town and Andy did not know his name. He crouched in a corner, watching the man with suspicion.

"Shhh. No one knows I'm here. I'll be in trouble if anyone sees me," the man whispered.

"What do you want?" Andy asked.

"Listen, I was at the boat dock today. I saw those two men shoot the King and I saw you try to save him. I know you're innocent."

Andy crawled over to the man and grabbed the iron bars between them. "Can you get me out of here?" he pleaded.

"No, it's too dangerous. But I brought you a blanket. Here, pull it between the bars."

"Thanks," Andy said, tugging on the blanket. "What's your name?"

"Never mind. Here's a loaf of bread and a flask of water. It's the best I could do. They weren't even going to feed you."

"What about King Strang? Is he alive?"

"He was when they took him to his house. That's all I know."

"Did you see Sarah Strang?"

"Nope. Never saw her."

"Do you know anyone that can get me out of here?"

"Maybe, but I can't make any promises," the man said. "You're going to have to be patient."

"I'll try," Andy said. "Thank you for the food. I'll pay you back, I promise."

"Don't worry about it. You'll need that blanket. It's going to get cold tonight."

Before Andy could reply, the mysterious visitor disappeared into the night. The blanket, food, and encouraging words cheered Andy considerably. He was still trapped, but at least one person on the island knew he was innocent. Tomorrow someone would find him and he would be released. Butch Jenkins had no right to lock him up. He wasn't the sheriff or even a deputy.

Andy tore off a big hunk of bread and stuffed it in his mouth. He hadn't eaten since early that morning so he quickly finished almost the entire loaf. After taking a long drink from the flask, he stretched out in a corner of the cage and covered himself with the blanket to ward off the night chill. Help would surely come in the morning. As soon as he got out, he would find Sarah and tell her everything that had happened. Together they would expose Tobias Humphrey's plot to kill the King. He could identify the two gunmen, so he would testify against them when they were brought back to the island. All three of the men would be spending a long time in prison. If Tobias Humphrey went to jail, he and Sarah would not have to leave the island after all. With this comforting thought, Andy closed his eyes and dozed off to sleep.

Sarah would have no rest that night. After the men were gone she and Elvira tightened the rags on King Strang's head to make sure the bleeding had stopped. Then they cleaned up the blood that had soaked his hair and streamed down his neck. In addition to his head injury he had been pistol-whipped, so his face was a mass of bloody bruises. They could to nothing but cover the wounds with wet rags to ease the pain and reduce the swelling.

The King had not moved or spoken but he was breathing steadily so they were hopeful that he might survive. Even though he had lost a lot of blood, they both believed that the head injury was only a deep scalp wound and that it would heal with proper care.

Late in the afternoon they heard the back door slam and steps in the hall. In a moment Edith Watson came bustling into the room.

"I heard what happened. I'm sorry I couldn't get here sooner," she exclaimed. "What can I do to help?"

Sarah and Elvira both ran to her side, grateful to see the older woman.

"We've done everything we could," Sarah said. "We don't know what else to do."

"Well, let me see," Edith said. "I did some nursing before I became a schoolteacher. Do you mind if I take a look?"

"Please," Elvira said. "His head was bleeding. We put a bandage on it."

Edith lifted the sheet covering King Strang's face. She paused and took a deep breath, shocked at the sight of his injuries.

"Has the bleeding stopped?" she asked.

"Yes, mostly."

Edith poked and pulled at the bandage. She lifted up a corner and looked at the wound.

"It is a long and deep cut, but it can be stitched together. You did a good job, ladies."

Sarah and Elvira came over to the bed to watch Edith make her examination. She looked carefully at the King's face, gently running her fingers over the bruises. She stopped at his right cheek and massaged the swollen tissue, feeling with her fingers. Just below his eye she located a small hole and deep in the flesh she felt a solid lump.

"I have bad news," she said. "He's been shot. See there? Before they beat him, he was shot in the face. The bruises mean nothing, but there's still a bullet in there. I can feel it."

"Can we get it out?" Elvira asked.

"No, it's too deep and too close to his eye. Only a doctor could get it out, and I'm not even sure about that."

"But there's no doctor on the island," Sarah said.

"We need to get him to a hospital on the mainland," Edith replied. "He's stable now, but there's no telling how long he will remain so. He needs to go as soon as possible or he may die."

"But how—"

"Wingfield and I met with Tobias Humphrey and some of the brethren after the *Michigan* departed. Tobias was at the dock this morning so he saw what happened. He offered to take King Strang and a few passengers to Milwaukee on his schooner, the *Lumber Baron*. There's a hospital there and Tobias knows a good doctor. This may save the King's life. Sarah, will you go?"

Sarah hesitated. For the first time since morning Sarah thought about her ordained betrothal to Tobias Humphrey, her plans to run away with Andy, and her father's last-minute decision to break off the engagement. Had her father had a chance to talk to Tobias? If so, was Tobias angry? If not, would he still expect her to marry him? Sarah did not know. She only knew that right now her father needed her.

"Sarah?"

"Yes, of course I'll go." It was the only answer she could give. She must do everything she could to save her father's life.

Throughout the evening and into the darkest hours of the night Sarah, Elvira and Edith kept vigil over King Strang's prostrate form. They kept his wound covered and patted his face with damp rags, but there wasn't much else they could do. His breathing was steady and he didn't seem to be in any pain, so they were all hopeful that he would be able to survive the long trip to Milwaukee.

As dawn began to break over Paradise Bay, Sarah prepared a travel bag for herself and her father. She included blankets, pillows, extra clothing, and a bag of medical supplies that Edith prepared for her. Although she had not seen nor heard from Andy all night, she fully expected to see him at the boat dock. Indeed, she planned to ask him to accompany her on the *Lumber Baron*. She knew Tobias would not like it, but at least if Andy were along he could help her. Not knowing if her father had broken off the engagement, Sarah had her misgivings about Andy being on board, but she missed him so much that she was willing to risk the wrath of Tobias Humphrey.

Several men arrived to transport King Strang to the *Lumber Baron*. As they were carrying him out the front door, King Strang spoke for the first time.

"Don't go, Sarah," he said in a weak voice. "Don't get on the boat."

"Did you hear that?" Edith said. "He's getting stronger already. Don't worry, Sarah, he'll be better soon and you'll be back before you know it!"

Something in her tone made Sarah doubt that Mrs. Watson believed her own words. She looked around desperately for Andy. Not seeing him anywhere, she had no choice. She hurried after the men carrying the stretcher and walked beside her father as they headed toward the *Lumber Baron*.

Andy woke to the sound of activity down at the dock. He rolled over and saw the masts of the *Lumber Baron*. Several sailors were unfurling the sails. It looked like they were getting ready to take on another load of lumber for shipment to Milwaukee. He expected them to begin loading the vessel but instead most of them went below. A couple of men remained on deck and loitered around as if they were waiting for someone. One of them sat down on a hatch cover and lit a pipe.

Andy wrapped the blanket around his shoulders. Stiff and cold, he lay back down and closed his eyes. He thought of the visit from the mysterious stranger during the night. This would be his last day in jail, he was sure of that. Someone would be along soon to release him.

After dozing for about an hour, Andy heard a commotion. The sailors had congregated on the dock and a group of Mormons had joined them. Andy recognized most of them. They had all been on the dock when King Strang was shot. Andy saw that Butch Jenkins was among them, holding a shotgun and watching the crowd.

Several men came into view, carrying a stretcher shrouded with blankets. A hooded figure, much shorter than the rest of them, walked beside the stretcher. Andy realized immediately that King Strang was on the stretcher and that the hooded figure might be Sarah, tending to her stricken father. As the group approached the dock, the waiting men gathered around them. Several of the men brandished pistols and shotguns.

Andy quickly surmised what was happening. Dead or alive, they were taking King Strang away on Tobias Humphrey's schooner. Sure enough, when they reached the end of the dock they carried the stretcher up the gangplank and laid it gently on the deck. He watched the hooded figure standing next to King Strang, his hands gripping the bars that imprisoned him. The figure kneeled and the hood fell away. It was Sarah! She spread a blanket over her father, raised her head, and seemed to be looking around the harbor. She looked pale and distraught. Andy waited for her to stand up and get off the boat, but she remained kneeling and turned her attention back to her father.

Two figures emerged from the crowd of Mormons on the dock and boarded the boat. It was Tobias and Gurdon Humphrey. They stopped at the prostrate form of King Strang and looked down at him. Gurdon appeared to speak to Sarah, but she did not look up, so he turned away and went into the ship's cabin. Tobias Humphrey waved his arm and shouted something to the men on the boat. They jumped to their feet and began hauling in the dock lines.

Andy watched in horror. They were taking Sarah away with them! When they got to Milwaukee, they would keep her prisoner and pretend to be concerned about King Strang. If he lived, they would force her to marry Tobias Humphrey. If he died...well, they probably didn't care if King Strang lived or died. Either way, Humphrey had what he wanted. He was kidnapping Sarah and he would make her his bride!

Andy grabbed the bars and pulled at them in a desperate attempt to escape his cage. He pounded his fists against the hatch and tried to spread the bars with his shoulders, but they would not budge. "Sarah!" he shouted, "Sarah, don't go! Get off the boat!"

She could not hear him. The men on the dock pushed the boat away and two sailors raised the main sail. The sail filled and the boat turned into the wind and began to move out of the harbor.

"Sarah, don't go! Don't go!" Andy screamed. He pounded with fury against the prison bars that held him.

No one heard him. No one, that is, except Butch Jenkins. Jenkins looked up and turned in Andy's direction. He lifted his shotgun, pointed it at Andy and fired. The men on the dock all laughed and several of them also raised their guns and fired. Andy heard bullets whistling overhead and he dove for cover, burying his face in the dirt.

When the men stopped shooting they ambled away, laughing among themselves and pointing at Andy. Andy raised his head and peered out the corner of his cage. His heart sank and he watched in despair as the *Lumber Baron* sailed out of the harbor.

After his raging attack against the bars of the cage and his dive for cover from the shotgun blasts, a deadly calm settled over him. It's a perfect set up, he thought to himself. Humphrey hires two men to assassinate King Strang. They fail in their attempt, so he uses the injured Strang as a lure to capture Sarah and take her away. Meanwhile, he leaves Butch Jenkins and his men to rule the island until his return. Jenkins will drive the last of the Irish fishermen off the island, and he will do it by force, not by persuasion. When Humphrey returns, he will rule the island, and he will have Sarah as his bride.

Another horrible thought occurred to Andy. Humphrey and Jenkins had an extra benefit which they probably hadn't counted on. They had him, Andy, locked in jail. They would charge him with the attempted murder of King Strang, thus taking all suspicion away from themselves. They would try him before a Mormon judge and jury, testifying that he jumped King Strang and held him down just before the shooting began. Jenkins had taken great pleasure in leading a posse to kill Tom Bennett. He would take even greater pleasure in watching Andy hang from an oak tree.

Andy grabbed the bars and pulled on them with all of his might. "I'm getting out of here," he vowed. "I'm going after them and I'm going to rescue Sarah. If Tobias Humphrey even touches her, I'll kill him!"

CHAPTER 18:

Escape

King Strang was bleeding again. His wounds had opened during the short trip from his house to the *Lumber Baron*. Sarah desperately wrapped new bandages around his head, but they kept falling off. She barely had time to look back at Beaver Island as the schooner crossed Paradise Bay and approached the open waters of Lake Michigan. Tobias and Gurdon had already gone below and the sailors were busy setting the sails. No one seemed willing to help her.

The captain of the *Lumber Baron*, a kindly man with a long white beard, saw Sarah struggling and came over to help. "Here," he said, "you hold the rag in place and I'll tie the knots."

"Thank you," Sarah replied, looking up at him gratefully. She held her hand on the rag while the captain tore several thin strips off another rag. He then wrapped the strips around King Strang's head and tied them neatly under his chin.

"That's better!" the captain proclaimed. "There's nothing like a couple of square knots to keep things shipshape, I always say."

Sarah sighed in relief. "Thank you so much," she said. "I couldn't do it by myself."

"You look mighty young to be doing this alone," the captain said. "Don't you have any help?"

Sarah glanced over at the hatchway leading to the main cabin.

The captain sat down beside her. "You'll never get anything out of those two," he whispered. "You come to me and I'll help you as much as I can. We'll get your father to Milwaukee safe and sound, I promise you."

After the horrible events of the previous day and the sleepless night at her father's side, Sarah's heart was warmed by the charitable actions of the captain. Her feelings of helplessness vanished and now she felt confident that she could keep her father stable until they reached Milwaukee. With good medical care she was hopeful that his injuries would heal quickly.

Several hours later the *Lumber Baron* cleared the south end of the island and the captain set a course toward Milwaukee. King Strang seemed to be resting peacefully, so Sarah walked to the stern to look back at her island home. On a high bluff she could see a tall white spire rising above the trees. It was the Beaver Head Lighthouse, built only a few years ago by the U.S. Lighthouse Service. The sight of the lighthouse cheered her, for she knew that soon she would be returning to the island and the lighthouse would guide her back to Andy and the life she was leaving behind.

⁓

Andy rolled over, trying to get comfortable. It was his second night in the cage and a chilling wet dew had settled on his blanket. He heard a faint sound and opened his eyes. Somebody was outside the bars, lurking in the shadows. Andy was suddenly wide awake.

"Psst! Psst!"

"Who's there?" Andy asked, rolling to his knees and crouching in the far corner of his cell.

A voice whispered in the dark. "It's Oren. Oren Whipple."

"Oren! What are you doing here?"

"I've come to let you out."

"Let me out? But—"

"Listen," Oren whispered, "I saw the whole thing. I was standing by the woodpile, right behind you. I saw you push King Strang out of the way just before he got shot. Butch Jenkins thought you were attacking the King, but you probably saved his life."

"So he's alive!" Andy exclaimed with relief.

"Yeah, but he's hurt real bad. He's got a bullet in his head."

"Where are they taking him?"

"To a doctor in Milwaukee."

Andy jumped to his feet. "How can you get me out of here?" he asked, grabbing the bars with both hands.

"I have a key."

"A key? Where'd you get a key?"

"My father had it. He's King Strang's bookkeeper, so he keeps all the keys in a safe. I just borrowed it for the night."

Andy clutched the bars and rattled them. "Let me out, quick! I'm going after them."

"Listen, Andy, before I let you out I've got to tell you something. I heard Jenkins talking to the sheriff. They're going to charge you with robbery—"

"I don't care about that," Andy snapped. "Sarah just loaned me some money—"

"—and attempted murder," Oren said. "You'll be charged with murder if King Strang dies. If you're convicted, they'll hang you."

"Murder!" Andy cried. "What about the two guys who shot him?"

"They're gone. They were taken prisoner on the *Michigan*. Now it's your word against the Mormons. You won't stand a chance."

"Then I'll just have to get off the island before they can catch me," Andy said. "My father will take me across in the *Emma Rose.*"

"That won't work. Jenkins' men are watching your boat."

"Why? They've already got me locked up."

Oren paused. "I'll explain that later," he said. "You just can't go home now."

"Then I'll hide in the woods. He can pick me up in the *Emma Rose* out on Whiskey Point."

Oren was silent. He was only a shadow in the dark, so Andy could not see the expression on his face.

"C'mon, Oren, let me out of here," Andy said. "They'll never catch me. I'll leave the island as soon as I can. I'm going after Sarah!"

"You can't leave the island."

"Why not?" Andy asked, rattling the bars again.

"Listen," Oren said, "I saw them beat you up and throw you in here. If they catch me they'll charge me with helping you escape. My parents left with King Strang, so I'm on my own too. You can hide at my house, but you have to do as I say. I've got food and you can get some sleep, and then we'll talk."

"But I don't want to sleep. I want to go after them."

"You have to promise to follow me or I won't let you out," Oren said. "I'll explain everything in the morning."

"All right, all right, just get me out of here!"

Oren pulled a key out of his pocket and fumbled around in the dark until he found the lock. He opened it with a click and the cell gate swung open.

"Shh. Follow me," Oren whispered. "I know a secret trail."

Andy squeezed past the gate and followed Oren. He desperately wanted to take off on his own, find a boat and rescue Sarah, but for once he realized that he would be better off to curb his impulse and stick with Oren, at least until morning. He was famished from hunger and fatigue, and he was still sore from the beating he had taken from Jenkins and his men. They would be sure to come after him as soon as they discovered the empty cell. If Jenkins caught him again he would end up right back in jail, probably with a worse beating.

Oren led the way to the woods and crouched under some low bushes. Andy crawled after him and they both disappeared into the forest, swallowed by the darkness of the night.

Andy woke to the smell of frying bacon. At first he did not know where he was. His head was throbbing and his mouth was full of the bitter taste of dried blood. He opened his eyes and saw that he was in a small cabin, darkened by sheets draped over the windows. Oren Whipple was standing by a woodstove cooking breakfast. Andy pulled back his blanket and sat up on the edge of the bed, groaning as a searing pain shot across his back.

Oren heard him and turned around, a spatula in his hand. "You look terrible," he said.

"Thanks," Andy replied, holding his head. "I feel terrible."

"There's a bowl of water on the nightstand if you want to wash up. You've got blood on your face. They beat you up pretty bad."

"Yeah, I know. I hurt all over." Andy picked up a washcloth and scrubbed his face and neck while Oren returned to the stove, flipping pancakes and turning the bacon.

"Is this your house?" Andy asked.

"Yeah, but don't worry. No one will look for you here."

"Where are your parents?"

"I told you already. They left on the boat with King Strang."

"Oh, I forgot," Andy replied, splashing water on his face and wondering why they left the island without taking Oren with them.

"Here's some breakfast," Oren said, bringing over a plate stacked high with pancakes and bacon.

"Hey, thanks! I'm starving," Andy said. He threw down his towel, grabbed a fork, and dug into the pancakes. After two days in jail without a roof over his head, he was ravenous.

Oren returned with a cup of steaming hot coffee and sat down across from Andy.

"Let's go over to the *Emma Rose* after breakfast," Andy said, taking another bite. "My father will be wondering where I am."

"Not now," Oren replied. "Maybe tonight after dark. I snuck over there before you woke up and Jenkins has two men watching the place. They're sitting right on the dock."

"Oh, I'm not afraid of those guys. King Strang is gone. What can they do now that I'm free?"

Oren reached over and grabbed Andy's fork out of his hand. "You should be afraid of them," he warned.

"Why?"

"You know the answer to that. Without King Strang, Butch Jenkins is in charge. He's crazy."

"But he'll have to catch me again."

Oren sighed, got up from his chair, and peeked out the window. "Listen, Andy, after you ran away from the dock Jenkins sent six men out to look for you."

"Well, they didn't find me, did they?" Andy said, taking a swig of coffee.

"No, but they found your father. He didn't know where you were and he wouldn't tell them anyway, so they got in a big fight."

"So? He's pretty tough."

"Not against six lumberjacks, he isn't. Andy, they almost killed him."

Andy put down his mug and stared at Oren. "What happened?"

"Well, for one thing, he's blind. His face is so swollen that you can't even see his eyes. And he's probably got a concussion. They beat him with clubs. They knocked out some of his teeth and cut his lip real bad, so he can hardly talk. I don't even know what else they did, but Nathan thinks a couple of ribs and one of his wrists are broken."

"Damn!" Andy shouted, jumping to his feet. "I've got to help him!"

Oren grabbed Andy before he could reach the door.

"You're not going anywhere! They'll just throw you back in jail."

"But he needs me!" Andy said, struggling to break free of Oren's grasp. He had forgotten all about King Strang and Tobias Humphrey. He even forgot about Sarah for a moment. All he could feel was anger and guilt for running away and hiding while Jenkins' men went after his father.

"Listen, he's going to be all right," Oren said. "He's in bed at Patrick's house. Mrs. Watson is nursing him and Patrick is guarding the door with a shotgun."

Andy finally stopped struggling. Oren let go, but he leaned against the door, watching him warily.

"Well, when can we go there?" Andy asked.

"Like I said, tonight, if the coast is clear."

"All right, I guess I can wait." Grimacing, he reached around and put his hand on his back. His shirt was torn across his shoulders.

"You'd better let me look at that," Oren said. "Turn around."

Oren lifted Andy's shirt and saw an angry red streak across Andy's back, jumping from shoulder blade to shoulder blade.

"Man, are you lucky. You almost got killed."

"What is it?" Andy said, alarmed. "It can't be that bad."

"You've got a gash across your back from a bullet. When they shot King Strang, they shot you, too. It's not bleeding anymore, but it's all red and swollen."

"Yeah, it hurts."

"I'll bet it does. I can't do much for it, but you'd better save that shirt. That's your lucky shirt now."

"I guess it is," Andy said. "Hey, thanks for rescuing me from that jail, Oren. You didn't have to do that."

"It's a good thing I did. Those other two guys got away, but the Mormons might have hung you."

"Do you really think so?"

"Yes, I do, and you're not out of danger yet. They'll be looking for you."

"What should I do today?" Andy asked.

"Just stay here in the cabin and lay low. I'm going into town to see what's happening now that King Strang is gone. I'll be back this afternoon, so why don't you try to get some sleep? We'll sneak over to your house tonight after dark."

"Yeah, I'll feel better by then. Thanks, Oren."

Andy crawled over to his cot and climbed under the blanket. He was still weary and sore from his ordeal in the Mormon jail. He closed his eyes and in a few minutes he heard the front door open. It closed with a thud and the cabin was silent.

Andy tried to sleep but his mind was reeling from the events of the last few days. He could hardly believe that he and Sarah had been on the verge of escaping the clutches of Tobias Humphrey. Now, in just one day, Sarah's father had been shot and his own father was blinded and crippled by a severe beating. Even worse, Sarah was on a boat headed for Milwaukee and possibly an early marriage to Tobias Humphrey. Andy could only hope that Humphrey would at least be decent enough to wait until Sarah was able to nurse her father back to health. If King Strang managed to survive his gunshot wounds he would surely need time to recuperate. That might give Andy time to make his way to Milwaukee to rescue her.

But then Andy thought of his own father lying in bed, blind, injured and helpless. Just a few days ago he was talking about building a bigger house to replace the one the Mormons burned to the ground. How could Andy even think of leaving the island at a time like this? His father needed him. Sarah needed him. He was a fugitive, hunted by Butch Jenkins and his men. It was no wonder he couldn't sleep.

Late that night, Andy and Oren slipped out the back door of Oren's cottage and crept into the darkness. Oren seemed to know his way all around the harbor, whether in broad daylight or in the middle of the night. He moved silently along a hedgerow behind his house and picked up a faint trail that led in the direction of Whiskey Point.

"Oren, which way are you going?" Andy whispered.

"I'm going to swing around to the back side of your barn to make sure there's no one prowling around your dock," Oren replied.

Andy followed him, keeping up as best as he could. Andy had learned to respect Oren after he had rescued their wagon at Cable Bay. Now Oren's parents were gone, and he was on his own. It took a lot of courage to open the jail cell in the middle of the night and let him out. And with Butch Jenkins and his men on the prowl, Andy still felt dependent on Oren, at least for the time being. They reached the back of the barn, and Oren motioned for Andy to wait. He disappeared into the darkness and Andy paused on the side of the path.

In a few minutes Oren returned. "I was right," he whispered. "There's two of 'em out on the dock."

"Did they see you?" Andy asked.

"Nah, they're slumped over. I think they're asleep. If we sneak around the back of Patrick's house we should be able to crawl through a window. That's how I did it before."

"Lead the way. I'm right behind you."

They retraced their steps, cut through a grove of trees, and came out of the woods behind Patrick's cabin. A dim light shined through a single window, cut high in the logs of the cabin.

"Boost me up," Oren said.

Andy lifted him to his shoulders and Oren slithered through the narrow opening. Inside, Patrick and Nathan had heard the creak of the window and they were waiting for him.

"Oren, you're back!" Patrick said. "What news do you have?"

"I brought company," Oren said, dropping to the floor.

"Andy!" Nathan cried out, looking up to see Andy climbing through the window.

"Are we ever glad to see you!" Patrick said, grasping Andy by the arm and helping him down. "Where've you been? Tell us what happened."

"I will," Andy said, catching his breath, "but first tell me about my father. Can I see him?"

"He's asleep right now. We managed to get him to drink some soup and Mrs. Watson stopped by earlier today to change his dressings."

"Can I see him?"

"Sure, but his face is still wrapped up."

Andy picked up a candle from the table and tiptoed across the cabin to the bedroom door. He looked back at Patrick and quietly entered the room.

Ian was lying in bed, covered in blankets to keep away the evening chill. He was breathing fitfully and making hoarse guttural sounds in his sleep. The lower part of his face was wrapped in dressings. His head was also wrapped, and Andy could see a dark stain of blood seeping through the cloth, but it was the exposed upper half of Ian's face that was most shocking. Ian's cheeks and eyebrows were so swollen and discolored that his eyes were completely hidden except for two purple gashes on either side of his nose. Patrick came up behind Andy and put his hand on the boy's shoulder.

"Is he blind?" Andy asked, his voice choking.

"Let's go back out by the fire," Patrick said gently, leading him by the arm. "I've made some tea."

In a daze, Andy turned around and went back into main room. Oren and Nathan were sitting at a table near the fire. Nathan pushed a steaming cup of tea over to him. Patrick closed the door and joined the boys at the table.

"No, he isn't blind, Andy. Fortunately his eyes were not injured, but his face is so swollen that he can barely see. Mrs. Watson has been applying ice packs to try to get the swelling down. She thinks it will subside in a couple of days."

"But what about the rest of him?" Andy asked.

"It's going to take some time," Patrick said, "but I think he'll get better in a few weeks as long as he doesn't get an infection."

"Where else is he hurt?"

"Well, they worked him over pretty good. His jaw is broken and he lost a couple of teeth. He broke his hand in the fight and he's probably got some broken ribs. Other than that, he's just got a lot of bruises and a nasty cut on his head."

"Oren told me that they beat him with clubs."

"They started to, but I put a stop to that," Patrick said.

"How did you stop all six of them?"

"With my rifle. I threatened to shoot them."

"Oh," said Andy, surprised that Patrick would ever pull a gun on anybody. "I guess that would work."

Patrick folded his arms across his chest and looked across the table at Andy, who was slumped in his chair. "They were dead serious, Andy. They told Ian that you tried to kill King Strang and they wanted to know where you were hiding. Ian wouldn't hear a word of it. He told them to get off his property and he added a few choice words of his own. That's when they went after him. He got in a few good licks but there was too many of them. They beat him half to death."

Andy's face flushed with shame as he thought of his father fighting for his life while he was hiding in the woods. He should have stayed at the boat dock and fought those men. He felt like a coward for having run away.

Oren came to his defense. "They lie! Andy tried to save the King. There were two other men hiding behind a log pile. They shot King Strang, not Andy."

"Who were they?" Patrick asked.

"They were both Mormons, or at least they used to be," Oren said. "They were arrested and taken away on the *Michigan*."

"Well, that certainly doesn't help Andy's case much, now does it," Patrick replied.

"That's why he's staying at my house. We've been hiding."

"I guess you'd both better tell me the whole story," Patrick said, leaning forward and sipping his tea.

"I saw the whole thing," Oren said. "Andy was sitting on top of a pile of lumber. He just—"

"I went to the dock to see the *Michigan*," Andy interrupted, finally deciding to talk. "I had no idea what was going on. I just wanted to see the boat."

"What happened when you got there?" Patrick asked.

Andy proceeded to tell the story, from the moment he tackled King Strang until he was caught by Butch Jenkins in front of Strang's house and thrown in jail. He left nothing out, even telling them about how he ran away and hid in the woods.

"Why did you go over to Strang's house?" Nathan asked. "If Jenkins' men were after you, wouldn't that be the last place you'd go?"

"I wanted to see if King Strang was all right, and I wanted to see if —"

"You wanted to see if Sarah was there." Nathan completed his sentence.

Andy squirmed under the gaze of his friend. "Yes," he said.

"Oren, tell us what you saw at the dock," Patrick said, turning in his chair. "And tell us how you both ended up at your house."

Oren described the assault on King Strang. He told them how Andy jumped on the King and pushed him aside as the two men fired their guns, beat him with clubs, and ran to the *Michigan* with a mob of Mormons chasing them.

"Who were the two men? Did you know them?"

"It was Thomas Bedford and Alexander Wentworth."

"Why would they shoot their own King?"

"Bedford used to be a Mormon, but he was excommunicated from the church. He hated King Strang. I'm not sure why he even stayed on the island, unless it was for revenge. I don't know about Wentworth. He was never much of a Mormon. For all I know, he did it for money."

"So then you let Andy out of jail in the middle of the night and now you're both hiding at your house?"

"Yeah, that's about it," Oren replied.

Patrick cupped his chin in his hands. "Where are your parents, Oren?"

"They left with King Strang on Tobias Humphrey's schooner."

"Did they even tell you they were leaving? Why didn't they take you along?"

"No," Oren replied. "I guess they were too worried about King Strang."

"So you and Andy are alone at your house? Are you safe there?"

"I think so. I keep all the shutters closed and the doors locked. Everyone probably thinks I left with my parents."

"All right, then, let me think for a minute." Patrick stood up and walked to the window, his back to the boys at the table. He tugged on the shutters, making sure that they were tightly closed. Then he took a few steps across the room and checked the lock on the door. After he was satisfied that the house was secure, he returned to the table, blew out the candle, and sat down again.

"Boys," he began, "I'm afraid you're in a heap of trouble. We're going to have to get you off the island."

"Maybe if—" Andy began.

Patrick held up his hand for silence. "Listen," he said, "here's what we're going to do. Tomorrow Nathan and I will get the *Emma Rose* ready to sail. Jenkins' men will be watching us, so we'll act like we're just going fishing. Oren, you and Andy go back to your house and stay inside. Keep the door locked and the shutters closed. Then sneak back here tomorrow night after dark and bring your bags. Whatever you do, don't get caught. We'll sail out of here about midnight."

"What about those men on the dock?" Oren asked.

"I'm hoping they won't come around again. If they do, we'll have to distract them somehow."

"What about my father?" Andy asked. "We can't leave him."

"We're going to have to, Andy, unless you want to face a Mormon lynch mob. I'll have Mrs. Watson look after him. She takes better care of him than I do anyway, and I'll be back in a few days."

"But what about us? Where are we going to go?"

"Mackinac Island. We'll go straight to the authorities, and you can tell them the same story you just told me. I'm hoping that the *Michigan* will still be in port with Bedford and Wentworth in custody. Andy, you may have to be a witness against them, do you understand that?"

"Yes, sir."

"That may be the only way we can clear your name, in a court of law."

"Then can we come back to Beaver Island?" Andy asked.

"Maybe, but we'll have to wait and see. With King Strang gone, there's no law here anymore. If Butch Jenkins catches you he'll take the law into his own hands. I'll come back alone, and if I have to I'll smuggle Ian off the island on the *Emma Rose*. We'll just start over somewhere else."

The three boys were speechless. Beaver Island was the only home they knew.

"All right then," Patrick said, "Andy and Oren, you'd better be off. They'll be around here again looking for you in the morning, so you better hurry."

Andy and Oren put on their shoes and jackets. Patrick boosted them up to the window and they squeezed through the opening and disappeared into the night. As soon as they were gone, he closed the shutter and latched it.

The two boys huddled in the dark until they could see the shadows of the trees around them. The forest did not seem so hospitable after the warmth and comfort of Patrick's cabin.

Oren touched Andy's arm. "I'm going to see if those two guys are still out on the dock. You wait here," he whispered.

Andy nodded and watched Oren creep away. He thought about his father lying inside the cabin just a few feet away and wished he could climb back through the window instead of crawling through the woods like a hunted animal.

Oren reappeared out of the darkness. "They're gone! The coast is clear."

"Maybe not," Andy whispered. "Maybe they just moved."

"I don't think so. I didn't hear a thing."

"All right, but let's be careful. They could still be around somewhere."

"C'mon, let's get out of here," Oren said.

He turned and took off through the wet grass, crouching and running as he skirted around the side of the barn to the edge of the woods. Andy struggled to keep up with him, stumbling along in the darkness.

"Oren, wait!" Oren stopped and Andy almost ran into him. "I can't keep up."

"Sorry," Oren said, crouching low behind a pine tree.

"I thought I heard something back there."

"Naw, they're gone. I checked."

"No, over that way. Listen!" Andy said, pointing through the woods.

They both stood still and listened. Sure enough, in the distance they could hear the sound of muffled voices. A stick cracked and some bushes rustled. The sound was a long way off, but there was no doubt that someone was making their way through the forest in the middle of the night. Whoever it was, they were making no attempt at secrecy.

"Who is that?" Andy asked, his hand on Oren's shoulder.

"I don't know, but they're sure not Mormons," Oren replied.

"They're making enough noise. It sounds like they're drunk."

"That's why I don't think they're Mormons."

"Well, whoever it is, they'll never catch us with the racket they're making."

"Maybe not, but it sounds like there are a lot of them. We'd better head to North Beach and follow the shore back to my house. They're headed in the other direction, toward the harbor."

"We can circle around them," Andy said. "Lead the way."

Oren headed off into the woods and Andy followed close behind him. They entered an area of tall pine trees. There wasn't much undergrowth, so they were able to weave between the trees at a rapid pace even though it was very dark. Soon the sound of the mysterious voices faded away, and they heard only the wind in the trees and the eerie call of a distant whip-poor-will.

The ground began to get hilly as they approached North Beach. They climbed the back of a steep sand dune, pulling themselves up by grabbing saplings and bunches of grass. When they reached the top they could see the entire beach and a dim horizon of open water. Offshore, just beyond the waves, a schooner rested at anchor, a mere shadow in the vast lake. A solitary man could be seen on board, carrying a dim lantern and walking back and forth on the deck.

"So that's where they came from," Andy said. "See that rowboat pulled up on the beach? They must have made several trips. Look at all those tracks in the sand."

"They may have been drinking, but at least they had sense enough to leave a watchman on board," Oren observed.

"I thought I knew all the boats around here, but I've never seen that one before."

"Do you think this has anything to do with King Strang getting shot?" Oren asked.

"I don't know, but they're up to no good, that's for sure," Andy replied. "Otherwise they would have just sailed into the harbor."

"Are they from Mackinac Island?"

"Could be. I've seen boats like that over there before."

"I'll bet they are, and I'll bet they know that King Strang was shot."

"Do you think they're Irish?" Andy asked.

"Yeah, I do. I think it's all those fishermen the Mormons ran off the island. They still fish around here and they still want to use the harbor, but the Mormons won't let them."

"I sure hope you're wrong, Oren," Andy said, shivering in the chill night air. "We've got enough problems. Listen, let's get back to your house. This place is making me nervous."

"Me, too. There are too many people prowling around in the dark to suit my fancy."

Andy and Oren made their way back to Oren's house and slipped inside. They immediately locked the door and closed and latched all the windows. It was dark inside the cabin, but they were reluctant to light even a small candle, so they climbed up to the loft to try to get some sleep.

Andy lay in the dark and thought about Patrick's plan. The trip to Mackinac Island on the *Emma Rose* would take all night, but if they got there in time the *Michigan* might still be tied up at the dock. If it was, they would seek out the captain and confront Bedford and Wentworth. Surely some of the ship's officers must have seen what happened on the dock. They would all agree that Andy had nothing to do with the assassination attempt and that he tried to save King Strang. With this final thought, Andy fell into a deep sleep, exhausted by the events of the last few days.

After two days of sailing south against contrary winds, the Captain of the *Lumber Baron* decided to seek shelter and wait out the poor weather and rough seas.

"We're not making any progress and the ship is taking a pounding," he said. "We'll pull into the lee of Manitou Island and wait for a fair wind."

He ordered the sailors to change course and soon the *Lumber Baron* was sailing in smooth waters and approaching a wide protected bay on the east side of a small island. Shortly after the anchor was set, Tobias Humphrey came on deck.

"How is our patient today?" he asked.

"As well as can be expected," the Captain replied.

He's not bleeding anymore," Sarah said, "but his face looks awful. I'm worried that he might get an infection. How long will it take to sail to Milwaukee?"

"We'll lay up here for the night," the Captain said. "I'm hoping for a favorable wind tomorrow, and then it will take two or three days to get there. I'll have the men set every sail."

"Don't worry, Sarah," Tobias said. "The *Lumber Baron* makes good time when she's not loaded down with cargo. As soon as we arrive I'll rent a two-room suite at the best hotel in town. We'll put you in one room and set up a bed for King Strang right next door. I'll find a doctor and have him examine your father immediately. He'll know what to do. We'll get the best medical care possible for King Strang, and I'll spare no expense, I promise you that!"

"Thank you so much, Mr. Humphrey," Sarah said. "I appreciate everything you have done for my father."

"It is nothing, my dear," Tobias replied. "After all, he is King of the Mormons, and you are his daughter and my fiancé. How could I do anything less?"

Sarah froze and the color drained from her face.

"I know this has been a difficult time for you, Sarah, but perhaps while your father is recuperating we might have time to discuss our wedding. It will be the biggest and best wedding ever held on Beaver Island, I can assure you of that. We must set a date soon."

"But, I don't...I can't..." Sarah stuttered. She realized her worst fear was true. Her father had never told Tobias about Andy and never broken the engagement. He was shot down before he had a chance. Now she was miles from home and trapped on a boat with a man who expected her hand in marriage. She had been promised to him months ago from the pulpit of the Mormon Church. Now more than ever, she needed Andy. But where was he? He never would have let her leave the island alone with the Humphreys. Surely he must be following them in another boat. Sarah could only pray that Andy would find her soon.

Tobias looked at her with a benevolent and clueless smile. "Of course we will wait until your father has recovered his health and is able to attend. After all, we must have our King to officiate the wedding, wouldn't you agree?"

Sarah slumped to the deck and covered her face to hide her tears and despair.

"Come, come," the Captain said, "can't you see the child has taken ill? She has had no rest since we left the island. I will give her my stateroom tonight." The Captain helped Sarah to her feet and guided her down the companionway to his berth at the stern of the ship.

"You lie down here," he said. "I'll get you a pillow and a blanket."

"Thank you," Sarah murmured as she climbed into the bunk. The Captain covered her with a blanket and tucked her in.

"Young lady, you are exhausted. I want you to get some rest. No one will bother you in my cabin and I will look after your father."

It was true; she was exhausted. She had been caring for her father the last two nights with no rest at all. Sarah was dozing off to sleep before the Captain even closed the door.

In the early hours of the morning, Sarah woke up with an uneasy feeling that something was wrong. Her body was pressed against the wooden hull and she could hear water lapping a few inches from her head. The bunk, which had seemed so spacious and inviting, now felt cold and claustrophobic. She tried to roll over but she could barely move. Reaching out in the dark, she instantly realized that someone was in the bunk with her. Was it the Captain? Had he crawled in with her? Afraid to move and unable to sleep, she lay silently in the dark, counting the minutes and praying for daylight.

Sarah must have dozed off, for when she awoke at dawn she was pinned against the bulkhead and a cold hand was under the blanket caressing her thigh. Startled and suddenly wide awake, in the dim light she saw who was in her bed. It was Gurdon Humphrey!

"Aughh!" Sarah cried. "Get off me!" She lashed out with arms and legs and pushed Gurdon off the narrow bunk. He landed with a thud on the deck below.

Before Gurdon could move there was the sound of heavy footsteps coming down the companionway.

"How dare you!" the Captain shouted, grabbing Gurdon by the throat. "I'll not have anyone sneaking around in my cabin. You'll bunk in the fo'c'sle and scrub pots and pans for the rest of this trip. I don't care who you are!"

Gurdon broke away and scrambled up the companionway with the Captain chasing after him. Sarah heard the sound of loud voices and stomping feet on the deck. Above all the others, she recognized the voice of Tobias Humphrey, who was bellowing at the Captain for attacking his son. It was at this moment she realized she would have to take care of herself for the rest of the journey. She was the only woman on board the *Lumber Baron*. She must protect herself, take care of her father, and somehow avoid the Humphreys until they reached Milwaukee. Only then could she hope that Andy would find the *Lumber Baron* and rescue her.

CHAPTER 19:

Expulsion of the Mormons

"Andy! Wake up! Look at the harbor. It's full of boats!"

Andy yawned and rubbed his eyes. He looked over at Oren, who was peering through a small window at the end of the loft. Although the cabin was set back in the woods, the boys could see the harbor through a clearing in the trees. The morning sun was rising over Whiskey Point, illuminating a fleet of boats floating at anchor.

Andy was wide awake in an instant. "Look at that. There must be thirty boats out there. It looks like a navy."

"I recognize the *Iowa* and the *Louisville*," Oren said.

"Yeah, and those other two big boats are the *Buckeye State* and the *Prairie State*. I see them out on the lake when we're fishing, but they never stop at Beaver Island."

"What about those smaller boats?" Oren asked.

"Those are all fishing boats from Mackinac Island."

Oren grabbed Andy by the arm. "Andy, what's going on? You know those fishermen. What are they up to?"

"I think they are invading the island. When the *Michigan* left a couple of days ago it sailed straight to Mackinac Island. I'm sure word spread fast that King Strang was shot and maybe killed. What you see out there in the harbor is a giant posse. I think they're going to chase the Mormons off the island."

"Do you really think so? That's a little hard to believe."

"Yeah, I do," Andy replied. "I've heard them talk about it before."

"Oh, great," Oren said. "The Mormons are after you because they think you tried to kill King Strang, and now the Irish are after me because I'm a Mormon. Not only that, Butch Jenkins will be after both of us when he finds out I'm the one who let you out of jail. We're a real pair, aren't we?"

Andy almost laughed at their predicament, but he could see that Oren was truly frightened. Andy was frightened, too, when he thought about Butch Jenkins and his men. They must know by now he had escaped from jail, so they would conclude he was guilty. If they caught him they would probably lynch him on the spot.

"If we can just stay hidden today and sneak over to the *Emma Rose* tonight, we'll be able to get off the island," Andy said. "Patrick and Nathan will protect us. Patrick has a rifle and several pistols. Don't forget, he drove off six of Jenkins' men by himself."

"But what if they come here looking for us?" Oren asked.

"I don't think anyone will think to look here. Your house is so far back in the woods that the fishermen will never even notice it. As for the Mormons, they must think you left the island with your parents and King Strang. Isn't that what you told me?"

"Yeah, I guess I did," replied Oren, scratching his head.

"But just to make sure, let's get a rope and keep it by the back window. If anyone comes to the front door, we'll slide down the rope and take off into the woods. They'll never catch us."

"That's a good idea. I'll go see what I can find downstairs."

While Oren went to look for a rope, Andy returned to the window to watch the drama unfolding in the harbor. By now, the *Louisville* had tied up at the dock and about two dozen men had disembarked. Several of them had shotguns and one man was struggling to hold a pack of dogs, all of whom were straining on their leashes. The *Buckeye State* was pulling up to the other side of the dock and several sailors were tossing dock lines to the men on shore.

Oren returned with a rope, coiled it on the floor near the window, and tied one end to a beam in the rafters. "There," he said, "now we have an escape route. What's going on out there?"

Andy could not take his eyes off the scene in the harbor. "Do you remember that mob of Mormons we saw down at Cable Bay when they shot Thomas Bennett?"

"I don't think I'll ever forget that," Oren replied.

"Well, it looks like that, only with a lot more boats and a lot more men."

"You don't think they're going to shoot anyone, do you?"

"I sure hope not," Andy replied. "Look, they're all headed up to Johnson's Store."

The boys watched as the mob approached the store. They heard a distant thud as two men broke down the front door and a crash of breaking glass as the front windows were punched out. The men poured into the store and a stream of boxes and groceries came flying out the windows. They were ransacking the place, destroying Johnson's Store.

"Look at that!" Oren cried out. "We've got to stop them!"

"There's no way we're going to stop that mob. Look, the rest of the boats have landed on the beach."

By this time all of the boats had either tied up to one of the smaller docks or simply coasted up to the beach until they ran aground. Men jumped into the shallow water and waded ashore, joining up with men from other boats. They all headed into the village and disappeared from view after passing Johnson's Store.

"Where are all the Mormons?" Oren asked in despair. "Why aren't they fighting back?"

"They'd be crazy to fight that mob. They probably all headed south to hide in the woods somewhere."

"Did you recognize anyone on the dock?"

"Naw, they're too far away. I've seen some of those boats, though. They used to tie up out at Whiskey Point. They're from Mackinac Island."

"They got chased away by King Strang and now they're back for revenge," Oren exclaimed.

With the mob out of sight beyond Johnson's Store, a temporary calm settled over the harbor. A few men remained in town to guard the boats, and others picked through the debris in front of the store. There was not a Mormon in sight. Even the print shop, normally the hub of Mormon activity, was quiet and empty. The two boys kept their vigil at the window, but there was not much to see for most of the day.

Late in the afternoon Andy spotted a dark plume of smoke south of town. Someone must have set fire to a barn or one of the Mormon cabins. Andy, who could never forget the day he sailed around Whiskey Point to see his own house in flames, felt sorry for the Mormon family who must now be losing their farm. As he watched black smoke curling into the air, he saw a procession approaching the village on King's Highway. At first, he thought the fishermen must be returning from their day of mischief, but then he realized that this gathering was way too large. As the crowd got closer, he could see that the Mormons were in the center of the road, strung out in a line and pushing wagons and wheelbarrows piled high with their belongings. On either side Andy could see men on horseback holding rifles pointed in the air.

"Oren, come here, quick," he called.

Oren, who had been dozing on a cot at the other end of the loft, hurried over to the window. "My God, look at that!" he exclaimed. "They've rounded up every one of 'em, all in one day."

"Why aren't they fighting back?" Andy asked. "They're just walking."

"Hardly any of them have guns," Oren replied. "Anyway, they probably don't know what to do without King Strang."

"Couldn't they just hide in the woods?"

"Some of them probably did. I don't see Butch Jenkins or any of the lumberjacks anywhere."

"You're right," Andy said. "I forgot about him. He's probably still out there somewhere looking for me."

As the two boys stood transfixed at the window, the crowd disappeared behind the Mormon Church and the print shop. Before the last stragglers were out of sight, the first of the wagons appeared in front of Johnson's Store and stopped on the grassy beach near the boat dock. A crowd of frightened people followed them on foot, carrying their possessions and looking around in bewilderment. There were older couples, families with children and babies, and single men and women. Behind them there were more wagons with wheelbarrows piled high with clothing and blankets. A young girl pulled on a rope holding six goats. A dog nipped at their heels, making them run in all directions while the girl hung on.

After the last wagon came to a stop, several more men appeared in front of Johnson's Store. They all had rifles. A few of them were watching the Mormon families gather on the beach. The rest were gathered in a tight circle, apparently guarding some prisoners who were lined up against the side of the building.

Oren peered carefully at the men lined up along the wall of the store. "Isn't that Butch Jenkins right in the middle of all those men?"

Andy looked over his shoulder. "It sure is! That's him, all right, and I see the two men who threw me in jail."

"I think they're prisoners. Look at that one with his hands together. He's wearing handcuffs."

"They all are, I think. They must have arrested all of them." Andy was elated. "I'm free! No one will come after me now."

Oren was not so sure. "Maybe they're the only Mormons who put up a fight. There's still a strong case against you, Andy, and you had a motive to kill King Strang."

Andy ignored him. "I'm going down there right now."

"I wouldn't do that if I were you," Oren said. "We don't really know what's going on yet."

"Sure we do. They arrested those guys. I'm safe now."

"Who arrested them? Another mob? How can you be sure you're safe?"

"Oren, those are all Irish fishermen down there. I probably know about half of them. They're not going to do anything to me."

"Andy, listen to me. Right now there are two mobs on this island, one Mormon and the other Irish. A few days ago the Mormons were in charge and you were in jail. Today the Irish are in charge and you are free. Who knows what's going to happen tomorrow?"

"But they're all handcuffed," Andy said.

"I don't care," Oren replied. "Patrick and Nathan are getting the *Emma Rose* ready to sail to Mackinac Island. They're expecting us tonight, so we need to stick with our plan. When we get to Mackinac we'll find the sheriff and he can take us to the *Michigan*. Once we get you cleared we'll come back to Beaver Island and you can go on to Milwaukee or do whatever you want, but don't forget that your house got torched and your father is blind and lying in bed. If you go down to the dock now you might get in trouble again and you won't be able to help your father. Do you want to take that chance?"

"Oh, yeah..." muttered Andy.

Oren sighed with relief. "At least I didn't have to tackle you to make you stay put."

As evening approached, the last of the Mormons straggled into town, escorted by more armed men on horseback. The Mormons shuffled along as if they were in a daze. Some of them appeared to be in shock and they had to be prodded along. They had been hiding out all day in the forest to elude capture, but they had been hunted down and herded up like animals. When the captives reached Johnson's Store and saw the encampment by the dock, they stopped in their tracks. The fleet of boats in the harbor could be there for only one purpose. They must have realized they were being driven off the island.

Some of the earlier arrivals in the camp had set up lean-to tents tied between the wagons. The men had gathered wood along the beach and started a campfire and the women were preparing an evening meal with the scanty provisions they had managed to bring with them. As Andy and Oren watched from their distant lookout, the Mormons huddled together in their makeshift encampment. Without a leader they looked lost and confused. All they could do now was try to look out for one another.

Later in the evening, well after dark, Mormons were still standing around their fire. It was hard to tell from a distance, but judging from the fleeting movements of their shadows, they were not in any hurry to settle down for the night. Someone threw a large log on the fire, and a burst of sparks flew up into the air.

"What do you think they're doing?" Andy asked. "It looks like an Indian pow-wow."

"I imagine they're trying to figure out what's happening. They're probably talking about the attack on King Strang."

"Do you think he's dead?"

"Probably."

"Maybe they're trying to pick a new leader."

"Andy, you don't understand the Mormons," Oren replied. "King Strang wasn't just their leader. He was their prophet, called by God to lead them. He brought them to this island to start a better life. If he is dead, then everything those people believe in is gone. They are going to lose everything; their homes, their farms, and their faith, all on the same day."

"Do you believe he was a prophet?" Andy asked.

"It doesn't matter what I believe," Oren replied. "I already lost everything when my parents left on that boat a few days ago."

Andy gazed silently at the surreal scene in the harbor. He found it hard to believe that the Mormons would leave the island without even a protest. It didn't make sense. Ever since he could remember they had been forcing the fishermen off the island to create their own kingdom. Now they were just going to pack up and leave without a fight. Maybe King Strang really did have some kind of power over them.

After a while the campfire began to burn low. Most of the men drifted away to their wagons for the night. Some of them rolled out sleeping blankets underneath the makeshift tents stretched between the wagons.

"We'd better get out of here," Oren said. "We're lucky no one found us today."

"Let's get our bags and go," Andy replied. "I've seen enough."

"Do you think Patrick still wants to sail to Mackinac Island tonight?" Oren asked.

"I'm sure he does," Andy said. "At least we won't have to worry about Butch Jenkins and his gang. We know exactly where they are."

Oren agreed. "I'm probably safer over at Patrick's house than anywhere else. If anyone catches me here, I'll be put on one of those boats tomorrow with the rest of the Mormons."

The two boys climbed down from their lookout and finished packing their belongings. Oren took one last look at his home, and they both slipped silently into the night.

Patrick's house was dark when they arrived. They had seen no one in the woods and there were no lookouts on the dock. After waiting in the shadows for a few minutes they decided the coast was clear, so they walked up the path and knocked on the front door.

"Who's there?" a muffled voice inquired.

"It's Andy and Oren."

"You haven't been followed, have you?"

"Nope. Everyone's down at the boat dock."

Inside the house they heard a thud and a clunk as the bar on the door was released. The door swung open and Nathan poked his head out.

"We thought you'd come to the back window again."

"Naw," Andy replied. "There's no one around."

"Well, get in here quick so I can shut the door."

Nathan opened the door and held it while Andy and Oren squeezed past him. As soon as they were inside, Nathan closed the door and shoved a stout piece of wood through the handle. Patrick appeared from the shadows of the next room.

"Welcome back, boys."

"How's my father?" Andy asked.

"He's sleeping. He could see a bit today, but he says everything is blurry."

"Did you see what's happening at the boat dock?" Nathan asked.

"Most of it," Oren said. "We watched from an upstairs window in my house."

"They caught Butch Jenkins and his men and tied them up," Andy said. No one will arrest me now."

"I wouldn't be so hasty, Andy," Patrick replied, "and even if you're safe from Jenkins and the Mormons, what about Oren here? We're going to have to keep him out of sight, with all these crazy people running around the island."

"We tried to watch what was going on," Nathan said, "but it's too far across the harbor for us to see much. We figured we'd better stay here with Ian and just wait it out."

"Are we still going Mackinac Island tonight?" Oren asked.

"No," Patrick said, "but the boat's all ready. I want to go into town in the morning and find out exactly what's going on before we leave Ian here alone."

"Yeah, let's all go!" Andy said with excitement, "and while we're there I want to tell Butch Jenkins a thing or two."

"Absolutely not!" Patrick replied sharply. "I've got enough worries already without watching you, Andy. I want you to stay here and look after your father. Something tells me that Mrs. Watson won't be around much longer to care for him. Nathan, tomorrow while I'm gone I want you to check over the boat one more time just in case we have to make a fast getaway."

"Yes sir," Nathan replied.

"Now, let's everyone try to get some sleep. It's going to be a big day tomorrow."

In the morning, Patrick reminded Andy and Oren to stay indoors and keep the door locked while he was gone. He instructed Nathan to load some extra food on the *Emma Rose*.

"If we go to Mackinac Island, we may be there a few days. Nathan, if I'm not back by early afternoon, come and get me. Andy and Oren, you stay put while I find out what's going on. Don't open the door for anyone."

Patrick put on his cap and jacket and looked out at the harbor. The *Louisville* and the *Buckeye State* were still tied up on either side of the dock and several other boats were clustered around the end of the outer pier. Patrick could see that the two larger boats had already put on a head of steam, as if they were getting ready to depart. The drama was unfolding faster than he had anticipated.

"I'll be back," he said, closing the door behind him.

Patrick heard a couple of gun shots before he even arrived at the dock. When he reached the front porch of Johnson's Store he saw a crowd larger than any he had seen since arriving in New York. It was a chaotic scene of angry men, crying children and barking dogs. The fishermen, all with guns or clubs, had encircled the Mormon encampment and were forcing the Mormons out on the dock. One man had a bullwhip and kept cracking it in the air.

Patrick saw a man whom he recognized as a fisherman who had often stopped at Whiskey Point to sell his fish.

"What's going on here?" he asked.

The man looked up in surprise. "Don't you know? We're running these damned Mormons off the island."

"By force?" Patrick asked.

"Whatever it takes. They chased us off Beaver Island and now we're chasing them off."

"Where are you sending them?"

The man shrugged. "Chicago. Milwaukee. I don't care."

"But don't you think—"

Before Patrick could finish his sentence the man pulled out a wooden club and disappeared into the crowd, brandishing his weapon over his head. Patrick tried to stop him but he was jostled around by a surging crowd of Mormon and Irish men, all shouting and threatening one another. He could not retreat, so he held his hands over his head and worked his way over to the edge of the mob. When he finally managed to reach a quieter area behind a pile of lumber, a young woman approached him and tugged at his arm. Patrick recognized her as a Mormon who often brought eggs and vegetables to sell at Johnson's Store.

"Please, Mr. O'Donnell, she said tearfully, "Can you help me? I can't find my husband."

"I'm sorry, ma'am," Patrick replied, "I haven't seen him."

"But can't you do something? They're putting us on the boats. Can't you stop them?"

"Ma'am, I'm only one person. There's no way I can stop this mob by myself."

The woman looked up at Patrick with pleading eyes. "I remember when you helped build the school. Now you're just going to stand here while they take our homes and send us away?"

The woman's words hurt, but there wasn't much that Patrick could do. He gently lifted her hand from his arm. "You wait here. I'll go see if I can find your husband. Maybe he's already on one of the boats."

Patrick left her and shouldered his way through the mob toward the *Buckeye State*. As he approached the edge of the dock, he heard a familiar voice bellowing over the noise of the crowd. It was Wingfield Watson, standing by his wagon and team of oxen. He was brandishing a stout log, waving it back and forth. Several men had surrounded him and were eyeing him warily. Wingfield was a formidable figure with his long gray beard. He stood a head taller than the men circling around him. Patrick had never seen Wingfield get angry, but now he was red in the face and his hair was flying about as he waved the log over his head. No one wanted to be the first to take him on. It was a standoff.

One of the men finally stepped forward and pulled out a revolver. He pointed it at Wingfield's feet.

"We told you, mister, put down that log, get away from those oxen, and get on the boat, damn ye."

"I'll do no such thing. Where'd you take my wife and baby."

"They're already on the boat. You'd better get on that boat yourself if you want to see them again."

"Not without my oxen and my wagon."

"The oxen and wagon stay here. That's the price you pay for stealing from us."

"I never stole anything from you, mister."

"You're a Mormon. That means you're a thief just like the rest of them. Now get on the boat, right now."

The man raised his revolver and pointed it at Wingfield's chest.

Wingfield shook his log and raised it over his head. "That's pretty hard, mister. This is all I've got left in the world since you burned down my barn, you son of a bitch." He was so mad that the veins were standing out in his neck. He wasn't going to give in.

"You say that again and I'll shoot you."

In a flash Wingfield grabbed the gun from the man's hand, and threw it over his shoulder. Then he picked the man up like a sack of potatoes and tossed him off the end of the dock. The other men were upon Wingfield in an instant, grabbing his arms and legs and throwing him to the ground. Wingfield fought back, but there were too many of them. They pinned him down and shoved his face in the dirt. It took four of them to hold him.

"Put him on the other boat," one of the men said. "This boat's going to Chicago and the other one's going to Milwaukee. That'll teach him."

Patrick saw the man who had pulled the gun climbing out of the water with fury in his eyes. His weapon was gone, but he picked up a big stick and marched toward Wingfield. Seeing the danger, Patrick started toward him, but before he could take a step he was shoved aside by a burly man who grabbed the stick out of the man's hand.

"You've done enough to these people already," he shouted at the men holding Wingfield. "Can't you see he has a wife and a baby? Why can't you just put him on the boat with his family?"

"We want to see how long it takes him to find them when he gets to Chicago and they're in Milwaukee," sneered one of the men holding Wingfield.

"I said, put him on the boat with his family. Do it, right now."

"Who the hell are you?"

"I'm Obediah Newton."

"I ain't never heard of you. Why should I do what you say?"

"Tell me, mister, how did you get to Beaver Island last night?" Newton asked.

"I came over on the *Eliza Caroline* from St. Helena Island, not that it's any of your business."

"It sure as hell is my business. I guess you don't know me, but I live on St. Helena Island and I own the *Eliza Caroline*. Now unless you want to get marooned here, you put that man on the boat with his family right now."

The man paused and slowly released Wingfield's arm, which he had pinned in the dirt with his foot.

"All right, we'll let him go, but we're keepin' the wagon and oxen."

Wingfield scrambled to his feet and ran up the gangplank of the *Buckeye State*, where Mrs. Watson was waiting for him. She put his arms around him as soon as he stepped on the boat. Two sailors shoved them aside and pulled in the gangplank. The ship was ready to depart.

Wingfield leaned over the rail of the boat and shouted, "I'll be coming back for my oxen, and when I do I'll be looking for you, mister."

"It won't be hard to find me," the man shouted back. "I'll probably be living in your house."

"Get outta here, ya damned Mormon," another man shouted at Wingfield.

Patrick stood among the crowd as they jeered and shouted at the Mormons on the deck of the *Buckeye State*. He tried to catch Wingfield's attention, but Wingfield and his wife had already retreated to the far side of the boat. The rest of the Mormons soon followed them, and the *Buckeye State* backed away from the dock.

"Damn it," Patrick said. He had forgotten to search for the husband of the young Mormon woman. Beaver Island was going to be no place for a woman without her husband, Patrick was sure of that. He hoped that she had found him.

The burly man who had saved Wingfield from a beating stood beside Patrick and watched the *Buckeye State* head out into the lake with its cargo of Mormons.

"I never thought it was going to be like this," he said. "If I had known how these people were going to be treated, I wouldn't have come here."

"You saved a good man from a beating," Patrick said to him. "He's one of the most honest men I've ever met."

The man spat in the dirt and wiped his mouth on his sleeve. "I don't know how much I helped him. He still lost his wagon. Looks like he could've whupped all those guys, if you ask me."

"Yeah, you're probably right. He's pretty tough."

The man turned to Patrick and introduced himself. "My name's Obediah Newton. I'm from St. Helena Island, about halfway between here and Mackinac Island."

"I've heard of it. I'm Patrick O'Donnell. I came here from Ireland, where people were starving to death, and I never saw anything like this."

"Things got out of hand, that's for sure," Obediah replied.

"We've got to stop them before someone gets killed," Patrick said.

"It's a mob. You ain't gonna stop a mob."

Patrick and Obediah looked around at the scene on the dock. With the departure of the *Buckeye State* it had quieted down on one side of the dock, but on the other side there was still a gang of men with clubs and guns forcing Mormons to board the *Louisville*. Patrick noticed that an armed posse was escorting Butch Jenkins and his men up a gangplank at the stern of the boat.

Jenkins was in handcuffs and the rest of the men had their hands tied behind their backs.

The Mormon camp on the beach was almost empty now. A few men and boys were picking through the abandoned belongings littering the ground. A stray dog pulled at a bone in the campfire.

"I've seen enough of this," Obediah said. "I'm going back to my boat. Half of these men are drunk. When they sober up they can find their own way back to Mackinac Island. To hell with them."

"Where's your boat?" Patrick asked.

"It's anchored off the North Beach."

"I live over that way. Mind if I walk with you?"

"Not at all. You seem to be the only person on this island that ain't crazy."

"After today, I'm not so sure," Patrick replied.

The two men kept to the far edge of the pier, avoiding the commotion at the *Louisville*. The last of the Mormons were forced at gunpoint to board the boat, and two sailors were already pulling in the dock lines. Patrick and Obediah took one last look at the jeering mob on the pier. There was nothing they could do. They left in stunned silence, appalled at the brutality they had just witnessed.

"Where did all these people come from?" Patrick asked, as they reached the main road through the village and headed toward North Beach.

"Most of them are from from Mackinac Island," Obediah said.

"I can't believe they would do this."

"I can't either, but they did."

"Most of the people here are just simple farmers."

"Yeah, but some of them deserved it."

"To be driven off the island at gunpoint? That's a little extreme, isn't it?"

"Maybe it is, but think about it. The Mormons took land that didn't belong to them. They chased just about everyone off the island who wouldn't join their church, and kept everything they owned."

"The Mormons were burning buildings," Patrick admitted. "They burned my brother-in law's cabin and beat him near to death."

"That's what I mean. They forced everyone out and now they're getting forced out. I just didn't expect it to be so nasty. I can't say I'm proud of the way they were treated, especially the women and children."

The two men had reached the path that led to North Beach. They looked back at the harbor and saw the *Louisville* steaming past Whiskey Point. Many of the smaller boats had already pulled anchor, and the men on board were raising sail.

"Isn't anyone going to stay here?" Patrick asked.

"Naw, it's too near the end of the season," Obediah replied. "But you'll see lots of people move back here next spring. This is the best harbor in Lake Michigan."

"How about you? Will you be coming back?"

"Maybe, but I've got too much invested on St. Helena Island."

"Well, if you do, you're always welcome at my house. I live about halfway between here and Whiskey Point."

"Thank you. I'm sorry we had to meet under such circumstances. Good day to you, sir."

Patrick watched Obediah walk away into the woods. He wondered how such a man could have gotten mixed up with a mob. Then he began to question his own actions on the pier, and his thoughts turned back to the tearful Mormon woman who had pleaded with him to find her husband. He looked back at the harbor. The *Louisville* was now past the point and well out on the lake. Beyond the *Louisville*, the *Buckeye State* was only a black smudge on the horizon.

Patrick shook his head sadly and headed for home, thinking about what he should tell the boys, who would be waiting in suspense to find out if they must abandon their island home.

CHAPTER 20:

Trapped

"We're staying," Patrick said, his hands still on the door. "Most of the Mormons have been run off the island. It's a miracle no one got killed today. Mrs. Watson is gone, so now Ian needs us more than ever. Andy and Oren, I think you'll be safe now, but I want you both to lay low for a few days. Oren, you should stay here with us for a while, and you're welcome to stay as long as you like."

"But what about Bedford and Wentworth," Andy asked. "They got away—"

"There's nothing we can do about them. They're in the hands of the government," Patrick replied. "Like I said, Andy, your father needs us now."

A few days later, Patrick left the boys and walked to Saint James. Johnson's Store had re-opened, so he bought a few provisions, but mostly he wanted to find out how many people were left on the island. He discovered that there were still a few Mormons living in a small settlement several miles out King's Highway. Some of them had escaped capture by hiding in the woods, and some had been able to convince their captors that they had forsaken the Mormon faith.

A few of the fishermen who helped drive the Mormons from the island had remained and moved into abandoned Mormon homes. One man had managed to acquire Wingfield Watson's team of oxen and he planned to skid logs over the winter. Another man had taken over the Mormon print shop and he was converting it into a boarding house. Both men told Patrick they expected the island population to grow dramatically now that the Mormons were gone. It never occurred to either of them that they had stolen someone else's property.

Ian remained bedridden. Without Mrs. Watson around to look after him, he was not healing as quickly as everyone had expected. His vision gradually returned as the swelling on his face subsided, but other wounds were still troublesome. His biggest complaint was dizziness and severe headaches caused by the blow to the back of his head. It was going to take some time before he completely recovered from his injuries.

Knowing that Oren's parents had abandoned him, Patrick took Oren under his wing and made him part of the household. Oren and Nathan worked together on the *Emma Rose,* making repairs and putting away fishing gear. At night, Oren bunked in the loft with Andy and Nathan.

As for Andy, he spent most of his time with his father. He changed dressings, washed bedding, and prepared meals. Andy took good care of him, but his thoughts were elsewhere. The day of Sarah's departure on Tobias Humphrey's schooner was the most dreadful day of his life. The final scene of Sarah kneeling beside her father with Tobias and Gurdon Humphrey looming over her was almost more than he could bear. He knew what they both wanted, and it had very little to do with getting King Strang to a doctor in Milwaukee. Until his father recovered he would have no chance of following her. He was trapped on Beaver Island.

By now Ian knew the story of the assault on King Strang and Andy's capture, imprisonment, and escape. He also knew of the departure of the *Lumber Baron* with King Strang, Sarah, and Tobias and Gurdon Humphrey on board. For a long time he had been aware of Andy's feelings for Sarah. Ian saw his son's sadness and knew it was caused by Sarah's departure, but she would likely return soon, or so he thought.

But Ian did not understand that Sarah had been kidnapped. He did not know that King Strang had promised Sarah's hand in marriage to Tobias Humphrey from the church pulpit, or of the secret pact made between the two men. Nor did he know the true depth of despair his son felt while trapped in an iron cage and watching Sarah sail away.

The *Lumber Baron* arrived in Milwaukee without further incident. As soon as the boat was tied to the dock Tobias disembarked and disappeared into the city. An hour later he returned with another man in a carriage led by a team of fine horses. A second team followed behind, towing an open wagon. Both teams stopped at the curb and the two men hurried out the dock and up the gangplank. Sarah was tending to her father when they came on board.

"Sarah, this is Dr. Wilson," Tobias said. "He has agreed to examine King Strang before we attempt to move him."

"Hello," Sarah said. "Thank you for coming."

"So you are the daughter of King Strang," Dr. Wilson replied. "I am very pleased to meet you. Now let's have a look at your patient."

Sarah stood up and made room for the doctor. After kneeling beside her father for so long she suddenly felt dizzy, but she was thankful that help had finally arrived.

Dr. Wilson knelt beside King Strang and opened his medical kit. While Sarah, Tobias, and the Captain watched, the doctor carefully examined the king. He peeled back Sarah's bandage and looked at the scalp wound, gently spreading the swollen tissue and peering into the open gash. Then he looked at the bruises and abrasions on the King's face and peered into both eyes. Finally, he examined the dark hole in the King's cheek. All the while, the doctor murmured to himself and occasionally wrote down a few notes.

"Did he bleed profusely?" he asked, putting down his notebook.

"Only from the head wound," Sarah replied. "We were able to stop it."

"Has he spoken?" he asked.

"Yes," Sarah said, "but only a few times. I could not understand him."

Dr. Wilson stood up. "I must examine him in more detail," he said, "but I have made some preliminary conclusions."

"Yes?" Sarah asked.

"The facial bruises and lacerations are trivial. They will heal themselves. The head wound is quite severe, but you have handled it well and I commend you. I will add some stitches so it will heal faster. Also, he may have a concussion, so there may be some temporary mental and speech loss."

"Thank you," Sarah replied, breathing a sigh of relief.

"However," the doctor continued, "I am very concerned about the bullet wound in his cheek. It is quite deep and there is danger of infection."

"Can you get the bullet out?" the Captain asked.

"No, not at this time. He is very weak after the long trip from Beaver Island. If I did it now it would probably kill him."

Sarah gasped. "What should we do?" she asked.

"I understand Tobias has arranged some accomodations," Dr. Wilson replied. "I recommend we take him there and allow him to rest for a few days. If he gains some strength back, I would be willing to attempt to remove the bullet, as long as you understand the risk."

Sarah looked over at the Captain, who nodded silently.

"I have rented a suite of two rooms at the hotel on Front Street," Tobias said. "We will set up a hospital bed for King Strang in one room. Sarah, you may have the adjoining room so you may be close to your father. Also, Dr. Wilson's nurse has agreed to stay with you. We will set up a cot for her so she will be able to watch the king day and night. Her name is Abby, and she has been instructed to attend to your every need."

Sarah nodded. "Thank you," she murmured. An awful thought had just crossed her mind. Ever since Gurdon had climbed into her bunk on the *Lumber Baron*, Tobias had been attentive and helpful to her in every way. There had been no mention of their engagement and Gurdon had been confined to the bow of the ship. But somehow it all seemed contrived. Was Tobias sincerely concerned about King Strang or was he simply trying to win her favor?

Either way, there was nothing she could do. She must take care of her father and she could not do it without the aid of Tobias and Dr. Wilson. Andy had not appeared at the dock, as she had hoped. She could only pray that he would arrive soon.

Under the direction of Dr. Wilson, two sailors picked up King Strang's cot and carefully placed it on the wagon. Dr. Wilson took the reins of the wagon himself and led a slow procession along the streets of Milwaukee, with Tobias following in the carriage.

At the hotel, Tobias led the way and the sailors carried King Strang into a luxurious suite with a hospital bed in the center of the room. Dr. Wilson and

Abby, who were waiting inside, gently transferred him to the bed and covered him with warm blankets.

"Sarah, I will leave you now so Dr. Wilson can complete his examination," Tobias said. "You must be very tired. Abby will show you to your room."

Dr. Wilson agreed. "You have had a long journey. I suggest you get some rest. Abby and I will look after your father and I will see you in the morning."

Abby took Sarah by the hand and led her into the adjoining room. It was beautifully appointed, with a desk, a dresser, a washstand, and a large bed made up with soft linens and pillows. Towels and a flannel nightgown were neatly folded at the foot of the bed.

"I will be here all night," Abby said. "If you need anything at all, just call for me." She left the room and gently closed the door behind her.

Sarah looked around the room at the fashionable decorations. She had never seen such luxury, but she was too tired to appreciate it. Changing into the nightgown, she pulled back the sheets and climbed into bed. In a few moments she fell asleep, praying for her father and dreaming of Andy. She needed him so much. If only he would come soon.

In the morning Dr. Wilson and Tobias arrived together. Dr. Wilson had brought a complete medical kit in order to conduct a thorough examination of King Strang. With Abby's assistance, he cleaned the head wound and put in several stitches. Then he carefully cleaned and examined the bullet wound. Throughout the examination Tobias stood at the foot of the bed, watching and listening and helping out whenever he could.

When he was finished, Dr. Wilson closed his medical kit and gestured to Sarah and Tobias to join him in a corner of the room.

"He seems to have more color today and I suspect he slept well now that he is off the ship. Perhaps he is a little stronger. It is hard to tell as long as he remains comatose. I have examined his cheek and I regret to say that the bullet penetrated deeper than I thought. It is lodged under his cheekbone. Some of the bone will have to be removed to extract the bullet."

"Can you do that?" Tobias asked.

"It will be difficult. It is critical that he regain some strength. I shall be back again in the morning to check on his condition."

After a few private words to Abby, Dr. Wilson departed, with Tobias at his side.

"What did he say?" Sarah asked.

"He is worried about infection," Abby replied. "He wants me to keep the wound clean and covered."

"Is my father going to die?"

"I don't know, Sarah," Abby said, touching her arm. "We just have to do the best we can if we want to save him."

Every morning for the next several days Dr. Wilson and Tobias arrived to examine King Strang. Dr. Wilson could do nothing until the King regained some strength, and it seemed to Sarah that Tobias was becoming more distracted and impatient with every visit. He often waited outside while the doctor tended to his patient.

On the eighth day Dr. Wilson arrived alone. After completing his examination, he sighed and beckoned Sarah to a corner. "Your father has not progressed as quickly as I had hoped," he whispered. "In fact, every day he is weaker. There isn't much more I can do for him."

Sarah felt tears of grief and frustration welling up in her eyes. "Couldn't you just try to remove the bullet? We've been waiting so long."

"If I did, I would be violating my sacred oath as a physician. I am quite sure he would not survive the procedure. I am very sorry."

Dr. Wilson gathered up his medical kit and left the room, closing the door quietly behind him. Abby came over to Sarah and put her arms around her, holding her for a very long time.

Late in the afternoon Tobias arrived, this time with Gurdon following behind him. Sarah recoiled when she saw Gurdon enter the room. She had not seen him since the night on the *Lumber Baron* when he had crawled in bed with her. Cringing at the thought of his hands on her body, she could barely stand the sight of him. After all the years of rude gestures, vulgar remarks, bullying and fighting, it was too much for her to see him in the same room as her dying father.

"How is our patient today?" Tobias asked Abby.

"He is very weak," she replied.

"Well, I hope you are taking good care of him, because as soon as he is better—"

"Or dies," Gurdon interjected.

"—as soon as he is better," Tobias continued, "we will be having a wedding."

"He's not going to die!" Sarah cried, appalled at Gurdon's remark. "I can't believe you would say such a thing."

"Gurdon can say anything he wants. He's my son."

"Yeah, I can, and he *is* going to die. Just look at him."

"I have spoken to the doctor, but it doesn't really matter, Sarah," Tobias said. "If he lives or dies, we are having a wedding. King Strang has decreed it, and I am getting impatient. I promised to take care of him and I have done so. Now it is time for you to fulfill your father's promise to me."

"But he changed his mind!" Sarah said, blurting out the words.

"Oh, really?" Tobias sneered. "May I ask when that happened?"

"It was the night before he got shot. He never had a chance to tell you."

"How convenient. Why would he change his mind after he made me a promise?"

Sarah took a deep breath. "Because I told him I was already engaged to someone else."

Tobias jumped to his feet, towering over Sarah and glaring down at her. "Who would that be? Another Mormon? I'll put him in his place!"

Sarah couldn't stand it any longer. "He's not a Mormon! It's Andy McGuire. He asked me to marry him last summer, and I said yes."

Gurdon exploded. "That Irish piece of trash? That murderer? He's not fit to marry a dog. What about me? You were supposed to marry me!"

"He's not trash! You're the trash, Gurdon. I wouldn't even dream of marrying you. I can't stand the sight of you. I hate you!"

At this outburst Tobias raised his hand and slapped Sarah, sending her reeling across the floor and crashing into her father's bed. Her cheek stinging in pain, she saw a look of evil in Tobias' face, the same look she had seen in Gurdon's face so many times.

"You will never speak that way to Gurdon again, do you understand me?" he shouted. "Your father is mortally wounded. He cannot recover and he probably is going to die. As for this Andy McGuire of yours, he tried to kill your father. He was captured and thrown in jail before we even left Beaver Island. He tried to kill your father so he could have you to himself!"

"He did not! He would never do such a thing. We were going to run away. He loves me!"

"He didn't get very far, did he?" Gurdon smirked.

Tobias pushed his son away. "You are a young and gullible child, Sarah" he said. "You need to be protected from these foreign gentiles who are destroying your father's kingdom. Do you really want to marry a poor immigrant boy who assaulted your own father, after we have been trying so hard to drive them off the island? Do you realize he might hang for what he did?"

It was you!" Sarah cried. "You burned Andy's house down! You burned it down to get rid of him. You should be in jail, not Andy!"

At this, Tobias yanked Sarah to her feet and struck her again, this time with a closed fist. Sarah cried out in pain, collapsed to the floor, and crawled under her father's bed, the acrid taste of blood filling her mouth. King Strang, still unconscious, let out a dreadful moan, raised his arm above his head, and let it drop weakly back to his side.

Tobias and Gurdon both crouched down and peered silently at Sarah, who was whimpering in the shadows.

Tobias finally spoke, his eyes bright with passion. "Oh, yes, you will marry me, Sarah Strang, and I will teach you how to behave like an obedient Mormon wife. Your own father, King of the Mormons, has decreed it. Gurdon and I have been without a wife and mother for too long. Poor Gurdon does not even remember his mother. He has sought your hand in marriage, and you reject him! Such a hurtful thing to do! But now I see what to do. Since your father has five wives it is only fitting that you, his eldest daughter, should have two husbands! Therefore, we will have a double wedding; you will marry me and at the same time you will marry Gurdon. As the King himself said, it is the duty of all Mormon men to produce as many offspring as possible. With you as our wife, we will have the biggest Mormon family on Beaver Island. You, Sarah, shall be the mother of our children!"

It was at this moment Sarah realized that Tobias Humphrey was not a Mormon at all. He was a lustful, sick old man. He was bound to possess her, to force his desires on her, and to share her with his perverted and malevolent son. Sarah shivered in pain and fear and cowered under the bed. Her heart cried out for Andy, but where was he? Surely Tobias must be lying. Andy would have known that she left the island and he would have followed her. Perhaps he had already arrived in Milwaukee and was seeking her out this very day. Sarah could only pray, for if he did not come soon, her worst nightmare was about to become her destiny.

Tobias stood up and put his hands on his hips. "If King Strang remains alive, the wedding will be in three days," he announced.

"But what if he dies?" Gurdon asked.

"If he dies we marry immediately. There's a church right across the street. They'll do the job."

Tobias and Gurdon both headed for the door. As they were leaving, Tobias turned to Sarah. "In case you were thinking of escaping, all of the doors have been locked and the windows have been nailed shut. Also, Butch Jenkins — you remember Butch— has just arrived from Beaver Island. He's the one who captured Andy and threw him in jail. Now he will be guarding you, day and night. He'll be right outside, waiting in the hall."

They slammed the door and locked it. Abby, who had been cowering in a corner, quickly rushed to Sarah and pulled her out from under the bed. Sarah slumped into her arms, consumed with pain and horror and trapped in an empty room with her dying father.

CHAPTER 21:
Funeral and Wedding

Early in the morning, Abby awoke Sarah. "It is time," she said. "I am so sorry. He died in his sleep about an hour ago. He is at peace with the Lord."

"Somehow I knew," Sarah said, still in shock from the previous evening. "May I see him now?"

"Yes," Abby replied, "but I should warn you, there are many other people in the room."

"What people?" Sarah asked, startled.

"His followers. They have been waiting outside all night."

Abby opened the door for her. The outer room was dark, with only one candle on a nightstand. King Strang lay on his bed, now covered with a white sheet. The far wall was lined with Mormons from Beaver Island, all standing quietly out of respect for their king. Sarah was amazed that so many of the brethren had made the long trip to pay tribute to her father. She had no way of knowing that they had been evicted from their homes, herded on a boat, and abandoned on the wharf in Milwaukee. They were now refugees with no leader, no possessions and no place to stay.

Among the crowd, Sarah spied Wingfield and Edith Watson. Her first instinct was to run to Mrs. Watson, to be held, to be comforted, to be assured she would be safe. But at the foot of the bed she saw Tobias Humphrey, Gurdon Humphrey, and Butch Jenkins, all standing erect as if at a military parade. She would have to squeeze past them to reach her friends. All she could do was to go to her stricken father, take his hand, and let the tears flow.

Abby came forward, eyeing the three men at the foot of the bed and sensing the tension in the room. Gently she led Sarah away, and they both retreated to the other room. "We'll come back later when you can have some time alone," she whispered. She closed the door and led Sarah back to bed.

Several hours later someone knocked on the outer door. Sarah, now alone and still in bed, covered her head. She did not want to talk to anyone. The second knock was softer, the third knock softer still.

"Who is it?" she finally asked.

"It's Edith Watson," a muffled voice replied.

Mrs. Watson! Finally, a friend, someone she could talk to, someone who would listen, someone who could help her.

"I can't open the door," Sarah called. "They've locked me in."

"I have a key," Mrs. Watson said.

Not pausing to ask why she had a key, Sarah rushed to the door and listened while Mrs. Watson fussed with the door lock. Finally the door opened and she swept into the room, carrying a large box. Sarah rushed into her arms and burst into tears, overcome by all of the pain and fear of the last several days.

After holding Sarah until her tears subsided, Mrs. Watson released her and held her at arms length. "Sarah, Wingfield and I am so sorry about your father. You must have had a terrible journey, all alone with those rascals."

"Please help me..." Sarah said, still choking back her tears.

"I'm going to help, but first let me look at you. Now tell me, what happened to your face?"

"Tobias hit me. At first they were nice to me, but after we got here they said awful things. Tobias told me I had to marry him. When I told him about Andy, he hit me and I crawled under the bed. He said Andy was in jail for attacking my father, but I know it isn't true. Then Gurdon called Andy a murderer and Tobias said I had to marry both of them. Oh my God! You have no idea what they're going to do to me...It's hopeless..."

"Now calm down, Sarah. We'll talk later, I promise," Mrs. Watson said, "but now we have a lot to do. First, let's get you cleaned up."

Mrs. Watson went over to the nightstand and came back with a washcloth soaked in warm water. She sat down next to Sarah and gently washed her face, removing the dried blood from her cheek. Then she pulled out some cream and applied it to Sarah's bruises, rubbing it gently into the skin on her face and neck to reduce the swelling. Finally, she brushed her hair, picked out the tangles, and combed it back over her shoulders.

"There," she said. "Now you look better. How do you feel?"

"I feel better," Sarah replied." I'm just so sad about my father, and what am I going to do about—"

"We're sad too, my dear...Oh Lord, I didn't even lock the door!" Mrs. Watson exclaimed. She rushed across the room, pulled her box inside, and locked the door behind her.

"What's in the box, Mrs. Watson?" Sarah asked.

"It's your wedding dress."

Sarah's heart sank. Was Mrs. Watson helping Tobias Humphrey? "But I thought—"

Mrs. Watson grabbed Sarah by both shoulders and looked her in the eyes. "Wingfield and I are going to try to get you out of here, but you have to do exactly as I say, do you understand?"

"Yes," Sarah said hesitantly.

"You are going to have to trust me completely. Can you do that?"

"Yes."

"Good, because we only have one chance and we don't have much time. Now listen carefully. Tobias insisted on having the wedding today, so Wingfield persuaded him to let me help you get ready. I bought you this wedding dress, and if everything goes as planned you won't need it for long. Now here is the plan: Across the street there is a church. At four o'clock we are going to walk to the church arm in arm with you wearing this dress. On the corner you will see a tavern. I expect that you will see Tobias and Gurdon and probably Butch Jenkins and some of his men on the porch. They will be dressed in suits and they will be watching us, so just hang on to my arm and look straight ahead. When I squeeze your hand, I want you to look over at them and smile and wave."

"I don't think I can do that," Sarah said.

"You must! That will assure them that we'll be waiting in the church. Maybe they'll even go back into the tavern for another drink. Then we'll have more time. When we go into the church, I'm going to shut the door and lock it. I want you to run as fast as you can up the center aisle. Beyond the pulpit you will find a small door. Go through that door and you'll be outside, behind the church."

"But what about you?" Sarah asked. "Aren't you coming with me?"

"I'll be staying by the front door. I'll hold them off as long as I can."

"But—"

"I cannot say any more simply because I don't know exactly what will happen, but we are doing everything we can to rescue you. You must trust me. You must go out that door!"

After Mrs. Watson left, Sarah went into the adjoining room to pay her last respects to her father. The room was quiet and dark. She sat alone at the foot of her father's bed. Even in death, she could feel his charismatic presence. Solely by the power of his words he had created a kingdom and carved it out of a wilderness. Along the way he had attracted many loyal followers and made many bitter enemies. Sarah knew her father was not a saint, but she could not understand how anyone would wish to harm him. Some would defy his edicts, ignore his proclamations, and seek to leave his kingdom, but why would anyone want to kill him?

Sarah remembered how cruel he had been to her mother so long ago. She thought of his wicked plan to wed her to Tobias Humphrey simply to secure his own stature on the island. On both counts he had been a selfish and greedy man. But in the end his love for her had prevailed. He had opened his heart and seen her love for Andy and he had given her his blessing. No matter what fate awaited her now, she forgave him and she would always love him.

At the appointed hour, Sarah and Mrs. Watson came out of the hotel and stood on the porch, arm in arm. Sarah looked beautiful in her wedding dress and Mrs. Watson was dressed in her finest Sunday attire. Just as Mrs. Watson had predicted, a group of men were standing in front of the tavern. In the front was Tobias Humphrey, wearing a black coat with long tails and a string tie. Behind him stood Gurdon and Butch Jenkins, both also dressed in black. A group of men were loitering on the porch, many of them holding a glass.

Mrs. Watson held Sarah's arm. "Now we're just going to start walking," she whispered, her lips held in a tight smile. "Stay with me and we'll be fine."

Sarah nodded, her heart in her throat. Clinging to Mrs. Watson, she gingerly stepped into the street. Together they walked, looking straight ahead. When they reached the center of the dusty street, Mrs. Watson squeezed her arm.

"Now, Sarah," she whispered.

Sarah, in a daze, was staring at the church.

Mrs. Watson pinched her. "Sarah, you must!"

Sarah turned, pulled her lips into a grimace that looked like a smile, and raised her arm in an imitation of a wave. One of the men smiled and raised his glass.

"Good! Now let's keep walking."

Together they continued their journey, across the street and up the steps of the church. It seemed to take forever and Sarah could feel the eyes of the men upon her. She knew that soon they also would start walking across the street, with Tobias leading and Gurdon and Butch Jenkins following behind him.

As soon as they entered the church Mrs. Watson whirled around and locked the door.

"Run, Sarah, run!" she exclaimed.

Sarah scurried down the aisle, holding up her dress as she ran. She ran past the pulpit, stumbled through a row of choir chairs, and stopped at a narrow door in the back wall. Yanking it open, she was instantly blinded by the late afternoon sun.

"Over here!" a deep voice called.

It was Wingfield Watson, standing next to a wagon and a team of horses. He grabbed Sarah by the arm and led her to the back of the wagon, where she saw two barrels, one open and one sealed with a wooden lid.

"Get in the barrel," Wingfield ordered, glancing over his shoulder. "Be quick about it! They'll be here any minute."

This time Sarah did not hesitate. She climbed up on the wagon and jumped into the barrel. Her wedding dress caught on the rim, tearing the delicate fabric. Wingfield slapped the lid in place, picked up a handful of nails and a hammer, and nailed it to the barrel. Sarah huddled in the bottom, smothered by stifling darkness and the dank stale smell of salted fish.

"There's a blanket for you and two airholes in the bottom," Wingfield said, his voice muffled. "Hang on. It's going to be a rough ride."

Confused and bewildered, Sarah cried out to him. "Where are we going?"

But Wingfield did not hear her. He had already jumped up to the seat on the front of the wagon and was calling to the horses.

"Giddy-up, there! Giddy-up. Let's go!"

The wagon lurched forward, rocking the barrels and knocking them against each other with loud wooden thunks. With nothing to hang on to, Sarah bounced back and forth, first smacking her head and then flying forward and smashing her face into the rough wood. She cried out in fear and pain, but she knew that with every bump the wagon was taking her farther away from the church and marriage to the Humphreys, father and son.

Wingfield did not waste any time. He urged the horses onward, going as fast as he could through the cobbled streets of Milwaukee. On the outskirts of town he turned south on a country road. He whipped the reins, pushing the horses to their limit and making the wagon bounce over every bump and crunch into every pothole. The jarring ride rattled the barrels and shook Sarah in every direction, but Wingfield did not let up until they were well out of town.

After passing several farms he finally slowed down to a steady pace, but he did not stop, wishing to cover as much ground as possible. After about an hour they left the farmlands and entered a dark forest. The road had smoothed and Sarah had finally found a stable position inside the barrel. Wingfield stopped the horses in the shade and listened intently.

"I think I hear them," he finally said. "Yes, they are coming."

Sure enough, in the distance Sarah could hear the pounding hoofbeats of approaching horses.

"I was afraid of this," Wingfield said, his voice faint. "Sarah, you're going to have to trust me. You must remain absolutely silent, do you understand?"

"Yes," she replied, feeling helpless and terrified.

Wingfield shook the reins and the wagon moved forward, this time at a slower pace.

The hoofbeats got louder until they passed the wagon on either side. Sarah guessed that there must be several riders. They stopped in front of the wagon and Sarah could hear the horses breathing heavily. She froze in her barrel, listening and waiting to see what would happen.

"Stop right there," one of the riders shouted. Sarah heart sank when she recognized the voice. It was Butch Jenkins.

Wingfield reined in the horses and the wagon stopped. The riders dismounted. Sarah could hear them walking around the wagon and kicking the wheels. Another man spoke. It was Tobias Humphrey. Sarah cringed, knowing she was about to be discovered.

"Well, I'll be damned. It's Wingfield Watson. It seems like we just saw you this afternoon, Watson. I believe it was near a church back in Milwaukee."

"It could be…" Wingfield muttered.

"And your wife, too. Yes, I am quite sure we saw both of you today."

"I don't know…"

"I saw her, too!" another voice shouted. "She was with Sarah. They went in the church together. I'm sure of it!"

Sarah almost cried out, for this third voice was the voice of Gurdon, her tormentor and worst enemy of the three men. There could be no escape now. They would drag her back to Milwaukee, lock her up, and haul her back to Beaver Island for a life of abuse and misery. She held her hands over her mouth to stifle her sobs, but she could not hold back her tears as they ran down her cheeks.

"You took off mighty fast, Watson," Tobias said. "Why were you in such a hurry to leave?"

Wingfield hesitated. "Well, I…"

"Where is she?" Tobias demanded.

"Who?"

"Sarah Strang, you idiot."

"I don't know," Wingfield lied. "I haven't seen her."

"Butch." Tobias gestured to Jenkins. Jenkins pulled his revolver and pointed it straight at Wingfield's chest.

"Please, I have no idea where she is," Wingfield said, a tremble in his voice. "The last time I saw her was yesterday in King Strang's room. I didn't even talk to her."

"So why'd you leave town so fast?"

Wingfield hung his head. "I just had to get away..." he murmured.

"Speak up, man. I want the truth."

"I just had to get away....from that woman. I can't stand another day of wailing and whining and crying. That's all she's done for a month, ever since King Strang was shot. You'd think the Lord himself had died. I can't stand it anymore."

"You're running away from your wife? Is that what you're telling me?"

"That's the truth of it. I have no idea where Sarah Strang is, I swear."

Butch Jenkins started to laugh, a mean vicious laugh.

"What's in the barrels?" Tobias demanded.

"Fish. Salted fish," Wingfield replied.

"I don't believe you."

"It's true. I'm going to sell them in the next town."

"Do you have an axe on this wagon?"

"An axe? No, I don't"

"What's that behind the seat?"

"It's just an old hammer."

"That'll do. Butch, open those barrels. I want to see what's inside."

Jenkins jumped up on the wagon and grabbed the hammer. Sarah cringed, waiting for the first blow.

"Don't do that!" Wingfield pleaded, stepping between the drums. "The fish are—"

Jenkins ignored him. Taking a stance, he raised the hammer and took a mighty swing. He hit the first barrel with a thud, splintering the wood. Sarah, cowering in terror in the other barrel, buried her head in the blanket and covered her ears. Jenkins swung again and again, splintering the wood. A stream of yellow liquid began to flow out between the barrel staves. Jenkins kept swinging and suddenly the end of the barrel broke away in shattered pieces. A deluge of rotten fish guts and fish heads poured out, spewing across the wagon and splashing Tobias and Gurdon with slimy ooze.

"Aghhh!" Tobias cried, recoiling from the slobbery mess. "What is this crap?"

Wingfield looked at them sheepishly. "I tried to warn you. They're a little old…"

"A little old! They're completely rotten!"

"I can't help it. I need the money."

"You were going to sell them?"

Wingfield was silent.

"You're running away from your wife and on your way out of town you're going to sell these rotten fish to someone, is that what you're telling me?"

Sarah, still cowering in the drum, listened intently, but Wingfield did not say a word.

Tobias was furious. "Watson, you're a liar and a thief. You Mormons make me sick. How you could stay married to that windbag all these years is beyond me. Take your rotten fish and get out of here. You ride this wagon straight down this road as far as you can go and never come back. I don't ever want to see you again. If you show up in Milwaukee or on Beaver Island I'll kill you myself. I swear to God I will. Now git!"

"But what about Sarah?" Gurdon asked. "We still need to find her, don't we?"

"Yer damn right we do. She's probably with that old hag Edith Watson, hiding somewhere near the church. We'll find her, don't you worry about that! Let's go, Butch!"

The three men grabbed their reins, saddled up, and took off at a full gallop back toward Milwaukee. The sound of the hoofbeats got fainter and fainter until there was silence along the country road.

Wingfield began to whistle a tune. At the sound, the horses began to pull. The wheels creaked and the wagon moved again. He did not say a word to them, nor did he speak to Sarah. He just kept whistling the same tune, over and over. Her heart still pounding in fear, Sarah understood Wingfield's message. The imminent danger was over, but the men on horses might return and if they did they would not be so forgiving. She must remain in the barrel, remain silent, and trust Wingfield to deliver her to safety. She still did not know their destination, but the steady sound of the horse's hooves calmed her.

After what seemed like hours the wagon slowed, turned, and stopped. Sarah felt the wagon shift as Wingfield climbed down and then she heard the sound of a gate opening. The horses moved ahead and the gate closed, squeaking on rusty hinges.

In the distance a woman's voice called out. "Who is it? Who's there?" Then the voice was closer. "Wingfield? Wingfield Watson? Is that you? What on earth are you doing here?" Even though it had been five long years, Sarah instantly recognized the voice. It was her mother, Mary Strang!

For the first time on the trip Sarah's trembling fear gave way to acute claustrophobia. She had to get out of the barrel! "Wingfield!" she cried, "Open the lid! Hurry! Get me out of here!"

Wingfield obliged, grabbing the hammer and pounding on the lid. The wood began to crack and split and Sarah saw her first beam of sunlight. After a few more whacks the lid began to splinter and fall away. Wingfield tore off the last few boards and tossed them aside. Sarah vaulted out of the barrel, rolled off the back of the wagon, and landed face down in the dirt. She was still wearing her wedding dress, now covered with blood, dirt, and fish slime.

Mary, who had come up to the wagon, stopped in her tracks. "Oh my God, Wingfield, who is this poor soul?" she exclaimed.

"She's—" Wingfield started.

"Mother..." Sarah whimpered, slowly raising her head.

"Sarah! Is that you? Good Lord, child, what has happened to you?"

"She's got some cuts and bruises, but she's safe now," Wingfield said.

"Safe from what?" Mary demanded.

"Well, it's a long story."

Mary helped her daughter to her feet and held her in her arms. "There's time for that later. First let's get you out of this horrible dress and get you cleaned up." She helped Sarah along the path and led her to her home, a small cottage bordered by a white picket fence.

Wingfield turned back to his wagon. He dumped both empty barrels in the bushes and fed and watered his horses. Then he climbed into the seat of the wagon, whistled a few bars of a familiar tune, and let out a long sigh of relief.

The next morning Sarah felt like a new person. The night before, Mary had stripped her of her wedding dress and given her a hot bath. While soaking in the tub, Sarah told Mary of her rescue by Edith Watson and of the harrowing escape from the Humphreys and Butch Jenkins. Her mother then tucked her into bed and Sarah had her first good nights sleep since leaving Beaver Island.

Over breakfast, Sarah continued her story, telling Mary everything that had happened on Beaver Island, including the conflicts between the Mormons and Irish, her arranged betrothal to Tobias Humphrey, Andy's plan to escape the island together, and the sudden and unexpected assault on King Strang.

"But what about Andy?" Mary asked. "If you were going to escape together, wouldn't he have followed you? Where is he?"

"I don't know, Sarah replied, holding her hands to her face. "I expected to see him in Milwaukee, but he never showed up."

"Sarah, I'm worried about him."

"Tobias said Andy assaulted my father and is in jail. Gurdon says he murdered him."

"Of course they would say that. Don't worry about it. We must find out what really happened. Maybe Wingfield knows."

At that precise moment there was a knock on the door. Mary opened it and there stood Wingfield Watson, his large frame filling the doorway. Sarah ran to him and hugged him. "Thank you so much for saving me." she said.

"Feeling better today? You had a rough ride yesterday. I'm sorry about that."

"Good morning, Wingfield," Mary said. "Come in and have some tea." Wingfield pulled up a chair and Sarah poured him a cup.

"We've been talking—" Mary began.

"I'll bet you have! It's not every day a daughter comes home in a barrel!"

Mary got right to the point. "Sarah and I would like to know what happened to Andy."

"Andy McGuire? I have no idea. I'm telling you, the last few days on the island were chaos."

"What happened the day my father was attacked?" Sarah asked.

"I was planting crops that day so I wasn't in town. The navy ship was at the dock and there was a big crowd. I heard that several men attacked King Strang while he was walking down to the ship. Shot him and hit him with clubs, so they say."

"Was Andy one of them?' Sarah asked.

"I don't know, but I can't imagine why he would have anything to do with it. The navy ship left that day and you left the next morning on the *Lumber Baron* with your father. A few days later all hell broke loose. A mob invaded the island. They came to our houses and made us load our wagons and head to town. The next day they forced us on boats and we had to leave. I lost everything."

"Wait a minute," Mary asked, "they forced *who* on boats?"

"All of us. All the Mormons. They took over the island."

"You mean there are no more Mormons on Beaver Island?"

"Nope, not that I know of," Wingfield said.

Mary and Sarah were dumbfounded. They had no idea that the island had been invaded. They were both silent for a moment, finally realizing that King Strang's kingdom had collapsed.

"Can I go back there?" Sarah asked, tears forming in her eyes.

"I wouldn't advise it," Wingfield replied, "not for a long time."

"But how am I ever going to find Andy?" she cried.

Mary put her arms around her daughter and held her. "Don't worry, dear, we'll figure it out. We'll find him somehow."

Sarah could no longer hold back her tears. "What about my father? Can we at least go back to Milwaukee to see him?"

"That would not be safe," Wingfield replied, "but I don't expect the Humphreys will stick around after they discover that Edith is gone. But just to be sure, we have someone helping us. She is watching the waterfront. As soon as the *Lumber Baron* leaves the dock, she will make arrangements to have King Strang's body brought here, where we can give him a decent ceremony and a proper burial."

"Who is helping us?" Sarah asked.

"Abby. She saw how you were mistreated and she wanted to help."

Mary looked at Wingfield with admiration and gratitude. "You planned every detail, didn't you," she said.

"Nah, it was mostly Edith," Wingfield replied. "She's a remarkable woman."

"But aren't you worried about her? Those men must have been very angry when they got back to Milwaukee and still couldn't find Sarah. They might have harmed her."

Wingfield chuckled. "Don't worry about Edith. After the Humphreys took off after us, she high-tailed it down to the waterfront and boarded a ferry to Chicago. She'll spend the night there and tomorrow she'll get on a stagecoach. I expect we'll see her here about dinner time."

Sure enough, the next day a wagon arrived carrying a wooden coffin and followed by a large group of Mormons, all refugees from Beaver Island. An hour later a stagecoach arrived from Chicago and Edith Watson climbed down, still wearing her Sunday dress. In the evening a brief ceremony was held and several of the church brethren made powerful and passionate eulogies to King Strang, praising his leadership and faith in the Lord. He was buried in the local cemetery. His kingdom had lasted almost exactly six years.

~

As it turned out, Mary and Sarah did not attend the funeral. Mary could see that her daughter was exhausted, broken in heart and body. She would need time to recover from her ordeals and she would need some positive news to lift her spirits.

"Sarah, I spoke with Wingfield before he left for the funeral. He agreed to ask everyone he could about Andy. Surely someone must know something. Also, I have learned that not all the Mormons left the island. Some of them renounced their faith and were allowed to stay and others simply hid in the woods. I am going to write a letter to each and every one of them, and I want you to write to Andy. No matter who is living on the island, the post office won't be closed for long, you can be sure of that. Don't you worry, we'll solve this mystery. Together we will find him!"

The next day Mary brought out writing paper and pens and began to write to her old friends on Beaver Island. Sarah sat down across the table from her mother and wrote a long letter to Andy asking him to join her in Voree.

It would be the first of several letters she would write.

Ian McGuire was slowly recovering from his injuries. Not one to remain idle, he began to think about beginning work on a new house. It wouldn't be long before winter arrived, and they needed a place to live. "Andy, what does our old house look like these days?" he asked one morning.

"It's just a pile of burned logs and ashes. There's nothing left but the chimney."

"I've got an idea. Why don't we get started on rebuilding it?"

Andy looked at him, startled. "Right now? The whole house?"

"Sure, why not? We don't want to spend all winter in Patrick's house, do we?"

"No, I suppose not." Andy didn't even want to spend the winter on Beaver Island.

"We could cut down those trees back by the barn. Patrick and Nathan and Oren will help. We can get the walls and roof up before it snows, and then finish the rest over the winter."

"But you're not better yet," Andy said.

"I will be soon."

Andy took a deep breath, and then said what was on his mind. "Actually, I was thinking about going across the lake to Milwaukee."

Ian was not completely surprised by Andy's remark. He knew his son well, and figured that he would want to follow Sarah sooner or later.

"It's getting pretty late in the year for a trip like that."

"I know, but I could make it."

"Listen, Andy, I know you want to find Sarah, but we need a roof over our heads. She'll be back in the spring when her father gets better. She left once before for the winter and came back, don't you remember?"

"But it's different this time." Andy groped for the words to explain the urgency he felt. "King Strang might not get better. Sarah may never come back."

Ian put his hand on his son's shoulder. He remembered how he felt when he lost his wife back in Ireland, knowing he would never see her again.

"Oh, I think she will," he said. "Look, Andy, let's just start building this cabin so at least we have a roof over our heads. If the weather holds and a steamboat happens to pull in the harbor this fall, maybe you'll be able to hitch a ride. How does that sound?"

"All right, I guess," Andy said. But he did not feel at all comforted, knowing that Sarah was in the clutches of Tobias Humphrey somewhere in Milwaukee.

"Good!" said Ian. "We'll start cutting trees in the morning. I won't be much help, but I'll do what I can."

The next morning, before the sun even rose over Whiskey Point, Andy was out by the barn swinging an axe. He had already cut down a large pine tree when Ian called him to come and have some breakfast. Andy dropped his axe, ran inside, and gobbled his meal. He was back outside before Ian could even pour him a cup of coffee.

Later in the morning Patrick and Nathan and Oren all came out to help. By afternoon they had the burned cabin site cleared and they had the first log set on the old foundation. Ian had sketched out some plans for the new house. It would be the same size, but by adding an enclosed porch to the front, there was room for a small bedroom in the back.

Ian's health was improving rapidly now that he was working on a new project. "We'll make the roof steeper this time," he said. "It will add more headroom in the loft and we'll divide it into two bedrooms."

In several weeks the four walls of the cabin were completed and holes were cut for windows and a door. A foundation of stones had been laid for the new front porch. It was time to start building the roof. Andy and Nathan and Oren were dispatched to the woods to cut some straight cedar poles to serve as rafters. They gathered up axes and saws and headed to Whiskey Point, where they knew there was an abundance of cedar trees.

"Do you think King Strang is dead?" Nathan asked, looking around for straight trees.

"No one knows," Andy replied. "He was alive when they put him on Humphrey's boat and set sail for Milwaukee."

"I think he's dead," Oren said. "I saw him when they carried him up to his house. He was shot in the head and in the face. Thomas Bedford pounded his head in with the butt of his pistol. I don't think he could survive all that."

"If he's dead, I wonder if any of the Mormons will ever come back to Beaver Island."

"I doubt it," Oren said, wondering if he would ever see his parents again.

"Sarah will come back, won't she?" Nathan asked. "She only left the island to take care of him."

Andy didn't respond. All three of the boys knew that if King Strang died, Sarah might never be able to return to the island. Or, if she did return, it would be on Tobias Humphrey's schooner as his wife.

Finally Oren broke the silence. "Maybe Sarah went to her mother's. She lives in Voree, not far from Milwaukee. A lot of Mormons live there."

"I don't think so," Andy said. "Not while she's held captive by Tobias Humphrey. It doesn't matter if King Strang is dead or alive. He'll never let her go. That's why I've got to go and rescue her."

"Andy, it's pretty late—"

Andy suddenly stopped in his tracks. "I just had a great idea," he said.

"What?" Nathan and Oren asked in unison.

"Let's sail the *Emma Rose* to Milwaukee."

Nathan and Oren stared at him. "Are you crazy?" Nathan asked.

"This time of year?" Oren asked. "We'd all drown or freeze to death"

"Ian and Patrick would never let us do that," Nathan added.

"Why not?" Andy asked. "We're all good sailors. We know the *Emma Rose* and we know Lake Michigan."

"Not in November we don't," Nathan responded.

"Andy, the *Emma Rose* is your livelihood," Oren said. "If anything ever happens to that boat, you'll be working in Humphrey's saw mill."

"But nothing would happen. We could do it if we're careful."

The boys reached a thick stand of cedars. They selected a dozen of the straightest trees and marked them. Andy and Nathan cut the trees down while Oren cut them to length, stripped off the bark, and rolled the logs to the path. Throughout the day Andy kept talking about how they could rescue Sarah. Nathan and Oren thought the idea of sailing across Lake Michigan in November was suicidal, but Andy could not be dissuaded from his plan. He was quite certain that if they watched the weather carefully they could make it to Milwaukee in a couple of days, find Sarah, and sail back to Beaver Island without any trouble.

That evening Andy approached his father with his plan and asked if he could borrow the *Emma Rose*.

"In November? Are you crazy?" Ian asked, echoing the words of Nathan and Oren.

"But I'm a good sailor."

"I know you're a good sailor, Andy. That's why you should know better."

"We'd only be gone a few days—"

"You'd sink the boat and you'll all drown. I'm not going to let you risk everything we've worked for just because you're soft on some girl."

"We'd be careful and we'd stay near shore—"

"Andy, that's enough! I don't want to hear any more about it. If you really want to go to Milwaukee this fall, you're just going to have to find another way to get there."

Andy realized he had lost the argument with his father. He was not going to be able to escape Beaver Island on the *Emma Rose*. He crawled up the ladder to the loft, collapsed in bed, and stared blankly at the pine boards over his head. No more steam boats were likely to stop in the harbor this late in the season, he was sure of that. He was going to have to figure out another way to get across the lake.

The next day the boys hauled cedar poles from Whiskey Point and Ian and Patrick shaped them into rafters. In the afternoon they fitted four corner rafters and raised a ridgepole, attaching it with wooden pegs. Over the next few days they fitted the rest of the rafters, and by the end of the week they nailed the first row of cedar shingles on the new roof. Andy worked as hard as ever, but he wasn't talking much. His mind raced as he worked, still trying to figure out a way to get off the island. He even thought about waiting for the lake to freeze and walking to the mainland, but the ice would not set in for at least a couple of months. He had to act soon.

Soon the roof was finished. Plenty of work remained, but it was time to move into the new house. While Ian and Andy carried their belongings over to the new cabin, Patrick prepared a housewarming feast.

"Venison stew with carrots and potatoes! Come and get it!" Patrick hollered.

The three boys scrambled into the cabin and lined up at the table. Ian followed them, still limping and nursing his broken ribs. "Nothing like a cold fall day and the smell of fresh-cut cedar to give a man an appetite," he said, closing the door behind him.

Patrick dished out the stew and Ian proposed a toast.

"To our new home! May it last longer than the first one."

"Hear, Hear!" the boys all shouted

"I have a special treat today," Patrick announced. "Fresh bread and raspberry jam, which I made for the first time. It turned out quite well, if I do say so."

"Mmm, this smells good," Oren said, taking a large spoonful of the jam.

"Where'd you get the berries?" Ian asked.

"I found a berry patch this summer," Patrick replied. "It's in a clearing in the woods out by the North Beach."

Andy looked up, startled. He knew exactly where the berry patch was. He had spent many summer afternoons there with Sarah, munching on berries and talking about their future together. They were the happiest times of his life, but now they seemed so long ago. He spread the jam on a slice of warm bread and watched as it oozed into the bread and dripped over the sides. Then he raised it to his mouth and took a bite, savoring the sweet and succulent liquid. The smell and taste of the raspberry jam brought back memories of Sarah, and it suddenly made Andy realize what he must do.

Mary Strang kept Sarah inside and tended to her wounds. She made her rest, cooked some good meals, and kept a sharp lookout for any strangers that might be looking for her. Sarah quickly recovered from her injuries and soon she was helping Mary in her garden. Together they pulled weeds, watered flowers, and talked about the island. Mostly Sarah talked about Andy.

"How long do you think it will take for my letter to get to him?" she asked.

"I would say at least two weeks," Mary replied. "Maybe longer."

"So I won't hear back from him for a whole month?"

"I'm afraid not, but we may have some news sooner than that. Most of the Mormons who came to your father's funeral have settled around here and more are coming every day. We're sure to hear something. Who knows, he may even show up on our doorstep one day."

Sarah was comforted by her mother's words. She knew she must be patient, but she missed him so much. She was grateful to be reunited with her mother and safe from the clutches of the Humphreys, but all she wanted more than anything else was to be with Andy, to see him, to touch him, to hold him again.

~

Andy knew how to fish. Now that they were settled into the new cabin, it was time to catch some fresh lake trout. With fishing pole in hand, he left early, well before dawn. He hiked toward Whiskey Point to a dock that extended out to deep water. It didn't take him long to catch a full bucket of trout.

Just as the sun rose, he put down his pole and began to walk along the shore of Paradise Bay, staying out of sight among the bushes. It took him a while, but he soon found what he was looking for. He found an old boat, washed up on shore and hidden in the reeds. It was an open, single-masted sailing vessel. Too small for fishing, it must have been used to travel to the other islands, with possibly an occasional summer trip to Mackinac Island.

Andy had reasoned that in the confusion surrounding the expulsion of the Mormons, a few stray boats must have been abandoned around the edges of the harbor. After all, the dock had been crowded with wagons and tents, and most of those had been abandoned. Why not an abandoned boat? This one must have drifted across the harbor, and it was perfect.

The next day, after catching another bucket of fish and stashing it in the bushes, Andy went to work. First he bailed out the bilge water and dried the hull. Then he untangled ropes and rigging and laid the sails out on the grass, hoping they would dry in the weak fall sun. A couple of days later, he came back with some oakum and an old sheet of canvas. He went over every inch of the hull, filling even the smallest cracks. He spread the canvas over the bow, stretched it taut, and nailed it to the sides of the boat, making a small, weatherproof cabin.

He always left the house before dawn, so no one noticed how long he was gone. After catching a bucket of fish, he still had time to work on the boat and make it back home just in time for breakfast.

Andy was obsessed with his work, but he was not stupid. He knew what kind of weather an early winter storm could bring to the Great Lakes. If he was going to sail this boat across Lake Michigan in November, he'd better be prepared for severe cold, strong winds and big waves. He packed all the winter clothes he could find into a duffel bag and retrieved the luggage that he and Sarah had planned to take on the *Louisville* last summer. He packed several wool blankets in a trunk and stuffed everything into the makeshift cabin, along with plenty of food and an extra pair of oars. Carefully checking all the knots and ropes, he rigged the sails and furled them to the mast.

Andy knew his father would never let him sail away by himself, but he was sure he could make it as long as the weather held. Maybe he would only reach the northern coast of Michigan, but that was fine; he could travel to Milwaukee on land. After he found Sarah, they would stay with her mother in Voree and then return to the island in the spring.

November 10 dawned clear and calm, another mild day in what had been a warm fall. It was cold in the morning, but as the day progressed the sun melted the frost and warmed the air. Ian, who had been cutting firewood, took off his wool shirt and threw it over a stump.

"I won't need this anymore," he said. "It's almost hot out here. Hard to believe, for this time of year."

Nathan was helping him by stacking the wood between the cabins. "Maybe we've got enough," he said. "I've stacked two big rows already."

"Oh, we'll need a lot more wood, you can bet on that," Ian replied. "It's going to be a long winter. This stretch of good weather won't last, and when it breaks, you'd better watch out. We're going to get hammered."

"Do you think it's going to snow?" Nathan asked.

"I think it's going to do a lot more than snow. We're going to get our first winter storm, and it's going to be a big one. Look at the color of the sky over there. That doesn't look right, does it?"

Nathan had to agree that the sky in the west had an odd green color. Still, there was no wind and not a cloud in sight.

"By the way, where's Andy?" Ian asked. "I've haven't seen him this morning. He should be hauling this wood, not you."

"I don't know. I haven't seen him either."

"He sure has been moping around lately. I can't get a word out of him, and he's never around when I need him."

Nathan was surprised at Ian's remark. Ian never complained about Andy. "I'll look for him this afternoon," he said.

Nathan knew exactly why Andy had become so sullen. No boats had arrived in the harbor, so it looked like he was going to have to wait until spring to find Sarah. Andy was not good at waiting. Later that day, Nathan went to Saint James to see if he could find him. He checked in the Mormon school, which was empty now. He walked to the dock and then on to King Strang's house, which had been boarded up. Nathan checked for any signs of entry, but all the doors were locked.

On a hunch, Nathan returned home by way of Sarah's berry patch, but he found no sign of Andy anywhere. As he climbed down the bluff to the beach, he felt a puff of cold air on the back of his neck. Looking up at the sky, he saw a few high clouds overhead and an ominous black cloud bank moving in from the west. Ian had been right. A storm was rapidly approaching.

Before returning to his own house, Nathan stopped to see Ian. "No sign of Andy. I looked everywhere," he said.

"Maybe he went fishing on one of the inland lakes," Ian replied. "He likes to do that sometimes."

"Could be…"

"It looks like a storm is coming, just as I expected," Ian remarked.

"Yeah, the wind is starting to pick up."

"Well, he'll probably be home before dark."

"I'll let you know if I see him." Nathan closed the door and went over to his own cabin. Ian did not seem too concerned about Andy's absence, but Nathan had grown increasingly worried throughout the afternoon as he prowled around the empty houses in Saint James. Andy was independent, but he seldom vanished completely, at least not for very long. Nathan looked out at the harbor. The sky had turned dark gray and waves were already slapping angrily against the dock. By dusk he began to suspect that Andy had not gone fishing. Not this time.

Nathan woke in the middle of the night with a sick hollow feeling in his stomach. He had dreamed of a small boat, far out in the lake and unable to return to land. He waved his arms, but the boat sailed away from him and disappeared. Nathan got out of bed and peeked out the window. It was still dark and the wind was howling through the pine trees. It was the first storm of the season. He fell back into bed and closed his eyes, unable to sleep.

Just as the sky began to turn pink in the east Nathan put on his winter coat and boots, slipped out the front door, and headed toward Whiskey Point. He walked along the shore, casting his eyes back and forth amongst the reeds and bushes, searching for some kind of a clue. As the sky brightened he was able to cover more ground and soon he reached the old dock on Whiskey Point. He walked to the end of the dock, turning up his collar to block the wind and kicking snow into the swirling water below. Out on the lake, he saw nothing, nothing but waves and whitecaps.

On his way back home the light had improved. This time Nathan found what he was looking for. It was just a trace, a line in the windswept snow. He followed the line and found several broken reeds. Sweeping away the snow, he discovered a deep gouge in the frozen mud.

"I knew it!" Nathan cried. "This is where it was!"

Without looking any further, he ran as fast as he could back to the cabins. Ian and Patrick were sitting at Ian's table when Nathan burst in, wind and snow swirling through the door. Both men jumped to their feet.

"Where have you been?" Patrick asked.

"Did you find him?" Ian asked at the same time.

"No, but I know where he is," Nathan said. He was out of breath and covered with snow.

"Where is he?" Ian demanded.

"Do you remember the boat that Tom and Sam Bennett had down at Cable Bay?"

"Sure. It's hard to forget that boat. The Mormons used it to bring Tom Bennett's body back after they murdered him. Nobody wanted it after that."

"It was in pretty bad shape," Patrick added.

"Do you know what ever happened to it?" Nathan asked.

"What's this got to do with Andy?" Ian asked.

"What happened to the boat?" Nathan demanded.

"It was abandoned. I think it drifted across the harbor and washed up in the weeds out near Whiskey Point."

"Yeah, come to think of it, I saw it there this summer," Patrick said. "Why do you ask, Nathan?"

"I had a hunch when I woke up this morning, so I went out there to check on it."

"What for? It's freezing outside."

"Because I found where the boat used to be, but it isn't there now."

"What do you mean, it isn't there?"

"The boat is gone. Andy took it."

Ian and Patrick looked at each other in stunned silence. They were both thinking the same thing. Andy had taken the old abandoned boat and was attempting to sail across Lake Michigan in a November storm.

"He'll never make it," Ian said, slumping in his chair.

"Now, Ian, he's a good sailor," Patrick said. "We've been out in worse weather than this before."

"Not this time of year. Not alone in an open boat."

"He's a tough kid, Ian. He'll probably just run before the wind until he makes landfall somewhere on the mainland."

"Couldn't we launch the *Emma Rose* and go after him?" Nathan asked.

The two men stopped for a minute, mulling over the idea.

"She's already out of the water and sitting on her cradle," Patrick said. "In this weather, it would take a full day to launch her."

"We'd have to get the sails and rigging out of the barn and put them up," Ian added. "That would take another day. That's two days. He'd have a two-day head start."

"We don't even know what direction he headed," Patrick said. "He could try for Milwaukee, or he could run due east to the Michigan shore, or he could just hole up on one of the islands around here and wait out the storm."

"We'd never find him, Nathan," Ian said. "Not in a thousand years. "I just hope to God he knows what he's doing out there."

Patrick put his arm around his friend. "We'll pray for him, Ian. He's a good sailor. He'll turn up somewhere, alive and well. It may not be until the weather breaks, but he'll turn up somewhere, I promise you that."

The wind howled around the cabin and rattled the windows. Andy had vanished without a trace.

CHAPTER 22:
A Stranger Arrives

"Sarah, I have good news!" Mary said, arriving home after a trip to the village.

Sarah jumped to her feet. "What is it? Is it about Andy?"

"No, I'm sorry—"

"But it's been months!"

"I'm afraid we'll just have to wait until spring, Sarah. There probably isn't much mail delivery this time of year."

"I've written him three times."

"Maybe after the ice breaks up on the lake the mail will come through."

Frowning with disappointment, Sarah returned to her seat by the fireplace.

"I spoke with the headmaster of the Voree public school. They are in need of a teacher. With your experience you would be perfect. You could start right away."

"I don't want to teach. I just want to find Andy."

Mary came over and sat down next to her daughter. "Sarah, we are all looking for him, but there isn't much we can do until spring. It won't do any good to mope around all winter. Why don't you take the job; it will keep you occupied. When the boats start to run again we can send someone to the island to find out what happened to Andy."

Sarah didn't say much, but she knew her mother was right. The next day she went to see the headmaster. When he learned about her experience on Beaver Island he hired her on the spot. She would start teaching the following

Monday. It all seemed so permanent, so over the weekend Sarah wrote Andy another letter. She knew they all sounded the same, but it made her feel better and she hoped that one of the letters might actually make it to Beaver Island.

On Monday she reported to the school and was immediately confronted with a classroom full of unruly children. Remembering everything Mrs. Watson had taught her, she quickly restored order and within a week she had the students reciting the alphabet.

Sarah enjoyed her new teaching job. The children were learning quickly and it was fun to watch their progress. Every evening after dinner she prepared a new lesson plan and placed it in a folder by the door. Every night she hid under her blanket, hugged her pillow, and went to a lonely and private place of her very own. In her dreams she was on the island with Andy, walking to school or slipping away to their secret berry patch for an afternoon together. In her darkest nightmares Andy was gone: trapped somewhere, locked in jail, lost at sea, or dead, killed by Butch Jenkins and his gang. In the background, always hovering over her, were the dark figures of Tobias and Gurdon Humphrey.

All winter Nathan walked the shorelines of Beaver Island, hoping to find a clue in the ice or along the rocky beaches. Patrick traveled from Whiskey Point to Saint James to the outlying farms south of town, seeking out anyone he could find and asking them if they had seen or heard anything about Andy. He had no luck.

Ian kept his own lonely vigil, staying near the cabin and praying for the safe return of his son. In January, he and Patrick tried to walk across the ice to Garden Island to expand their search, but they were turned back by thin ice. As winter closed its grasp around the island, they finally gave up hope of finding him. All talk of Andy making it to the mainland had given way to the realization that he couldn't have sailed across Lake Michigan in a leaky old boat. If he was alive, he probably was marooned on one of the many small islands surrounding Beaver Island, and they would have to hold out until spring to try to find him. Meanwhile they were trapped on an island that seemed to share their desolation with every winter storm.

~

Spring arrived early in Voree. The last of the snowbanks had melted and the first daffodils were starting to bloom. One morning Wingfield Watson came to visit. "Good day to you, ladies," he called from the front porch.

Mary and Sarah both ran to the door to greet him. "Good morning, Wingfield," Mary said. "Please come in. How was your winter?"

"Well, it was long and cold, but I just leased forty acres of land just down the road, so I'll be farming again soon." Wingfield paused. "Sarah, I've come to see you. Have you heard anything from Andy?"

"No, nothing," Sarah replied.

"Neither have I, but I have an idea. Do you remember Oren Whipple?"

"Oren? Yes, I do."

"Good! Do you recall that Oren's parents were with you on the *Lumber Baron*?"

"They might have been. I really don't remember. I was too busy taking care of my father."

"Yes, of course. The Whipples were on the boat and they expected to return to Beaver Island, but they never did after they found out all the Mormons had been run off. They stayed in Milwaukee."

"What does this have to do with Andy?" Mary asked.

"Their son Oren remained on the island. They have not seen or heard from him. They have written letters and asked everyone, just like we've done. Gilbert Whipple has decided to go back to find his son. I told him of your predicament and he has agreed to look for Andy. Furthermore, if you wish to write a letter, he will deliver it. He no longer trusts the mail."

"He's a Mormon. Won't that be dangerous for him?" Mary asked.

"He doesn't care. He wants to find his son."

"May I go with him?" Sarah asked.

"Certainly not!" Mary replied. "Those wicked men are still out there."

"Maybe they are," Wingfield replied, "but I've heard that Tobias Humphrey bought another ship and has settled in Milwaukee to run his business."

"What about Gurdon Humphrey and Butch Jenkins?" Mary asked.

"Tobias fired Jenkins after Sarah escaped. No one knows where he went, and he hasn't been seen since. I'm sure Gurdon will follow his father."

"When is Mr. Whipple leaving?" Sarah asked, still amazed that she had finally heard some news after an entire winter of silence.

"As soon as the ice melts on the lake. He'll take the first steamboat."

After Wingfield left, Sarah sat down to write another letter to Andy. She stared at the page and fiddled with her pen, but for some reason the words would not come. Finally she put down the pen and went for a walk through the fields behind her mother's cottage. She wasn't gone long but it gave her time to think. It had been almost a year since she had come to Voree. Beaver Island now seemed worlds away. Why hadn't Andy followed her? Why hadn't he written or gotten word to her somehow? It seemed that she would never know.

After dinner Sarah tried again to write. She completed half a page before she crumpled up the paper and threw it on the floor. She picked up a new piece of paper and started another letter. This time the words came to her. This was a letter she knew she must write.

―～―

Spring finally came to the island, and with it came longer days, a warming sun and melting snow. It was time for Ian and Patrick to launch the *Emma Rose*. Even though the harbor was still partly frozen and there was still plenty of snow on the ground, they all got outside and went to work.

But winter was not done with them yet. There was one last storm looming on the horizon. After several days of unseasonably warm weather, the sky took on an eerie gray cast, and then a dark line of clouds appeared beyond the trees on the other side of the harbor. By mid-afternoon a fearsome wall of clouds had built up in the southwest, and soon it began to snow. It was a wet snow, and it was heavy. By nightfall the *Emma Rose* was buried and Nathan's wagon was covered in drifts. Then the wind began to blow. "We'd best get inside," Ian said. "There's nothing we can do out here."

"Let's grab some firewood," Patrick replied. "We're going to need it tonight."

Nathan and Oren brushed snow off the woodpile and they each carried an armload of wood into Ian's cabin. Soon they sitting around a warm fire and listening to the howling wind and the sound of tree branches breaking under the weight of heavy snow.

"I hope the *Emma Rose* doesn't get hit by those branches," Nathan said.

"I think she's clear of any big trees," Ian said. "I'm more worried about our cabins. There's an entire forest behind us."

Rather than venture out into the storm, they all decided to stay in Ian's cabin for the night, close to the fire. Nathan was up at dawn to check on the horses. After he fed and watered them, he went out to look at the storm damage. Every tree had lost limbs, and a few trees along the shore had been uprooted. Fortunately Ian had been right about the *Emma Rose*. She was only covered with snow, which would soon melt. Nathan saw that the strong winds had broken up the ice in the harbor. The whitecaps had returned, crushing ice against the shore with each surging wave.

But Nathan wasn't looking at the ice. He was looking farther out on the lake. He was astonished to see a frozen apparition appear beyond Whiskey Point and glide across the harbor. It was a sailboat, low in the water and covered with ice. It was the first boat of the season, and it looked like a ghost ship.

Nathan's first thought was of Andy. Could he be on board? Would they have any news of him? What about Sarah and King Strang? What about all the rest of the Mormons? Nathan couldn't wait for anyone else to join him. He immediately started out for Saint James, watching as the phantom ship cruised across the harbor toward Johnson's dock.

When Nathan reached the dock, he recognized the boat. It was the *Dolphin*, owned by Captain Bonner from Mackinac Island, a supply boat that made regular runs to Beaver Island during the shipping season. Captain Bonner must have taken advantage of the mild spring weather, but instead he encountered the unexpected storm. Nathan wondered why they had departed so early and risked their lives. They must have an important cargo, or passenger.

The pilot at the helm was bundled in coats and covered in ice. Nathan waved to him from the edge of the dock as two men stumbled out of the cabin.

"Ahoy! Would you mind catching our bow line?" the pilot shouted.

"Sure," Nathan answered, recognizing Captain Bonner. "Welcome back."

"We're mighty glad to be here," Captain Bonner replied. "That was the worst crossing I've ever made."

One of the men threw Nathan a bow line, and Nathan pulled the boat in and tied the line to the dock. The other man tied off the stern line, and all three of them stepped off the boat, relieved to be on shore.

"You must be Patrick O'Donnell's son," Captain Bonner said.

"Yes, sir," Nathan replied. "I'm Nathan O'Donnell."

"I have a passenger. This is Tom Appleby. He's the new lighthouse keeper for the Beaver Head Light at the south end of the island."

"Hello, Nathan," Tom said. "Pleased to meet you."

Nathan shook his hand. "I thought that lighthouse was abandoned."

"Not anymore it ain't," Captain Bonner said. "Tom's come all the way from Cleveland to get that light working before the shipping season opens. That's why we're here so early, but I wouldn't do it again after the storm we just went through."

"Is there anyone else on board?" Nathan asked.

"Nope. Just the three of us."

Nathan's heart sank. When he first saw the *Dolphin* enter the harbor, he had hoped that Andy might be on board. He thought of last fall, when a similar stretch of mild weather and a sudden vicious storm had taken Andy away. Now it was six months later, and the chance of Andy returning on this particular boat was very small, Nathan now realized.

"Listen," Captain Bonner said, "we're just about frozen. Is there a place where we can get a hot meal and a place to stay tonight?"

"Gibson's Inn," Nathan replied, coming back to the present. "It opened last fall in King Strang's old print shop, just a block south of here. Gibson serves three meals a day."

"That's just what we need," Captain Bonner said. "Grab your gear, men."

"Nathan, is there a way for me to get to the south end of the island?" Tom Appleby asked. "I need to get the lighthouse operating as soon as possible. The shipping season has already begun on the southern part of the lakes."

"Sure," Nathan replied. "I have two horses and a sleigh. We're delivering mail and provisions to Cable Bay tomorrow, and the lighthouse is only a few miles further. Why don't you hitch a ride with us?"

"Excellent!" Tom said. "Thank you for the offer. What time are you leaving?"

"It's a long trip. We'll pick you up at dawn."

"I'll be ready. See you then."

The three men grabbed their gear and trudged off to Gibson's Inn for a hot meal and a warm fire. Nathan hurried home to get the sleigh ready for a trip to the south end of the island.

Before dawn, Nathan arrived at Gibson's Inn. A cold wind was still blowing and a high snowdrift clung to the side of the building, covering the windows. He tied the horses up at the hitching post and went inside.

Not knowing which room Tom was staying in, Nathan called out, "Hello! It's Nathan O'Donnell, here with the sleigh. We're ready to go."

"Good morning, Nathan," a voice called from the shadows. "Here I am, ready for duty."

Nathan turned around. Tom was standing on the stairway, neatly dressed in a blue lighthouse keeper's uniform. Perched jauntily on his head was an official lighthouse keeper's cap with a gold rim and a Lighthouse Service emblem stitched in the cloth. Tom's lean figure and and neatly trimmed beard gave him a military air of authority.

He came down the stairs as Nathan admired his uniform. "Good morning, Tom. It's going to be a cold ride to the south end of the island. I hope you have a warm overcoat."

"I've got a wool coat and gloves hanging on the coat rack. My luggage is by the door, and there are some trunks on the porch."

"That's great," Nathan replied. "We'll load up and be on our way."

Tom grabbed his coat and they both walked out to the sleigh. At the hitching post, two horses stood patiently, breathing clouds of mist into the cold morning air. Oren was standing by the sleigh, kicking snow and slapping his hands to keep warm.

"Tom, I want you to meet my partner. This is Oren Whipple. He's kind of skinny, but somehow we manage, as long as I do most of the work," Nathan said with a smile.

"Good morning, sir." Oren came forward and shook Tom's hand. "Welcome to Beaver Island. We're sure glad you're here. The lighthouse was dark all last year."

"Good morning, Oren," Tom said. "Pleased to meet you."

"Are you ready to go? We should be able to make it to the south end of the island by afternoon as long as our driver doesn't get lost."

Tom laughed. "Yep, all ready. We just have to grab my luggage."

Oren walked over to the porch and picked up the largest of Tom's trunks. In one smooth motion he threw it on the back of the sleigh with a loud thud.

"Don't mind him, Tom. He's just showing off. After all that work for just one trunk he's going to have to rest for most of the day."

"Yeah, you bet," Oren said. "By the end of the day you'll see who does all the work around here."

Tom laughed and they all started loading the boxes of provisions for the lighthouse. When they had everything secured, Nathan untied the team of horses from the hitching post and hopped up on the driver's seat.

"All aboard," he cried. "First stop, Cable Bay to deliver the mail. Last stop, Beaver Head Lighthouse to deliver the new lighthouse keeper!"

"Tom, why don't you hop up and sit in the middle," Oren said. "It's a better seat and I won't have to listen to the driver jabber all morning."

Tom grinned. "Much obliged, Oren. I'll try to keep him quiet." He hopped up on the front seat next to Nathan and reached over and gave Oren a hand up.

Nathan shook the reins and called out, "Hey there, Guy! Hey there, Lois! Giddy-up!"

The two horses pulled together and soon the sleigh was gliding down the snow covered street. Tom was amazed at the smooth ride. He had never been on a sleigh. He was used to rough wagon rides over dirt roads full of potholes.

Down the street they passed several empty log houses. They turned up a hill and passed a large building, now covered in snow.

"That's the Mormon church," Nathan said. "Have you heard about the Mormons?"

"I've heard some," Tom replied. "Captain Bonner filled me in on the way over from Mackinac Island."

"So you've heard about King Strang. He held church services here every Saturday until he was shot last summer. Now the building is abandoned."

"Are there any Mormons here anymore?" Tom asked.

"You're lookin' at one," Oren said. "My parents were Mormon. That's all they ever talked about. They read the Mormon newspaper every day and before they went to bed they read a chapter of *The Book of the Law of the Lord*, written by King Strang. I never saw much sense in it myself."

"Where are your parents now, Oren?"

"They left with King Strang on the *Louisville* after he was shot. I haven't heard from them. I guess they joined the Mormon colony in Wisconsin."

Tom didn't know what to say. He sensed a wistful edge in Oren's voice. He was saddened to think that two parents would abandon their son on an island because of religious convictions.

"Look over there," Oren said, pointing to Johnson's dock. "That's where King Strang got shot."

Tom looked over to his left at a large pier stacked with cordwood waiting to be sold to passing steamers.

"Two men shot him and pistol-whipped him while he lay on the ground. They ran on board the *Michigan* and the boat left for Mackinac Island that afternoon. I hear that one of them is living there now, free as a bird. How's that for justice?"

"Oren needed a place to stay," Nathan said, "so my father took him in. We started this hauling business late last fall. We did pretty well until winter set in."

"I'm going to Wisconsin after I save up a little money," Oren said. "I want to start my own hauling business in Milwaukee. Lots of boats stop there. Maybe I can find my parents."

"We all may go there if business doesn't pick up this summer," Nathan said.

"Don't worry," Oren replied. "Tomorrow we have a whole week of work hauling barrels for the fishermen. As soon as this storm ends they'll be setting their nets and bringing in fish, and it's just the beginning of the season. Saint James is going to be the best fishing port on the Great Lakes in a couple of years."

"I think you're right, Oren," Nathan said. "But it's been an awful long winter. This is the first hauling job we've had in a month. I'm about ready to get off this rock if business doesn't pick up soon."

"What would you do, Nathan?" Tom asked.

"Back in Ireland we had some cows. Someday I want to start a dairy farm. Everyone says Wisconsin is a great place for farming. I'll probably go with Oren to Milwaukee and work for a while. There's a lot of good farm land around Milwaukee. Maybe I'll settle there."

"Why don't you tell him the rest of the story, Nathan," Oren said.

"That's what I want to do, start a dairy farm. With cows."

"Yeah, cows. And a girl."

"Now I'm interested," Tom said. "A girl, eh?"

"Aw, never mind," Nathan muttered, his cheeks flushing.

"He knows a princess," Oren said. "An island princess."

"Well, that's impressive," Tom said. "Would this be one of King Strang's daughters? I heard he had a big family."

"Her name is Sarah Strang," Nathan said reluctantly. "She went away with her father after he was shot."

"Some of the Mormons went to Wisconsin," Oren said. "We heard a rumor that King Strang died, but that's all we know. We haven't heard from Sarah or my parents or anyone else since they left. The rest of the Mormons were chased off by a mob of Irish fishermen from Mackinac Island."

"They weren't all Irish," objected Nathan.

"Most of them were, and now they're living in Mormon houses. A lot of other people left the island on their own. Nathan's own cousin took off without telling anyone. We don't even know where he went."

"He might have gone straight across to the mainland."

"Could be," Oren replied. "No one really knows. He could have drowned in the lake, for all we know."

"I don't think so," Nathan said. "He was too good a sailor."

"Yeah, you're probably right," Oren said. "Personally, I think he made it to Wisconsin."

Nathan did not reply. He stared straight ahead and snapped the reins. He missed Andy, but still the thought of Andy going to Wisconsin to find Sarah was unsettling. He and Oren were friends now, but Oren could not possibly know that he thought about Sarah every day and dreamed of her every night. He often daydreamed of meeting her in Voree and of starting a farm together. It seemed more and more like a dream as time went by, but even though it was just a dream, he had to find out. He was still planning to leave the island in the fall and go to Milwaukee.

By now the sleigh was headed south on King's Highway. The sleigh glided along past tall evergreens and open farm fields covered with a blanket of new snow. At the intersection of a narrow lane they passed several darkened log houses. The doors were wide open and one home had a broken window and a large hole in the roof, a sign of the rapid Mormon exodus.

"These were all Mormon houses," Oren said. "Some of them were burned to the ground, but you can't see 'em now because they're buried in snow."

The horses came over a rise in the trail and started down a long hill. Tom grinned as they picked up speed. The exhilaration of his first sleigh ride made him forget the cold wind and the daunting tasks awaiting him at the lighthouse.

After a couple of hours of travel through the woods, they came to a sign with neatly painted letters:

CABLE BAY

Below the sign there was a rough board with a scrawled message: *"No Mormons allowed."*

"Whoa, there. Whoa," Nathan called to the horses. "Here, Tom, hold the reins."

Tom took the reins and Nathan jumped off the sleigh. He grabbed the board with both hands, ripped it off the post, and threw it into the woods.

"This is Cable Bay, Tom," he said, walking calmly back to the sleigh. "Last fall my father and I delivered supplies here. I should warn you; this place can be a little rough."

"I'm not looking forward to paying another visit to Cable Bay," Oren said. "My last visit here didn't go so well."

"Don't worry, Oren. We'll just drop off the freight and be on our way."

Nathan took the reins and turned the sleigh down the trail leading to Cable Bay. They approached an open field sloping down to a small bay on Lake Michigan. Two fishing boats covered with crusted snow and ice were tied to a pier. A cold wind blew out of the south and kicked up whitecaps on the lake. Tom turned up his collar and shivered.

Several log buildings were clustered around the pier. The first building they passed was the saw mill. Two men were at work cutting barrel staves. Oren and Nathan waved at them and Tom tipped his hat. The men leaned against the open doorway and watched the sleigh go by.

"Fishing is so good these days that the barrel makers can hardly keep up," Oren said. "Nathan and I haul a lot of barrels down to the docks back in Saint James."

"Where do they send the fish?" Tom asked.

"Most of the barrels are shipped to Milwaukee or Chicago. The boat stops right at the pier several times a year. They pay cash. Good money, too."

Nathan stopped the sleigh in front of a low log building that looked like a bunkhouse. Smoke rose from the chimney and they could hear loud voices and laughter inside.

"This could be interesting," Nathan said. "These fishermen work hard, but when there's a storm they usually play cards and drink too much."

Oren reached behind the seat, pulled out a canvas mail bag, and handed it to Nathan.

"You go first," he said.

"Thanks." Nathan grabbed the bag and knocked on the door. There was no answer, so he picked up a piece of firewood and pounded on the side of the log building. A shutter in one of the windows flew open and a man with a grizzled beard glared out at them.

"Who the hell's making all that racket?"

"It's Nathan O'Donnell. I brought your mail and supplies."

"Nathan! Why didn't you say so?"

"You didn't ask. Good day to you, Walter."

"Where's your old man? He usually brings our mail."

"He's too busy in town. I came with my partner Oren Whipple and the new lighthouse keeper, Tom Appleby."

"Well, I'll be damned. A lighthouse keeper. What do you know about that? Top o' the mornin' to you, sir. That light has been dark for almost a year. Last time I was down that way, it looked like the light tower was taking a list to starboard. There's no foundation underneath it, you know. It'll probably fall down soon. Those crooks who built that place took the government for a ride, I'll tell you that."

"Yeah, well, Tom's going to take care of that," Nathan said. "He'll have that light burning in no time. The word is that the Lighthouse Service is going to build a taller tower next year, along with a brick keeper's quarters."

"You don't say," Walter said. "A new lighthouse, right here on Beaver Island!"

"That's right," Nathan said, shivering and standing in the snow.

"Hey, Nathan, why'd you bring the sleigh? Don't you know it is spring?"

"Sorry, Walter, I guess nobody told us."

"Well, come on in! Don't just stand there in the snow freezing your bejeebers off."

"We might think about it if you would be so kind as to unlock the door."

"Well, I'll be damned," Walter cried. "You just wait right there."

Walter slammed the shutter. From inside came the sound of a heavy thud and a crash, as if a chair had fallen over. Then there was more profanity and the sound of shouts and laughter. The door finally swung open, with Walter hanging on the doorknob.

"Come on in, boys," he said. "Watch your heads."

Nathan and Tom ducked their heads and stepped inside the cabin. It took a moment for their eyes to adjust to the dim room. A fire burned in the fireplace and a cloud of wood smoke hung near the ceiling. Oren blinked and stepped in behind them.

"Mail call!" Walter shouted. "Nathan O'Donnell's here. Who wants their mail?"

Several fishermen were sitting at a table playing poker and drinking whiskey. Nathan had often seen their boats in the harbor and he knew them all by name.

"Nathan!" one of the men called, "Have a seat. We'll deal you in."

"Good day to you, Charlie. No thanks. We're just dropping off the mail. Hello, Archie. Hello, Shorty. How's fishin' these days?"

"It's been real good this spring, at least until this storm came along," one of the men said. "Did you see our boats? They're covered in ice."

"Yeah, I saw them. It was a bad storm. It's still real cold out."

"Hey, Shorty," one of the men said, "maybe Nathan brought a letter from your wife. You ain't seen her in awhile."

"I got a wife?"

"Yeah, Shorty, you got a wife. She lives in town, remember?"

"Well, what's she look like?" Shorty asked, slurring his voice.

"I don't know, Shorty. Why don't you ask Nathan. He lives in town. He probably sees her."

"From what I hear, he sees her all the time," said another one of the men. "Ain't that right, Nathan. What do you think about that, Shorty?"

All of the fishermen burst out laughing. Shorty reached over and gave the man a cuff and knocked his hat off.

"Hey, boys," Walter said, "we got to be hospitable to our guests. You boys want some whiskey? C'mon in, come sit a spell. Tell us who your partners are, Nathan. You forgot to introduce us proper like."

"Well, thanks for the offer, Walter, but we can't stay. You all know Oren Whipple. We'll be working together this spring."

The men were silent. They all knew by his name that Oren was a Mormon.

"And this here's Tom Appleby. He's the new lighthouse keeper. He's going to get the light fired up again this year."

"Welcome aboard, mate," Archie said, shaking Tom's hand. "Good to have you here. We'll sure appreciate seeing that light burning when we're coming in with a load of fish."

"Thank you," Tom said. "From what I hear, I've got a lot of work to do."

"It's a bit rough living out here, but you'll like it soon enough. Too crowded in town, I say. You boys wanna play a hand of poker? You sure you don't want a drink? Hand me that bottle, Shorty. I'm runnin' a little dry."

"No thanks," Nathan replied. "We've got to drop Tom off and get back to town before dark."

A grunt came from a dark corner of the cabin. A burly man rolled out of a straw bed and landed on the floor with a thump. A whiskey bottle fell from his hand and hit the floor. He grabbed it and pulled himself up by the bedpost.

Nathan watched the man carefully, but he wasn't looking at his face. He was looking at his hands. One hand held the whiskey bottle in a tight grip. The other hand grasped the bedpost with only a thumb and an index finger. Three fingers were missing, leaving only disfigured stubs, red and swollen.

It was Sam Bennett, Tom Bennett's brother. In this very cabin Sam Bennett's hand had been shot off, and he had watched his own brother die under a fusillade of Mormon gunfire. Then he had been arrested and forced to sail to Saint James in shackles with his dead brother lying at his feet, awash in the bilge water of his own boat. Ever since that day Bennett had threatened to kill every Mormon he saw, and he had proceeded to drown himself in whiskey.

Nathan glanced at Oren. He moved over a step so he was standing in front of him.

Bennett walked unsteadily toward the men at the table. He was unshaven and his long hair was hanging over his face. His clothes and hair were covered with straw.

"Whipple," he snarled. "Is that your name? You Gilbert Whipple's kid?"

"Yes," Oren said. "Gilbert Whipple's my father."

The man turned toward Nathan with a ferocious stare. "What do you mean by riding in here with that kid? He's a Mormon! He ain't welcome here. Get 'im outside quick, before I get my hands on him."

Bennett stumbled out of the shadows and into the light of the fire. His voice was slurred and his body swayed as he staggered across the room. He grasped the whiskey bottle in his good hand and waved it over his head.

Nathan answered him sharply, "You bugger off, Sam Bennett. You all know Oren. Yeah, he's a Mormon, but he's never hurt anybody. Now do you want your mail and freight or not, because if you don't, I'm going to ride right out of here. I got to drop off our new lighthouse keeper. He's a lot more important than you, Bennett. Now what's it going to be?"

With a hoarse cry, Bennett lumbered across the floor. He raised the whiskey bottle in his good hand and with a roar he swung it at Nathan's head. Nathan didn't have time to duck. The bottle came crashing down toward him.

An arm shot over Nathan's shoulder and grabbed Bennett's wrist. The bottle stopped only an inch from Nathan's temple. Tom Appleby twisted Bennett's arm as hard as he could to make him drop the bottle, but Bennett was strong. Tom bit his lip to keep his arm from trembling. Bennett held on to the bottle and sneered in Tom's face, his breath reeking of whiskey. Then Tom took a deep breath and squeezed Bennett's arm, digging his fingers into the man's wrist. Very slowly, the bottle tilted away from Nathan's head, and suddenly it clattered to the floor. Tom let go, and both men stumbled backwards.

"I'm glad you changed your mind about that, mister," Tom said.

All of the men were leaning forward with their hands on the table, ready to pounce. Bennett reached down to his boot, pulled out a long knife with his good hand, and started forward again. This time he was headed toward Tom.

"You stop right there," commanded Tom. "I guess I'm the closest thing there is to a law man around here. I don't mind hauling you back to town and turning you over to the sheriff. Now stay where you are!"

There was silence in the room. All of the men remained poised in their chairs and Bennett stared at Tom with the same ferocious glare.

"Oren," Tom said, "why don't you pick up that mail bag and take it over and give it to those gentlemen."

Oren picked up the bag and walked over to the table and held it out. None of the men lifted a hand so he dropped it on the floor.

"Thank you for your hospitality, gentlemen," Tom said. "I have to get to the lighthouse and these boys want to get back to town tonight. We'll just leave your freight on the front porch."

Bennett stood motionless, holding the knife at eye level. Tom, Nathan and Oren backed slowly out the door, and Nathan quickly closed it behind them.

"Whew," Nathan said, taking a deep breath. "That was a close one."

"Let's just get these boxes unloaded and get out of here," muttered Oren.

Tom and Oren unloaded the boxes and stacked them on the porch while Nathan kept an eye on the door. Then they all pushed and heaved on the sleigh to turn it around. Nathan jumped up and grabbed the reins.

"Giddy-up, Guy! Giddy-up, Lois!" he shouted.

Tom and Oren hopped on just as the sleigh began to move. They passed the saw mill and immediately turned south, back on the trail to the lighthouse. None of them looked back.

CHAPTER 23:

Resurrection of the Lighthouse

"That was really something," Nathan said as they turned the corner and rode away from Cable Bay. "How did you do that, Tom?"

"Oh, I was watching Sam Bennett and I saw him start to swing the bottle. Just got lucky, I guess."

"No, I don't mean that. How did you get Bennett to back off and stay put? He had a knife and you didn't."

"Well, Bennett was pretty drunk. He wouldn't have done much. I think he was intimidated by my uniform. It's just a good thing he didn't hit you with that bottle."

"But what about all those other guys? Walter, Charlie, Archie and Shorty. They're a pretty rough bunch."

"We caught them off guard and we got out of there fast. You know, there were a lot of guys like that along the waterfront back in Cleveland. Some of them wanted to fight after a few drinks, but most just wanted to have a good time."

"What do you think, Tom?" Oren asked. "Do you think we could have taken all of them in a fight?"

"Nope. They would have whipped us pretty good, Oren. Or worse."

"You know, Tom," Nathan said, "you're going to have to go back to Cable Bay every so often to pick up your mail and provisions."

"That's true. I hadn't thought about that. Well, I guess I'll just have to wear my uniform every time I go, won't I?"

"Yeah, I guess," Nathan said, not at all convinced.

After a short distance the trail began to narrow as it entered a thick cedar forest. A rough log bridge crossed a swampy area and a small stream. The sleigh hit a loose log on the bridge and took a bounce. All three of them grabbed the sleigh and hung on.

"Sure would have been nice to get warm by the fire back there," Oren said. "It's freezing out here."

"Yup, it sure would," Nathan replied.

The road smoothed out again, and the sleigh picked up speed. None of them spoke again. They all were stunned after their close encounter. Tom was trembling, but not from the cold. He wondered what would have happened if he had not been able to stand up to Sam Bennett. Nathan would have had his head smashed in, and the fishermen might have ganged up on Oren. They might have even killed him. In his drunken state, Bennett certainly would have. Tom was appalled at the animosity he saw between the Irish and the Mormons. Even though the Mormons were gone, the anger lingered like a festering wound.

Meanwhile, Oren was thinking about what would have happened to him if Tom had not stopped Sam Bennett. At the very least all three of them would have been beaten badly. Oren was now convinced he must leave the island soon. Without the protection of people like Nathan and Tom, he didn't have a chance. Everyone else hated him, only because he was a Mormon. Oren wondered where his parents were. If only he could save enough money this summer, he could travel to Wisconsin and find them.

Nathan was not thinking about Sam Bennett or the lighthouse. He was thinking of Sarah Strang. He remembered back when she returned to the island after spending the winter in Buffalo. She had been so happy and carefree, even when surrounded by her extended Mormon family. Nathan knew Sarah had troubles at home, but she still had remained cheerful and full of life. Even after the difficulties on the island started, they had remained best of friends. Even after Andy began courting her, she always had a special smile for him. Nathan thought of all the times he had offered her a ride on his wagon. Mostly he remembered the touch of her hand as he lifted her up beside him. Now Sarah was gone and Andy had disappeared. Nathan shivered and closed his eyes for a moment. He felt very alone.

The sleigh glided between two cedar trees hanging over the road. White pillows of snow formed strange shapes on the branches. Occasionally a clump fell silently to the ground, crumbling to powder before it vanished. The trail soon turned west and followed the shoreline. Waves from the recent storm were crashing in a cascade of freezing spray and crunching ice. Beyond the waves, high seas were breaking in whitecaps all the way to the horizon.

"I sure wouldn't want to be out there today," Tom said.

"No kidding," Nathan replied. "That's as rough as I've ever seen the lake." They all turned up their collars as an icy blast ripped across the top of the waves and blew a cold spray over their heads.

After riding a few more miles along the shore, the trail turned behind a hill covered with trees. The trees blocked the wind, but the snow had drifted across the road. The weary horses plodded along, dragging the sleigh through the deep powder. Tom and Oren got out and walked in front to make a trail. Occasionally they had to remove large branches that had fallen across the road.They finally broke through the deep snow and came out of the woods. In the distance they could see the Beaver Head Lighthouse, rising above the trees in a burst of late afternoon sunlight.

"There it is!" Oren exclaimed. "There's your new home, Tom. We made it at last!"

Tom stopped to survey the lighthouse. A brick tower rose high above a two-story building with a wide wooden porch along one end. The entire structure looked weatherbeaten and unkempt. A year of neglect and a long winter had taken its toll. He noticed some winter damage, probably inflicted during the recent storm. Several windows were broken and many of the shutters were blown off. Part of the porch roof had collapsed from the weight of snow.

"This is going to take some work," he muttered.

The sun was dipping low on the horizon and the light tower made a long shadow across the snow. Nathan pulled the sleigh up near the porch and stopped the horses. In the shadow of the tower, the place seemed cold and gloomy. No one spoke for a moment.

Finally Oren jumped down and tied the horses to a post near the porch. "Let's get these trunks unloaded," he said. "It's getting late."

Nathan and Tom were still looking up at the damaged building. Hearing Oren, they grabbed the handles of a large trunk and carried it to the porch. Then they stacked the rest of the boxes against the wall, away from the snow. With three of them working, it took only a few minutes to unload the sleigh. Just as they lifted the last box, the sun dipped below the horizon.

It was time to say goodbye to Tom Appleby.

"Are you sure you want to stay here?" Nathan asked. "It's awful cold and it'll be dark soon."

"I'll be fine," Tom replied. "You and Oren need to get back to town."

"Well, we could at least help you haul these boxes inside."

"I can take care of that in the morning. It's late, and you boys have a long ride ahead of you."

"That doesn't matter," Oren said. "There's a moon tonight, and the horses know the way."

"I know, but you have barrels to haul tomorrow. It's your first big job of the season, remember?"

"What if we take you back to Cable Bay tonight?" Nathan suggested. "At least you'd be warm there. It's Oren they hate, not you. You could get a good night's sleep and a fresh start in the morning."

"Sam Bennett would probably slit my throat in the middle of the night," Tom said. "I don't think I'll be going back to Cable Bay for a long time. But don't worry about me. I'll be fine here. This lighthouse needs a lot of work, and I want to get the light in the tower burning as soon as possible. The ships will be heading north after this storm passes."

Seeing that Tom could not be persuaded, Nathan untied the horses. The three of them shook hands and said goodbye.

"We'll be back in a few weeks with more supplies for Cable Bay," Nathan said. "We'll stop by and see how you're doing."

"Thanks," Tom said. "I would appreciate that."

"That's the least I can do after you saved me from getting clobbered with that bottle."

"Aw, it was nothing," Tom said. "You'd better get moving. You've got a long ride."

Nathan shook the reins. "Giddy-up, Guy! Giddy-up, Lois!"

Tom watched as the sleigh glided away into the evening shadows. Oren turned and waved, and the sleigh disappeared into the forest. Tom waved, and then he looked back at the lighthouse and took a deep breath.

The front door to the building was jammed. The skeleton key given to him back in Buffalo didn't work even after he jiggled it in the lock several times. Tom cursed himself for not trying the key before Nathan and Oren departed. He walked to the front of the building to locate another door. A sharp blast of cold air hit him when he went around the corner. On the horizon, the waters of Lake Michigan were still raging from the storm. Below him, at the base of a steep bluff, waves were crashing on the shore. A small wooden boat had washed up on the beach and was partially buried in sand and snow. The sail still hung from the mast, but it was torn and flapping in the wind.

Tom looked past the sailboat at the pounding surf of Lake Michigan. Far in the distance he could see a dark speck on the horizon with a black plume rising above it. It was an approaching steamer, fighting the storm and belching smoke into the air. He suddenly realized that while he was traveling to Beaver Island, the shipping season had opened in the southern part of the lake. The boat on the horizon was headed due north, directly toward the shallow reefs extending out like jagged razors from the south end of the island. The waves crashing against the reefs could tear a boat to splinters in a few deadly moments. It was dusk, and darkness was rapidly closing in. Tom knew that he must get the light in the tower burning quickly to warn the approaching ship that it was headed for disaster. There wasn't much time.

He turned and looked at the front of the building, seeking an entrance to the light tower. He was appalled at what he saw. It looked like a winter hurricane had blasted this side of the building. A huge snowdrift rose to the second story windows. Shutters and shingles were scattered everywhere and all the windows had been blasted out by the furious winds. Some of them revealed white curtains inside, fluttering in the breeze. Others stared back at him blankly like dark frozen eyes. A huge tree limb had crashed through one window, its branches sticking out like a beckoning skeletal hand.

Tom looked up at the light tower. The tower was intact, but the small circular room at the top was heavily damaged. All the glass windows were broken and most of the roof was gone, blown away in the wind. All that remained was a steel frame and a few rafters. Icicles hung from the frame at weird angles, like knives piercing the wind.

Tom suddenly felt very alone. Glancing back at the road leading into the forest, he wished that Nathan and Oren would somehow reappear. The dark speck on the horizon seemed a bit larger. There was no doubt that the boat was heading directly toward Beaver Island. It was getting darker by the minute and a foggy mist was rising off the water.

"I've got to get that light burning!" he exclaimed.

He ran to the entrance to the light tower, floundering in the deep snow. A door lay in front of him, both hinges broken. He tossed it aside and plowed ahead. At the base of the light tower there was a heavy wooden door, ajar and creaking in the wind. Tom stumbled up the steps and gazed into the dark interior, his eyes wide with wonder. The entire entryway was filled with snow, buried almost to the ceiling. The high winds must have created a vortex, pulling frigid air in from above and filling the circular tower with white powdery snow.

Tom began to dig frantically. He dug with his hands and pushed the snow between his legs, kicking it backwards with his feet. The snow piled up behind him and spilled out the open door. He soon reached the first iron step of the circular stairs, but more snow fell from above and showered him with icy crystals. He pushed the snow away and finally cleared a narrow passage. A wall of snow faced him above the single exposed step.

"This will never do," he said in frustration. "I need something to move this snow."

Tom turned around and floundered back to the entryway. To his right was the door facing the lake, still ajar and half buried in snow. Straight ahead was a doorway that led into the lighthouse keeper's quarters. The thick door was slightly open and the wood was splintered and cracked along the edge. Tom looked at it carefully in the dim light.

That's odd, he thought to himself. The wind couldn't have done this. It looked like someone had broken in.

The interior of the building was pitch black. Tom peered into the darkness, waiting for his eyes to adjust, but it was too dark. He took a few steps into the room and hit his shin painfully on something hard. Reaching down, he felt the sharp edge of a wooden bench. He groped forward in the darkness and felt what seemed to be a duffle bag of clothing or possibly a lumpy pile of blankets. His hand moved forward to the end of the bench and he stepped carefully into the darkness, finally touching a wall and following it with his hands. When he reached a corner, he touched two wooden handles and circled his hands around them in the dark. The first handle was a broom. The second handle was a shovel!

Elated, Tom grabbed the shovel and groped his way back toward the dim outline of the doorway. Once he reached the entryway he started digging, throwing snow out the open door. Soon he found the first iron step, hitting it with the shovel blade with a sharp clink. The end of the wooden handle cracked and broke away. Disgusted, he threw the broken piece behind him and kept digging. Soon he realized that the shorter handle actually made the work easier in the confined space, as long as he didn't stab himself with the jagged splinters at the end.

Tom cleared a few more iron steps, moved back to the entryway, and shoveled the snow outside. Then he returned to the steps and dug some more. After clearing about a dozen steps, he tired of going back down to clear out the entryway, so he just kept digging and throwing the snow behind him. He worked upward one step at a time and the snow piled up behind him. Soon he was entombed in a cylinder surrounded by bricks and filled with snow. The only sound was his own breathing and the clink of the shovel as he found each new iron step.

Clink. He hit the next step. He shoveled it clear and pushed the snow behind him.

Clink. Another step and more snow.

Thud.

Now what? Tom thought. A wooden step? A hatch?

He reached up and swept away the snow to reveal a black surface. It was soft, like leather or rubber. He swept more snow away, exposing an elongated oval shape.

It was the bottom of a shoe. He grabbed the shoe and tugged on it but it would not budge. He began to dig into the snow to the left of the shoe, near the wall of the lighthouse.

Thud.

It was another shoe. He grabbed this shoe and tugged but it would not budge either. He dug carefully around both shoes. He found shoelaces, untied, dangling, and encrusted in snow. Then he reached up and felt an ankle!

Terrified, Tom jumped backward and fell over, tumbling and bouncing down the iron steps. He landed with a thud at the bottom, upside down and half buried. His heart was pounding in the white silence of the snow-covered tomb.

He lay still for a long time with his eyes tightly closed. He was horrified of what must be in the tower, only a few feet above him. Tomorrow, in the light of day, he might be able to face the task ahead of him. At least he would be able to see. He decided to go back to the keeper's quarters, look for a candle, and find a place to rest for the night as far away as possible from the frozen apparition awaiting him. He knew he would not sleep, but at least he could get warm and wait out the long night.

Then Tom thought of the boat he had seen on the lake, rapidly approaching the jagged reefs of Beaver Island in the darkness. There could be a lot of passengers on board. After the long winter, people would be traveling again, coming north to work or delivering supplies to outposts in the upper Great Lakes. The beacon in the light tower would remain dark for one more night if he retreated into the keeper's quarters.

"Dammit," Tom cursed, "I've got to get that light burning."

He scrambled to his feet, dusted off the snow covering his clothing, and grabbed the broken shovel. He began to dig again, snow falling away below him. Soon he uncovered the dreaded shoes. As he dug, he found skinny legs shrouded by baggy work pants tied at the waist with a rope. A denim shirt and an overcoat covered an emaciated chest. The snow fell away, and in the dim light he saw the face of a young man with unruly brown hair matted across his forehead. The face was pale and smooth, with a gentle melancholy smile and closed eyes, as if the man was asleep.

Tom kept digging and squeezed past the corpse in the narrow passage, scarcely daring to look, his heart pounding in fear. He shoveled franticly now, digging and pushing the snow behind him as fast as he could. The steps seemed endless as they curved above him in the darkness. He was breathing hard and his hands were freezing from the cold. With one final heave, he burst through the last layer of snow and thrust his head into the night air. Lunging upwards, he threw the shovel aside and fell on the platform, gasping for breath. Above him the stars and the moon brightened the sky, casting a dim light on the peak of the lighthouse tower.

~

Out on the lake, the *Louisville* churned through the water on its way to Beaver Island. The storm had passed but huge waves were still marching up the lake from the south, driven by three days of strong winds. The following seas lifted the stern, sending the boat surfing down the front of each wave. Then, as the wave passed, the stern settled into the trough almost as if it were sinking. A new wave came along and lifted the boat again and drove it forward.

The *Louisville* had departed Milwaukee three days ago, venturing into the heart of the storm. It was the first trip of the year, and the owners were anxious to get an early start for the 1857 shipping season. The trip up the lake had been very rough. High waves had carried away two lifeboats and destroyed the stern railing. The captain had been forced to take shelter behind a small island. But he was impatient, and after spending only one night at anchor he ordered the ship back into the big lake, hoping that the waves would diminish.

The pilot house was dark. The only lights came from the captain's pipe and a candle illuminating the ship's compass. The needle on the compass pointed due north and the wheelsman held his course with an occasional turn of the spokes on the ship's wooden wheel. He peered intently into the darkness as the wind blew spray across the windows, blocking his vision.

Earlier in the afternoon, the *Louisville* had safely passed North Manitou Island and the Fox Islands. Now they were out on the open lake, well to the east of Beaver Island and heading north to Saint James, or so the captain thought. What he did not realize was that the wind and waves had pushed his vessel far to the west, and he was now on a collision course with the south end of Beaver Island.

Tom brushed snow off the huge glass lens and the delicate light mechanism. It was still intact, despite the broken windows and the collapsed roof. He turned to look out at the lake. In the distance he could see a light, the bow light of the approaching vessel. It was much closer now, and it was still heading straight toward the rocky reefs stretching out beneath the waves.

With trembling frozen hands, Tom got out his trimmer, reached inside the glass lens, and carefully cut the rough edges of the lamp wick. He a filled a container under the lamp with a flask of oil he had carried with him. Then he opened a valve that supplied oil to the wick, struck a spark with his flint, and watched with apprehension as the wick began to burn weakly with a dark orange color. As the oil slowly saturated the wick, the flame grew larger and changed from orange to bright yellow. He waited a few moments and then gradually opened the supply valve to provide the maximum amount of oil to the flame. Soon the wick burned bright with a white flame and shined through the glass lens, sending a powerful beam of light piercing across the night sky for the first time in over a year.

Tom looked in satisfaction at the flame in the lamp. He had done it! The lamp was burning and still growing brighter. He had completed his first assignment as a lighthouse keeper. Of course there had been training sessions back in Buffalo, but this was different. Here, he was alone. It was very dark, very cold, and there was a frozen body below him on the stairs.

Tom looked out at the lake. He could still see the light of the approaching vessel. It was closer now and it was still headed directly for the island. He prayed the sailors would see his warning beacon in time and alter their course. If they did not turn soon, they would run aground on the rocks and huge waves would quickly pound the boat to splinters, spilling the passengers into the freezing water. There was no way that Tom would be able to save them in the darkness.

Gilbert Whipple stood on the bow of the *Louisville*, clinging to the railing with both hands as the boat rose and fell with each passing wave. He was not a good sailor. He had been frightened during the long voyage up the lake, and all day he had been nervous about the proximity of the boat to the Manitou and Fox Islands. Now he was fearful of the approaching darkness and another night on the lake. As he peered ahead, it seemed to him that there was a dark mass on the horizon, but he could not tell if it was another island or just a low cloud formation or a fog bank.

A sailor approached him in the darkness. "Mr. Whipple, you'd best come below for the night. The waves are still running pretty high, and you'll be safe in the cabin with the other passengers."

"Yes, I suppose you're right. But doesn't it seem to you that there is something out there ahead of us?"

"I can't see anything in this darkness. Don't worry, I'm sure the captain knows what he's doing." A large wave hit the side of the boat and splashed both men with freezing water.

"All right, I'll go below," Mr. Whipple said, sputtering and wiping his face with his coat sleeve.

The two men walked back along the deck, holding the railing. Just as they reached the door to the cabin, Mr. Whipple turned and took one last look toward the bow of the boat. His eye caught a pinpoint of light in the darkness. He grabbed the sailor's arm.

"Look," he said excitedly. "Did you see that light?"

"What light? There's no light."

"Look right there, straight off the bow."

The sailor watched carefully. Sure enough, after a few seconds he saw a tiny flash in the blackness. He watched again, until he had seen the flash six times. He counted off the seconds under his breath as he watched. Each flash came at a three second interval and each flash seemed a little brighter than the last.

"Good God! That's a lighthouse and we're heading straight for it! You wait right here." The sailor scrambled up the stairs to the pilothouse and pounded on the door.

The captain peered out a window. "What do you want?" he snarled.

"A light, sir. Mr. Whipple saw a light, dead ahead."

"You think I care what a passenger saw? Get him back in the cabin and quit bothering me."

"Begging your pardon, sir, but I saw it, too. It looks like a lighthouse. The light has a three second interval. I think you should look at it, sir."

"Dammit," swore the captain. He pulled on his overcoat and stomped out on the stairway. Staring into the darkness, he watched carefully until he too saw the flash of light.

"By God, sailor, I think you're right! Get me the telescope," he ordered. The captain watched the light through the telescope and counted the seconds under his breath.

"Wheelsman! All stop on the engine. Hold your course."

"Aye, aye, Captain."

The captain clambered down the stairs and walked rapidly to the bow. He listened intently as the *Louisville* began to slow down and settle into the water. In the darkness he could hear a deep rumbling sound.

"Dammit, those are breakers!" The captain ran back to the pilothouse. "Wheelsman, turn hard to starboard. Make it fast!"

As Tom tended the light and watched the vessel out on the lake, he pondered the mystery of the frozen body resting below him on the stairs. He thought about the stories he heard of the murder of King Strang and the rapid departure of the *U.S.S. Michigan* with two assailants aboard. The mortally wounded king had been carried to another ship and had departed the island, accompanied by several of his followers. Later all the Mormons were forced off the island with nothing but the clothes on their back and a few meager possessions. Tom wondered if the body in the lighthouse was somehow connected to these events.

He checked the light again and saw that it was burning brightly. Out on the lake he could still see the dim light of the approaching vessel. It seemed that the light had moved ever so slightly to the east. Could it be that the vessel had seen his light beam and was altering course? Tom watched the tiny light and held his breath.

When the wheelsman heard the captain's order, he instantly turned the wheel hard to starboard. The captain charged into the pilot house, slammed the door behind him, and grabbed the signal to the chief engineer.

"Engine room! Full speed!" he shouted. "Let's make this boat turn, and fast."

The engine picked up speed and the *Louisville* turned sharply into the waves and began to roll from side to side. The big paddlewheels churned the black water and the boat plunged forward. Off the port side, the lighthouse flashed brightly and the dark shape of an island emerged out of the mist. The clouds broke for a moment and the rising moon lit up the whitecaps and surf pounding on the rocky shore.

The wheelsman gripped the wheel with both hands, fighting to keep the *Louisville* on course. He licked his lips and glanced nervously over at the captain.

"Steady there, sailor. Steady as she goes. We can make it."

Both men held their breath as the boat headed due east, still rolling in the waves. The captain stood in the open doorway, listening to the crashing surf and watching the flashing light from the lighthouse. After timeless minutes that seemed to last forever, the light began to recede behind them until it was flashing off the stern quarter of the *Louisville*.

"I think we're clear, thank God. Good job, wheelsman."

"Thank you, sir," the wheelsman said. He took a deep breath and wiped the sweat from his brow.

"That must be the Beaver Head light, on the south end of Beaver Island," the captain said. "I don't understand it. That lighthouse has been dark for over a year. Someone must have lit it. Whoever it is, they saved our lives tonight."

"Yes, sir, captain. Must be our guardian angel."

"I believe you are correct, sailor. That was our guardian angel back there, tending that light."

The captain sat down on the bench along the back of the pilothouse. He was sweating underneath his heavy overcoat. He knew how close they had come to becoming a shipwreck. Everyone on board would have perished.

—⁊—

Tom checked the flame again. It was burning well and getting brighter by the minute. The flash of the powerful beacon caught his eye and momentarily blinded him. He turned away and looked out at the lake but the dim light of the boat had disappeared. Had the boat hit a reef and sunk in such a short span of time? Tom stared intently into the darkness, fearing the worst.

In a few moments his night vision returned and finally he spotted the light off to the east. The boat had changed course just in time. It now appeared to be heading out into the open lake. The sailors must have seen Tom's light at the last possible second and made a sharp turn, avoiding a shipwreck and certain death on the rocks.

Tom slumped down on the deck and took several deep breaths as the light shined brightly over his head. From the shadows he watched the tiny light out on the lake and wondered what kind of boat it was and how many souls were aboard. There must have been quite a commotion when someone first spotted the beacon from the lighthouse. He could almost hear the captain cursing and shouting orders to his crew.

For twenty minutes the *Louisville* headed due east, rolling in the deep troughs of the waves. The sky had cleared and the moon illuminated the south end of Beaver Island. The *Louisville* was now far away from the threatening breakers.

"We're clear of the island now," the captain said. "You may turn due north. Set a course for Paradise Bay. We'll be in Saint James tomorrow."

"Yes sir! Paradise Bay it is, sir!"

Tom tended the light all night long and kept it shining brightly even though he saw no more ships and suffered terribly from the cold. At daybreak he extinguished the flame, covered the wick, and began the dreaded plunge into the stairway below. The passage was mostly clear of snow, but he descended slowly, step by careful step. He soon reached the frozen corpse in the narrow passage. Afraid to look, he squeezed by, keeping as far away as possible and searching with his foot for the next step. As he passed the body he trembled and he could feel the hair on his neck rise. He scurried down the rest of the stairs to the entryway and retreated into the keeper's quarters, slamming the door behind him.

The room was now bright with the early morning sun shining through a window. Tom could see that it was a cooking area with a wooden table and benches. There were two duffle bags on the benches along with some rumpled blankets. Tom suddenly realized how exhausted he was. He had been up all night at the top of the tower, standing in the cold and tending the light. He lay down on one of the benches and pulled the blankets over his shivering body, using one of the duffel bags as a pillow. Soon his fear gave way to fatigue and he fell into a deep and dreamless sleep. Outside, the sun rose high in the sky and the last of the clouds moved off to the north. The snow on the roof began to soften and melt, dripping steadily from the eaves.

That night the light shined again from the Beaver Island lighthouse with a bright and steady beam. Other vessels, far out on the lake, saw the beacon and made the long turn safely around Beaver Island.

CHAPTER 24:

Reunion at the Boat Dock

athan and Oren were up at dawn. The *Louisville* was expected to arrive from Milwaukee so they had a full day of work ahead of them. They would have to unload a delivery of salt and then load barrels of fish, all before the boat departed the following morning.

The *Louisville* steamed into the harbor at about noon. As the vessel approached the dock, Nathan and Oren arrived with a load of fish. After they rolled the barrels off the wagon, they stopped to watch as the gangplank dropped and passengers began to disembark. Several fish brokers, a crew of lumberjacks, and a few spring visitors walked down the gangplank and headed toward the village. Nathan noticed a short middle-aged man who looked familiar.

"Hey, Oren, isn't that—"

Oren glanced over at the passengers. "Father!" he shouted. He jumped off the wagon and ran across the dock. Gilbert Whipple saw him and immediately dropped his luggage and jostled his way through the line of passengers.

"Oren!"

Oren ran up to his father, his worn shoes kicking up snow. "Father, what are you—"

"Oren! Thank God I found you!"

"Where's Mother? Is she all right?"

"She's fine. She's in Milwaukee. We've both been so worried about you."

"I've been here—"

"I came back on the first boat of the season to find you."

"I've been staying with Nathan O'Donnell. You remember Nathan, don't you?"

"Of course I do. Hello, Nathan," Mr. Whipple said with a smile. He held out his hand to Nathan, who had just joined them in the crowd.

"Hello, Mr. Whipple," Nathan said, shaking his hand. "Welome back to the island."

"Nathan and I are hauling freight together," Oren said. "Mostly we haul barrels of fish, but yesterday we delivered a load of supplies to Cable Bay and took the new lighthouse keeper down to the Beaver Head Light."

"That explains it!"

"Explains what?" Oren asked.

"We saw a light last night," Mr. Whipple said. "It must have been the Beaver Head Light. I don't know how close we came to the island, but the captain turned the *Louisville* as soon as he saw the light. It was a rough ride, I'm telling you."

"We had a big storm a couple of days ago," Nathan said.

"I'll say," Mr. Whipple replied. "It took us three days to get here. Half the passengers were sick."

"Yeah, and it's still cold," Oren said. "Why don't we go to the house and warm up? We can come back later and load these barrels."

"To our house?" Mr. Whipple asked. "It wasn't burned down? We heard all the Mormon houses were burned."

"Some of them were. They missed ours, I guess."

"Thank God for that!"

A few minutes later Mr. Whipple and the two boys were seated in the Whipple's cabin. Nathan put a log on the fire and Oren poured some hot tea.

"You've taken good care of the house, Oren," Mr. Whipple said.

"Mostly I stayed over at the O'Donnell's," Oren replied, "but I come over here a lot during the day."

"Mr. Whipple, tell us what happened after you left the island," Nathan asked.

"It's a long story, son," Mr. Whipple replied, taking a sip of tea. "As you know, we left the island on Tobias Humphrey's schooner with King Strang. We were all convinced he would survive with proper care and we planned to be back on the next boat. In all the commotion and panic that day, I don't think anyone really gave it much thought. We just got on the boat to protect the king and get him away from his attackers."

"What happened to King Strang?" Oren asked.

"He had some horrible injuries. He was shot in the head and he had another bullet lodged in his cheek underneath his eye. At first he seemed to be getting better, but the wound in his face became infected. He died about two weeks after we got to Milwaukee. There was nothing anyone could do. We gave him a Mormon funeral and buried him near his parents' home in Voree."

"What happened to everyone who went with him?"

"Well, there was a dilemma. When King Strang died, we lost our prophet and leader. Everyone began to question their Mormon faith, because we all thought he was our immortal savior, descended from God. After he was gone there was nothing left of the church. But your mother and I had a more immediate problem. We left the island without our belongings, with very little money, and with no way to support ourselves. Your mother took a job cleaning rooms in a hotel in Milwaukee. I was without work until January, when I got a job as a bookkeeper for the shipping line that owns the *Louisville*. We were both worried about you, but there was nothing we could do until we saved some money. There were stories about how all the Mormons were chased off the island. A lot of Mormons did arrive in Milwaukee, but you were never among them. We feared the worst when you did not reply to our letters."

"I never got any letters," Oren said.

"Oren, don't you remember the rumors we heard about the new post-master?" Nathan said. "Everyone said he was throwing mail with a Mormon name on it into his woodstove."

"That would explain it," Mr. Whipple said. "I'm sure glad I came up here in person. The owners of the *Louisville* have been very good to me. They even gave me a few days off to come to Beaver Island to find you."

They were all silent for a moment. Then Oren asked, "Father, are you completely safe here? There are a lot of folks on the island who don't exactly like Mormons."

"Your mother and I were a bit worried about that, but now that I'm here with you and Nathan I feel perfectly safe. I just cannot stay for long, in fact I must return tomorrow."

"Don't worry, Mr. Whipple," Nathan said. "You'll be safe with us."

"Oh, I almost forgot, Nathan. I have some correspondence for you."

"Correspondence?"

"Yes, a letter." With a flourish, Mr. Whipple reached into his coat pocket and drew out a small envelope and handed it to Nathan.

Nathan turned it over in his hands. On one side it said simply, "Nathan O'Donnell, Beaver Island, Michigan."

"Who is it from?" he asked.

"I believe it is from our newest schoolteacher in Voree, Wisconsin."

"Who—"

"A former resident of Beaver Island who entrusted me to deliver it personally to you. Open it, Nathan."

Nathan slipped his finger into the end of the envelope and carefully opened it. He unfolded the paper inside and saw that it was covered with neat cursive writing, written by a feminine hand. He turned the letter over. At the bottom of the page the letter was signed, "*Yours truly, Sarah Strang.*"

Nathan looked up. Mr. Whipple and Oren were staring at him expectantly. "It's from Sarah," he said.

"Ah," Mr. Whipple said, raising his eyebrows in feigned surprise.

Nathan turned away from them, his heart pounding. He turned the letter over and began to read the words on the page.

April 20, 1857

Dear Nathan,

I have entrusted this letter to Mr. Gilbert Whipple. He is traveling to Beaver Island to find his son Oren. I hope he will also find you. Please understand that he bears you no ill will, in spite of all the events of last summer. I fear he may be in some danger while on Beaver Island. Please protect him, as I know you would protect me.

I do not know if either you or Andy are still on the island. I wrote Andy several times but I have never heard back from him. I can only think that my letters were lost or destroyed at the post office, since both of them had the name Strang on the envelope. That is why I sent this letter with Mr. Whipple.

Nathan, so much has happened since I left the island. You probably heard by now that my father died of his wounds. The men who murdered him were released on Mackinac Island. They never even went to trial, because they killed a Mormon. Without my father, the church has collapsed and most of the brethren are scattered. There are only a few believers left and they are just trying to survive after losing everything.

Wingfield and Edith Watson have been such a blessing. Last fall they helped me escape from the Humphreys and Butch Jenkins and they took me to my mother's house in Voree. Now I am living with her and teaching at the new school here. It is small but there are many children. Every boat that stops in Milwaukee brings new immigrants, and many of them are settling here and clearing land for farms.

I have not heard from Andy since I left the island. The Mormon refugees that came here did not see him last summer. They say he disappeared after my father was attacked. There have been rumours that Andy was involved in my father's murder, but I cannot believe that. All I know is I have never heard from him. He never came after me or even wrote me a letter.

Nathan, it broke my heart to leave the island without saying goodbye to you. Please understand that I had no choice. I had to leave to take care of my father. I loved him very much.

I have been busy teaching school and helping my mother, but I still miss the island. Even after all this time, my thoughts often turn to you, and I think of you fondly. Please forgive me; I know it is not proper for me to be so forward. I only hope Mr. Whipple can find you and that you still have some small amount of affection for me.

Yours truly,
Sarah Strang

Nathan stood still for a moment, clutching the precious letter in his hands. His heart was so full that he could barely breathe. He held the letter to his chest, closing his eyes and thinking of Sarah. It had been almost a year, and she had written him a letter! All this time he feared she was gone from his life forever. He quickly turned back toward Oren and Mr. Whipple, who were both looking at him expectantly.

"I got a letter from Sarah," he said, his voice quivering.

"We know, Nathan. You already told us. What does she say?"

"She wants to see me."

"That's great. You were hoping to find her and I was hoping to find my parents. Now, in one day, my father is here and you heard from Sarah. It's everything we wanted."

"Then it's settled," Nathan said. "We'll go back with your father tomorrow on the *Louisville.*"

"Wait a minute. It's not settled at all. What about Guy and Lois and the wagon?"

"We'll just sell them," Nathan replied, still distracted by the letter.

"Listen," Oren said. "We hardly have enough money to pay the boat fare. We already have a month of work hauling barrels and the season just beginning. Do you want to throw all that away and travel to Wisconsin as paupers?"

"No," Nathan said, "but I want to see Sarah."

"I'm sure you do, Nathan. I want to see my mother, too. But let's be logical about this. If we work hard all summer, we can make enough money to take Guy and Lois and the wagon with us. If we save carefully, we may even have enough money to start up a freight hauling business in Wisconsin."

"But I want to start a dairy farm."

"You can, Nathan. You can do anything you want. But if we haul freight for a couple of years in Wisconsin, we can build up a good business. Then someday maybe I'll buy out your half. How else are you going to be able to buy land for a dairy farm?"

"But what about Sarah?"

"You'll just have to write her a letter," Oren replied. "My father is going back to Wisconsin tomorrow, so you can send it with him. She'll get it in just a few days."

"I guess I could do that," said Nathan hesitantly. "But...."

"But what?" Oren asked, exasperated.

"Well," Nathan said, "I've never written a letter to a girl before."

Mr. Whipple had been following the conversation with amusement. "Nathan, I will be glad to help you write a letter to Sarah. Then you sign it and I'll deliver it to Sarah personally as soon as I get back to Milwaukee."

"You would do that for me?"

"Of course I would, Nathan," Mr. Whipple replied.

"I guess it's a deal, then."

Oren smiled and breathed a sigh of relief. "Whew," he said. "I'm glad that's over!"

"Well then, it's settled," Mr. Whipple said. "Nathan, you can write Sarah this afternoon. I'll help you, and Oren can write to his mother. I'll deliver both letters as soon as I get back. Then, while you boys are still here hauling barrels, I'll look around for delivery work in Milwaukee. I'm sure that the *Louisville* will have some work picking up freight at the boat dock. Nathan, if I have time I'll look for some good farm land somewhere between Milwaukee and Voree."

They all stood up and shook hands. Nathan clutched the letter from Sarah to his chest. Oren stood shoulder to shoulder with his father, beaming at his friend.

The next morning Nathan and Oren were at the dock before dawn. By sunrise they were hard at work, rolling barrels of preserved whitefish and lake trout on the *Louisville*. It wasn't long before Mr. Whipple arrived. As soon as Nathan and Oren had loaded the last barrel, they came over to say goodbye. Oren didn't know what to say. He began to reach out his hand, but Mr. Whipple embraced his son and held him for a long time.

"Thank you for coming back for me, Father," Oren said, choking back tears. "Give Mother my love. I'll see you both in a few months."

Nathan shook Mr. Whipple's hand, "Thank you for bringing Sarah's letter."

"I'll deliver your letter right away, Nathan," Mr. Whipple said.

The whistle of the *Louisville* blew. Mr. Whipple stepped on board and climbed to the stern railing on the upper deck. He took the two letters out of his coat pocket and waved to them with a letter in each hand. Oren and Nathan waved and watched as the *Louisville* headed out into the lake. Nathan reached into his shirt pocket, put his hand on Sarah's letter, and pressed it against his heart.

After so many years of seeing Andy and Sarah together, it was hard to believe that she had written to him. Perhaps she was simply angry or hurt that Andy had not contacted her. Perhaps she just wanted to be friends, as they always had been, or perhaps she really did feel some affection for him. Nathan did not know, but he longed for her now even more than the day she left the island.

But where was Andy? Nathan knew he would never have deserted Sarah. The only reason he left the island was to find her. He had been willing to risk his life by sailing across Lake Michigan in November. Did he make it to the mainland? He had not been seen or heard from in over six months.

After watching the *Louisville* leave the harbor, Nathan suddenly realized that when Sarah got his letter, she would know for certain that Andy was lost. And though his letter might be awkward and incomplete, Mr. Whipple would surely fill her in on all he had heard about Andy's disappearance. Sarah would be heartbroken.

Nathan cringed when he thought about what he had done. He had informed Sarah that Andy had been missing since November, and in the same letter he had expressed his joy at hearing from her. But had he said too much? Had he revealed his true feelings for her, kept secret for so long? Would she be angry? Would she despise him now? Would she even answer his letter?

"Well," Oren said, breaking into Nathan's thoughts, "we'd better get these barrels of salt delivered. We've got a lot of work to do this summer."

By now many of the fishermen from Mackinac Island had returned to Paradise Bay, and they were already making record catches of whitefish and lake trout in the waters around Beaver Island. Every day Nathan and Oren stockpiled more barrels of salted fish on the dock, rolling them between stacks of wood waiting to be sold to passing steamers.

The *Louisville* normally stopped at Saint James every two weeks, but its return was delayed by more spring storms and high seas. Finally after three weeks the boat limped into the harbor, leaking badly and low on wood for fuel. When the *Louisville* tied up, Nathan was at the dock with his wagon. A sailor called to him, and Nathan caught the bow line and secured it to a piling. Another sailor jumped to the dock and tied off a stern line. A bell rang, a whistle of steam blasted out of a stack behind the wheelhouse, and the engine came to a stop.

"Yoo-hoo! Yoo-hoo!" a familiar voice called.

Nathan looked up. He saw Edith Watson, leaning over the rail. "Mrs. Watson! Hello!" "Hello, Nathan! We've had a rough trip, and we're mighty glad to be here."

"Did Mr. Watson come?" Nathan asked.

"No, he had to plant crops. But I do have a traveling companion. Now where did she go? You wait right there, young man. Don't move an inch!"

Mrs. Watson disappeared. Nathan smiled, remembering the days when Mrs. Watson ruled the classroom with her cheerful and commanding voice. He wondered why she had returned to the island and, if Wingfield wasn't with her, who was?

In a moment, Mrs. Watson re-appeared at the railing with Sarah Strang at at her side. Nathan froze. It was a moment he had longed for, but he had never expected to see her again on Beaver Island. For the last three weeks all he had been able to think about was his letter and how he wished he had never sent it. He had convinced himself that he would never hear from her again. And yet here she was, standing on the bow and smiling down at him.

"Sarah!" he called, shouting over the commotion on the dock, "What are you doing here?"

"I came to see you," Sarah called, cupping her hands. Nathan stared at her, and then stared at Mrs. Watson, who was struggling with a large suitcase.

"What are you waiting for, young man?" Mrs. Watson asked. "How about helping us with our bags? We've been on this boat for two days, and we're mighty sick of it."

Mrs. Watson and Sarah disappeared, and in a few minutes they came down the gangplank. When Sarah reached the dock, she ran over to him. "Nathan, it's been so long. I'm so glad to see you!"

"I'm glad to see you, Sarah," Nathan replied, waiting for her to ask him about Andy.

Sarah turned and looked around the harbor. "It's so beautiful here," she said. "I'd forgotten how beautiful the island is in the spring."

"We've had a lot of stormy weather in the last few days," Nathan said. "You must have had a rough boat ride."

"It was awful! Most of the passengers were seasick."

Mrs. Watson came up behind them. "All right, that's enough idle chit-chat, boys and girls," she said. "Here, Nathan, you can carry Sarah's bag."

"Where are you staying, Mrs. Watson?" Nathan asked.

"The captain recommended Gibson's Inn. It must be new, because we never heard of it."

"Gibson's Inn? They just opened this spring. It's in the old print shop."

"My father's print shop?" Sarah asked, startled.

"Um, yeah," Nathan replied. "It's an inn now."

"Is my father's printing press still there?" Sarah asked, putting her hand on his arm. "It was in the back room, wasn't it?"

"Yes, it was. Near the fireplace."

Nathan didn't respond, suspecting the press had been vandalized or destroyed. The two of them walked in awkward silence, listening to Mrs.

Watson chattering away. When they reached Gibson's Inn, she turned to face them.

"I'm bushed," she said. "That boat trip just about did me in. Now why don't you young 'uns take a walk somewhere, get to know each other again."

"Right now?" Sarah asked.

"Sure, why not?" Mrs. Watson replied. "I'm going to get a room and take a nap." With that, she grabbed her bag and went inside, leaving Nathan and Sarah standing on the porch.

"Would you like to walk over to the school?" Nathan asked.

"Sure," Sarah said. "I'd love to see it again."

They stepped off the porch and followed a path they had both walked many times before, but now it was overgrown with weeds.

"I got your letter," Sarah said.

"Sarah, I can explain—"

"It was lovely, Nathan."

"It was?"

"Yes. It was the most beautiful letter I've ever received."

Nathan thought that Mr. Whipple must have changed his words. "But what about—"

"Andy?"

"That's the reason you came back, isn't it? To find him?"

"No, it isn't."

"Then why—"

Sarah stopped on the trail and looked at him. "In your letter you told me Andy left the island in a small boat last November. That was the first news I heard of him."

"But what about all last winter? Weren't you worried?"

"Of course I was. I was sure he would follow me. I expected to see or hear from him every day, but I never did."

"He couldn't leave, Sarah. He had to stay and take care of his father."

"I know that now, but he could have at least written me."

"Maybe he did; I don't know," Nathan said. "But the way things were last fall, I doubt if any mail was leaving the island, especially if it was addressed to you."

Sarah was silent, not understanding exactly what he was saying.

"With your last name, I mean, with a Mormon name." Nathan stopped, thinking he had hurt her feelings. But Sarah let it pass.

"Nathan, I have to ask you something."

"Yes?"

"Did Andy have anything to do with my father's murder?"

"No! He tried to save your father!"

"That's what you said in your letter, but I heard the most horrible rumors about how he was arrested and thrown in jail. I didn't believe any of it, but it still hurt to hear such stories."

"Sarah, believe me, Andy did try to save your father. He even got shot himself. Butch Jenkins' men caught him and threw him in jail. They would have hanged him if he hadn't escaped. When the Mormons were chased off the island Andy was hiding from Jenkins and his gang. At first, even I didn't know where he was."

"I feel better, hearing it from you in person," Sarah said. "Now I know the truth."

By now they had reached the school. The front windows were boarded up and high grass was growing around the building. They sat down on the front steps and looked out at the harbor.

"Didn't anyone go to school this year?" Sarah asked.

"Nope. There weren't too many people around."

"It's sad to see it empty."

"Yes, it is. We had some good times here," Nathan replied, thinking of the days when he and Andy had walked Sarah home from school.

"This is where Andy and I first—"

"I know," Nathan said, looking down at the ground.

"I'm sorry," Sarah said, reaching over and touching his arm. "I shouldn't have mentioned it."

"That's all right."

"Nathan, I have to explain something to you, so I might as well just say it. Andy was my first love. We were both very young, and I won't forget the times we had together. When I left the island I hoped he would follow me. I never heard from him, so I didn't know what had happened. It was just too long for me to be without him. For me, I lost him a little bit each day. I finally decided I had to go on with my life."

Nathan looked at her, not knowing what to say.

"With all the stories I'd heard, I couldn't come back to the island," Sarah continued, "so after my father died I got a job teaching school in Voree. I've learned a lot and grown up a lot since last summer. I needed some stability in my life."

"Sarah, I—"

"So that's why I came back to find you, Nathan. You've always been there for me, even when I ignored you or hurt you."

"You never hurt me, Sarah," Nathan said.

"Yes, I did," Sarah replied. "I hurt you when I spent so much time with Andy. I could tell by the look in your eyes."

Nathan was embarrassed. "But we were all friends," he said.

"Nathan, I could tell when you were hurt," Sarah said, turning and looking at him. "And I could tell how you felt about me."

Nathan's cheeks turned red. He had been flustered ever since Sarah had appeared at the railing of the *Louisville*. Expecting an interrogation about his letter and the circumstances of Andy's disappearance, now he was even more confused. But finally, looking into her eyes, his fears began to dissolve. And yet, even after a winter of dreaming of her, he still could not find the right words to say.

"Do you think you could learn to love me instead?" he finally blurted out.

Sarah took his hand. "Nathan, I do love you," she said.

"You do?"

"Yes, I do. I wasn't sure until I saw you standing on the boat dock."

"But that was only a few minutes ago," Nathan said.

"That's true," she said, "but I had all winter to think about it."

"So did I. In fact that's all I thought about," Nathan said."

"Nathan—"

"I love you, Sarah. I want us to be together."

"So do I, more than anything."

"I'm moving to Milwaukee in September, so we'll be able to see each other."

"Voree isn't far away. We can see each other on weekends and I'll visit you in the summer when school is out."

"Maybe I can find some land near Voree. We'll stay near your mother, build a place of our own, and start a farm. Would you like that, Sarah?"

"Yes, oh yes!" Sarah said. "That would be wonderful, Nathan. You've made me so happy!"

They both stood and Nathan reached for Sarah's hands, but Sarah walked over to the bell post and touched the weathered wood. The bell was rusty now and the rope hung in tatters, swaying gently in the summer breeze. With one last look at Paradise Bay, Sarah turned to face Nathan and the new life ahead of her.

EPILOGUE:

The Tale of the Lighthouse Keeper

O n the other end of the island, the Beaver Head Lighthouse kept a lonely vigil over the vast expanse of Lake Michigan for many years, warning passing ships of treacherous reefs and lurking sandbars. Tom Appleby continued to serve as the lighthouse keeper, diligently climbing the stairs and lighting the beacon every evening at dusk. Over the years, many other keepers and assistants came to the lighthouse, spending a few seasons on the island and then moving on to other posts around the Great Lakes. But Tom remained on duty until well after the turn of the century.

The mystery of the disappearance of Andy McGuire might have been lost in antiquity if not for a friendship between Tom and a young island boy. This boy was Benjamin Thill, son of the manager of the Wildwood Inn, a resort lodge built in 1910 on a bluff overlooking Cable Bay. Ben was fascinated by the Beaver Head Lighthouse. Whenever he got the chance, he hiked south along the shore until he saw the light tower rising above the trees. Tom befriended Ben, allowing him to explore the tower and even showing him how to light the beacon on summer evenings. But he never allowed him to stay after dark. Long before the sun set in the west, Tom escorted Ben back down the spiral staircase and sent him home to his family.

The Wildwood Inn did not last long, succumbing to a decline in visitors in 1912. The Thill family closed the inn and moved back to the mainland, but

Ben did not forget his friendship with Tom Appleby and he vowed to return to Beaver Island. It wasn't until a few years later, when he was a college student, that he finally got the chance. In June of 1916, during a summer break from classes, Ben took passage on the mail boat in Charlevoix, traveling across Lake Michigan to visit his childhood home.

When Ben reached Saint James he learned that Tom had retired from the Lighthouse Service and moved into town. He now lived in a cottage on Whiskey Point. Ben set out on a walk around the harbor to find the old lighthouse keeper. He passed fishing docks, a steam-powered saw mill, and stacks of lumber along the road. Before he reached Whiskey Point, he came upon several log cottages clustered along the shore. As Ben passed the cottages he spotted Tom working in a garden behind a white picket fence. His hair was white and he carried a cane, but he held his head high as he moved slowly among the flowers and vegetables.

"Hello, Mr. Appleby," Ben said.

Tom looked up, startled.

"I don't know if you remember me. I'm Benjamin Thill. My father used to manage the Wildwood Inn, just up the road from the Beaver Head Lighthouse."

Tom squinted into the evening sun setting across the harbor. "Benjamin Thill? Ben, is that you? Sure, I remember. You came to the lighthouse. Kept me company on many an afternoon, as I recall." He came over to the fence and shook Ben's hand. "You're older now," he chuckled. "Well, so am I, so am I."

Tom Appleby still had a commanding presence, even in old age. His eyes were deep gray and tucked beneath bushy white eyebrows. He wore an old blue jacket with brass buttons. The cuffs were worn but the jacket still fit him perfectly.

"I'm living in Chicago," Ben said. "I just finished my second year of college."

"That's mighty fine, son. I always knew you'd do well."

"Thank you, sir."

"Well, come in, come in. I'll make some tea. I just baked an apple pie this morning."

Tom opened the gate and Ben followed him into the house to a small dining room with a view of the harbor. "You sit here at the table and make yourself at home," he said. "I'll be right back."

Tom disappeared into the kitchen. Ben sat down and looked around with curiosity. The room was spotless, just as the lighthouse had always been. He noticed a broom leaning in the corner. Behind the broom, propped against the wall and oddly out of place, was an old shovel with a splintered wooden handle.

Tom came back with two cups of tea and and two slices of pie. He placed them on the table and settled into a chair.

"I made this pie with apples from Peiffer's orchard, just down the road from the Wildwood Inn," he said.

Ben picked up his fork and took a bite. "It's delicious," he said. "We used to pick apples at Peiffer's orchard."

"I don't get down there much anymore," Tom said. "A friend brings them to me."

"You must miss working at the lighthouse," Ben remarked.

"Oh, I do sometimes. I was stationed there a long time. My entire career, actually. The Lighthouse Service tried to transfer me a few times, but I wouldn't leave."

"When did you first come to the island," Ben asked.

"It was in the spring of 1857. I must have been about your age, Ben."

"It must have been exciting to be a lighthouse keeper."

"Well, to be honest, it was pretty boring most of the time. Boring and lonely. You just go through the same routine every night. There's not much to tell."

"What was it like when you first arrived?"

"When I first arrived? Ah, now there's a story I'll never forget. I remember as if it were yesterday." Tom stared out the window for a moment and then turned toward Ben with a sharp gleam in his eyes.

"I'd like to hear it," Ben said.

"I'm an old man, Ben. It all happened a long time ago. But I'll tell you my story, if you don't mind sticking around for awhile."

"Not at all. I've no where else to go this evening." Ben leaned forward and listened as Tom began his story.

He spoke of his arrival on Beaver Island in a snowstorm and his sleigh ride to the lighthouse with Nathan O'Donnell and Oren Whipple. He described their stop at Cable Bay, their escape from Sam Bennett, and his first view of the Beaver Head Lighthouse: gloomy and snowbound. Tom spoke in a calm and methodical manner, as if the events were common enough and could have happened to anyone. He spared no detail, telling of the light tower buried in snow, the lights of the approaching ship, and the frozen body on the stairs. He described the freezing wind, his frantic efforts to light the beacon, and his stunned relief when the ship finally turned away from the island.

Ben was sitting on the edge of his chair, mesmerized by Tom's story. "How close was the ship?" he asked.

"Damn close. It was hard to tell in the dark, but I'm sure it was just beyond the breakers. They turned just in time, that's for sure."

"What about the body? Did you ever find out who it was?"

"Oh, yes, I figured it out the very next day."

"How——"

"Let me show you something." Tom went to the kitchen, came back with a box, and handed it to Ben.

Ben opened it with curiosity and lifted out a book about the size of a small textbook. "McGuffey's Reader," he read aloud.

"That's an English grammar textbook. All the kids had them back then. I even had one myself when I was in school."

Ben pulled out another small book titled, "A Poetry Primer."

"Look inside."

He opened the cover. On the front page, written in neat cursive writing in the upper corner, was the name 'Sarah Strang.'

"Was she King Strang's daughter?" Ben asked.

"Yep. Sarah was King Strang's oldest child. She left the island with him after he was shot."

Captain Appleby reached in the box and pulled out a long object sealed in paper and handed it to Ben. Ben unwrapped the paper and put it aside. In his hand he held a tapered knife with a solid wooden handle. He recognized it as a knife used for cleaning fish.

"Look at the handle."

Ben turned the knife over. Neatly carved in the handle was the name "Andy McGuire."

"Andy McGuire was Nathan O'Donnell's cousin," Tom said. "He vanished from Saint James in November of 1856, six months before I arrived on the island."

"So it was Andy's body you found in the tower?"

"Yes, it was. You see, when I awoke in the kitchen of the keeper's quarters the next morning, I found two duffel bags. One bag contained these two books and Sarah Strang's clothes. The other bag contained this knife and some old work clothes. That was Andy's bag. I actually slept that night covered with Andy's blankets and I used Sarah's bag as a pillow.

"What happened then? What what did you do with his body?"

"Well, Ben, I had a problem. I was alone at the lighthouse and I had to keep the light burning. There was no way to get back to Saint James and I had no idea when Nathan and Oren might return with their wagon. The only other alternative was to walk to Cable Bay, but after my unpleasant reception the day before I wasn't about to stroll into Cable Bay with a dead body. Sam Bennett would have killed me; at least that's what I thought at the time."

"So what did you do?" Ben asked with trepidation.

"I really had no choice. I buried him."

Ben looked at Tom with shock.

"I gave him a good Christian burial. I had a Bible with me so I read from the scriptures and said a prayer. You see, in some ways a lighthouse keeper is like a ship's captain. He is the one who performs weddings and funerals at sea. In 1857, at the far end of the island, I was obliged to show the same respect for Andy McGuire."

"Where exactly is he buried?"

"Do you remember those bluffs overlooking the lake just east of the lighthouse?"

"Sure, I used to hike there."

"On the tallest hill I put up a white wooden cross and planted trillium over his grave. The cross is gone now but the plants have spread over the years, so they cover the entire hill. I believe they are in bloom right about now."

"But how did Andy end up at the lighthouse with two duffel bags?" Ben was still baffled by Captain Appleby's remarkable story.

"When Andy disappeared, everyone thought he sailed to the mainland and made his way to Milwaukee. There were a lot of rumors about what happened to him, but I learned the truth. Andy found a leaky old sailboat in Saint James and tried to sail across Lake Michigan in November. He only made it to the south end of Beaver Island where he was blown ashore and shipwrecked. He broke into the lighthouse to try to find shelter, but it was too late. He froze to death in the tower and his body remained there all winter."

"But that's crazy. Why would he try to sail across Lake Michigan in November, and why did he have Sarah Strang's bag with him?"

"Andy McGuire was in love with Sarah Strang, but Sarah was betrothed to an older man, a Mormon named Tobias Humphrey. Andy and Sarah had been planning to escape the island and they had their duffel bags packed and ready. They were going to stow away on a steamboat and start a new life in Wisconsin, but their plans were interrupted when King Strang was shot. Sarah was forced to leave the island on Humphrey's lumber schooner with her injured father, leaving Andy behind. He must have felt marooned without Sarah and he was desperate to follow her. He finally left in late November. It was suicide to try to sail across the lake in an open boat, and he only made it as far as the lighthouse."

"How do you know all of this, Tom?"

"Well, it took a while to piece it all together. In June I finally managed to make my way to Saint James and I immediately sought out the sheriff. We went to see Andy's father, Ian McGuire, and we broke the news to him. Ian was a fisherman so he knew what the lake is like in November. Even so, he was devastated.

"I stayed in Saint James for several days and met Andy's uncle, Patrick O'Donnell. We all sat down together and told Nathan about Andy. I think Nathan took the news harder than anyone. They were cousins and they had been through a lot together. It was Nathan who told me the story of Andy and Sarah. He said that Andy was heartbroken when Sarah left the island and obsessed with finding her. According to Nathan, Andy found an abandoned boat in the harbor, patched it up as best he could, and sailed off alone without telling anyone. There's no doubt about it, Andy died trying to follow Sarah."

"That's quite a story," Ben said. "Do you really think he loved her that much?"

"I often wondered why Andy was in the light tower, halfway up the stairs," Tom said. "He must have been just about frozen to death when he washed up on the shore. I think he tried to climb the tower so he could have one last glimpse across Lake Michigan. He wanted to look toward Wisconsin, toward Sarah. That's how much he loved her. He died for her in that tower."

Tom paused and then continued his story. "Later in the summer we had a memorial for Andy. Patrick spoke, and I remember his last words to this day:

'Andy's dream shall forever live
In the bricks and mortar of this lighthouse.

God bless our youthful skipper
Who sailed away for love.'

"What happened after the memorial?" Ben asked.

"The next day everyone headed back to Saint James and I went back to tending the lighthouse. We all had work to do."

"No, I mean after that. Did they all stay on the island?"

"Well, at the end of the summer Nathan and Oren sold their wagon and moved to Milwaukee, where they started their own freight company. After a couple of years Oren took over the business and Nathan and Sarah got married. They bought a dairy farm and settled down near Sarah's mother. Patrick later moved to Voree and he went to work on the farm with his son. As for Andy's father, he stayed here on Beaver Island. He fished for a while, but his health never recovered from the beating he received from King Strang's henchmen. He died a few years after Andy disappeared."

"Why did you stay here for so long, Tom? Didn't all of this bother you?"

"Ah, the first year was a little rough," he replied, "but soon folks started to visit me at the lighthouse and in a couple of years I knew just about everyone on the island."

"But didn't you get lonely living all those years at the south end of the island?"

"Naw, not too often. I kept busy tending the light. When times got hard I thought of Andy buried up on that hill. He's the one that was lonely, not me. Once in a while I'd climb up the hill and sit by his grave. To this day I often wonder how many lives would have changed if he had made it across the lake and found Sarah."

Tom had finished his story, so they sat in silence for a long time. Outside, two fireflies danced in a rising spiral, flashing their tiny lights high above Paradise Bay.

Author's Notes

The _King's Daughter_ is a book of historical fiction, based upon events on Beaver Island in the years 1849 to 1857. Many of the main characters in the story are fictional, including Sarah Strang, Ian and Andy McGuire, Patrick and Nathan O'Donnell, Tobias and Gurdon Humphrey, Gilbert and Oren Whipple, Butch Jenkins, and Tom Appleby, lighthouse keeper of the Beaver Head Light.

The character of Sarah Strang was inspired by a daughter born to James and Mary Strang in 1838 in the village of Ellington, New York, where James Strang served as postmaster for several years. This child, also named Mary, died at the age of five. If she had lived, she would have been eleven when her family first moved to Beaver Island in 1849 and seventeen when her father was assassinated in 1856. In this novel I have brought Mary back to life as Sarah Strang, the king's eldest daughter.

All other characters in the book were real people, including James and Mary Strang, Elvira Field, Alva Cable, Wingfield Watson, the Bennett brothers, and Alexander Wentworth and Thomas Bedford, the two assassins of King Strang.

James J. Strang was crowned king of the Mormons on Beaver Island on July 8, 1850 and ruled for six years over the only kingdom ever to exist within the borders of the United States. During this time he also served for two contentious terms in the Michigan State Legislature. He was shot on Beaver Island on June 16, 1856, and died on July 19, 1856 near his parents' home in

Voree, Wisconsin. Two of his wives, Betsy and Phoebe, were with him, as were several faithful Mormons. When King Strang died, he had five wives and ten children. Four of his wives were pregnant.

Two ships play an important role in *The King's Daughter*. The *U.S.S. Michigan* was the first iron-hulled war steamer in the U.S. Navy. Built in 1843, the *Michigan* bridged the gap between wind power and steam power, and between wooden sailing ships and modern steel warships. She sailed the Great Lakes for 106 years, eventually serving as a training ship. Sadly, the *Michigan* was cut up for scrap in 1949. Only the bow and ship's wheel were saved as memorials to this historic vessel.

The *Dunbrody* was built in 1845 in Quebec to deliver timber from Canada to New Ross, Ireland. In 1849, at the height of the Irish potato famine, she ferried 179 emigrants from New Ross to New York City with no loss of life. A full-scale replica of the *Dunbrody* was completed in 2001 and is now on display in New Ross. The ship houses the *Dunbrody* Famine Ship and Irish Emigrant Experience, a museum honoring the 1.5 million emigrants who traveled from Ireland to distant points around the globe.

In *The King's Daughter* I have made every effort to maintain accuracy while weaving a fictional story into real historical events. Although all of the dialogue and most of the scenes in the book are fictional, I have endeavoured to present them as if they could have happened within the context of known historical events. On rare occasions I have taken liberties with precise dates for dramatic literary effect. Any other omissions or inaccuracies are my responsibility alone and are no reflection on the generous and knowledgeable people who assisted me with this novel.

Daniel Hendrix
Traverse City, Michigan